P9-AFT-621

"[An] auspicious debut . . . Earling handles her subject with keen insight into human nature and with reverence for the stark beauty of the American West and the venerable traditions of a native people torn between two ways of life."
—*The Advocate*

"Like Louise Erdrich, Earling has a mythic quality in her writing that beautifully suits her tale. Earling draws on her intimate knowledge of the vast and unforgiving country and its people to weave this dark and moving tale."
—*The Denver Post*

"A startlingly spiritual novel of the lives and loves and heartbreak on a Montana Indian reservation. The characters, especially the strangely destructive lovers, Louise and Baptiste, are so sharply drawn that they will bring tears to your eyes. And the landscape, the richly detailed backdrop against which these characters play out their roles, adds a dimension that borders on mythic. . . . Earling is a truly gifted writer, and *Perma Red* is a wonder-filled gift to all of us."
—James Welch

"Earling's deliberate pacing gives an otherworldly feel to the grim circumstances of the time, and makes real the hypnotic effect of this slim, green-eyed woman on the men around her."
—*The Seattle Times*

"Earling has done something magical. She has imbued *Perma Red* with a sense not of universality, which usually sounds phony, but of permanence. . . . The way of telling is what makes *Perma Red* so good. The way of telling is what makes it art."
—*The Salt Lake Tribune*

"Like Michael Dorris and Louise Erdrich before her, Debra Earling transforms the bleakness of her characters' lives with the power of poetry, but also with the power of heartbreak."
—*The Austin Chronicle*

"From the first page, tragedy looms in the dark corners of this story. . . . Earling's prose is searingly beautiful. . . . The reader holds on, hooked and hoping for a shred of redemption, grateful when it comes."—*St. Louis Post-Dispatch*

"[An] elegant debut . . . Stunning."
—*Seattle Weekly*

"You will be so mesmerized by this novel that you will not want to answer the phone."
—*Taconic NY Weekend*

continued . . .

"Earling follows the literary trail blazed by Louise Erdrich.... The plot veers between hallucinatory, poetic descriptions of reservation life and tumultuous romantic encounters ... First-rate characterizations ... There's little doubt that Earling has considerable potential." —*Publishers Weekly*

"In the deep wells of compassion for her people, and with her stunning eye for the rituals of their existence, Earling reminds us again that the greatest writing is always about matters of the human heart." —Larry Brown

"A love story of uncommon depth and power, a love story that is as painful as it is transcendent, a love story in which the lovers, like Birkin and Ursula in Lawrence's *Women in Love*, are unwilling to diminish themselves in the act of joining together but are equally unable to turn away.... Coming-of-age novels set on reservations are a rich part of contemporary literature, of course, and Earling's effort fits securely into the tradition of Welch, Erdrich, and others, but it stands on its own just fine. The Lawrentian psychodrama that emerges ... gives the novel a richness that transcends the story's time and place but that, simultaneously, brings the large theme of cultural clash into even sharper focus. Let's hope we hear much more from Earling."
—*Booklist* (starred review)

"In this beautiful first novel, set on the Flathead Reservation of Montana in the 1940s, Earling traces the youth and young adulthood of Louise White Elk and the men who try to win her heart and soul.... This novel will stand proudly among its peers in Native American literature and should have strong appeal to fans of Louise Erdrich." —*Library Journal*

"Like the finest of wines, *Perma Red* has reached the peak of vintage with a lyricism that makes most other books on the average bookstore's new-release table look like cheap bottles of bad wine ... a book as permanently beautiful as the Montana landscape itself. I find it hard, if not impossible, to shake Earling's book from my mind. To paraphrase another Big Sky writer, Norman Maclean, I am haunted by words." —*January* magazine

"Seems destined to be included in future lists of the fine novels crafted by writers of Native American descent ... a powerful first novel of love, loss and landscape." —*Seattle Post-Intelligencer*

BLUEHEN BOOKS

New York

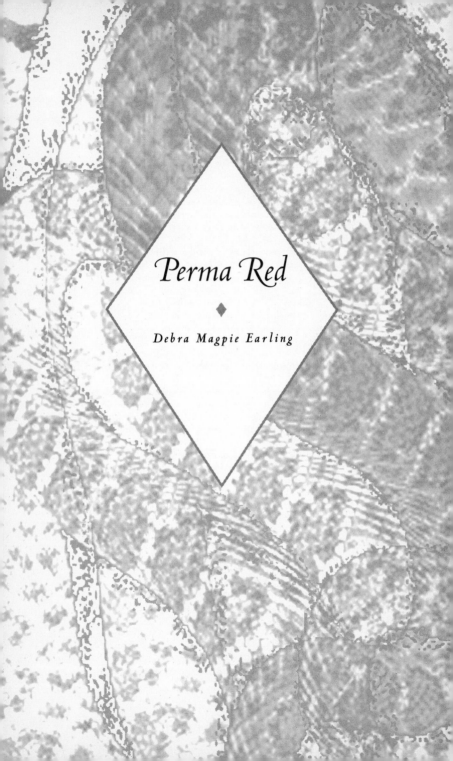

Perma Red

◆

Debra Magpie Earling

BlueHen Books
Published by The Berkley Publishing Group
A division of Penguin Group (USA) Inc.
375 Hudson Street
New York, New York 10014

Portions of this novel have appeared in different form in
Cutbank, Northeast Indian Quarterly, Ploughshares, and *Talking Leaves:
An Anthology of Contemporary Native American Short Stories.*

Copyright © 2002 by Debra Magpie Earling
Book design by Stephanie Huntwork
Cover design by Honi Werner

First BlueHen hardcover edition: June 2002
First BlueHen trade paperback edition: June 2003
BlueHen trade paperback ISBN: 0-425-19054-4

The Library of Congress has catalogued
the BlueHen hardcover edition as follows:

Earling, Debra Magpie.
Perma Red / Debra Magpie Earling.
p.   cm.
ISBN 0-399-14899-X
1. Flathead Indian Reservation (Mont.)—Fiction.   2. Salish
Indians—Fiction.   3. Indian women—Fiction.   4. Montana—
Fiction.   I. Title.
PS3605.A75P47   2002   2001056586
813'.6—dc21

Printed in the United States of America

10   9   8   7   6   5   4

For my mother and father
who give me the loving gift of their stories
and
For my sister Cheryl in memory of her mother, Louise,
Perma Red no more

Acknowledgments

◆ I owe many thanks to many friends who have helped me over the years to make this book a reality. I thank James Welch for being my teacher, a constant source of inspiration, a brilliant light. Amy Crewdson for her counsel and determination. William Kittredge, Annick Smith, and James Crumley for their unfailing encouragement. Greg Glazner and Jon Davis for all those years of good words and support. I thank all my friends. Laura Stearns for a faith that recalls my childhood wonder. Andrea Opitz who keeps me sane. Larry Brown for all those songs. Melissa Kwasny who graces my life. Mark Medvetz my blood brother. Ledoux Hansen my kindred spirit. Anne Appleby, Steve Eby, Fiona Cheong, Judy Blunt, Sandra Alcosser, Theresa Ferraro, Colleen O'Brien, Terry Ryan, Joy Lewis, Henrietta Mann, Margaret Kingsland, Mary Bentler, Kim Barnes, Mary Sale, Dixie Reynolds, Georgia Porter, Barbara Theroux,

Craig Lesley, Susie Castle, Jeffery Smith, Richard Ford, Emma Jean Rouillier, Judge Louise Burke, Cora Stubblefield. My colleagues, Deirdre McNamer, Kevin Canty, Katie Kane, Hank Harrington, Bob Baker, Bill Bevis, Bruce Bigley. I am grateful for the support of my family, my brother Robert who rescues me, my brother Dennis who keeps me humble, my brother James Bureau whose good heart shines, my great-grandmother Cecille Magpie Charlo who loves me beyond death, all of you. I thank my editor, Greg Michalson, for his brilliant insights and long patience. My agent, Sally Wofford-Girand, for her utmost professionalism and sincere friendship. I thank my teachers Dan McCall, Ken McClane, James McConkey, Henry Louis Gates, Jr., and Mary Ann Waters. I humbly thank St. Jude for prayers answered. And I thank Robert Stubblefield for being a blessing in my life.

Flathead Indian Reservation

Louise and Yellow Knife

◆

The Old Marriage

When Louise White Elk was nine, Baptiste Yellow Knife blew a fine powder in her face and told her she would disappear. She sneezed until her nose bled, and Baptiste gave her his handkerchief. She had to lie down on the school floor and tilt back her head and even then it wouldn't stop. She felt he had opened the river to her heart. The cloth he had given her was wet with her blood. She felt hot and sleepy. Sister Thomas Bernard pulled her up and told her to go to the bathroom and wash her face. Sister pinched the bridge of Louise's nose. Louise kept the handkerchief pressed to her face, embarrassed by all the attention she was getting. She could feel her blood cool in slow streams between her fingers. She remembered at one point Baptiste Yellow Knife had knelt down beside her. Her head was empty. She imagined the veins in her temples quivering. Her skin draining color. Her face glowing, a candlelit egg. Suffering. A saint. Awkward Baptiste. Pigeon-toed and dusty Baptiste was kneeling beside her cradling her head with his cool, dry hands, his voice tickling her ears. He was leaning over her, whispering to her, whispering a story. His voice was in her ear. She felt Sister Bernard pull Baptiste away from her. The back of her head danced with silver stars and Louise fell back into dreaming, a snagged fish released again to water.

Grandma squeezed her hand as she blinked awake. Louise's hands were cold. "We got this back," Grandma said. She held up the handkerchief that Baptiste had given her. It was crumpled, stiff and black with her blood. Louise didn't understand at first and then she remembered Baptiste standing close as the school nurse lifted her into the car. He shyly asked the nurse for his handkerchief back. As they pulled out of the school yard, Baptiste smiled at Louise and lifted his bloody handkerchief up so she could see all he had taken from her.

Her grandmother had told her to stay away from him. He was the son of Dirty Swallow, the rattlesnake woman. Baptiste Yellow Knife's mother could direct the rattlers to do her bidding. Last summer a rattler had tapped the back of her grandmother's skirt as she sat on the stick-game lines. Her grandmother had won too much of Dirty Swallow's money, and she wanted it back. Now the son of Dirty Swallow wanted something from Louise.

There was something about Baptiste. Baptiste was from the old ways and everybody hoped he would be different from his mother. He knew things without being told. He knew long before anyone else when the first camas had sprouted. He would inform his mother the night before the flower would appear and he was always right. He knew stories no one but the eldest elder knew but he knew the stories without being told. "He knows these things," her grandmother had said, "because the spirits tell him. He is the last of our old ones, and he is dangerous."

On the day Louise's great-grandmother had died Baptiste foretold her death. It was in the spring, on a day so clear clouds faded overhead like wide ghosts. Louise's great-grandfather was branding horses in the high field and, she remembered, Baptiste had come over with his grandfather to watch. Louise was six years old at the time but she still remembered Baptiste, because it was one of the few times she had seen him out of school then. But she remembered him most because of what had happened that day. And that day Louise sat up on the hillside with her mother, her grandmother, and Old Macheese—her great-grandmother. Louise thought at first Baptiste was frightened of Old Macheese and had chosen to sit away from her.

Old Macheese had survived everything, even smallpox, but her grandmother said her face had always been pitted. Louise could still remember Old Macheese's face, places where disease had died beneath her skin, bruised places where the blood had pooled for good. Old Macheese liked to rub her knuckles down Louise's spine, liked to laugh at her when she tripped or cried, whenever she hurt herself. And after the old woman died Louise's grandmother had told her Old Macheese was just that way, mean.

Louise had wondered if there was something wrong with Baptiste that day, because he stared at her, and even when she made faces at him, he did not stop his watching. She had heard stories about him, how he could see and hear things other Indians could not, how his mother had the rattlesnake power. He sat away from the others, rocking back and forth, digging his slender fingers deep into the black soil while his grandfather worked. He wasn't called down to the corral like the other boys. His grandfather had let him be alone and quiet on the hill.

Old Macheese had just started to tell a story when Baptiste had stood up, so thin the dirty seat of his pants hung almost to his knees. Old Macheese spoke up, saying he probably had tuberculosis. He wore a belt that had once been his grandfather's horse bridle. He had two white splotches clouding his face and still he was the darkest Indian Louise had ever seen, a beaver-dark boy who stood with a strange certainty Louise recognized even then as trouble. When his grandfather saw Baptiste stand, he slipped the knot off the colt he was holding and headed fast toward Baptiste. Louise remembered the old man had leaned over Baptiste, listening and nodding. But Louise could not hear Baptiste.

"Baptiste has seen a salamander," he called, "a lizard turn red."

Louise's great-grandfather, Good Mark, shut the corral gate and made his way up to Baptiste. Louise stood silent beside her grandmother. The other men had stopped working and had turned to see what was troubling Baptiste. The horses crowded one corner of the corral as the workers gathered at the bottom of the hill. The men crouched suddenly to the ground. They were patting the dirt, searching, feeling for something. She could see Good Mark weaving his fingers through the faded grass, his white braids were tucked in his belt. Louise's mother shook her head, then cupped her hands together on top of her head. Louise's grandmother tapped Louise. "Look for a lizard," she had told Louise, half-whispering. "See if you can find the lizard."

Louise got down on her hands and knees with the men. She combed the grass with her fingertips. She picked up a branch and brushed the ground but she saw nothing. Baptiste Yellow Knife crept up behind her and Louise looked up to see his knife-bladed hair, his dark face. "You won't find it," he said. She pushed at his feet, but he did not budge. "Move," she said. She didn't like being told by Baptiste, a boy she barely knew, that she couldn't do something. "You're in my way," she told him. She turned over stones, picked at the sage and grass, looking. She glanced at Baptiste and noticed his watching was dim. His eyes lazy. His lashes flickered and she saw the glare of black irises swirling back in his head, and then only the whites of his eyes, spooky, almost blue. "It won't do no good," he said, his dizzy eyes closed. "Someone will die." Louise saw the dirt in the slim cuff of

Baptiste Yellow Knife's pants. She saw clouds bleaching to wind, a haze of dust changing light like silt changes water. She saw her great-grandmother standing on the hill, and then Old Macheese was falling back, falling, while the wind lifted her olive scarf from her head.

Louise asked her grandmother how she had gotten the handkerchief back. How did the old woman manage to snatch back her blood from Baptiste Yellow Knife's tight fist, his ugly smile? Grandma didn't answer her. Louise imagined many things and settled on Sister Bernard and her hard thumping knuckles. She wouldn't let the boys play with dead rattlers or poke at the mouths of dead birds with sticks. And she wouldn't let Baptiste keep a blood-soaked handkerchief.

Louise had a dream that followed her from a long night into morning. It was a familiar dream. She heard a Salish voice, neither a man nor a woman's voice. The voice did not speak to her but to the dream she cupped in her small hands like a million water-colored glass beads.

It is cold. Snakes sleep in deep holes trapped by snow. We tell our stories now. Rattlers are quiet. It is so far back your blood smells like oil in the tongues of your grandmothers. The snow is frozen so hard it can bruise. The snowdrifts are razor-edged. Snow shines. We're locked here. Outside Grandma's house, a naked man stands near a red fire. His face the face of a woman, smooth and deep-planed. His back is lean with ribs. His hips are narrow. Flames light high on the roof of Grandma's house. Base-blue tongues of flame burn buckskin tamarack. Black wood dust to white wood ash. The naked man blows through teeth, his cracked lips whistling to fire. His whistle calls a great wind up from snow.

Firelight becomes one small candle. It flickers, then fails white, then fails, fails white to smoke. Steady wind scatters white ash to thin choking sheets of hot dust. Snow and timber powder, hot and cold. The man stands before the white stars, the endless snow.

His white light is turning to morning.

Louise never asked her grandmother about the handkerchief again. She knew who had brought it back. She remembered stories of her great-grandfather: the secret training rituals of medicine people sent to find a single pin in a night that pressed to forty below, one pin dropped deep in snow, miles from where they stood, shivering and naked. Her grandfather had saved her. Somehow he had picked her blood from the dark hands of Dirty Swallow. And she knew it had been at a great price. She would never talk to Baptiste Yellow Knife again.

When Louise was fourteen, Baptiste snuck up behind her and slipped a rattler's tail in her hand with the slick skill of a small wind passing. She wasn't sure what to do with it. She stared at it for a long while, then dropped it deep into her pocket, hoping it would fall out of the hole she hadn't mended. But the tail became a power she was afraid of, a feeling she had never had before.

"Why didn't you just get rid of that when he gave it to you?" her grandmother asked.

Louise didn't answer. She looked at her feet as her grandmother was talking. She didn't know how to tell her grandma that once the rattle had gotten into her pocket, it began moving, as though the whole snake was still attached. She felt the rattle twitching on her leg, like a new muscle, and she was afraid of it in a way that made her strong.

Grandma made Louise bury the rattle on the hill and mark the spot with three red-colored rocks. "That way we can avoid it," she said. Louise took her time burying the rattle. She found the nicest spot on the hill under the shade of a juniper tree. She dug a deep hole that was sweet with the smell of new roots. She carefully wrapped the rattle with a glove she had worn thin to fool it into feeling she was near. Then she covered the hole up as fast as she could with the sweep of her arms and the clawing cup of her hands. She walked slowly away from the small rock mound, pacing her steps, careful not to look back and reveal any desire to stay.

All that night dreams swallowed her. She was falling. Tall grass shot up around her and whispered with heat. Smooth flat rocks near Magpie Hill were shining with sun. She felt the warm breath of her mother and curled down into a dark sleep.

Louise found a power in ignoring Baptiste Yellow Knife. He no longer existed for her. She pretended she did not hear or see him. She stopped listening for the whisper of scales beneath the thin slat steps of her grandmother's house. He had less presence for her than the ghost of her sister's dead cat. Sleep was good, and she began to feel at ease. When he came close behind her from any direction, she sidestepped him and talked as if he wasn't there. The only time Baptiste could secure her attention was when he rode his horse Champagne. He had even named the horse for her when he had overheard her say she wanted to try champagne. When she had stopped to pet the horse, Baptiste began telling everyone at the Ursulines' that he was going to marry Louise. "Stay away from her," he would say. "She belongs to me." The more she denied him, the more he would follow her. She would look for him, she told herself, so she could stay clear of him.

At the stick games in Dixon she hid beneath Charlie Kicking Woman's tribal-police car for almost an hour with everybody staring at her, because Melveena Big Beaver had told her Baptiste was looking for her. She lay half under the engine-hot car in a stain of oil that ruined her good dress, only to find Baptiste walked past her holding hands with Hemaucus Three Dresses. When Louise stood to shake the dry grass from her hair, Baptiste did not look at her or even shift a glance her way. Only his mother, Dirty Swallow, eyed Louise. Dirty Swallow sat in the dirt of the stick-game line without a blanket. Her eyes were small and steady and though she kept playing the game she kept her eyes on Louise, opened her palm to reveal the black-rimmed bone.

Baptiste was animal and dark and when he smiled at Hemaucus he almost looked handsome. Louise felt relieved and pulled breath deep into her lungs, but the moment of relief came to her with the feeling she had lost something. She lit a cigarette and tried to attend the scar of juniper trees near the road. She looked over at the both of them. Baptiste rubbed the back of Hemaucus's brown hand on the side of his thigh then led her to the stick-game line. Louise saw the two of them smiling at each other.

She didn't know how to feel. She wondered if everyone was feeling sorry for her because Baptiste Yellow Knife had managed to find someone new, someone better. She knew she didn't want Baptiste Yellow Knife and his attentions, had run from him for years. She had dodged his every whisper, averted his every glance. She stood next to the dusty trees feeling dry-handed. The oil stain bloomed on her dress. Louise thought the people were looking at her because they were thinking she should be jealous of Hemaucus. And in the stinging light of a summer day passing, Hemaucus's hair hung heavy, so shiny it seemed to be water. Hemaucus was an older woman but she quieted her laughter with her hands when she looked at Baptiste. Her waist was full and her smooth arms were tight-lined with muscle.

Louise felt small. She could feel the hard lines of her ribs. Her stomach was sinking and hollow. The bones of her pelvis caught the thin fabric of her dress. She had heard the old women telling her grandmother to watch her. "Make sure she hasn't got TB," they said. And, standing in the field, the grass white and brittle at her ankles, she felt her big-boned knees. She felt tired and foolish. Maybe she had fooled herself into thinking she looked better than she did. When Melveena Big Beaver walked by with her sister Mavis, when they both looked at Louise and turned their heads covering their smiles, Louise kicked dust at them.

Louise realized she had kept no distance from Baptiste. All of her focus, all of her attentions had been and were still directed toward Baptiste. Ignoring him had only made him present in her life. Now that he had given up on her she began to wonder if he had really chased her. He was in love with someone else and she saw him only on occasion but he no longer looked at her. She told herself she may have been the problem all along. She had nothing to worry about. And when Louise saw Baptiste Yellow Knife alone again, she was in the safety of Malick's store, safe among rows of peanut butter and preserves, crates of fresh eggs. She walked down the main aisle, passing him. He said her name as she was heading for the counter, and for the first time in years she turned to him and smiled. She had no way of knowing the power she had given him again, not until she glanced at him from the smoke-stained window as she was leaving. He stood just outside the store, his arms lank at his sides. Louise watched him for a long time, but he did not move from his place. He would not surrender his vigil. She wondered if he was waiting for Hemaucus but she realized too late her grandmother had been right. He was waiting for her. She should have ignored him forever.

Louise had only one nightmare in all the months she had denied him. In her dream, Baptiste was an old man swimming against river water. His shoulders were harnessed, pulling something she could not see. He estimated each swell, each hesitant wave. Watching. She heard the slap of water against the pockets of his body, to rock, to water, to rock. Up from a swell of water, silver as winter rain, he reached for her. He had not gotten her then and he would not get her now. Louise swallowed a deep breath of stale grocery air and stepped outside to face the hot sun and Baptiste Yellow Knife.

"Louise," he said, and she hesitated in her walk. It had been a spring without rain. She could smell the autumn edge of leaves. The fields gave up the morning in great pulses of heat. She felt his desire in the dense heat of her breasts, a thousand snelled hooks pulled by little sinkers weighed the tips of her nipples, the heavy lobes of her ears. She placed her hand on her scalp and felt her blood beating. The sun was so hot she could count the strands of hair beneath her palm. A heaviness settled in her lungs like green water. She stopped and shifted her feet to brace herself against the son of Dirty Swallow. His presence was odd, like a pressing wind she had to lean into to gain strength.

"You don't talk to me," he said. "Do you hear me talking to you?"

Louise knew something was wrong. She felt heavy on the spot where she stood. She stamped her tongue against her front teeth and tried to think of Roger Mullan, his long yellow teeth. His own mother said he could eat apples through a picket fence. She strained to hold the image.

Baptiste tugged at the swell in his crotch as he talked to her. She focused all of her attention on moving away from him. He struck a match on the zipper of his pants to a yellow flame and lit a pipe of kinnikinnick leaves. Now that she had his full attention again he did not look like the Baptiste who had held Hemaucus's hand. She could tell he had been drinking. He'd been drinking for days. His breath was bitter. She glanced at his face but would not meet his gaze. It occurred to her, like a push, that Baptiste could be both handsome and ugly to her. His voice was slow water moving deep in the channel, pulling her. She knew he wasn't touching her but the rasp of his swollen tongue grazed her left breast. She turned to him and he was grinning. He blew smoke through his lips like a kiss and her eyes watered. She believed he knew what she was thinking. Around the brown hub of his eyes the whites rimmed yellow as if they'd been boiled. She felt an urge to move closer to him, a strange urge she didn't understand, the same urge she had to look close into the small mouths of dead animals. She would cross the highway again for a closer look at a bone-broken deer. And she knew she would move closer to Baptiste.

"Louise," he whispered. Her name was thick in his mouth. She could feel a wet heat rising from his collar. She surprised herself when she leaned forward to touch the tip of her tongue to the fat lobe of his ear. He tasted sour with old body salt. He pressed his cheek to hers, leaving a damp imprint. Louise pulled back. She would not kiss him. He smelled different up close. Sweet, warm earth and the faint, odd smell of burning lime that covered everything unclean. He crooked his head toward her as if he could hear her heart beating. He opened his mouth to reveal his tongue red as a salamander.

The back of her head felt tight as if every pore had shut down. Louise tried not to look behind her. She breathed in slowly and listened. The wind was still. She imagined her head was as smooth as the translucent round moon rising high above their heads.

And, like the moon, she saw the world as if from a great distance. The fields were brittle with weeds. She saw Baptiste Yellow Knife below her, smaller than a hummingbird, his tiny heart beating down the thin, thin walls of his heart. One hundred yards from him Malick's store hid neatly stacked cans of soup, vegetables, baskets of penny candy. He could no longer touch her. The thought made her breathless as clouds. She looked down over the sun-silver hills and saw something moving. She sucked her breath full of wind. She saw the root cellar of her grandmother, the hill mound of rocks weathered smooth by rain, and, deep inside the cellar, the fat rattler that had outsmarted her family for years hiding behind fruit jars and gunnysacks of jerky, leaving the pale ghost peel of himself that grew longer and longer each year. She saw the hiding snakes in all their places.

In the damp shade of Grandma's woodpile a slim rattler was sleeping. She saw the Ursuline school and the snakes in the field close to the playground. Lorraine Small Salmon, just five years old, turned jump rope while, close to the tips of her shoes, a brown rattler hummed. She saw her sister chase the rooster toward and away from the bottom land where the tender-fanged mouths of one hundred snakes waited in the weeds. She saw a fisherman she didn't know, as vulnerable as his sunburned pate, at the Jocko, surrounded on all sides by brown rocks and rattlesnakes thick as lichen. She saw the dead snake the boys had hung on the cross of the French nun's grave. She saw the road snakes that had been sliced and smashed by passing cars, their eyes lit with the hard, black backs of flies, and beyond them, more snakes. She saw the milk-white eyes of a thousand August rattlers. She saw Dirty Swallow walking toward her grandma's rain-blistered door. Behind her, rattlesnakes trailed like a wedding train.

From a great distance she heard Baptiste Yellow Knife say, "Marry me." Louise stepped back from him to leave. The air was clean and hot. A sudden wind snapped her dress tight to the backs of her legs. She shielded her watering eyes from the grit of dust. He never stopped watching her, and for one small moment, she felt bad for him and bad for herself. She could hate him enough to pull him inside of her, to melt his bones to water. She turned from him and began to run. She dropped her small bag of groceries to run faster, to run home, more afraid of Dirty Swallow in her grandmother's house than of any field or road rattler.

Her sister, Florence, was squatting on top of the lean-to where the wood was kept. Florence put her finger to her lips and motioned for

Louise to stop. The back door of her grandmother's house was wide-open but the day was so bright Louise could not see into the darkness of the kitchen. The windows of the house were glazed with white sun. Louise glanced up at the narrow shade line below the eves, saw the twitching tails of sparrows hiding from heat. She felt a dull-fisted warmth in her throat and she tried to swallow. She stepped carefully through knee-deep sage, lifting her skirt up from small snags of cheat grass. She saw the last edge of bush grass, the scuff-smooth cow trail that led around the pond toward home. There was a rhythm of water moving slowly around the creek. She thought of rainbow trout, their dense eyes watching, the scales ringing along their backs as they bit up toward the small white wings beyond water. There was a pause in the reed grass as a deep breeze pulled dust toward a higher place. The red-winged blackbirds were quiet. She looked closer at the bloated cotton-wood roots that stretched to the pond edge. A slow current writhed silver and then green in the sleeping shade. She threw a rock toward the pond, saw a sudden lap of water, then more waves, the smooth familiar wiggle parting grass, small hiss. She had come to know the language of the fields, the thin weave at the roots of grass. Snakes.

Louise knew Dirty Swallow was inside the house. Dirty Swallow had come to Old Macheese's wake, and she had come to visit the day Louise's mother had died. The dry weeds had crackled with rattlers. Both times Florence had scrambled to a place where the rattlers couldn't get to her. As she came closer Louise could hear Dirty Swallow's voice. Dirty Swallow was walking, pacing her grandmother's kitchen in circles. As Louise stepped on the porch she heard the dry-rice sound of a rattler retreating.

"Get out of my house," her grandmother was saying to Dirty Swallow, but Dirty Swallow was not listening to her. Dirty Swallow stood still in the center of the kitchen. There was a sense of movement around her, a draft of spinning air. Her skirt was soft over her fat hips and worn so thin in places Louise wondered if she was seeing flesh, certain she could make out Dirty Swallow's dirt-dark skin beneath her pale skirt. The woman wore a belt of snakeskin and rattlers, her very presence a rustling noise that hushed the room. One rattle on her belt almost swept the floor and Louise tried to envision the length of the snake it had come from. A coolness whispered the linoleum floor, a vague scent of cucumbers split by sun was rising from the damp corners of the room. Louise heard the ticking shift of rattlers beneath the house.

"Go now," her grandmother said to Dirty Swallow. "You're not welcome here with your threats."

Louise had heard that Dirty Swallow wore a live snake around her waist, a big brown rattler with yellow eyes. She tried not to look too closely at the woman's hips, afraid she might see the shifting pattern of a diamondback. Dirty Swallow gazed out the open door and Louise turned to see a snake belly up the steps toward her. Dirty Swallow clicked her tongue and the snake stopped and coiled on the porch, its rattle lifted. Her grandmother was eyeing the broom propped in the corner. Dirty Swallow faced Louise with the squinting eyes of a mean drinker, hard poised and grinning, unpredictable because she was not a drinker. "I want you to answer my son," Dirty Swallow said. "Agree to marry him or someone in your family will be bit."

"You old bitch," Louise said loud enough to be heard.

"I see you're not raising your granddaughters right," Dirty Swallow said. "It doesn't surprise me."

"I won't make Louise do anything she doesn't want to," Grandma said. Dirty Swallow clapped her hands together once. The rattler slid back down the stairs leaving a belly trail in dust, silent and soon invisible at the edge of the weeds, and Louise knew then that Dirty Swallow had made her decision.

Louise stood on the porch and watched as Dirty Swallow cleared the field and met the highway. She bit her nails and watched the dragonflies tip downward to touch the weeds. This is the modern age, Sister Simon had told the class, we can't rattle bones to cure fevers. Hair clippings and toenails aren't going to save you from blizzards. Louise wasn't afraid of Dirty Swallow. She wasn't afraid of snakes. She was afraid of herself, she thought, afraid of the feelings Baptiste called up in her. She didn't want to live on the reservation her whole life. She wondered if there was something more, something beyond her grandmother's small house, something beyond the same roads she walked every day, something beyond Baptiste Yellow Knife. She looked at the hills. The river was motionless. In the heat the sky was tired, drained of color, everything seemed to be sleeping in the afternoon sun. She could see Dirty Swallow still walking in the distance. She walked steadily, and sometimes the pitch of the road would sink her out of sight and then she would appear again farther away, and when she passed over the last hill Louise could no longer see her. A scorched wind pulsed at the door.

Louise expected her grandmother to scold her but her grandmother came outside to help Florence get down from the lean-to. "Don't be such a coward," she heard her grandmother say, and for a moment Louise thought her grandmother was speaking to her. "You can't run from the things you're afraid of," she was saying to Florence.

Louise looked far off to the Mission Mountains, so hot, dizzy beads of blood spun black in her vision. Even with her eyes closed she could see the red sun. Old thoughts returned. She remembered her mother as she was being carried from her room. Charlie Kicking Woman had lifted her up from the bed and as he turned toward the door Louise saw her mother's face. Her face was swollen, the color of water-washed wood, pale, gray. She had looked so frail to Louise, almost holy, like St. Bernadette. She could see the delicate veins along her mother's jawline, the veins the color of turquoise at her temples.

Fever had frayed her beautiful hair but, as she passed Louise, her hair had brushed Louise's face and she had felt the sweet touch of her mother once more for the last time.

In the huckleberry summer after her mother had died, she remembered listening outside the open kitchen window to her grandmother and her aunt talking about the choices of men, of bad medicine and the power of the old marriage. She was a young girl standing barefoot to a long summer just beginning, and she imagined a skin bag dark with the oil of many hands, curling around the singed tips of her hair. Even then she had been thinking of Baptiste, Baptiste leaning over her as she lay on the schoolroom floor, her blood leaving, a heavy black smoke rising white from his teeth, a whispering, his breath inhaling her blue, blue heart. She wanted to believe that if her mother was still alive, her mother could tell her what to do. She wanted to jump down from the porch, run fast toward the mountains. But she had no way of knowing if she ran toward or away from him. Baptiste was everywhere.

They walked toward Perma. Grandma had promised Florence a bottle of Orange Nesbitts if she walked all the way there without complaint. Louise had chased her sister and they were laughing so hard Grandma said they would be crying soon. "Mrs. Yellow Knife," Florence called Louise. "Mrs. Yellow Knife." Louise ran from Florence like she was running away. Her breath was high in her chest. The magpies talked on the fence posts, and the sun shimmered over them. The black-eyed daisies were thick by the roadside and Grandma had stopped to pick the tender shoots before they blossomed. Louise remembered jumping the barrow pit. She had turned to see Florence midleap behind her. She heard the flutter of paper against weeds. She saw a grasshopper land on Florence's shoulder. Grandma was peeling the flower stems. She offered each of them a taste of Indian celery. "I love the spring," Grandma said to them. Florence tried to slap the stem from Louise's hand. "Don't dawdle," Grandma said. She had walked ahead of them. Louise ran to catch up to her. She walked beside her grandmother and it felt good to be walking.

Heat waved at the end of the road. "Why do we see water at the end of the road," she asked her grandmother, "when there is no water?"

"That's to keep lazy people walking," Grandma said.

Louise looked back at Florence. She appeared to be limping. "Hey, Lazy," Louise called to her. Florence smiled back but her walking was unsteady. Her hair hung in two heavy braids in front of her. She seemed pitched forward, dizzy. Her face shined with sweat. Grandma stopped and, when she turned to see Florence, she dropped her flowers and hurried back to her. Florence was hopping on her right leg, and Louise wondered if she was just trying to get some attention. "I think I got stung by a bee," she told Grandma. Her left leg was so swollen her heavy stocking had begun to split. Grandma squatted down beside her and tugged Florence's stocking down. Louise was running toward them. She saw the two small fang pricks that bled at her sister's ankle. Her sister moved slowly to sit down. Grandma took her handkerchief from her head and dabbed at the bite. Florence's leg was as purple as the Mission Mountains, so tight, Louise felt the blood dim at the base of her skull. The fields were whining.

"Am I going to die?" Florence asked. Louise noticed her sister's eyes were slow and calm as if she had just woken from a fever sleep. Louise felt afraid.

"Go get help, Louise. Run," her grandmother said.

Her knees felt too weak to support her so she pumped her arms. She ran to catch the water at the end of the road. She ran to save her sister's life. She ran with the sun so hot in her throat the miles slowed before her. This isn't the Dark Ages, she could hear Sister Simon saying, people travel from one end of the earth to the other just for vacation. Men are civilized. We have telephones and typewriters. Electric mixers and wash machines. Indoor plumbing. You Indians must understand. We can talk to wild animals until we're blue in the face, but a bird is never going to tell you how to build a nest. Snakes won't bite our enemies because we tell them to. I'm here to liberate you from the darkness of superstition. Wake up, the sister had told the Indian children when their lips trembled at her ideas, wake up to the world.

Charlie Kicking Woman

◆

The Bite

It had been a slow day on patrol. I hadn't seen another car on the highway for hours. Nothing but the late-spring smell of sage and hay. I figured I would drive on over to the Magpie place. It was a hot day for spring. My uniform was burning like steel wool. I hadn't seen much of Louise lately. I had heard the rumors about her and Yellow Knife, stories that he'd been hanging around her, stories that he planned to marry her. I was hoping against that possibility. Baptiste Yellow Knife had turned into a mean, sullen man, a drinking man. I thought I might just take Louise out to my car and show her my log chart, show her all the times I'd picked Yellow Knife up. Drunk and disorderly, trespassing, assault, drunk and disorderly, drunk and disorderly, creating a public nuisance. The list was long. I thought about showing her grandmother too. Louise wasn't easy to convince.

I reminded myself that soon I would have license to chase her again. She was a truant, one of the half-breeds we had to round up every year for school. It was my job to hunt her. She ran away often, sometimes twice a week, and over the years she had become a headache to me. I wanted to save her. I believed if I kept corralling her, eventually school would stick. I don't know if I imagined what she would become with an education but I knew what she would become without one. I didn't want to see Louise White Elk in the poorhouse, a husband like Baptiste beating her on weekends, ten squalling kids and another on the way. I wanted something different for her and sometimes my wife accused me of wanting her for myself.

The BIA social worker Mr. Bradlock had tried everything. Once he placed her in the Dixon school with all white students. Then they placed Louise back in the Ursulines', then back again to Dixon. She didn't like it much at either place, and ran away every chance she got. Last fall, she had hooked up with Georgette Small Salmon in St. Ignatius and the two of them ran off to Hot Springs together. I picked Louise up two days later, smelling like cigarette smoke and alcohol. She was wearing sunglasses. Georgette had punched her because Louise had been acting as though she was better than everybody else. Louise, Georgette told me later, was acting like a white woman. I guess when Louise asked Georgette what made her think acting like a white woman was acting better than everybody else she got slugged. The bruise around Louise's eye looked like the fat, split seam of a plum.

Mr. Bradlock thought Louise's grandmother would be old-fashioned, someone he could reason with. "You may be talking to an old woman," I told him, "but this is an Indian grandmother you're talking to."

"That's right," Mr. Bradlock had said, "I'm going to talk to the girl's grandmother." And I knew he was imagining a strict woman in a high collar, an old woman who baked cookies. Louise's grandmother did wear long skirts and high-topped moccasins. She covered her braided black hair with a bright kerchief, and her hair had silvered at the temples. She was also a gambler, stayed up all night for days on end to play stick game. She still rode the horses at the Kalispell horse races. She could chop wood and walk twenty miles to Mission to go to mass. She put up her own food, jerked beef, and fished in summer and winter. She stood about five feet tall but she could work like a man. She had different ideas for her granddaughter. "That's one grandmother," I had told Mr. Bradlock, "that won't be turning her granddaughter over to us, even if it is for Louise's own good." But he didn't listen to me.

I had to go with Mr. Bradlock to Grandma Magpie's house. It was a mistake. Mr. Bradlock told Grandma Magpie her granddaughter was wild and uncontrollable, that he'd placed her in every school from Mission to Dixon to help her, just to have her run off to Hot Springs like a floozy. The old woman had tossed us both out of the house.

Mr. Bradlock was right in some ways. There was a wildness about Louise. I'd seen her outrun the fastest boys at the summer powwow. Once, on a dare, she swam the white, churning waves of the Flathead River. I saw her dive down between the boulders that writhed the furious current. She had jumped into the deep pond at the Magpie place to save her grandmother when she broke through ice. There were times I wished I could be like Louise.

I drove the road that day not seeing, my ideas too big in my head, not thinking I would see Louise on the road when I caught a glimpse of her running toward me. Once again, I felt like I was the one caught by her. My heart was pounding fast. I pulled my hat down over my eyes, thought she could read me. My heart raced whenever I saw Louise. And whenever I drove out near Perma I looked for her whether I was supposed to or not. I'd told myself that looking for Louise was my job, and usually it was, but it wasn't my job that Saturday.

I rolled down my window. She was breathing hard. Her neck was wet with sweat. Her hair curled around her face. She leaned over ready to talk and tried to open the back door. "Let me in," she said. I hesitated, wondered what she was trying to pull this time. She kicked the door. "Charlie," she said, and I liked the sound of my name on her tongue. I was trying not to smile because I believed I had her then. "Please," she finally said.

I got out of the car and had her scoot over in the front seat. She pointed down the road. I was still thinking about my log sheets, the things I was going to tell her.

"There," she said, her breath almost a wheeze. She was looking down the road. I smiled a bit. I looked a long ways down the road knowing her bull. "What you got going there, Louise?" I said. I put the car in neutral. I rolled down my window the rest of the way and took a long breath of the day, knowing I was smelling her. I crossed my arms and couldn't keep from smiling.

"What are you doing?" she said, still breathing hard. She hit my shoulder. "Charlie," she said, her eyes were wide. I held the mike to my mouth to tell the dispatcher where I was. "Drive," she said, her voice sighed. "Drive." She bent over and grabbed her ankles and for a moment I wondered if she was trying to hide from someone. She reached over to me then and squeezed my knee with a strong hand. "My sister's been bit by a rattler," she said so fast I could hardly get what she was saying. "Hurry." She pointed down the road and I could see the heartbeat in her throat. I felt the kick of my own stupidity. I threw the car in forward, but something in me was only half believing her. She had tricked me before. She studied the road, her hand to her forehead, and I looked sideways at her. The day had taken a fast turn.

We covered five miles, and each clocked mile I kept thinking to myself that she had run this mile, measuring myself against her strength and falling short. Louise waved her hands at me, but I had spotted them too. The grandmother and Louise's sister. Florence didn't look well. I was half relieved because Louise had been telling me the truth. I got out of the car and swung open the back door to let them in. I noticed Florence's left leg. It was so swollen it looked like an extension of her torso. It wasn't good. Her leg was so big it looked as if it would split open. I stared at it as I struggled in my pocket to find my good knife. I squatted down next to her. I told Grandma Magpie to cover Florence's face.

I've seen every stretch of this ground. I've walked the Jocko in the thunder-heat summer. My ankles have grazed the nests of a hundred rattlers, but in all my time I have only heard about one rattlesnake bite that wasn't just story. A white man from Thompson Falls got the bite about eight years ago. Poison clutched his heart. He died.

"This won't hurt too bad," I said to Florence, knowing it would hurt like a son of a bitch.

"Hold her leg," I said to Louise. The sun was so bright the back of my head ached. Louise sat right down in the dirt next to her sister and held on to her leg. I brushed my arm past Louise. I could hear the dryness of my skin against hers and it made me gulp breath, and I felt ashamed, halfway neglecting my job, thinking about Louise when I should have been thinking about her sister and the task at hand. Louise smelled like lemon and salt, sweet almost. I felt the gooseflesh rise on my arms.

The grandma told me the bite was just above the anklebone on the inside of the leg. I turned Florence's foot out. It seemed her leg would squeak it was so tight with blood and water. My fingerprints stayed on her ankle long after I let go of her. I used her grandmother's red scarf as a tourniquet. I could see the double prick of the bite where the lightning lick of fangs could have shot enough venom in the girl to kill a six-foot man. I held my breath for a minute and prayed for both of us. I hadn't seen a bite before but I had heard the stories. With some the cool venom soaks the brain, with others the venom rides the nervous system like lit gasoline, short-circuiting, functions failing. I had never heard of an Indian dying from a bite, and I didn't want to be the first to witness it.

I cut down deep into the bite trying to think of the five-and-a-quarter-pound Brown I'd caught at Ninepipes the week before. The head of that fish was so big I had to swing an axe just to split it from the spine. A fish so big the ducks were in danger. I held this thought as I leaned over the red blood of Florence's leg to suck poison through my teeth. I closed my eyes and sucked hard. I could taste the iron-slick blood. I thought of that Brown lifting its head from the water, pulling a small wake behind itself. I could smell blood in my nostrils. My stomach quivered. I spit three times. I spit until my saliva stringed, and I wiped my mouth on the sleeve of my uniform, and then I sucked some more.

I could feel the hot sun on my scalp. The weeds buzzing hard. I clamped my mouth down tight over her leg and gave it one long pull rolling my eyes up to see Louise looking back at me. My tongue was salt. I sucked again harder. There was a sudden stinging taste in my mouth. I thought of all of that poison curdling my watering tongue. I looked up to see Louise still watching me, and I felt foolish for caring what she thought. I sucked blood until I was breathless. And then I had to take a breather. I had to stand in the dizzying sun and look away from Florence. I had no way of knowing if I had saved her. I looked off toward the sun-bleached fields, down the long road to Mission. My chest was trembling.

I took a deep breath and squatted down next to Florence. "Put your hands around my neck and hold on," I told her. I pulled her next to me and hoisted her up and over to the car. Her grandmother got in back with her. Louise sat in the front seat before I could get a leg in. I switched on the siren with no car in sight for miles, with only magpies fanning the low marshes. I floored that car like a sheriff. One hundred miles an hour all the way to Mission. The windows sang with wind.

I wanted to stay with them, to sit with Louise, but I had another call and I left them. I thought about the time Louise tricked me. Then I was new to the force and Louise comes along, all of thirteen years, and rooks me into giving her a ride home. At one point, I remember, she put her bare feet up on the dash and she opened the ashtray, and I knew she was trouble. She's trouble now. I can figure that out. I got back to my office like I'd done a good deed and learned that Louise was a runaway, that the superintendent was looking for her, had been for days. The chief of police heard me talking about her, called me into his office proud I'd detained her, commending me even. Me, green-horned and grinning with authority until I figured out the chief thought I still had her, that I had locked her up or turned her over to the state. It seems she'd left the boarding school. She'd been running, they told me. We can't catch the little shit. I stood there, suddenly in the backwash of my own incompetence, with my uniform hat in my hand, my big badge gleaming on my chest, remembering how Louise had smiled at me when she waved good-bye. I'd waved back, feeling good. She had to hurry home, she had said. I remembered the dust print of Louise's toes stamped on my dash.

Our property intersected the old Magpie allotment so I had watched Louise grow up. We would burn the fields at the end of summer, mend the wind-worn fences. I remember seeing Louise out in the fields, skinny and smart but definitely nothing to look at. She was a tomboy with straggly hair. She must have been about eleven years old when she broke her grandmother's horse. I watched Louise crawl up on that stallion's broad bare back without a bridle, and the horse gave her a ride, the kind of ride I've seen cowboys take when they're looking to win, a bucking hard ride that would land Louise flat on her bony ass. But the next day she was riding smooth, the horse and Louise like one. No chomping bit, no ass-slapping ride, just grace. Her nose was snapped near the top by a tumble from that stallion, but the break has served as a reminder of her fine bones and her tough spirit. Because of that break her nose looks delicate now. She was a roughneck child, ugly even, but now there's not a soul that can hold a candle to Louise. I often think about the day when she made a fool of me, when she was just thirteen and I was taking her home, the hot wind blowing through the open windows, the flush on her face. I found myself looking at her. She is beautiful and she is not beautiful. I compare Louise to the land, connect the idea of her somehow to when I was a kid and we'd have to go to wakes in Camas Prairie. God, I hated that country. It was hot and dry, nothing but weeds or cold stinging wind at thirty below. A couple of trees. An August dust so fine it powdered your knees when you walked, or sand-snow drifting across houses and roads, brutal and blinding. That was Camas Prairie. Now I drive that stretch of road in winter and summer. I come down into that valley and the fields are pale and the sky is pale and peaceful with a sun that lights even the ragged weeds, every distant hill, every rock shimmering a different color. I can see for miles and I can't stop looking or thinking about how lucky I am to see this country, to belong here. I can't stop looking at this land and I guess that's what Louise is like to me. She's always changing. I can't get a fix on her. But because we have shared close to the same plot of land, because we are from the same tribe, we are alike. Something about Louise and something about all the Indians here is something about me, a blood kinship, a personal history shared.

Aida, my wife, is Yakima Indian. She grew up far from the Flathead, and sometimes that makes me feel distant from her, as if something is missing between us. Aida can live here the rest of her life, speak pretty much the same language, but her home place is different from mine. I hold no remembrance of the people and places of my wife's past. Louise, on the other hand, has always been a part of everything I have known and loved. She is a part of me.

When I was a young man my uncle asked me a favor. His back was weak and he had a chore for me. I didn't know until we pulled up to the Magpie place that I was being asked to perform a task I wasn't quite up to. Annie White Elk had passed away. Pneumonia. She had gone to look for her husband, thinking he was out hunting. He wasn't. He was shacking up with Loretta Old Horn. Annie was gone for three days, and the rain was so heavy it poured in a thousand silver streams from the low sky without let up. Then it turned warm, that spring of '36. The bees were out everywhere, hovering around the porch and buzzing in the barn-board rafters. It was the cold rain and sudden heat, they say, that took Annie White Elk at twenty-nine years of age. She left her daughters, Louise and Florence, to the care of her mother. I had to carry her body down the stairs to the kitchen where Grandma Magpie was waiting to dress her daughter for burial. They had made a table for the body out of rough planks laid over sawhorses.

It was about the time I started noticing things a person should never notice. I walked into their house that afternoon and was surprised at how the sunlight lit the kitchen, a warm yellow light glowing in a sad room. I didn't know much then. I thought all the Indians were poor, because we seemed to be, but we were not poor compared to the White Elks. My father worked in the lumber mill in Dixon. We slept in the same room but we had beds and bed frames. They had flour sacks filled with cattails sewn together, no frames. They slept on the floor, the cold seeping through cracks, chinks of light poked through walls without plaster. Wallpaper was old catalog cutouts. They didn't have sheets, only rough wool blankets that had belonged in better days to horses. I tried not to stare.

Grandma Magpie pointed to the stairs. My uncle visited with her. "Go on, son," he had said to me. I needed coaxing. The steps held no railing, just a steep box of stairs turning toward a hole in the ceiling. There was a powdery smell along the stairwell, a smell I knew had not been there before. I had gone to many wakes. I had shaken the hands of the dead but the dead I had seen were prepared for viewing. Annie White Elk had just passed away. There was a smell in the room I have come to recognize as death. There is no other smell like death, though some things can remind me of it. My uncle told me we were like animals because we can smell death for the first time and know what it is. When I reached the last step I looked down to see my uncle looking back up at me. He nodded his head and then looked away from me.

I could hear their voices. They were saying something about how Indians begin to see ghosts just before they die. To this day I dislike the sayings that accompany visits to the dead. The hallway was dark. A silver light thread through a crack in the ceiling and traced the path I walked to the small room. It was cold upstairs because the rafters weren't sealed. When the wind began blowing it made a sound that caught inside me, and then a scent filled the hall, sudden and sweet in my throat. It wasn't home like I knew. It wasn't the hiss of day-old coffee on a hot stove. Not that smell. It wasn't the quiet heartbeat of clocks that has its own smell too or the smell of fry bread put to grease. Not that either. It was the damp smell of cold rain, water stains and water-swollen wood. I could smell pine needles and alcohol. I remembered my mother had told me that Annie White Elk had rubbed vanilla into the heat of her wrists and my mother had frowned on that luxury for a woman who had little to eat. I heard the wind again and the smell was gone as suddenly as it had shown up. The back of my throat was tight. There was only this small house for them that the wind claimed like a channel. Rain bled the walls to rust, and the newspaper wallpaper curled back from the ceiling. There were spots along the hallway, like warm spots in water, then a coolness again that made me gulp breath. I walked slowly down the hall, stalling, feeling my way with my hands.

I was surprised that the door to where Annie lay was glossy and I could see my face on its smooth surface, and I looked like the intruder I was. The body was on the floor. I didn't know Louise was in the room. She must have hidden behind the door as I entered. I saw

Annie's feet first, small and shoeless. Her feet gleamed like polished wood. A rough blanket was pulled up to her chin. I could feel the prickle of heat in my armpits, a heat flushed my neck as I bent over her. I tried to pick her up, bending from the waist, but I couldn't pull her to me. I knelt on the homemade bed, heard the dry rustle of cattails beneath my knees. As I was lifting her up from the floor the blanket slipped from her. She was naked. I scrambled to reach the blanket but was afraid of dropping her. I had to lay her back down to secure the blanket around her. I couldn't help staring at her dark breasts, but after all these years I can remember only the white bones of her ribs pressing up through her brown skin, that I could count them, each rib, as if she was holding a full breath, as if she was still afraid she could be hurt. I had heard the dead were heavy but she was so light I felt she would lift from me, so light I seemed to be holding her spirit. When I looked up I caught a glimpse of Louise hiding behind the door, a small, skinny kid who'd just lost her mother. I carried Louise's mother down that hall and down those steps. Annie had only asked for one thing, Grandma Magpie said, her daughter had asked to be buried in a homemade pine casket with a green satin lining. I helped my uncle build her coffin. I felt proud to be a man. I think that event sealed in me the desire to help others.

I try to think back, will myself to see the girl behind the door, but as hard as I try I cannot see Louise's young face then. The image of Louise that most sticks in my mind was years later. I'd been called in to check out the death of Ernestine Chief Spear, a young girl who had choked to death in a fit, the nuns called it. Ernestine died at the Ursulines'. I took my time to check on the matter. I wasn't up for it. I drove around back of the Ursuline building to park. I adjusted my hat and pulled out my mileage log. I tried to do anything to avoid the inevitable. I had wanted to sit there for a minute, breathe in the clean April air. I knew Chief Spear's family up near Pistol Creek. I had to drive there too, pull up as a policeman scattering their other kids to the hills, to tell her family she was dead. I was new to the job, thinking the nuns should have had the chore of breaking the news to the family, not me, but I had to be the one to tell Ray Chief Spear his daughter was dead. I had to punch that family with the news their thirteen-year-old girl had died. As I was driving up their road I knew I had to hide my own imaginings from them. They could see their daughter in my eyes, their sister dying in a dark room with floors so polished they gleamed like water. I couldn't stop myself from seeing Ernestine chok-ing to death in a night-black room while the nuns were probably singing or praying by candlelight.

When I told the Chief Spear family I was sorry I realized I wasn't sorry like I should have been. I wasn't sorry I drove a big official car because even the reservation problems began to look good from behind a windshield. I wasn't sorry I had more food to eat these days than I ever had. I would never be so hungry I would choke on the food I was eating as, I suspected, their daughter had. I wasn't sorry the whites treated me better when I put on the badge and that sometimes I thought I was better too.

The worst part is deep down I knew even then I wasn't any better than any other Indian with a job. Going to the Ursulines' just reminded me of my own failures, because after only a few minutes in the Sisters' company I found myself blaming Ernestine Chief Spear for her own death. I had listened to the nuns, and what they told me was Ernestine Chief Spear was bad, and because she was bad she had died. They didn't say that to me with their words. They told me every-thing with their sternly crossed arms, the sagging twist of their mouths. It was Ernestine's own fault she had been locked up, the bru-tal hint being she got what she deserved.

And I stood there, dumb to the nuns. I stood there with a pencil and a hardback report and I couldn't make sense of any of it. It just seemed to me the more good the white man tried to do for us the more trouble we had. The government thought it was a good thing for the Indians to attend the white man's school, to be instructed by a group of women who had never known love. Women who were more lost than we were as a troop of wild-eyed Indians, homesick, lousy, smelling like wood smoke. Women who came from France, women who came from Germany. Women who were more like us Indians than they cared to admit. Women who had lost their identities too, even their names, like our names, were lost to them. Nuns. Sisters who were not sisters. Their hands so white there was a gray look about them.

And I used to think they hated us. I'd been struck by these women, had my ears slapped for laughing, had been cuffed so hard I bit through my lower lip. But I felt sorry for these women and their lonesome lives. I used to walk up behind the school and look at the graveyards of all these women buried far from their families, knowing that long after we had left the Ursulines' they would stay.

I've got a lot of problems to deal with here, more than I liked. I had to accept the nuns at their word. Their uniform would always be more commanding than the one I wore. Their story ached in my ears, because I was telling myself the same story, because somehow the blame rested with me, because I was Indian too. And Ernestine Chief Spear died, I thought, because she was Indian. She died because she was Indian, and Indians are stupid. Stupid, stupid, the whole while I attended the Ursulines' the nuns told me how stupid Indians were, again and again, so many times that I began to believe we were stupid. The idea sank to my heart and I would go home and sulk at the hard life I couldn't escape, knowing my grandparents must be stupid too, because they were so proud to speak a language that couldn't be written. Illiterate. To the nuns we were all hopelessly stupid, unteachable, lost.

I'm not even sure why I chose to believe what the nuns told me when I was growing up or why sometimes their words still sting. Even Baptiste Yellow Knife refused to believe most of what they said. The nuns couldn't get to him like they got to me. When Yellow Knife draws a sober breath he still says the old ways of our people are the best, the right path is simple and the right path is still living in the ways of our people. I can't stand his self-righteousness. I'm seeing too many of our people stumbling toward an early grave and he's one of them. I'm seeing too many Indians who may be as stupid as the nuns gave them credit for. If the old ways are the best, the best is losing, and I want to win.

"When did you last check on Ernestine?" I asked.

Sister Simon told me Chief Spear had only been checked once that morning when her door was unlocked for breakfast. "We lock them in," she said, "because Louise White Elk and Ernestine Chief Spear were climbing out on the fire escape or sneaking down to the boys' corridor to smoke. " She squinted at me, suggesting something more. She handed me a key from her deep, black pocket and nodded her head toward the door at the end of the hall.

When I opened the door Louise bolted. I saw her run past Sister Simon. She was barefoot and my first instinct was to chase her. She ran so fast she was gone before I knew it. I stood for a while watching the empty stairwell. I'm not sure what I was thinking at first, not thinking at all, I guess, though I remember I could not shake the image of Louise running from that room. I had expected only to see a dead girl. It never occurred to me that the nuns would lock Louise back up in the room with Ernestine after they had found Ernestine dead. I removed my hat to enter the room.

There was a smell in the room, the familiar smell of death again, too sweet, not like flowers, more like potatoes, frozen potatoes, the kind we used to eat when there was nothing else to eat. Ernestine

Chief Spear was captured in a knot of sheets. Old sheets strangled her arms, wrapped her ankles, bound her so tight the rigid arch of her back suggested a struggle to free herself from the grip of the sheets rather than the struggle to regain her breath. Her hair was dry and snarled. A small froth, like egg whites, beaded her mouth. Her eyes were open, clean as glass. I felt a flutter in my chest and I swallowed hard. My mouth was thick with saliva. My chest was tight. I turned back to Sister Simon. She was still standing in the doorway with her hands folded in front of her. Her black habit was chalk-stained. I expected her to be praying, but she was looking at me like I was supposed to clean up the mess instead of investigate.

"You locked Louise back up in here with her?" I said, turning again toward Ernestine. Sister Simon was calm and justified. "We didn't want her out in the halls," she said. "We didn't want her to scare the others." I nodded, knowing cruelty would never be a crime around here.

I checked the room to distract myself. The lamp by the bedside had been broken. There was no other source of light in the room except the window, and it had been partially boarded; a bad jail for a grown man let alone two girls in the throes of puberty. It had been dark in here all night. Kick marks marred the bottom of the door and the shellac had been scratched off. Louise. Places in the wall clawed. Bloodstains. I looked away. "You must have heard something," I said, "the door banging?"

"Nothing," she said. "If the students heard anything, they haven't said."

I saw myself again, a young boy, my ear pressed to the heavy door, frightened and silent. I imagined Louise. It had been a full moon the night before, maybe just enough light came through the cracks of the board for Louise to witness the struggling face of Chief Spear. Louise must have called for help. She had banged on the door. She had clawed at the walls until her fingers bled, and no one came. And even when they did come, even when they did see what Louise was calling for, they shut her back up again in this dim room with death. She had been alone all night and all morning in that closed room. The smell. The smell of bad death in a sealed room. I left there with a tight knot in my throat, not for Ernestine Chief Spear who had died without comfort, but for Louise who had lived through Ernestine's death. I felt for Louise that day. Some people just seem to draw trouble and Louise is one of them.

Florence recovered quickly. I went to see her in the hospital several times hoping, I guess, to see Louise. I found Louise there once without her grandmother. Louise kept her face hidden behind a fashion magazine, and didn't even look up when I cleared my throat and offered her a ride home. Summer glared through the big hospital windows. They'd put Florence's leg in a shining silver cast that caught the light. I had to squint across that brilliant cast to catch a glimpse of Louise's legs. I looked until my eyes watered.

It was June when they released Florence. I made it my duty to give the whole family a ride home, sure that I would be traveling with Louise. But Louise slipped from the room while Grandma Magpie was signing Florence's discharge papers. I ended up riding with Grandma and Florence. My heart fluttered as we passed Louise on the highway. She lifted her hand, but when I stopped the car to offer her a ride, she pushed herself away from the window. "I'm walking," she said. I drove away reluctantly, watching the distance engulf her, the edge of the mountains fading, the shine of the river dulling in twilight, finally turning forward to stare at the open road stretching ahead of me for miles. I had hoped she would be afraid to walk the road after what had happened to her sister, but I would never be that lucky. It was clear she had other thoughts in her head.

Jules Bart and Louise

♦

The Cowboy

After the snake bit her sister, Baptiste was scarce. "I should
think he'd be ashamed of himself," Grandma told Louise.
"Their bad medicine is spinning back on the two of them. They'll be
laying low for a while." Louise had grown weary of Baptiste and talk
of Baptiste. "Be careful anyway," her grandmother warned her. "The
two of them are up to something." Louise had her fill of Baptiste. The
summer spread out before her and she felt restless. She spent time
alone sighing in tall grass, watching shadows of clouds pass over the
blond hills of Perma. Her grandmother would press her wrist to
Louise's cool forehead, make her drink juniper-berry tonic. Louise felt
like she was in love, in love with herself. Even Perma looked interesting. Louise would stand above her grandma's house, high on the hill,
and hold her arms out to catch the cool breezes of the short summer
nights. Sometimes she would sit on the porch of the Dixon Bar and
listen to the jukebox. She liked the songs about brokenhearted lovers.
She enjoyed listening to Eddie Arnold singing his cattle song because
it reminded her of the man who lived at Milepost 108, the champion
rodeo roper who'd recently returned home to the old Bart place.

He was a cowboy and she was an Indian, and Louise would sometimes imagine they would end up together because she knew it would never happen. The cowboy wasn't interested in her and that made him interesting. Jules Bart the Cowboy and Baptiste the Indian were at opposite ends of her world. She wanted something more than a dusty Indian man from Perma who drank his days away. She allowed herself to think of breaking from Baptiste with someone she imagined was tough enough to whip him, but she didn't really want either man. She wanted that summer to herself. She wanted to like whomever she pleased and for now she liked Jules Bart. As much as Baptiste Yellow Knife's interest in her repelled her, Jules Bart's disinterest attracted her.

Jules Bart's ranch was hidden behind the hills of Perma, but his fields were alongside the highway where she would often see him. Some nights, the warm nights, the breeze felt like water and Louise would watch him working in moonlight. He was long-legged and narrow-hipped. She had seen him drop his shirt from his shoulders and knot the sleeves around his waist to hang like a breech clout over blue jeans. Jules Bart was not like Baptiste Yellow Knife. Jules Bart had an easy patience about him. The moon would shine on his smooth skin and make her forget about Baptiste. In the dark grass she was only a whisper, close enough to hear the sound of his breathing.

Everything smelled good near his house. Spearmint and anise cradled deep pockets of grass. Even the fodder smelled good. The sweet, blood smells of farming were heat in her lungs. And all these smells and all the things around his place became a part of him, a part of a new life she imagined. She lay down in the cool grass to listen to him moving beneath stars. Irrigation pipes were throats on his back singing with wind. Sometimes she would hear him singing too. He would strum his guitar, sing mournfully about women and cows.

She had seen him buying oatmeal and mousetraps in Malick's store. Jules Bart had long-fingered, rein-bitten hands, and the bills looked small in his palms. As he leaned up against the counter she could see the boots he wore, golden leather roses on powdered elk skin. She had seen the same boots in the store catalog, but she had never seen anyone wearing them or anything like them. They were fancy riding boots that called attention to a man, and she imagined he'd have to be a fighting man to wear them. But Louise couldn't tell what type of man Jules Bart was. He was a man people liked to talk about but didn't seem to know. Louise had watched Jules Bart leaving the store. Sunlight was rose-colored and changed his skin to a shade near her own. She turned to Mr. Malick, feeling the heat rise to her face. She wondered if Jules Bart was aware she had been watching him that summer. She had learned that secrets were rare in small towns on the reservation. Everyone knew your business.

"Works out by your grandma's place," Mr. Malick had said, and Mr. Malick had puffed up proud to tell her that Jules Bart was a champion rodeo roper as if he himself claimed the honor. "Who doesn't know that?" Louise had said, and then felt ashamed of herself.

That same week she saw Jules Bart again sitting on the tailgate of Eddie Taylor's pickup eating a sandwich and wearing a different pair of boots. She walked past him kicking the warm dust with bare feet. She crossed the street pretending to be going to the Dixon Bar but the nearness of him made her feel awkward. Who cares if he's here, she told herself. Her knees hit together so she swung her arms more. She coughed, cuffing her hands together. She looked at him once and pretended to be looking somewhere else, because he wasn't looking back at her.

Eddie Taylor came out of the bar and whistled at her. Jules Bart glanced at her and then got in the pickup with Eddie. At that moment, she hated Eddie Taylor with his funny pinched nose he claimed was snapped when the hooves of a bucking horse had punched him in a fall. Whenever Eddie told the story he spoke with such serious eyes Louise could tell he was lying. Louise could see them a long way down the road. She watched the truck as it blended with the thinning trees that lined the hills to Perma.

It was the first summer Eddie Taylor had let her into the bar. He had poured her a beer so cold it made her teeth sing.

"Don't matter your age," he had told her. "Your looks will boost business." He had poured her another beer, then another, until the bar air spun cool and sweet over her head and the warm talk buzzed her ears.

Eddie had slammed some nickels into the jukebox and she had danced with a rancher who snagged his work-worn hands on the seat of her skirt. It was her first time in the bar drinking, and school was out. Baptiste seemed gone and the hot day sun leaned through the barroom window. She felt a new strength. She half hoped Jules Bart would find her there, that he would pull her up to a good jukebox tune.

That afternoon when she left the bar Eddie Taylor had walked her to the screen door, and with a wet smile, told her to come back. And she did go back, sometimes to have a pop, sometimes for a beer, but always with the hope she would see Jules Bart up close. She became a bar regular, returning so often Charlie Kicking Woman began to scout for her there.

It was a cold night without wind, a rare summer night cracked by winter, the next time she saw the cowboy. She had counted the days between seeing him, had marked each chance time on the outhouse wall with the stub of her cigarette. The cowboy had become a way to lift routine for her. Jules Bart was deliberate and slow that night. He no longer moved the way she remembered him, the way that relaxed her. He wasn't the man she had watched in the fields. He had become almost ugly and dull in the gray bar light. It was a new side to him that fascinated her with disappointment. She wondered how some men could change so quickly, become someone different because the night was long or lonesome, or because they had had too much to drink.

His lips were wet and his teeth were so white she thought of chalk. She glanced back pretending to be watching the door and saw him lean back too far on his bar stool. She took a hard swallow of beer. It was flat and left her throat dry. She heard the crack of wood as he hit the floor. No one moved to help him. She told herself again he wasn't the man she knew. The man she knew could lift himself up with one gathered movement, a cat reaching from sleep. He was anise and corn silk, the rough smell of water trickling in dirt troughs rutted deep by thirsty cattle. He wasn't the smell of smoke and barrooms and vinegared eggs.

She pushed herself back from the bar. Eddie Taylor shined a single glass until it squeaked. Louise walked over to Jules Bart. She could feel grit beneath the toes of her shoes so she walked hard placing each foot flat on the ground. He sat on the floor loose as an old woman's jowls. His head lolled forward. She breathed in and slipped her arms beneath his armpits, pulling up. She felt the lugging strain of him in her groin, in the bones shifting in her back. He wheezed forward, gathering the momentum of ten extra pounds.

"If anybody can, you can," somebody called to her.

She kneed Jules Bart hard in the back once, and he burped and sat up. She could feel the muscles in her legs flex hard. She squatted down for leverage and tightened her arms around the barrel of his ribs. His face was hot to her cheek and rough with whiskers. She pulled up and heard the dry whisper of his beautiful boots on the wood floor. She had him close to standing when Dag Bailey moved past her.

"I got her," he said.

And Louise watched him lift the man to standing. Jules Bart stood for a moment unassisted. In the wavering light Louise saw pale smoke rise up, a watery mist behind him. At the nape of his neck his dark hair curled with sweat. His jaw was slack as a child's near sleep. She saw Jules's head droop to Bailey's shoulder. For one brief moment, his eyes focused on her and then rolled back white.

A woman sniggered behind her. "I think he likes you."

Louise turned to her and saw grinning Marjorie Canfield, a thin white woman with bleeding gums who always ate U-No chocolate bars and drank tomato juice and beer from midafternoon till closing time.

"Piss up a rope," Louise said.

Jules Bart had drooled on her hand and she rubbed it in her skin like glycerine. All the men in the bar were looking at her. Louise straightened her skirt, ran her fingers through her hair, then lit a cigarette. She ordered another beer.

Dag Bailey had taken Jules Bart outside. She saw the red brake lights of Bailey's truck as they were leaving. She imagined Jules's face illuminated by the dim panel light, an angry sleep deep inside of him and his limp hands vulnerable as a wide, open wound. She looked again at Marjorie Canfield to measure a response.

"Honey, I'm not looking for a fight," Marjorie said. Louise sat down at the bar long enough so no one could recognize her broken heart.

She knew now he would never touch her thigh or arch his back into the lean darkness of her ribs. She did not have to be hiding in tall grass for him not to see her. She imagined she was invisible to him. He did not see her slide her skirt up the smooth length of her thigh. He did not see the button left unsnapped or the deep shadow between her breasts as she bent forward to order again and again. He looked toward her and saw only the road beyond, the failing smoke of her cigarette. She felt thin around him, thin enough to see through and beyond. And the thought made her feel distant from herself. Unrecognizable. She wondered if she had been defined by both men. Baptiste because he saw only her, Jules because he could not see her at all.

Jules Bart and Baptiste Yellow Knife were a shifting of light, a different way of seeing. They could each be beautiful, and ugly. She wanted things to be different from what they were. She didn't want Jules Bart to be just a man, like Baptiste Yellow Knife. She saw herself standing before twilight watching her image in water, the bottomless pond gurgling. If she could see herself in the shadowy dusk at the moment darkness eclipsed her face she would see her real self. But that moment never came. Only Baptiste Yellow Knife would come for her. The man she despised was the only man thinking of her.

Before sleep she would hear the dry cattails near the pond, the cottonwoods, the steady sucking squawfish. Sometimes she would get up from the warm sleep of her sister to pump a glass of cold water, careful of her sister's shifting. In the moonlight her slip glowed a ghostly blue that chilled the length of her arms. She sank down against the white light feeling loneliness at the hollow of her knees, her throat swallowing the burning smell of sweet nettle. Hearing the steady breath of her sister in sleep, the sudden jerk, the pulling away, arms meeting knees, a forehead to back, a settling in toward the absence of her body.

The sky was gray with morning when she heard someone calling to her from the screened door. She knew it was Baptiste. She recognized his hard, insistent voice. She pulled on her skirt and slipped her arms into a blouse. She stepped out on the porch and frowned at him.

"Louise, don't be mad," he said. "I've missed you. I've brought you a surprise." He disappeared behind the house and came back with his horse. Champagne was a beautiful horse, a quarter horse stallion that everyone envied. Baptiste had several horses but he knew this horse was her favorite. She could see the sun over the mountains, golden trails of light lit the high hills. Her grandmother was still sleeping but she would be up soon, would have been up hours earlier had she not waited up for Louise to come home the night before. Baptiste was on the horse in one easy movement. He reached for her.

"Come on," he said. "Ride with me."

She thought about Jules Bart, drunk and sleeping still. Men, Louise thought, were all the same. "Before I come with you," she said, "we have to get one thing straight."

Baptiste bent forward to hear her.

"If you ever harm anyone in my family again," she said, "I'll kill you."

He leaned back on Champagne and smiled at her and it came to Louise that he was different. He hadn't been drinking.

"OK, Louise," he said. "I believe you would."

She grabbed his hand then and he pulled her up on the broad, bare back of the horse. She hugged his waist tight and dug her knees into the barrel of the horse. She thought for one brief moment and then she clutched his balls hard enough to make him squeal. "I'm serious," she said. "I'll kill you dead."

"I understand," he said. "I get your point." She let go of his crotch then, and Champagne was running. Baptiste slapped his thighs and Champagne ran faster. They were running dead speed, the ground passed quickly beneath them, pale rocks, twigs, sage, the highway, the railroad tracks gleamed beneath them. She felt light. Her hair whipped her face. She had never ridden a horse so fast. She heard the spray of gravel, the hard ground was passing. She held her breath and held on.

Charlie Kicking Woman

◆

The Hard Truths

Being a tribal officer was never easy, but the job was hell when I was working with Officer Cliburn Railer, a white police officer from Lake County. Railer didn't like me either. Old Railer got wind of my connection to Baptiste Yellow Knife, not something I like to admit even to the Indians who know we're related. Yellow Knife's my cousin. My auntie's husband was a Yellow Knife and, according to the old ways, that bonds me to him. Just last week Railer referred to Baptiste as the troublemaker, the troublemaker my blood brother. Railer saying that to me made me realize again how much I had in common with Baptiste Yellow Knife, and how stupid the white man could be. Railer was imagining I had mixed blood with Baptiste by choice; Boy Scouts behind the outhouse rubbing self-inflicted cuts, pledging oaths. I wondered how the white man could be civilized if they didn't know their relations. How did Railer know his wife wasn't his sister; his mistress, his cousin. For a moment, I felt superior. For a moment, I believed the reason the white man had become so crazy was because they were an inbred people. I considered the story of Adam and Eve the nuns would tell us, how that story shamed me when I was a young boy dreaming of girls and letting myself imagine parting the warm thighs of my cousin Eileen. For a while I figured if we were all related to Adam and Eve we were all brothers and sisters, first cousins. The idea allowed me to shame myself, to entertain for a few short years the idea of bedding all my beautiful cousins. And the idea soiled me, made me grim-nailed, leering and disrespectful. An idea that still has the power to shame me, can make me lower my eyes in Eileen's company, turn my back to family gatherings.

I couldn't deny even to Railer that Baptiste was my relation. I'm still shaming myself by trying to deny the connection. My mother used to encourage me to help Baptiste, to be a good example to him. When Baptiste was younger I'd tried to have a man-to-man talk with him. I was twenty-some years old and Baptiste must have been about thirteen at the time. Baptiste was smoking kinnikinnick outside the Dixon Bar. I sat down next to him on the stoop. He was just a scrawny kid but he turned his back to me. He was bare-chested and the day drifted to the edge of cold. His skin welted with goose bumps, but he squared his shoulders to the cold and most likely to me. "Look Baptiste," I had said, "Auntie tells me you got some problems." He pulled on his homemade cigarette, and I heard the tough snap of a seed exploding. He faced me and blew smoke out his nose like a tough guy. I thought I had his attention. "You can talk to me, you know," I had said. "If you got problems, kid, you can talk to me."

"Yeah," he said, lifting his eyebrows to me, and I felt good then, hopeful, like I was making a difference. "I've got a lot of problems." He drew hard on his cigarette again, then opened his fingers to let it drop to the ground. Before I could stop him he stepped on the stogie with the ball of his bare foot and rubbed it out. He didn't flinch or even show discomfort, and I thought what a kid he really was. "A lot of problems," he said looking me in the eye. I was nodding, urging him on. "And you're number one," he said. He had taken me off guard. He stood up and I saw how thin he was, scrawny, long-armed and legged, his thin pants high-water. His belt was looped with a woman's red scarf. He looked pitiful.

I put my hand on his shoulder and he pulled away from me with such force it startled me. I felt the heat of his shoulder, the strength of his frame. "Don't be getting funny with me," he said. And he walked away from me then. I don't know how long I sat on those cold porch steps in my polished shoes and ironed shirt, my good intentions turned sour. I could hear the bar customers at my back talking about the price of cattle, laughing about their hard luck, and I wasn't even good enough to step into that bar and wash down Baptiste's sour words with a beer. I wasn't even good enough to walk behind Baptiste. I sat there for a long time until I believed I had shaken the connection. I was wrong.

I'd been called in for an accident backup outside of Perma. A Studebaker had struck a guardrail post and flipped over on its top. Railer had made it to the scene first. I saw the red glare of his cherry light. It was early afternoon and the sun was beating off the bumper. The top of the car was almost flat. It was going to be rough, I thought. I stopped my car and reached for my flares.

"I got cones in the back of my vehicle," Railer said. He was standing casually next to the wreck, his arm resting on the underside of the car like he was leaning on a fence chatting with a neighbor. I detected a grim smile on his face and I thought he was a cruel bastard. I avoided looking at the vehicle upside down on the hot pavement. I had to steady myself. Railer got a kick out of me when I got sick by the roadside. He'd seen me more than once heaving my lunch into the weeds. And he feels free to comment on my predicaments. "See you had egg salad for lunch," he would say, and his comments would make me sick all over again. I guess he thought he was funny. He's a sick

SOB. I took some deep breaths. "Try the trunk," he says to me. I grabbed the keys from the ignition. I saw a magpie flutter to a fence post, the sky was the blue of blue veins, the blue of a white man's eyes. I could smell hot road tar and a faint whiff of wild rose. I wanted to be out in that field. I felt a particular swell of lonesome. Since I began working for law enforcement I saw the landscape differently, littered with glittering chrome, beads of broken turn signals, busted head-lamps silver in sunlight, steering wheels teetering from the high branches of a tree, hub screws, baby bottles, schoolchildren's note-book papers, lipstick holders, car registrations, love letters. We found them all. The miles were haunted. I rubbed my neck and grabbed the cones. Railer was squinting at me. I heard then the high, shrill voice of a man. "Get me out of here," he screamed. Railer hunched down by the car door and grinned into a few inches of squashed window. I dropped the cones quickly, almost relieved. I could see the red face of a white man. His tie fluttered with his breath when he spoke, spitting directions at us. I surveyed the door.

"Are you feeling any pain?" I asked the man as I crowded next to Railer and checked the door. "Steering column's pinching my nuts," he said. Railer wiped his hand over his mouth trying to hide his grin. I looked at the ground, checking for gasoline. Radiator fluid gleamed on the road, and I smelled the dense sweet scent of it, felt the throb of my head. I'd come to hate that smell.

"Get me out of here," the man yelled. "Get me out of this frigging car now."

"We got an Indian brave to help us now," Railer told the man, always the funny guy. "We'll have you out in no time." I was too tired to feel even a small well of anger. The man shot me a look. "I don't care if you got the whole damn tribe or the U.S. Cavalry," he said, "just get me the hell out of here."

"Not to worry," Railer said. "We'll have you out in a jiff." Railer stood up and tipped his head for me to follow him. I ignored him. I could see the door was stuck tight, buckled to a weld. I reached to pry the door with my fingers but Railer grabbed my shoulder. "Kicking Woman," he said and motioned again for me to follow him. "We got some equipment in the car, big fella," he said. The man arched his neck to see me, his eyes mournful and bulging.

"Sir," I said, "just relax."

Railer stood by the side of his car. "I called for the fire truck," he said, "but they're out on a call. It's just you and me, friend."

I glanced back at the car. I could hear the man wheezing. I was thinking he'd give himself a stroke.

"Got any ideas?" Railer said. He had pulled a toothpick from his jacket pocket and he was teetering it between tight teeth.

"We could get a crowbar," I said.

"I thought of that," Railer said. "It isn't going to work. You got a winch on that heap?" he said.

I was getting nervous. I didn't want to kill a man who stood every chance of living except for a stupid call on our part. I shook my head no.

"Look," Railer said. "I got a chain in the car. We can leverage it on a guardrail post and use your car to right the vehicle."

I knew Railer was suggesting we use my car for fear of damaging his own, but it was pointless to fight him. A man was hanging upside down in a car. "OK," I said unwillingly. The early afternoon had turned into a long stretch of day and we were in the middle of it. I held my stomach and turned back to my car.

"What's going on?" the man asked. I could detect fear in his voice. His anger had gone. I saw the sheen of slobber on his cheeks. He was close to shitting himself.

"Take it easy," I said. "We're going to pull you right-side up. We'll be able to pop you right out of there." I could see his tight hands clutching the steering wheel. He'd lost any faith he had in our abilities, and I had too. Railer was unwinding the chain and securing the underside of the truck. We looked busy anyway. I could hear the tick of the chain as he threaded it through the drive train.

I backed up my cruiser and surveyed the hillside. I would have to get around to the passenger side. I was looking for a down side. I found a low incline and drove down. I heard the scrape of weeds, the squeal of rocks beneath the floorboards of the car. For a moment I had the idea that our scheme just might work. Railer strapped the chain to my tow bar and then gestured for me to begin the pull. I took a deep breath and held it. I gunned the engine, heard the chain roll, then felt the jolt of the catch. It slammed me in my seat. I had gassed too quick. I could smell the burn of motor oil. I saw the car rock and then it was dragged. I heard the screech of metal on the hard road, a loud screaming of man and car. Sparks of fire flew from the roof of the car. I saw Railer's tight face, Railer's referee arms. "Stop," he was yelling, "stop." I'd already lifted my foot from the pedal but Railer's face told me to slam the brakes. I stomped the brakes hard in a split second making a slip judgment call I would never live down.

I could see the surprise in Railer's face, feel the burn of surprise in my own chest. I had stomped on the gas pedal instead of the brakes, a dumb grinning kid in a farm truck. The chain snapped, recoiled back to slam my hood. The flattened car spun around and around, a ton top squealing metal sparks. I could hear the jagged spin of it, see the man's startled face quick and quick again, a mean carnival ride, a coyote trick. I felt the panic of hilarious laughter in my throat. Railer had jumped to the side to avoid being hit. The car stopped. I caught myself thinking the trapped man was laughing but I was slammed with the sound of his wailing cry. Railer took off his cap and threw it to the ground. And then Railer was at my side door yelling, "You dumb prairie nigger," he yelled. "Damn dumb prairie nigger." My hands were shaking as Railer yanked me out of the car. I thought he was going to hit me but he just stood close to me, loose-limbed, chest heaving. He put his hands to his hips and lifted his fingers to the man who had not taken his hands from the wheel of his car. It was suddenly quiet except for the man blubbering, his red face had turned white and puffy, his breath hoarse and heavy.

I stood stiff at attention wishing Railer was still yelling at me. The man's crying was unbearable, and I was responsible. We just stood there, Railer and me, caught up in our asinine plan with no more answers. Brute wind caught us up, rocked the car. We stood. Wind rushed at us, cracked the dry grass. I felt someone behind me. I looked at Railer but he was looking at the man, the wreck we had turned into a disaster. Railer was unaware that we had company but I knew. I crooked my neck, feeling the tight draw of muscles in my jaw. There on the hillside, big as life, big as a roadside warrior, a movie hero to the rescue, was my cousin Baptiste Yellow Knife on his faithful pony.

He sat straight in the saddle, a smirk on his face. He looked at me and held my gaze. I thought he was alone but when he shifted his shoulder I saw Louise on the back of the horse. At that moment she had never looked more beautiful. Yellow Knife dismounted. His horse was not even captured by a bit. He held the reins of the halter in his dark hands and without taking his eyes from mine reached up to help Louise down. I saw the shine of her long legs. Railer cleared his throat and I could see him looking at her too, the trapped man forgotten.

Louise glanced at us and without hesitation walked over to the man in the car. She squatted down beside him and lifted the hem of her skirt to dab the tears from his face. I couldn't understand what she was saying but her voice soothed all of us, low and cooing. The man's breath stuttered. I saw the man smile at Louise and roll his wet face in the folds of her skirt. When he looked up again he was lovestruck.

In the sunlight Louise's hair seemed firelit. We were all gawking at her but she only looked back at Yellow Knife. "Baptiste will help you," she said. "He'll get you out of here."

"Thank you," the man said.

"Don't worry. Don't you worry," she said.

"Yes," the man said, spellcaught, "yes."

"You have a rope?" Yellow Knife asked, though he did not appear to be addressing either Railer or me. I didn't fight. I went to my trunk and came back with a rope. "We've already tried to right the car," I said. "I see that," Yellow Knife said. As always, he had me. I shifted my weight, tried to look important.

"Aren't you going to help him?" Railer said to me. "Go help him."

"Boys," Yellow Knife said, "help like yours he doesn't need."

"What are you going to do?" I said, too eager. I realized I must have sounded childlike to him and to Railer, too ready to submit to his authority. I was glad that Yellow Knife ignored me. He harnessed the horse quickly and then gathered the rope up as he made his way to the side of the car. "Easy," he said to the horse though the horse hadn't budged. Yellow Knife tied a strangle knot to the door handle and worked it down tight while the man squinted up at him with admiration. "It's going to be fine," Louise said to the man, and he saluted her.

"Step back now, Louise." Yellow Knife put his arm up and corralled her behind his back. He clicked his tongue and without further prompting the horse began stepping back, pulling the rope taut. "Easy now," Yellow Knife said. We heard the rope tick. "Easy, easy," Yellow Knife said. I watched the horse whoa back, throwing his head up. I could see the muscles straining in the big stallion's chest. The horse heaved back and I heard the door screech and then loosen. The hinges of the door were broken. I worried that the door might break loose and crack the man but I decided to shut up. I had lost my power over the situation. I'd done enough damage to chime in with my two cents. The door held tight.

"Damn," Railer said. I could hear the sound of a car coming but before I could move Railer was on the road. He retrieved his hat from the ground and was straightening the bill as the car peaked the far hill. Railer met the car with his palm flat, his arm outstretched. The wrecked car was creaking. Railer rolled his hand for the passing car. He pointed to the far lane but the car stopped. The Two Teeth family leaned out the windows. "Baptiste," they called, waving. I lifted my hand but they met my hello with grim faces. I caught Yellow Knife watching as the car passed us. I was not the hero here. I wasn't even important enough to be the enemy. The family ignored me. I wasn't an Indian to them. I was a traitor in blue uniform. I forced a smile anyway and hoped Louise was not watching me too. The car rocked again. The man yelped, his face dangerously close to pitching to pavement. "It's coming," he said. "Keep her coming," he said to the horse. "Keep her coming." I was worried we were letting Yellow Knife kill the man.

"Hey, Charlie. Be good for something, will you?" Yellow Knife called to me. I saw then that the door was coming loose. The door was giving way. I stepped up to brace the door and Railer helped me. "Back it up, back it up," Yellow Knife said, and the poor animal strained. I could see the shine of sweat on its withers. "Pop the door, will you?" Yellow Knife said to me. I moved reluctantly. I was surprised when the door pulled off easily. The man breathed a loud sigh.

"Let me get you," I said to the man. "Let me help." But even though he was still hanging like a bat he shrugged away from me. "No," the man said. "You get away from me," he said. "If anyone's going to be helping me, it's going to be that guy," he said, indicating Yellow Knife. I didn't want to look up at Yellow Knife. I had lost this round.

Louise

◆

Years of Summer

*S*he *had* *to* *return* to school at the end of August, long before
summer would surrender. She had outgrown her clothes and the
nuns wouldn't allow brassieres. The nuns gave Louise tape to hold
her breasts, but the days were warm and soon the adhesive would
slip off, and she would feel her breasts loose. She had spent a long
summer away from school. She had drunk with men twice her age.
She had been told she was beautiful. The swell of her breasts was
admired. Here the nuns told her she was immodest. Cover yourself,
they would say to her crossing their arms over their own breasts. She
had no defense, no underclothing. She had felt the changes in her
body. The changes seemed to come sharp and fast. Overnight her
clothing shrank. She could feel the groaning of her bones before
sleep. A new longing settled in her by degree. It wasn't just the blood
of her growing that ached in her and stained her clothing. She had
changed. She was a woman.

The boys began to recognize her womanhood too, but at the
Ursulines' she was safe from the boys because of the constant threat
of Baptiste Yellow Knife. She could count on Baptiste to rescue her.
When Joseph Garlic had tried to kiss her Baptiste had saved her. He

came out of nowhere, they said, and he had knocked Joseph down with such force he skidded a ways on the blacktop. When he got back up, Baptiste punched Joseph so hard his eyes purled white and his head rested for a time too long on the pavement, his arms splayed, palms up, his left cheek swelling. The rest of the boys stood back looking away from Joseph, not wishing to take on Baptiste Yellow Knife. Louise had run back into the school not stopping even to look at Baptiste. She wished they would have beaten up Baptiste too, humiliated him, held his head to dust and bared his buttocks. She was afraid Baptiste was her constant, and yet she felt relieved knowing he had become her savior.

She was afraid of change. After one long summer Louise returned to school to find everyone had changed. The tomgirls giggled now and the boys were tough. They had all outgrown playground and curfews. They had worn out the idea of heaven and hell and carnal sin. The girls in classes behind her had grown breasts. Most of the boys were taller than the tallest nun. Rumor was that Melveena Big Beaver wasn't just fat, she was heavy with child. They were growing too old for childish pranks. They were growing too old for a school that hid their longings. Some girls wore red lipstick at the powwows. And their silk stockings and panties hung on the bushes with their boyfriends' sighs. The boys smoked without choking now. They stood in the back of the school yard sharing invented stories, broad shoulders huddled together, faces haunted by cigarette smoke and thoughts of women.

The nuns held them all in check, slapped at the girls' round hips, bound their breasts with tape, sniffed the boys' sheets, separated the fidgeting boys and girls in quiet rows they forever paced with the metal-edged threat of rulers.

She found herself waiting for Baptiste at times, holding on to the chain-link fence with one hand, letting her body swoop toward the pavement while her fingers grasped the metal links, becoming a semicircle drifting, hoping to be saved from the nuns, ignoring school, waiting for something or someone to save her. When Baptiste did show up she took to standing outside with him, neither talking nor listening to him, but waiting still until Mr. Bradlock sent her away to the all-white school in Dixon, to save her.

From the all-white school in Dixon Louise was sent to the all-white school in Thompson Falls, because the Dixon boys had lifted the back of her skirt to find she wore no panties. She had fought the Dixon boys, slapped their hands and scooped her skirt down tightly to her knees while the teachers had stood by or clapped their hands but made no real attempt to stop the boys who were attacking her. Louise had kicked at them, had spat at them, punched and scratched them. She felt a boy's fingers in her hair and she had slammed the butt of her palm into his chin until she heard the pop of his jaw. She caught one weasel-faced boy in the groin with the heel of her shoe, and he had bent over wheezing, and still no one came to help her. The boys had lifted her skirt high up over their heads, a tent, a worn umbrella, and finally she had stood still and let them have their look, let them see her bare ass. And she had been the one sent away, not the hooting boys who swooned at her lean nakedness.

Her only friend at Dixon was Myra Vullet, but even Myra stayed clear of her at school, watching her with a broad face smooth as river stone. Louise had no place here. At least at the Ursulines' she could count on Baptiste. She was no longer a child. She had outgrown schoolboys and schoolgirls. She had outgrown geography, and home economics had nothing to do with her life. She felt more comfortable in the bar in Dixon than she felt in the classroom.

At the Dixon school she ran away three times. Each time was a simple decision. She had no stockings. Her only pair of shoes was worn so thin she could count the stones beneath their soles. She had three dresses and she had outgrown all of them. The buttonholes of her favorite dress strained so tight you could see skin. Ten days into the school year she could take almost anything but she had grown tired of being the only Indian in the all-white school at Dixon.

The Dixon school was so close to home Mr. Bradlock, the BIA social worker, decided it would be best to place her in Thompson Falls again, with a family that would watch her, that way she'd have to think twice about leaving. He drove her to Thompson Falls himself. It was a cool day in the early part of September, but it wasn't cold, and Mr. Bradlock kept the car heater running so high she felt dizzy. She rested her wet palms on the nape of her neck. "Don't get any ideas," he told her. But she did have ideas. She wanted him to stop just once so she could get out of the car and run from him, run from his oily peanut-colored suit, run from his large and balding head. But he didn't stop. He didn't stop once.

When they passed her grandmother's house she looked at the floorboard, hoping Mr. Bradlock would not see her face. She saw the rock hills rise above his car. She felt the shifting curves. The river was slow and green. She felt a flutter in her chest and she wondered if she would ever get back home again.

Lately Louise woke from dreams that Mr. Bradlock would send her away and she would never come back, like Dolores Pretty Feather. Dolores was dying. Louise knew because Baptiste had told her. Dolores had been sent to Portland. And whenever Louise had passed the class photograph in the Ursulines' hall she thought Dolores's face looked ghostly, locked forever behind the glass pane, her eyes glazed upward as if she was watching a bird passing.

Louise had heard from Octave Good Wolf that Dolores was so sick she had collapsed in Mission before they sent her away. Dolores coughed up so much blood it was rumored Mrs. Moniker passed out at the sight of it. Stuffy Mrs. Moniker passed out in front of the Teepee bar. There was so much blood, Octave said, the dogs licked at the spot for days. So much blood Octave's mother told him to walk home on a different street.

"She's afraid I'll get it," he said. "Tooberculosis."

There were stories they put Dolores in bathtubs of ice to keep her blood slow, to keep her lungs from rupturing. In her sleep Louise would see Dolores in a long, white, porcelain tub of clear ice, Dolores's head resting on the lip of the tub, the shaved crown of her scalp gray with cold. Dolores in a room without windows. Dolores with eyelashes so long she had curled them with a butter knife.

Louise would wake thinking of Dolores and the old white woman from Paradise who had put her newly dead husband in a tin tub of ice in the living room to save herself funeral costs. So many Indians Louise knew were being sent away to hospitals for TB. They disappeared and nobody ever visited them or came back with news of how they were. Her father's new wife, Loretta, carried a picture of her sister Rosalie in her wallet. The photograph had been pushed and pulled in and out of Loretta's wallet and touched so many times, you could hold it up to the window and see through the lines and cracks of its finish. It wasn't an old picture but Rosalie looked far away, the way that people can look distant and dead in a photograph.

All the Indians began wondering why so many of them had the disease. Why so many of them were disappearing. Her grandmother thought they were all being killed off slowly. And there was evidence. Last month the health nurse had brought her grandmother a bottle of iodine and told her to put a drop of it in her drinking water each day. "It's a good idea," the nurse had said. "It will keep you healthy." But her grandmother had looked at the skull and crossbones on the small green bottle.

"These people think we're not smart," her grandmother had said.

Her grandmother told her Mr. Bradlock wanted to break her like a horse, make Louise a white woman. And Louise could believe this was true. She had heard Mr. Bradlock talking about her. "She's a beautiful girl," he had said to Charlie Kicking Woman. "I just can't have her living like a damn Indian." And when Charlie looked at him, Mr. Bradlock had fumbled with the sleeves of his jacket and turned away from Charlie, but he had not apologized. She had heard Charlie say in a soft voice that surprised her, "You are Indian. You are." She didn't need Charlie to tell her she was Indian but somehow it made her feel stronger.

Mr. Bradlock took Louise to Mrs. Shelby Finger's house in downtown Thompson Falls. He pulled up in front of a small pink house in the middle of town and a young woman clopped down the steps of the house in a pair of big white pumps.

"That'll be Arliss Hebert," Mr. Bradlock said. "Maybe she can teach you a thing or two about manners."

Louise felt a small claw of panic tighten her throat. She knew the name too well. Arliss Hebert. Was this the same Arliss, the Arliss that used to live in Hot Springs? She had known Arliss. She had known Arliss for years. Arliss used to sit outside her mother's house in a dirt-stained dress, a small ugly girl who would cuss at the Indians who were headed to Camas to bury the dead. Arliss was dirty inside and out, Louise's grandmother used to say. And now here she was again. And Louise would be living in her house.

When Mr. Bradlock was leaving Louise wished she were going with him. "Here's your big chance," he told her. And Louise wasn't sure what he meant by his comment. She listened to his car, the high whining of the last shift of gears, and then he was gone. She stood beneath the changing light of a maple tree. She could hear the tattered whisper of leaves high over her head, but when she looked up she saw the tree was still hard green.

Mr. Bradlock had thrown Louise's clothing on the damp lawn, a small wad of clothing rolled and wrapped in twine. Arliss stood over

Louise balancing one foot on the edge of her white high heel. Arliss stared at her. Louise felt the sting, the swelling at the back of her throat. She fanned her face and looked down the road. She was tired. She wondered how long it would take to walk back to Perma. A long time, she thought. Arliss made a sound with her tongue, uncrossed her arms, then walked back into her mother's house. Louise sat down on her clothing and looked down the road again.

Mrs. Finger finally opened the door and motioned to Louise. "Get in here," she said. "What are you doing?"

Mrs. Finger was a small, skinny woman. She reminded Louise of a field cat ready to scratch. She wore so much lipstick her mouth looked sore. "They're not paying us enough money to feed you," she said to Louise, "but I am sure your lunch will be more food than you're accustomed to anyway." Louise did not let Mrs. Finger know that what she had said was true. Sometimes her grandmother had fry bread, sometimes dried meat, and sometimes beans, but Louise was always hungry. At the Ursulines' it was the same, except worse. She had fought for her food at the Ursulines', had knocked down some other hungry girl for a piece of chicken or half a sandwich. Louise had been hungry for years.

When Arliss and her mother sat down for dinner Louise would sit out on the porch steps hoping someone she knew would walk by. She even watched for Baptiste Yellow Knife, waited for him, imagined him coming up the walk, imagined rattlers slinking through the grass, slipping through mouse holes, curling around Mrs. Finger's backyard trellis, rattlers entering Mrs. Finger's kitchen, sleeping in circles on her bathroom rug, twining around the foot of Arliss's pink vanity. Louise could see Baptiste in his old clothes smelling like wood smoke, looking in the windows at Arliss undressing, looking at Arliss's wide, white ass and smiling. She would imagine Jules Bart passing by, lifting his hand to Louise, the sunlight warm in his eyes, opening his door to her. She missed Grandma and Florence. She missed home. She dreamed of Baptiste riding up the drive on Champagne, hissing at Arliss, carrying Louise away while Arliss stood in her scuffed white shoes, open-mouthed and envious on the steps of her mother's house.

At Thompson Falls, Arliss had grown into a young lady who wore white ankle socks and violet- and rose-flowered dresses. Louise noticed that Arliss's high forehead seemed to bleach whiter in the sun. She had pale spider veins that mapped her temples and faintly edged her jawline. It seemed to Louise that Arliss had cracked her face, forever fussing in the mirror, tapping her cheeks and checking her big teeth, smearing her lips with petroleum jelly. She kept her thin skin so powdered and creamed it resembled tissue paper. She seemed silly to Louise but Louise began to learn from her, Arliss Hebert with her small shoulders and broad hips, Arliss with her hair gathered back in different-colored crocheted snoods she had made herself. None of the boys seemed to like Arliss, and even made fun of her as she walked by them in the hall. But Arliss Hebert had made her meanness count in life. Arliss recognized others' misfortunes and would use their hardships to her benefit. Louise noticed that even though no one seemed to like Arliss at school they tried hard to stay on her good side.

On Louise's first day of school at Thompson Falls Arliss hissed at Louise. "Dirty Indian," she said, "dirty, dirty Indian," loud enough for the others who stood on the school steps to hear. "You don't belong here. You don't deserve to live in my house." Louise knew she could take Arliss, roll her down the hard steps watching her skirt fan over her dimpled thighs, punch her powdered face until her eyes turned black. Louise could take care of Arliss but she chose to keep quiet.

Louise knew she didn't belong at Thompson Falls. In the early morning she would sit outside on the steps of school and smoke the cigarettes she had stolen from Mrs. Finger. The students would stand at the windows to gawk at her until the teachers would come outside and yank her up by her elbows. But even if she sat at her desk with her hands quietly folded, the other students would point and whisper. The boys would dig each other's sides and grin at her. And when she would pout they would lean close to her.

One long day when the sun was too hot at the windows, Mrs. Teeter, the teacher, smiled toward Arliss and announced to the class that Arliss Hebert was a lady. Louise watched chalk dust hover in the window light and remembered the day they had passed Arliss's house on their way to the burial of Louise's mother. Arliss had stood, tight-fisted, in her yard. It was a hard, strange day, a rain-heavy day that would not rain. Earlier the sky had been blue and the day had been warm, almost hot. Passing through Hot Springs the sky was charged yellow and Arliss's frayed hair stood out against the lightning-lit hills. Arliss's face was strained from yelling but all Louise could hear was the steady rattle of her mother's coffin in the back of the buckboard. She had heard Arliss before, Arliss too many times when they had gone to Camas Prairie for someone else's burial. When Louise wrote to her grandmother she did not tell her she was staying in the house of an enemy.

She planned to run away. She would leave school and follow the river. She could make it to Paradise before they figured out she was gone. She began to conjure Baptiste Yellow Knife, willing him to find her. She imagined the details of his face, saw clearly the sharp lines along his cheek that dimpled when he smiled, and made him almost handsome. At night she would see his face before sleep, his eyes were round and huckleberry-dark. She would imagine meeting him beneath the river willow, just outside of Plains, the place where the water swirled and slowed and big trout rested, the place where she often hid from the world. She would see him, picture him there with her again and again. And when she would wake up she would whisper his name.

During the long school day she would imagine Baptiste Yellow Knife waiting for her by the river. She knew Baptiste would hide her from Charlie Kicking Woman and Mr. Bradlock.

Louise carefully planned her day of escape from Arliss and Mrs. Finger's and then she waited for the days to pass. She remembered how she had counted the days of not seeing Jules Bart. She was good at waiting. The days held out sunny and warm but the nights ached with coolness. Mrs. Finger commented to Louise that she loved the fall days. She even told Louise that her father had called these warm days Indian summer and Louise felt good enough to smile at her. She knew she would be leaving soon. The days were melting down but it was still summer to Louise and she didn't want to be in school. Mrs. Finger stood at the door twisting the rings she wore on her fingers, straightening her skirt, dabbing at her hair, applying more lipstick. She would turn from her faithful watch whenever a car would pass the house, pretending to be busy and aloof. When the car was gone she would turn again to the window. She was waiting too, Louise thought. She was always waiting for her boyfriend, Warner Phillips.

Warner Phillips was a thin man, thinner than Mrs. Finger, and together their thinness made them appear stingy and dangerous. There was no warmth in either of them, so when they sat together on the hard sofa the room was cold and angular. When Warner Phillips was around, Mrs. Finger had a habit of crossing her legs, rasping her high heel off of her foot again and again. She seemed to like telling Warner Phillips he was funny but she never laughed at the things he said. If Arliss and Mrs. Finger and Warner Phillips stayed in the same room together, one of them would brood or they would suddenly fall to silence. Warner Phillips rubbing his small hands together. Mrs. Finger clicking her fingernails. Arliss jangling her charm bracelet.

Louise knew something about them she did not want to know. Whenever Warner Phillips appeared, Louise noticed, Arliss would rush to her bedroom to put on her highest high heels. Louise had seen Arliss squirreling her bare feet into her shoes. Arliss would step back into the living room stilted forward, her feet heaved together so tight in the point of her shoes that her toes had cleavage. Too many times Arliss would bound from her bedroom in just her slip when Warner Phillips would arrive. And each time Mrs. Finger would shoo Arliss from the room like an old tomcat. Warner Phillips would shake his head and remove his cap trying to give Mrs. Finger the impression he understood the company of women. There was something going on.

Louise could taste something in the room when they gathered together, a taste like aluminum, or water from a rusted cup. Louise had seen the way Warner Phillips looked at Arliss, pretending he was not. Louise had seen him rubbing himself on Arliss when he got the chance, acting as if he was only reaching for his keys or another ciga-rette. Mrs. Finger would sit watching them, a loving smile perched on her lips. For all the attention Mrs. Finger gave Warner Phillips Louise was surprised she didn't see him at all.

Louise was surprised too when she began to feel a small smirk of sweetness for Mrs. Finger. Her grandmother had always told Louise there was some good in everyone. With Mrs. Finger Louise under-stood she could like someone who wasn't worth liking.

When Arliss was visiting her girlfriends, sometimes Mrs. Finger would invite Louise to sit at the kitchen table with her. It made Louise nervous to sit across the table from Mrs. Finger. At first Louise kept her legs crossed and her hands still in her lap. But after a while she dis-covered Mrs. Finger wanted nothing more than to talk to someone, even if it was Louise. And Louise would watch Mrs. Finger as she talked. She talked without breath, one story and then the next. She talked the way some of the old ranchers talked at the Dixon Bar. She talked at times with urgency, leaning toward Louise, making her eyes wide and wider as if that would make Louise understand what she was saying. She talked as if by talking she could make sense of herself. Louise imagined Mrs. Finger running these thoughts through her narrow head with no one to listen to her. Mrs. Finger sighing as she applied her lipstick, as she patted her oatmeal meat loaf. Louise thought she had become Mrs. Finger's sanity, an endless vent, a constant nodding head.

In the early sleepy evenings Louise would find herself idly thinking of Jules Bart as Mrs. Finger spoke of Warner Phillips. Louise would shift in her chair when Mrs. Finger's stories somehow conjured too many thoughts of Baptiste Yellow Knife. But Louise looked forward to her visits with Mrs. Finger. Mrs. Finger would set out soda crackers and strawberry jam. As long as Mrs. Finger would talk Louise could eat.

Mrs. Finger talked about many things. She talked about her old boyfriends, about Arliss's father, about her ideas for furniture, her special beauty tips, her pimple remedies, but all her stories and all her thoughts returned again to Warner Phillips as if he was the enchanted key to her life. So many sighing thoughts that little by little Louise began to see not Warner Phillips but the Warner Phillips Mrs. Finger had invented. Warner Phillips the movie star, more handsome than Tyrone Power, as beautiful as summer twilight and just as rare and fleeting, invented somehow by years of longing and loneliness, no longer a man but the dream of a man, more and more like her own dashed ideas of Jules Bart.

But Louise knew the man Warner Phillips. She knew he held no magic or dreams. He would never be a champion or work a hard day to night. If Warner Phillips dreamt at all he dreamt of Arliss, her fat fanny, her plump thighs and matchstick waist. He dreamt of her thin, powdery skin, her hair falling from her pastel snood. Mrs. Finger was too invested in her own ideas to see what was going on between her daughter and her dream man, too caught up in her own desire to believe her Warner Phillips was creeping his hands up her daughter's legs, lipping his thumb into the elastic of her panties. But Louise knew. And the day was coming soon when Louise would leave this house and Mrs. Finger. She could feel the tick of tension in the kitchen clock, in the radio hum.

Louise had spied on Arliss only once and she wished she hadn't. She wished she had left her ideas to suspicions but she had seen. She had seen them together. Warner Phillips and Arliss Hebert.

Mrs. Finger had gone to bed early with one of her headaches. Five minutes after Mrs. Finger had lain down in her dark room and asked Louise to close her door Arliss had snuck outside. "If she asks where I am," Arliss hissed at Louise, "tell her I've gone to a girlfriend's." Louise looked out the window to see Arliss lady-trot in her high heels across the shadowed backyard. He hadn't had the good sense to park far from Mrs. Finger's house or even to pick Arliss up and take her somewhere else.

Warner Phillips had parked his truck on the backside of Mrs. Finger's junk-filled garage, almost hidden but not. Louise had snuck up on the two of them. She hid for a while behind a corner of the garage and watched them until they slipped down into the truck cab out of sight. Louise crept up on them slowly, carefully, the way Baptiste had taught her to walk, so quietly the birds wouldn't fly from her footsteps. She had looked in the rear window of Warner Phillips's truck to see the two of them together.

He was slipping a candy necklace past Arliss's thick ankle. He rubbed the necklace as far as he could up her leg to her dimpled thigh until the candy buttons were wide apart. "Spread your legs, Princess," he said to her. Arliss was grinning at him, her skirt bunched up to her waist, her legs splayed limp to him. Louise heard the gurgle in Arliss's throat as Warner pressed his head to her thigh. Louise felt sick. She crouched down beside the truck to leave them. "I'm going to eat it," he kept saying but the only sound Arliss made was a strange, wet gurgle, almost a giggle low in her throat. Louise ran back to the house holding her breath.

She was startled to find Mrs. Finger in the kitchen ironing a blue dress. "I just couldn't rest," she said to Louise. Her eyes were small and troubled. A pot of coffee boiled on the stove. Just past the kitchen wall, so close she could have heard them if she listened, the man Mrs. Finger loved was betraying her. Louise knew all this trouble would rise like a dead fish to the surface. It was happening now: even while Mrs. Finger still waited for Warner Phillips to trap her in his arms, to kiss her like a movie dream, to redeem her pitiful life, her daughter was giving herself away to Warner Phillips in Mrs. Finger's backyard.

Louise went to bed. That night the cool sheets on her back-porch bed felt comforting. Louise tried to write to her grandmother but she felt dirty, as if she herself had spread her legs to Warner Phillips. She knew Arliss would arrive at the door soon, smug and flushed and eager to lie. Warner Phillips would tail her a short time later, skunk-shouldered and twitching, angling his gaze toward Arliss's door as he wheezed himself into the perfumed body of Mrs. Finger.

Louise wondered if it all came to some sense after all. Mrs. Finger made no attempt to hide what she and Warner Phillips did. After Louise and Arliss went to bed Louise could hear the couch thumping. She could hear Warner Phillips grunting. Even worse she could hear the noises Mrs. Finger made, funny noises like she was snacking on cake. Louise would hold her pillow over her head. She wondered what Mrs. Finger was thinking when she made love to Warner Phillips while her daughter lay just a few feet away behind a wall thin enough to rattle with voices. It disturbed her to think of Arliss listening to them, that from her bedroom Arliss Hebert could hear even more than what Louise was hearing. Louise thought of her sister, Florence. She thought of the warmth of their cattail bed, how she liked to listen to her grandmother before sleep settled. The snow would fall soon. The woodstove would crack with fire and her grandmother would tell them stories. Mrs. Finger and Warner Phillips had brought this trouble on themselves. Louise was ready to leave this place. Relief settled in her chest. Her time at Arliss Hebert's house was closing. She had stayed long enough to convince Mr. Bradlock she was finally settled. She made a point of telling her teacher she liked Thompson Falls. And Mrs. Teeter grasped the idea and took credit for Louise's adjustment. Louise tried to convince them all she was changing. She hummed to herself now when she sat out on the porch steps at suppertime. And sometimes Mrs. Finger would even offer her a plate of leftovers with a smile. Louise was fooling them all. The days were racking up in her favor. She held to her plan to leave in one week. But three days before Louise's secret date to leave them all Mrs. Finger's dream of Warner Phillips exploded like an August weed set to fire.

"I'm going to visit my sister," Mrs. Finger told Arliss. "You'll be fine. I'll just be gone one night," she said. Then she packed her makeup case and put a pair of panties in a paper sack. Louise hadn't wanted her to go. She hadn't wanted to be alone with Arliss for even one night. It was a sunny Saturday morning when Mrs. Finger left them. "Stick to home, you," she said to Arliss before she drove off.

Louise stayed out on her porch bed hoping to avoid Arliss. She read Mrs. Finger's *True Romance* magazines until her eyes ached. She played solitaire on the bed. It was turning colder and the wind hissed through the window cracks, chased dust across the rough porch floor. She could feel the bite of winter and she wondered if she were to stay here if they would let her freeze to death on their back porch. The lamp beside her bed offered a dim ring of light. She could see her breath now. Her sheets were so slick and cold she placed them on top of her blankets to avoid their chill. The wool scratched her face but held the warmth to her. She tugged the blankets over her nose, pulled her knees to her chest, and closed her eyes.

When she heard the screen door open then bang shut, she wondered if Mrs. Finger had returned. But the house was quiet, too quiet. Louise rolled over facing the house wall. She lifted her head from the pillow but stayed still. She listened. She heard nothing. But she could feel Warner Phillips in the house. She listened harder with her eyes open. She could feel Warner Phillips's shoeless feet press the linoleum floor. She thought she could hear the teeth of his zipper unhitching, his clothes dropping to the floor. She heard the groan of Arliss's bedsprings as Arliss shifted to open her covers to him. Louise pulled the blanket up over her eyes again but strained to hear them whispering. After a long while she slept.

She woke to a sound like a cat whine and then the house seemed to rock. It occurred to Louise that Warner Phillips was rocking the house with his lovemaking. Glass cracked then shattered. She thought she heard the voice of Mrs. Finger, shrill and distinct. Louise sat up. For one brief moment the house was very still. Then the hollow crack of gunfire numbed her ears. She grabbed a blanket around her shoulders and slipped out the porch door. Her heart throbbed at her throat. Her feet ached in the frosted grass. Every light in the house was on. Every light, even the kitchen lights scorched the black morning. Louise ran to the front lawn and then she moved slowly to the window. She could see Mrs. Finger trembling with light, her hands fluttering at her face. Louise saw the deer rifle already propped against the door to Arliss's room. She saw the white face of Arliss standing naked by her bed. And there was Warner Phillips bending over, ass blazing, as he fumbled to stuff his legs into his pants. The lights in the house across the street flipped on and then the house lights came on next door. If Louise could see them clearly she knew the neighbors could too. It was as if Mrs. Finger's dream had come horribly true. They looked like a movie screen, a movie stuck in an ugly scene and Mrs. Finger, Arliss Hebert, and Warner Phillips were the bright stars.

Warner Phillips tumbled out the door still pulling on his pants. Louise could not hide from him. But he ran past her blind. And he kept on running. He leaped into his truck and without shutting the door he lurched down the road leaving Arliss naked before her weeping mother, the neighbors looking on.

Louise kept her shoes on until the sun warmed the road. The sky was cloudless. She walked fast looking behind her. She stepped off the road and hid in the bushes or lay down in the tall grass when she heard the high hollow sound of a car approaching. The morning fields steamed. She felt like running. Before Paradise she stepped into an apple orchard just off the road and ate so many apples her mouth puckered. And then she kept walking.

It was midafternoon when she came upon the willow place. She was tired and a lonesome feeling was settling in her chest. Baptiste was not in sight. She put her feet in the cold water and rested. She closed her eyes and smelled the warm autumn grass. The day would be short. She would follow the river.

She put on her shoes and began walking the river line. The wind clicked the river bramble and skimmed over the water. She stood dazed for a moment watching the flashing water rippling. She heard the snap of old branches, the slight slough of field grass, someone walking. She hunched behind a gray log. She put her head down and pulled her hair to one side. Louise knew they wouldn't be coming for her for some time. Arliss and Mrs. Finger were too occupied with their own tough luck to think of her now. She took a long breath and let it out slowly.

Her grandmother had told her there were places along the river where water waited to be heard. River stories. They ice-fished the Flathead after her grandmother had made certain the ice was solid. She remembered the water gurgling in the steaming ice hole. And just before dusk a sound would wobble across the skim of ice, always a hard clattering like the river giving way, then a wire-pitched zinging close to her ears, a woman wailing. Her grandmother would smile then and tell them it was time to go. Louise would pitch the slick string of fish over her shoulder. Walking home Grandma would tell them it was the sound of Mali, the woman who fell into the river when Grandma was a girl herself. "Greedy," Grandma would say, "trying to pick berries over the river's edge."

She always thought her grandmother had told her those stories to scare her from water. Last spring when the water was high and silt-brown, she had slipped beneath the swirling water to escape Charlie Kicking Woman and water had shut over her like a door to a dark room closing. Water tightened around her throat and pulled her downward and then up. She felt the arms of water, the sting of river sticks and stray branches. She fought the current but after a while she let the current carry her. She was lifted to the surface downstream. She had heard Charlie calling her but he had seemed far away. Sometimes before sleep she would remember the burning cold of the river. Thoughts of an old woman with sticklike fingers leaning over her. Now she sat still, listening. She had never expected the things her grandmother had told her would prove true.

She had the uneasy feeling that someone was watching her. She looked around carefully. She could feel her breath heavy in her throat so she closed her mouth. She waited. She waited a long time and when she was sure she had just scared herself she stood up.

She didn't see him at first. He was still as a deer. Baptiste Yellow Knife sat on the bank watching the river. She thought if she looked away for a moment she would lose him, that he would blend away into the river grass. "I could see you," he said. He waved to her. "I could see you the whole time." He seemed almost shy to her. He was sober. She felt a sudden rush of relief push at her chest. She grabbed Baptiste's shoulders and squeezed him. She had believed Baptiste would know where to look for her and he had answered her thoughts.

"I waited here for you every day," he said. "I knew you'd come back to this place."

She tried not to reveal that she was puzzled. She looked away from him. "Oh," she said, "I thought maybe you knew I'd been thinking about you." She had wanted to see Baptiste here in this spot, had felt she had conjured him there, but was disturbed now to think Baptiste had spied on her in this place all along.

"I knew you'd come around to me. I did know that," he said and encircled her waist with his long arms.

"Not like that," she said, though for the first time it felt good to be close to Baptiste. "Not like that at all," she said and pulled away from him.

He did not move to touch her. He glanced toward the water. A bird fluttered over the far bank. Baptiste's arms were tight to his sides, his shoulders braced.

"I thought you were different," she said, "different in a way. Different like your mother."

He threw a small, round rock at the water. "What?" he said. "You think I can read your mind? Come on, you give me too much credit," he said. "If Indians like me had so much power we would have won."

She crossed her arms over her chest and looked at the slow curve of the river. Baptiste had known to find her here because he was an ordinary man, an ordinary man obsessed with a woman. She didn't know what to feel. She felt disappointed. Baptiste was right.

The birds stayed away from the weeds where she and Baptiste hid from Charlie Kicking Woman. They sat up on the hill in a thatch of rustling grass where they could watch Highway 200 and the Flathead River. To the east, Louise could see the Mission Mountains, the distant threads of snow that marked them. She could see the corner of her grandmother's house. Baptiste spotted Charlie first. Charlie's first stop was her home. She strained to hear the voice of her grandmother, the knock of the closing door, but she heard nothing. He soon appeared again, walking the fields to the root cellar. In the red dusk light of fall she could see the shine of his blue-black hair.

"Didn't take him long to sniff your trail," Baptiste said. "He wants you." Baptiste tapped her knee. She felt annoyed by him. She could see Charlie, how he circled the fields. They watched him for a long time and Louise yawned. She didn't believe he was going to be close to them before darkness closed the valley, if he found their trail at all. She watched Charlie Kicking Woman stop. He stood still for a long time and then he was walking back toward her grandmother's house.

"Cold," Louise said. "You're getting colder."

Louise lay back in the grass. "If he's looking for me," she told Baptiste, "I don't think he has a clue." She was exhausted from running, tired of it all. The wind had picked up and the tall, sleepy grass swept over her. The powdered moon was almost invisible. She began wishing that Charlie Kicking Woman would just go away and not only because she didn't want to be caught. She didn't want to make a fool out of Charlie again. She had seen Charlie drinking coffee in the Perma store. He was sitting with a group of suyapis, all of them in their uniforms. State police officers and Charlie the Indian by himself.

Louise had stopped just outside the screen door to listen to them. The white men were talking about Indians as if Charlie wasn't an Indian, or maybe Charlie wasn't a cop, or, worse yet, as if Charlie wasn't even there. Louise had snuck up to the window to watch Charlie. Their conversation was loud. It wasn't long before one of the white men stood up and put his hands on his hips. Charlie stood up then and put his hands on his hips too. He was nodding and laughing with those men like he had been places he'd never been. Charlie Kicking Woman began making fun of Indians himself when he looked up to see Louise. He had stopped talking then. He had taken off his hat and fumbled with some change in his pocket. He had shamed himself. Louise knew his shame. She had tried to pass herself off as white too many times so that she could spare herself ridicule and discomfort. She had denied her family and herself so she could have a drink with a white man. She didn't know what would happen if Charlie did find them. Baptiste always seemed to get the better of Charlie. She didn't want to be witness to Charlie's red-faced fumbling again. It would be better for all of them if he didn't find her.

Baptiste was still keeping watch, rigid and vigilant. She began to feel grateful to Baptiste, but when he tapped her leg again there was a rise in his voice that told her he was in this for himself. Baptiste liked to trick others. She looked up to see Baptiste rocking. He rubbed the top of his head. She could hear the whistle of his breath and when she sat up, Baptiste sidled up behind her and wrapped his arms and legs around her. Charlie had suddenly changed direction. He was moving up the hill quickly, with purpose. When he kept coming in their direction, she bucked up against Baptiste's arms, ready to run, but Baptiste had captured her tight. "Easy," he said to her, and she felt like he was talking to Champagne. She couldn't stop her heart from racing. She could feel Baptiste's voice at the nape of her neck and she strained to hear what he was saying but he was not talking to her then.

Louise watched Officer Kicking Woman as he walked a straight-line path to where they sat hidden in the weeds. He knows where we are, Louise thought and pressed the palms of her hands flat to the ground, ready to run again. Baptiste leaned his chest into her back, and snipped off a milkweed stem, split it open to white foam with his broad thumbnail. He took the watery milk and rubbed it on his hand. Charlie walked a distance away from them and then stopped. A web of grasshoppers shot up behind him. Charlie's shoulders pulled up tight to his ears. He glanced backward for a moment so short he must have felt the muscles stretch behind his eyes.

Charlie was close. She hid her face. She did not want to see him. She could hear a crease of wind slow. Baptiste turned to her. "He cannot see you, Louise," he said. "He is blind to us here." Louise did not believe Baptiste. She pressed her fingers to his lips to quiet him but he kept talking. She put her hands over her head and scrunched herself down into the weeds.

Baptiste's voice was heavy in her ears. Charlie would hear Baptiste and take her back to Thompson Falls. Weakness pressed deep into her chest. Her hands were trembling like the honeyed saplings at the thick base of the hill. Charlie had stopped walking. He rested his hand on his holster. And still Baptiste kept talking. Charlie was close enough to hear Baptiste, to see them in the weeds. But Charlie only tilted his head up as if he were hearing something far away. Louise looked down at Charlie standing in the open field. The sudden wind had brought back the heat of summer. Clear heat shuddered the long September grass, a heat that looked wet in the distance, a wavering, filmy heat that seemed to wash over him. Louise wrapped her arms around her knees and watched Charlie. Charlie began walking toward them again. She breathed through her mouth. "He can't even hear us," Baptiste told her, but Charlie kept walking steadily toward them.

She believed Charlie was playing a trick on them. He was letting them hide like children, letting them play their game, but as Charlie got closer she could see his face and she knew. His eyes watered with the hard setting sun. Baptiste tapped Louise's hand. "We are hidden," he said. He pointed toward the stiff juniper that lined the river. She looked carefully.

"See that," Baptiste said. "See."

She saw the large herd of deer as if she were imagining it. First a twitch. Then a rolling haze. A great shuddering movement like wind on grass.

She could see the gray highway, the stuttering light on the river. She could see light cradled in sweet grass. She could not remember seeing light as if it were more than just light. Silver light channeled down the rock face of Revais Hill. Light glanced off Charlie's smooth face. Louise wondered if the sun itself shed its skin to hide all the animals. "That's right," Baptiste said, and she wondered if he was answering her.

In this field, these hills, the sun ached over red leaves, hid bear and deer. Trout slept in the hazy shadow of early evening, safe. She wanted to believe she was safe too, that there was a place for her to hide from all of them, from Baptiste Yellow Knife, from Mr. Bradlock, from Charlie Kicking Woman's chase.

Charlie's shadow darkened the spot where Louise sat with Baptiste. Louise was close enough to Charlie to touch his gun. She felt like a snake coiled and ready to strike. She could feel the heat of his leg, smell the singed heat of his wool slacks. She looked up, saw the wind stiffen the hair up from Charlie's forehead. Baptiste looked up too. Charlie was so close Louise could hear the tight squeak of his leather holster. She drew her knees tighter to her chest and heard the blood beating in her throat. Charlie shook his head and kicked at a rock beside her, his boot skimming her thigh. She felt laughter curdle her stomach. The idea that Charlie could not see them in the cover of the weeds began to fill Louise.

Charlie scanned the base of White Lodge Hill. When he left, he walked carefully, turning back to gaze in their direction with eyes steady and unseeing. She thought Charlie held only the vision of certain trees, a few rock swells he could not distinguish from dirt, everything blending to nothing. Maybe Charlie saw the curve of her hip as only another slope of land, her fingers stark as the weeds that surrounded her. Maybe Charlie could not see the meadowlark in the pine branches, the distant white heat lifting, the separate river rocks, the sleek dark shale that rose from the hill. Louise could feel a low shifting breeze. Charlie turned his broad back to them. Baptiste held her safe. He was talking to her, telling her a story. She wanted to lie back in the prickle of weeds beside him and listen to his dry voice. She could still see Charlie but then he began running, running as if from a cold place where the only name spoken was his own.

The sun had moved behind them, a yielding light now that carried a tint of coolness. She began to believe she was there by herself. Alone, listening to her heart, the sound of far water.

Louise

♦

The Falling Place

She left Baptiste Yellow Knife at Dixon with the idea that she would head to Missoula and shake Charlie. She was surprised Baptiste had told her to go, had let her go. She thought if she could stay in Missoula for a while she could head back home and have a better chance of fooling Mr. Bradlock. She didn't get a ride right away and she was worried Charlie would spot her on the roadside with her thumb up.

The stranger had picked her up at the hour she imagined her grandmother was washing her face at the spring. The man was tall, big-boned, and broad-hipped. His thinning hair was widow-peaked and made his strain-lined forehead longer. After each curve he patted the steering wheel with the palm of his hand but said nothing to Louise. She closed her eyes to see the green edge of water clearing in the pool of her grandmother's hands. The gray dusk of cottonwood trunks turning the color of salt clay.

She could feel night cooling the road. The muggy smell of nettles and jimsonweed hissed through a window crack and made her lonesome. It was dusk and growing dark fast. It seemed things were moving closer. The fields and the highway, the trees and the river blended toward sky and to earth again. She put her hand to her forehead and pulled back her hair. Eventually they would find her and they would take her back to Thompson Falls, back to the scaled face of Mrs. Finger, the tight frown of Arliss, who would find a way to blame Louise for their problems with Warner Phillips. She remembered how Mr. Moxy, the music teacher, once put his hand on her shoulder and in a hushed voice more intimate than a whisper told her she could pass for white and had hooked his finger and nipped Louise's breast as if he were cuffing her chin to be proud. She had never told anyone about Mr. Moxy. She had learned to take care of her own problems. She kneed him hard in the crotch. He left her alone after that incident, although he would smile at her at times, a cool glimpse of a smile as if they shared a secret. They could take her back to Thompson Falls a hundred times. She would not stay there.

Her throat pulsed at the collar. She shifted in the seat and reached back quickly and unhooked the top button of her blouse. From a side glance the man smiled at her and when she turned to smile back he looked away. The green panel light of the car lit his pale brown hair, the angular planes of his cheekbones. He had looked older when he had stopped to offer a ride. Now she saw the smooth skin of his face, how his chin shined from razor burn. His forehead had relaxed with the hum of tires, the long straight road, the distance of a day passing toward evening.

He had a cowboy shirt on, fancy, but not store-bought. There were hand-embroidered cowboy boots on his cuffs, on his left shoulder a horse head with an eye too big. It had fine detailed stitching, like lasso roping for the yoke. The fabric looked wet and was the color of beans. He's proud of himself, Louise thought and pressed the side of her forehead and cheek to the cool door window. She could feel wind skim her scalp, it pulled a strand of her hair through the window crack. Louise leaned her head back on the seat and looked ahead at the path of his headlights. The moon could not light up this darkness. The land lay out blind to them. He drove his car too close to the edge of a hill. She saw the rapid eyes of a porcupine, the gray needles of his coat, then the night again, pinholes of stars, the road threading out, the weak moon.

They were leaving the town of Arlee and she was looking forward to Missoula. She pressed her tight back into the seat, lit a cigarette, and opened the ashtray. It was clean. She tapped it shut and rolled down the window. The man gripped the steering wheel. She could feel the smooth force of the car, the solid whining road.

"What's your name?" she said. The man swallowed. "My real name," he said, "is Vivian."

"What's your other name?" she asked. She could half-see his reflection on the windshield. He was rubbing his neck.

"Vance."

"Vance," she repeated, but she did not offer her name. They passed one car with a dull headlight low to the ground. The other headlight shot the windshield silver and for a moment there was only a blinding whiteness, then the sky beyond, dense as velvet. Louise listened to the man breathe. He turned on the radio. A voice from Great Falls listed midland farm prices, the price of corn, wheat, potatoes. The radio popped and hummed. She licked the powder off a stick of gum and stuck it back in her pocket to light another cigarette. She handed the cigarette to the stranger, saying nothing. He pulled a breath in slowly, his chest full, exhaling a sigh. She could smell his lungs, sweet from sips of Coca-Cola, and she tried to imagine him naked. He would live at home, she thought, a man whose mother sewed cowboy shirts for him, pressing detailed horses and lassos to his bowed shoulders. A man who would only be naked behind a bathroom door, his butt red from a hot bath. She smiled at him and he glanced at her, his eyebrows as thin as his nose. She felt a sudden warmth for him, sitting in his dark car smoking cigarettes, traveling over roads that had scorched her feet too many times. She could like him.

His headlights bleached a tunnel of light beyond Sleeping Child. She could see a thin glow over the haze of the hill, an edge of her heart turning silver. Stars settled closer. She rubbed a dull pain beneath her rib cage. Walking the barefoot miles to escape Thompson Falls had made her legs restless. She could feel the slow crawl of blood in her calves. She leaned forward to loosen her shoelaces. She kept her head down for a moment. She could smell the leather of his seats, his wood-sweet cologne.

The man shouted "Look," and she lifted her head eye-level to the bottom of the windshield. She held the deer in her vision like light. For one moment suspended in its leap. She could see its white throat, the hair bristled on its back. She heard first the thick hide buckling the smooth chrome, then the slow slide of the well-grazed deer over the wind-ridden hood. She pictured the break of the shiny hood ornament, a knife now slitting a straight edge of the deer's belly, the hood purple with blood.

The deer came through the windshield, and time moved slowly for Louise. She heard the wheeze of the stranger as the deer hooves cracked the windshield. She could hear the dull flesh blows to the man's chest, and she thought of jumping down to sawdust in moccasins, of fruit ripe and falling to hard ground. His voice was cushioned by the neck of the deer, little puffs of breath, then a whistling, a rattling bone caught in his windpipe, pressing. She covered her face with her forearms, felt the razor cuff of hooves at the back of her hands, blood rush to her elbows. She heard herself moan as the car bounced hard on rough ground. She saw the headlights shoot up toward sky then down again to sage and white grass. She counted these things in the pulse of her fingers. A hiss of steam rose white like a warm winter river above the hood. She closed her eyes as her forehead hit the windshield frame.

She noticed first the car had stopped running. The deer's heavy head was cradled in her lap. She felt its still tongue, rough and dry on her hand. The cupped moon was yellow through the frame of broken glass. A dim light pressed through the open front window, enough that she could see the stranger, his eyes half open and dreaming beneath the cover of the deer's warm back. She felt a chill at her neck. She half listened to the dry slide of broken glass falling from the smooth leather seats as she pulled herself out of the car. She heard wood snap in the field as she headed for the highway. The haze on the road met the tops of the trees. She could see car lights filter the highest pine branches, a great powdered light that seemed to gather the ground. She lifted her arms to the first car and was resigned to see Charlie Kicking Woman.

Officer Kicking Woman

♦

Here

*S*he *appeared in my* headlights, sudden and brilliant, an apparition I could taste on the tip of my tongue, bitter metal on the backs of my teeth. Louise. There was a slash-rip across her blouse, and her skirt was torn and ragged. It occurred to me after it was all over she must have been bleeding badly because all I remember when I think about seeing her that night is the red-wet back of her arm as she shielded her eyes from my car lights.

I had to stop the car and rest my arm on the steering wheel a moment, blow a long breath through closed teeth. It shook me up to see Louise on the roadside looking like my worst fears. Louise grabbed the door on the passenger side.

"Shit, Charlie," she said. "I knew it would be you."

I turned the dome light on and saw the pale frown of her mouth, her eyes black with pupils. I took my coat off and wrapped it around her shoulders.

"What the hell happened?" I said to her, knowing she was afraid of more than a highway accident, knowing she was afraid I would haul her back to Thompson Falls. She was shaking, a wet-dog shake that made me shiver in the heat.

"I don't know," she said. "Some guy got it down the road. The car's off that way," and she waved toward the low field. Her tongue looked swollen and tight against her teeth but there was no alcohol on her breath. Blood was slow on her arm. I looked at her closely. Her body seemed swathed in shock, jerky, oddly motioned, deliberate yet fast. Her mind had kicked in to save her.

"Let me take a look here," I said and clipped her wrist, holding her arm firmly between my thumb and index finger. Her heartbeat was strong and fast. There was a half-moon puncture on her inner arm, like a trout's mouth filled with blood.

Her hair was tangled at the base of her head, and her neck was loose and fluid. I grabbed a coil of white gauze and closed the wound with wrap. Her breath was smoke-heat and wind. I tried to picture her in the field before I found her on the highway, the road dark, fragments of cold stars falling. It bothered me to think of her being alone out here with no ride in sight and a long ways till morning. There is a darkness that presses in on you out here when your car slows or turns a hairpin curve. You can be stopped by a sudden nail, a low tire squeezed by a bent rim, or deer, elk, lazy bear, sharp rocks, thorns. There is always something unexpected just over the shoulder of one easy curve, a drop-off that can shatter your bones. A mist passing over the hood of your car can make you believe in your childhood ghosts. I've seen too much out here and every year that passes my own fears crawl farther up my neck.

"I think he's dead," Louise said.

"Boy," I said, feeling my heart rock, as always paying more attention to Louise than the duties at hand. I slid out of the car. "Hold tight there Louise, I'll be back."

I took my heavy flashlight and skimmed the area with light. I saw the LaSalle chrome shine first, like a stain of silver light in the darkness. A coolness lined the backs of my arms. I could smell engine oil and rock dust. My flashlight illuminated the shattered windshield, now an open pocket to sky. Light stabbed the great dead deer. I saw tufts of hide hair on the twisted frame of the window. I saw the stranger's still head, rock-heavy and resting on the couch seat.

I scratched my side but did not take my eyes off the front seat. I wanted the man to stir, show some sign of life, but he wasn't moving. I prepared myself for the task at hand. Check his pulse. Check his air passages. Check his pupils. I only wanted to go back to Louise, wash her wounds and wrap her in warm blankets, take her home. I wanted to sit with her in her grandmother's kitchen until the sun rose. I wanted to know her. Know her so I no longer cared one way or another about her. I wanted her to be ordinary to me so I could go back to thinking about my wife at home. But I had to attend to the wounds of a dead man.

I flashed a light toward the fragile dust tracks and made my way to him. I opened the driver's door, and the deer's legs pulsed toward me, then stiffened. I pushed the deer back enough to clear a breathing way for the man's struggling chest. I heard a thick gurgle and checked the man's ears for bleeding, wiped the run of blood from his nose. He might have a chance. I looked around the car frame to see if there was some way I could wedge the deer out enough to release the man. But the only way out for the sorry bastard was some meat saws and a lot of good luck. His chest was already swelling with wounds.

"You got a long time coming," I said. "Grab on." The man snorted and then I heard the snoring rattle of blood when he passed out again. I ran back to check on Louise and radio the state patrol. It would be a long night. I opened the trunk and took out two heavy blankets. I tossed one on Louise and headed out to the field to wrap the man. I was hesitant about looking in on him again but I could hear the man's breathing a ways away. I smoothed the blanket between the man and the deer and wondered about the man's legs, how his blood flow was doing. The pulse of his neck was sure and even. I tapped the man's cheeks. He was young, maybe had children. "What's your name, sir?" I asked. He moaned and his head lolled forward. "What's your name?" I said again. "I am Officer Kicking Woman," I said to him, keeping my voice sure and even and wondering if my name alone might scare him. "Help's on the way," I said. I caught myself trying to smile reassuringly at him in the darkness. The man moaned almost a sigh and set his head back to rest on the seat. "Easy now," I said. "I'll be close by."

I went back to my car looking forward to waiting with Louise even if she was sleeping. Louise was down in the backseat. I could hear the shift of her breathing. Now and then she would wake herself snorting blood too. Her nose was swelling and I guessed the deer had slammed its skull to her face. I looked out the windows toward the quiet highway. The moon gave off enough light that the road seemed to shine. When the breeze picked up I could see the tall grass shining too. Moonlight glinted on the road signs. And sitting quiet beside that roadside, unmoving, the land seemed safe.

I had covered every curve, every straight line of that road. I knew where to pump my brakes, where the road dipped and often changed. I knew the soft shoulders and the bends in the land that couldn't be fixed. There's even a place in the road outside of Dixon that looks as if it's a gradual hill but I have seen surveyors lay a level to the same spot for years and every time it comes out even as a concrete plane. And I wondered about that sometimes. I wondered how many other things were off-balance or different from what they appeared to be.

I heard Louise shift in the backseat and I uncovered her face to check on her but I really just wanted to see her face. Even in the thin moonlight, with her face swelling, she was beautiful. I looked at my watch every few seconds. I counted the median lines as far as I could see in both directions. I checked my watch again. Only ten minutes had passed since I had found Louise. I waited. I had too much time to think.

I remembered three years before, a family from Hot Springs had driven their car into the Flathead River at forty below. They must have been flying, their tires lifting above the drift of ice when they hit that dipped curve to soar airborne like a lover's thrill with seven occupants. The sheer weight of that '42 custom LaSalle broke the thick ice clean and they had disappeared like a flat dream of Christmas. They had settled, the whole carload of them, in the shallow elbow of the winter river. They froze there like a picture of themselves out for a Sunday drive.

Three weeks later the Reston brothers, a couple of white boys too dumb for pranks, the ding-a-lings we used to call them when their names were forgotten, the sorry sacks near the cutoff, told everyone they had found a carload of circus mannequins, circus dummies, in the water near the boundary curves.

It occurred to me two minutes after Railer that it was the Albin family. When I pulled up at the river Railer surprised me by motioning to me.

"You got to see this," he said to me, almost giddy.

It was a sight that called for more witnesses. Unbelievable and rare. The wind swirled the snow to smoke above our heads.

"Don't go telling your Indian friends," Railer had said to me, almost laughing. The sight stunned me so much I didn't answer. I had held my ears in the nip of cold. My eyes jelled. We stood on the dense green ice of the Flathead River and looked down between our slick-soled boots to the family trapped beneath us. This is what comes of accidents on a river curve at forty below.

The car had settled at an angle on its side. It looked to be almost up and running. From our keen vantage we could see all of them. Railer and I were no better than the cockeyed Reston boys.

I saw the baby clearly first because the baby was pressing at the passenger window. The baby was straining out of her mother's arms. The baby had pinned her pink mouth to the window like she was playing with us, like she was kissing us through five feet of ice. I brushed the snow away with the ball of my boot and looked down to see the mother, the young boys struggling in the backseat like they were still at play. One boy was looking upward, a painted statue, his hair rising from his head like thorns. The father had his right arm resting on the wheel, looking forward, as if he were still driving the highway. But I kept locking my eyes on the woman. She wasn't just pretty. Beneath the silver strands of ice that held her she was beautiful. Her blond hair had swirled up around her face in a halo of bubbles, caught just before the water had frozen. She was turned almost toward us, turning toward her baby, and she was smiling. She had dimples. She was smiling, I could tell. And there was something about that smile that even then reminded me of Louise. I told myself they were dead, had been dead for weeks, but I could still see the moment of their deaths. I couldn't take my eyes off the sight of all of them, stiff and unchanging, beneath hard water. I blew warm air into my hands although the deep-freeze cold had ended. The cold spell was broken, I told myself. Even as we stood on solid ice, the middle of the river was claiming a wider channel, broader than the length of that young mother's arms. I wondered if the car would break through its casing in February if we left it and travel on with its strange and happy family. "How can this be?" I asked myself because Railer had gone back to his car. Railer and I both had listed that accident as a river drowning. We had no other way to explain it, and I wonder now and then if that story happened the way I remember it. I'd never mentioned that accident to

Railer again. But one time I did ask my supervisor, in a roundabout way, how something like that could have happened. His look told me I needed a day off. He told me "something like that" wasn't possible. I wondered what was possible and what was not. I looked in the back-seat at Louise but she had slumped into the seat and had turned her face from me.

I hoped Railer would be off duty. Railer was not the highway patrol but if there was an accident he was the first to arrive. When there was a white man involved he had to assume the duties, but he would take over as if I had failed my job. He took all the credit for a job well done and blamed me for any problems. Any good work I have done over the years was a fluke to him, a stroke of good luck with no measure of my competence, something that fell into my lap. But I had something on him now. We'd both botched the highway accident out-side of Perma. The way I saw it Railer had nothing to gloat about. Yellow Knife had rescued us both.

Louise

◆

At Long Last Home

Charlie Kicking Woman threw the blanket over her head when Lake County Officer Railer finally arrived. She knew enough to be quiet, to stuff the blanket in her mouth to keep her teeth from chattering while Charlie Kicking Woman lied to the white man. He had not even told his dispatch she had been in the car accident. Beside that dim highway, in the wake of scattered gravel Charlie had risked his job and she wondered why. She heard him tell Officer Railer there was only a driver, a Caucasian. She knew Charlie would take her home and then hate himself. The night was thick with her near-misses, her lazy troubles, her wildness, her grandmother's downward glances.

They passed only one other car on the way home to her grandmother's. Her head ached. The bones of her hands seemed loose and rattling. She closed her eyes and tried to rest but she could not forget the furious hooves of the deer shattering the window, the smell of hot oil and the man's cologne, the strange, wild light scattering through a thousand broken edges of windshield glass. She felt the highway turns and the constant spine-aching rumble of tires on an uneven road. Now and again she thought she saw a farmer's porch light glance through the windows as Charlie drove on. She was aware of things disconnected. The green light of the dashboard. Charlie's stiff uniform collar. Charlie's ears. She heard the spitting static of the dispatcher's voice and Charlie's low, sure reply.

She wasn't sure how long the car had been stopped. The car lights shined on her grandmother's house and then the back door was opening and Grandma was reaching for her. Louise walked steadied between Charlie and her grandmother. Moon struck the pond, a dark ache of shine that made Louise stumble. "She's more shook up than anything," Charlie told her grandmother. Louise remembered how Charlie had stood for a moment at the door, turning his hard-billed hat in his hands. He almost looked sorry to Louise as if he had suddenly come to his senses and decided to be Indian. He didn't stay long. When her grandmother started to unbutton Louise's blouse he turned a shy face from them. He didn't say good-bye before he left. He was there and then he was gone.

Her grandmother put a war-grass poultice on Louise's arm and led her up near the cottonwoods. "I won't let them take you again," she said to Louise. Louise felt a rush of weakness in her shoulders, the backs of her legs. She fell asleep beneath the trees hearing the cold, high river of wind above her. Her grandmother and her sister, Florence, slept beside her out under the stars and she stayed warm. When she woke in the squinting light of morning her grandmother and her sister were gone. She remembered the leaping deer, the strange girlish scream of the stranger. She was stung with the idea that he had probably died. The bruises on her arms were the color of huckleberry stains. She scratched her head, picked small clusters of glass from her scalp. In places, her hair was only bristles where glass had clipped her. She tapped a grit of dust above her left eye and found she was still bleeding. Her forearms were swelling but her grandmother's poultice relieved the soreness.

She sat up on the hill above the small house, hidden in the trees. She could see her grandmother making her way up the hill. She brought Louise a jar of bitter, black, juniper tea. Louise knew her grandmother had boiled the juniper berries all night until the tea had turned to syrup. "I've been checking on you," her grandmother said. Louise rubbed her eyes. "You've been asleep on and off for two days now." Grandma handed Louise a newspaper cutout from the *Ronan Pioneer*. The headline read, "Butte Man Survives Road Buck." The stranger hadn't died. He lived with his wife and four children. She saw again his kicked arms, his swollen jaw, the hoof marks that slashed his ears. He would tell his wife this story a hundred times, leaving Louise out. She wondered if he even remembered her. She wondered if he slept with his eyes open and sightless now like he had the night the car trundled to a jolting stop, his vision turned inward toward highway shadows and women on roadsides. They had to saw through the deer to get the stranger out of the car. There was a picture of the car in daylight, the hood bowed, the window frame a maw of glass teeth. She found herself looking closely at the picture, looking down into the blurry grain of the photograph, looking for herself in the wreck, some clue that she had been there. For a moment she wondered if her life would be recorded at all, if anyone would remember her times of suffering or if she too would be cut away like a spine-broken deer that wouldn't even make it to a poor person's table.

It occurred to her that Charlie Kicking Woman was protecting her but his good will would only last as long as his short pangs of guilt. He had tried so hard to catch her and now that he had finally captured her he had released her.

Her grandmother pulled Louise up. Her legs felt weak and she felt oddly disappointed as if she had won a struggle that came to nothing.

"We have to get going," her grandmother told her. Louise noticed her grandmother had braided her hair wet. Her grandmother's hair was sleek and shining in the autumn sun. Grandma patted Louise's arm. "I know where to hide you," she said.

They followed the road toward Perma until they came to a thick grove of trees up on the hill. The brush was dense and cool. Beside a tree Louise could barely see the lean-to that her grandmother had built for her. "Florence will bring you food," she told Louise, "but you stay here for a while." Louise grabbed her grandmother's hands and held onto her for a moment. Louise had never hugged her grandmother. That was not Grandma's way. It was just enough to hold her hands, to look into Grandma's eyes. Louise liked the way her grandmother would always shake her hand with both hands like she had not seen her in a long time. "You be good now," her grandmother told her.

Grandma left her alone. She watched her grandmother walk up the hill a ways and then turn toward home. Her grandmother did not disturb the brush. She left no wake in the quiet grass. Louise had known her grandmother to pick huckleberries without staining her fingers. She was quick and limber. She was respectful. She carried the old ways in her. Louise realized she knew little of the things her grandmother had taught her and she felt ashamed.

Louise had shrunk back from the stink of brain tanning, even when Grandma called for her help. She hadn't wanted to boil tallow and pound chokecherries into meat. Lately Louise had become uncomfortable with the smell of buckskin tamarack and jerked meat. She remembered Mrs. Finger sniffing her clothing, how she had hung all Louise's clothing out on the white clothesline soon after she had arrived. Louise had sat in the house wrapped in a thin towel. She had watched Mrs. Finger through the glaring windows, the white flash of Mrs. Finger's diamond ring as she hung up Louise's few pieces of clothing. Mrs. Finger had made Louise feel that she was soiled, that her skin would never wash clean, that her dresses would always smell like wood smoke. And she wondered if she too had become like Charlie Kicking Woman, homesick at home, alone with thoughts that she was better and worse than everyone else.

Louise lay back on the rough wool blanket her grandmother had carried to this place. The day was cool and the deer-hoof moon was a smear of white dust in the sky. She watched the slow sun lift over the river, heard the scratching rattle of cattails down in the low field. As she closed her watering eyes she saw the shadowed branches of trees above her, heard the distant sigh of a car passing the highway.

She slept so hard the palms of her hands felt weak. She heard wood crack, the brush of branches pushed aside. She sat up slowly rubbing her left shoulder. She thought Florence was on her way up the hill but when she looked down she saw Baptiste Yellow Knife. She felt a blue lick of adrenaline skim her chest. He looked like he had a rough time reaching her, and he was drunk. His skin was oily with sweat and he had unbuttoned his shirt down to his belt line. His skin was shiny. His hair was dusty. He had a thick butcher knife strapped to his thigh with leather thongs and she thought for a moment he had stumbled on her by chance when he was out hunting. But she knew better. He had traveled miles from his mother's house to find her. She felt uneasy. Baptiste Yellow Knife was another man when he was drinking. He smiled at her when he stood over her and she noticed that he was weaving. When Baptiste Yellow Knife got drunk he was mean. His teeth looked big. She noticed he had tattooed her name on his hand with indigo pen ink. The tattoo was large, in wide block letters, blue pigment staining his skin forever with her name. Louise tried to imagine Baptiste poking the ink-dipped needle into his brown hand again and again, ink pooling beneath his skin, her name sinking into his blood.

He sat down next to Louise on her blanket and for a moment she was glad for the company. But even her boredom did not make Baptiste Yellow Knife a welcome visitor when he'd been drinking. He didn't speak to her and she didn't speak to him. It occurred to her that Baptiste had ways of finding things out that had less to do with his mother's medicine power and more to do with his desire. He had the clean whistling eyes of a screech owl. She believed he could look for her in darkness to hunt her out. She had trusted him to hide her from Charlie and now she wondered if he was expecting payment. She felt she had trusted him too much, because she couldn't count on Baptiste to stay away from the bottle. Baptiste Yellow Knife could find her, because he had memorized the shape of her footsteps in weeds and tall grass. He knew the brush of her hands past the huckleberry bush and wild roses. He knew the way leaves turned as she passed them, the way her scent fused with spearmint and sage. He knew the sound of her breath and the sound the wind made as it passed around her. He could trace her because he wanted her. He could sniff her out.

He had a pouch tied around his neck and Louise tried not to look at it, because his black hair curled blue around the leather straps and around his strong neck. She wondered if Baptiste could ever really change. Maybe being in the woods could cleanse his ways. Baptiste had told her the land brought us all back to our best selves. Now she wondered if he could make a change for the better. She could feel the warmth of his skin and she wanted to be close to him but she pulled her legs up to her chin. She let herself imagine. She saw herself kneeling beside him, opening her blouse to him, her nipples hard in the cool shadow of the cottonwoods, letting him suckle her, the gooseflesh rising on her arms, letting him have what he wanted. No one would know. Hidden in the dark trees, the scent of them drifting, then gone. No one would know. She looked down at her shoes.

Baptiste stood up over Louise. She was dwarfed by his standing, his strong, lean legs. He stepped around her slowly, almost carefully. She let go of her thoughts and felt the brutal toe of his boot barely touching her buttocks. He turned his back to her and she heard him unzip his pants. She kept quiet. She did not want Baptiste to know she was afraid of him just as she didn't want him to know she was drawn to him. She heard the low sound of Baptiste's voice as he pulled back from her. "Don't worry," he said. "Your luck has run out." She wondered what he meant. She wished his foot was still at her back. She was afraid to turn around.

She heard the dense patter of urine and she tightened her arms around her legs. Baptiste walked slowly, circling her, peeing like a dog marking territory. Louise wanted to hide her face in her lap but she kept her head up. She had a desire to pull her blanket tight around her but she made no attempt to move. She could see the stream of his piss. She could smell the dry soil, then the pine needles startled by brief moisture. His pee seeped slowly into the pale dust, leaving a dark clay stain.

She wanted to shove Baptiste's skinny butt down the hill. She wanted to slap at his head, chase him away from her. She looked down at the highway and wished she could make a run for it, yet she knew there was no running from Baptiste. She remembered that Baptiste, even with his smoking and his hard whiskey ways, could outrun the high school athletes. She had seen him running hard, never winded, hurdling barbed-wire fences as easily as a deer. He could stand dead-stop on solid ground and leap like an antelope over the high school fence. He could bolt full-speed when he wanted nothing. And she knew he could jump her like a cougar if she tried to run from him—and would. Her grandmother had told her to back slowly away from him if she was frightened by him. She had run from him before and her sister had been bitten by the rattler. She pulled in a sigh and waited.

Finally Baptiste turned back toward her and shook his penis dry. "Scare you?" he said, grinning. Louise watched him zip up his pants and wished she had the power to make him catch his cock.

He sat down beside her and whispered to her. "Don't you know animals are afraid of human scent?" He batted her arm with the tips of his fingers. "You wouldn't want a skunk in your bed, would you?" Louise swatted at her ear as if she were slapping a mosquito. She gave Baptiste the same look her grandmother gave her when she came in from a night of drinking.

Baptiste leaned over close to her and before she could duck him his teeth clenched the top of her ear. He bit down hard enough to sting her. She seized his jaw and pushed him back from her. She grabbed the branch she kept by her blankets and swung at him. He jumped over her first strike, laughing until she cracked him hard on his backside. When he put his hand to his back she struck a hissing blow to his face. She could see the white welt rising on his cheek as he stood back from her.

She watched his face, afraid he would hit her. He stared at her. He stared at her for a long time until she had an urge to rub the back of her neck, to look away from his staring. She sat still with the thick branch still raised in her hand. "You shouldn't have left me," he said. "Did you think you were rid of me?"

She heard the crackling of brush and knew from the sound that her sister was coming up the hill. The welt on Baptiste's face was pinched and puffy but he did not flinch. "I'll have you," he told Louise. "I'll have you yet. Sweetheart," he said, as if he could touch her heart, as if he could taste it. She turned from him pretending she couldn't hear what he was saying. She would not let him know that he had flicked her heart, that he had made her giddy and shy, that he had made her breath come fast. She did not want him to know she could hate him enough to be full of him. Baptiste was like a brief cool breeze, a sudden thicket of darkness on a hot day.

When her sister called her name Baptiste pulled himself up and crouched down. "Someday," he said to Louise in a low, whispery voice, "you'll be mine." And then he headed farther up the hill and he was gone. When Florence came up the hill she was breathless. She carried a sack of fry bread and a small jar of sugar. She sat down next to Louise and pulled out a piece of bread. Louise looked up the hill. She could not see Baptiste. She stood up to look but he was gone. "What?" Florence said. Louise shook her head and sat back down. She was hungry. Her sister held out a piece of fry bread and was sprinkling sugar on it. Louise looked at Florence. She was thick-framed but not heavy. She had a delicate nose and large black eyes. She took after Great-grandpa Magpie. Her skin was fine-toned and radiant and kissed with freckles. Her hair was black and usually long, but now it hung past her knees. Every summer for years Florence would go to old Suset to get her hair chopped off but Grandma had asked her to let it grow. Now her hair seemed a nuisance to her, thick and heavy, braided tight and still too long for her. She had tied her braids behind her head.

Florence could handle an axe with ease even though she was just a kid. There was a strength in her, in the way she smiled, in the way she moved. Louise thought she was beautiful, and envied the way Florence never strayed from their grandmother. Louise thought it was funny that Florence was easy to frighten. Small sounds startled her. She was afraid of the dark and she had once lit Grandma's tent on fire with matches. Florence had been afraid of the tent. She said the tent was dark and she felt as if she were suffocating. Grandma had understood her fear. Florence had not been punished for the tent fire. Louise remembered the flare of red flames, the thick smudge of smoke, the hot, sick smell, flames ticking like static as the tent seared to sky. Florence had stood behind the house, her teeth chattering, watching the fire. Louise looked at her sister as she ate her fry bread. She would not tell Florence she had seen Baptiste.

Louise saw the slim shine at the edge of the river, the sheen of waterlight outlining every tree at the moment of dusk. Her sister talked on as the wind rattled the bushes and the smooth stars began to appear above the pale hills. She wondered if she had just imagined Baptiste Yellow Knife coming to her. She picked up the stick she had hit him with and poked around the dirt he had peed upon but the ground was dry. She could find no trace of him. She brushed a strand of hair from her face and looked up the hill. A few leaves trembled in the breeze. She could feel Baptiste Yellow Knife was far from her.

"They're looking for you," Florence said. Louise sat up with interest. "Even Mr. Bradlock is scouting the hills. Grandma and I saw him. He can hardly make it across the field without his face turning red." Louise thought of Mr. Bradlock. The sour dampness of his heavy jowled face. She knew he would not find her.

"What about Charlie?" Louise asked.

"He's mad at Grandma. He says you'll die out here. He's saying now he should have taken you to the hospital."

"He would have taken me back to Thompson Falls," Louise said. She knew he was looking for her again. She pictured him in his patrol car, spotlighting barrow pits and bushes, Charlie scrambling up the wrong hills, breathless and turned-around. She knew Charlie would never find her. A hundred people could find her, but not Charlie.

Florence stood up. "I brought you more water," she said. Florence brushed a leaf out of her hair. Louise had an urge to grab her sister's hand tightly and hold on but she did not. Louise smiled at Florence and stood up to watch her walk down the path. "Stay down," Florence said, looking back. And Louise sat back down and tried to figure out what she was wishing for. She had run out of wishes.

The night cold settled around her, a cold that seeped through the blankets and ached at the small of her back. Her spine felt brittle. She could feel the tender bruises on her knees, the drawing of the deep cut on her arm. She wondered if Charlie had been right. She pictured herself on a long sterile bed, wrapped in white gauze. She looked at the rough blanket beneath her. She thought of Baptiste pissing around her. There was a weak rumble in her stomach. She had lost her hunger. Her arms felt weary and useless but she had to prepare for the night. She got up and gathered the leafy branches her grandmother had taught her to use. She folded her blanket lengthwise and covered the top with sage and the branches. She buried herself beneath the sweet boughs and then pressed her head down into the covers and soon she fell asleep, a sleep that forgave the wind, the moaning tree trunks, and the crying coyotes, a sleep that called her. The moon was too thin to offer light and the night closed around her.

A breeze shook the branches and they clicked above her. The bum smell of bear gripped her. She heard rustling, familiar and close, a snorting sound growing distant. The smell retreated. She lifted her head and remembered Baptiste, how he had peed a circle around her, and then the thought of him passed. She was not thinking about Baptiste Yellow Knife. There was only the smell of dampness settling. She closed her eyes and saw again the silver gleam of spiderwebs, miraculous, the cotton cocoon of moths blown up from a thousand branches floating above her like light.

She sees the moon moving high above the fields, catching light in sleeping pockets of water. The valley is winking with smooth ponds. The water light. All the fields are dry now. The clouds lit by the moon are water, passing. It is close to harvest. And she is dreaming beneath this moon the way her grandfather dreamed, his cap of magpie feathers pressed to sky. With power she feels the movement of things and even the still night air has weight. Louise feels the night in her throat, in her skin, water-heavy.

In the distance he is glazed in quiet light. She dreams of Baptiste Yellow Knife moving toward her but never touching. He is watching her. The night air is cold as creek water and though he is far from her, she feels his breath. He is warm. She feels the heat of his passing like his horse lathered from running. She smells him. He is the smell of all the things she loves without awareness. The smells pass her like childhood: the river smell, spring sage before lightning, juniper and jack pine, the deep smell of dirt and worms after winter, camas flower and chamomile, her grandmother's hands.

All summer long he has tended his horses. He is brushing Champagne's mane. He is cutting Champagne's tail straight and knotting it to silk. She hears a low sound and realizes someone is singing. The sun is white heat. She can't remember the moon. And she is naked, sighing in the dry grass. He is far from her. He is wearing his dancing silks. He is ready for marriage. She lifts her hand. But he rides away from her. She yells to him, waving her arms. He is leaving her. She knows now. She is running. She hears the dull slam of his thighs to the horse, the hard kicking of his heels. Dust worries at the edge of the field, lifting heat to sky. She is sweating in this heat. She squints to see. He is riding toward the rock rise of shale. He shouts to her. She can't hear him above the swift sound of wind in the high pines. She sees only his shirt, fallen to dust. It smells like rust-blood. He is gone from me, she thinks. He is gone. And she turns back to see him ride toward the black highway. His back is broad and shines with sun. All she sees now is the white gleam off the top of his shoulders. The fields and the grass are white with sun and the miles and miles of fences.

Louise woke in darkness, breathing hard. Her eyes settled on the pale moon. She lifted herself up on her elbow. She saw the thick net of branches that concealed her legs and remembered where she was. She thought of Baptiste. She lay back down and let her breathing quiet. She closed her eyes. A thought came to her and she looked up but could only see darkness, a blur of branches tangled above her.

When she had walked home her thoughts focused on Baptiste Yellow Knife. Thompson Falls had made Louise think there were worse things than Baptiste Yellow Knife. After all this time of ignoring Baptiste, looking away from him, running past him without a glance, hating him, pushing him, punishing him, using him, Baptiste had persisted. He wouldn't let go of her. And though Baptiste could be mean, Baptiste had insisted on loving her with no love in return.

Louise thought of Jules Bart, how for a short time she had let the thought of him devour her sad life. Yet he took no more time to think of her than the time it took his heart to thud his chest once. And he had turned out to be another lonesome drunk, wanting nothing. At least, she thought, Baptiste wanted her. She swallowed hard, felt the dry rasp of her throat. She reached for the jar of water her sister had brought her and wished for one cold beer. She gulped the water too quickly and for one moment she felt dizzy, almost drunk. She flattened her palms to her sides to brace herself, and found she was rocking. She felt the raw flush of her longing.

She lay back down wanting to say aloud "Go away." She could turn away from Baptiste for a hundred years but she wondered now if he would always be there. All that night she had prayed to be left alone and she realized now she was alone. She was alone and the slow morning revealed only the curving branches of the ragged junipers, the highway spilling toward places that would not accept her. The cottonwoods were curving toward the loneliness that cupped her but could no longer define her. She would not run again. She would go home. She felt the leap of the deer again, heavy and sudden in her lap, its beauty and crushing pain.

Louise

♦

The Burning Fields

Mr. Bradlock had knocked on the door at four in the morning and while her grandmother and Florence were at the window, fleeing, Louise had stood up calmly. She picked her dress off the floor and laced her shoes. She could hear Mr. Bradlock at the door. She knew that even at four in the morning he would be in his suit, his thin hair oiled and grimly shining. "Don't run from me," Mr. Bradlock yelled through the door. "Louise," he said.

"I'm not going anywhere," Louise said. She did not raise her voice. She imagined Mr. Bradlock pressing his ear to the door and listening. Knocking. Listening again. Her grandmother had wanted her to flee the house but she had refused. Grandma and her sister would be up the hill by now. Their breath would rise from them in the darkness. They would not come home again until they saw Mr. Bradlock drive away.

Louise opened the door to Mr. Bradlock. She had thought about this moment for a long time. She was no longer afraid. She did not feel the dense thud of her heart. She did not feel a weakness in her neck. She was ready to face him. He stood at the door and then turned slightly. "You can't run again," he told her. She saw that he was looking at the bruises on her arms not knowing she had been in a car accident. "Come on now," he said.

"I'm not going," Louise said. "I'm not going with you ever again."

She saw Mr. Bradlock trace his hairline with his fingertips as if he thought he would enjoy this fight. She stepped back from him and he grabbed her arms. She felt the blood squeeze of his stubby fingers but she refused to let him know he had hurt her.

"I'm not going," she said.

Mr. Bradlock rubbed his chin and she could hear the whisper of stubble on his cheeks. Louise leaned forward, close to his face and looked him in the eyes. He scattered his attention, looking at the cook stove, looking at the cattail bed on the floor, looking at her eyes and then away again. Louise spoke low to Mr. Bradlock. "I'm getting married," she told him. He dipped his ear to his shoulder as if the puff of her breath had tickled him. Then he looked up at her, meeting her eyes, a hard grin lifting his face, his temples, his fleshy forehead green in the shadowy kitchen light. He looked at her like he knew he had caught her in a lie that would embarrass her. He rested his hands on his hips, half smiling, half laughing. Louise waited.

"Who'd marry you?" he finally said. "Who'd have you?"

Louise felt the anger rise in her throat but she felt she had him. She smiled at him, the slow, lazy smile she gave to men at the Dixon bar when she wanted them to buy her a drink. Mr. Bradlock put his hands in his pockets but he continued to watch her. "I'm ready to go here, Louise," he said.

Louise pulled the kitchen stool to her and put her foot on it. She bunched her dress up to her thigh and bent down to tighten her shoelaces. She had to think. Mr. Bradlock played with the change in his pockets. She could see the squint of his watching so she pulled her dress back down.

"Who is going to marry you, Louise?" He had taken two quarters from his pocket and was rasping them together. She pulled the hair back from her face and stepped back from the stool. She dabbed at the corners of her mouth. He dropped his change and slapped his thigh.

"No one would have you," he said. The room fell to silence.

"I'm going to get married," she said again. He grinned to himself. He wiggled a little bit in his suit jacket and Louise felt a sickness crawl her chest. This old man in his baggy-butt trousers, his belly heavy with food even at four in the morning, this man older than her father was telling her no one wanted to marry her. He leaned up against the door frame and looked at his keys.

"I'm marrying Baptiste Yellow Knife," she said, and the words gripped her, because she realized it was true. She would marry Baptiste Yellow Knife.

Mr. Bradlock placed his hand over his belt buckle and coughed. "Louise," he said, "I've tried to save you." He looked at the toes of his shoes and then out the window. He tugged his trousers up too high over his waist. He wouldn't look at her. "Not worth the time," he said. His face was white-welted as if he had been cuffed by a hard fist. She had disappointed him. As he was leaving he stumbled on the door-jamb and pulled a handkerchief from his shirt pocket and waved it. He had surrendered to her.

Louise sat down and waited for her sister and her grandmother. Mr. Bradlock had not questioned her answer, had not pressed her any further to see if she was lying to him. He had accepted her answer with a sure and certain resignation, as if the thought of marrying Baptiste was too terrible to lie about. And now the idea of her marriage to Baptiste hovered around her. She would wait to tell her grandmother. She had yet to tell Baptiste.

When she entered the house, her grandmother did not ask Louise what happened. "You're staying," was all she said, and Louise nodded and smiled. Her sister came up behind her and whispered, "I thought you were a goner."

"Maybe so," Louise answered her.

They heard a vehicle pulling into the field. Louise saw Charlie and Aida Kicking Woman sitting for a moment in their worn truck and she found herself calm and relieved. She knew even Charlie would no longer come for her and she wondered when Mr. Bradlock would hit him with the news of her impending marriage. Charlie got out of the truck. He was on his annual mission. He carried a can of gasoline. His face was pulled into a grin of determination. Florence leaned on the window frame and watched them. Her grandmother looked out the window with Louise. "Every year it's the same," she said.

It was five in the morning and color was returning to the land. For the first time in longer than Louise could remember she felt she wasn't running from anyone but the feeling did not rest in her like she had hoped. No one would send her away anymore. No one would look for her on black nights. No one would find her on the roadside. Charlie Kicking Woman would search for another Indian. She sat down and listened to Charlie and Aida yelling to each other over the first spark of fire. Louise knew her running would not stop but no one would be chasing her now.

Charlie started the fire that would burn the fields close to her grandmother's house. The fields hissed under the lick of red fire. The fire gathered heat so fast there was a sucking sound close to the ground as if the fire or the grass was wheezing. Louise walked out on the porch with her grandmother and watched the fire run the hill, a red line of light that even outran the smoke. Her grandmother looked at the field rushing with fire. "I don't think they know what they are doing," she said. Louise said nothing. She sat down on the porch steps and looked at the charging flame.

Aida Kicking Woman ran toward the field chasing the fire and then the fire would switch direction like an angry snake, to chase her. She looked like a young girl with short stubby braids leaping over licks of fire. Charlie finally grabbed her by the collar of her coat and pulled her back to the truck. They could hear Charlie Kicking Woman even over the sound of fire. "How many times do I have to tell you, sweetheart, to stay by the truck?"

Aida's shoulders slumped and she looked small and disappointed in the open door of the truck. Louise suddenly felt sorry for her. She wasn't Flathead Indian. No one knew her or spoke much to her at powwows or Indian doings. She was only known as Charlie's wife. Louise knew she spent a lot of time alone while Charlie was out on call. She wondered if Aida got lonely in her small blue house. She did not have any friends, as far as Louise knew.

Louise watched the fields. A great wind was chasing the tall grass and sagebrush. The wind was spinning low to the ground, gruff-voiced and angry. Louise listened to the crack of weeds. Little licks of flame rounded the swamp grass and sizzled to smoke. Smoke grew in the fields. She watched the small frozen moment when every tendril of sagebrush glowed red, each small leaf outlined before the weeds exploded, before the sagebrush fell to fire. The sky was rose-colored with fire now, delicate as powdered clay, a smudge of color that grew wistful as memory, deep orange and then fading. Louise sat on the steps until the fire grew quiet, until the smoke grew quiet and hung heavy. Louise felt that she could stare at the fields all day and not ever find the place in all that heat and smoke that could hide her from Baptiste Yellow Knife. He had chased her and now she was rounding back on him.

Night grew like smoke over the hills, resting in the fields. A gunpowder haze closed over the river and then sheathed the highway. Louise thought of all the snakes in the fields, roasted, without power.

She thought of Baptiste Yellow Knife and wondered where he was. She hadn't seen him for a few days and yet she wondered if he was hiding from her in the dense smoke. She went into the house uneasy, wondering if somehow Baptiste had overheard what she had said to Mr. Bradlock that morning. She felt as if her words had given Baptiste even more power, that somehow the words she had spoken had lifted from her like a tattling bird. She thought of Baptiste moving in the darkness toward her, circling her. She would glance back suddenly to see the ragged chintz chair at the window, the rattling hollyhocks hugging the house.

Her sister and her grandmother worked in the kitchen. It was still light outside when she went to bed. The smoke made her bleary-eyed and sleepy. She felt thick in the slow haze that settled over the house and entered their rooms. She carried the thought of Baptiste to sleep with her. She woke dreaming he had called her. She got up carefully out of bed, lifting the sheet from her sister's shoulder, breathing softly through her mouth. She stood looking out into the darkness until she could see light. The moon lit the valley. Just across the cattails and swamp grass the field was lit red in places. The moon was rosy, ruddy, and peculiar, bleeding like a bar sign on a rainy night. She watched the distance, looking for Baptiste. She studied the black junipers on the ridge. She looked at every strand of grass in the murky light but she did not see him.

She stepped outside to make the trip to the outhouse. She sat for a while on the rough boards. She smoked a cigarette. Baptiste was not around. She felt a small pressure on her chest, a small ache of loneliness, as if he too did not want her. She left the outhouse and began to walk back to the house. She could smell smoke. The field was crusted black, cracked in places where red embers still held fire. A small wind could carry the fire to her. She could feel the heat on her bare arms. She stood for a moment and that was when she saw him. He stood at the edge of the blackened grass. He was watching her. She felt the chill of Baptiste Yellow Knife. She could hear his voice but she couldn't understand what he was saying. She walked a little faster toward the house. When she got to the porch she heard him calling her. His voice was rough and husky, scorched. She stopped and turned toward him.

She could feel the heat from the fields. She could see the outline of Baptiste in the murky light. He was stretching his arms behind his head. She knew he was smiling. Suddenly she wanted to go back inside. Pull the smoky blankets over her head and close her eyes. She felt the edge of her teeth clicking. She wondered what he would say to her. She feared his sudden mean nature.

Louise unbuttoned the top of her nightdress and pulled it over her head. She would play with Baptiste. She would gain the power. A wind blew. Flames cowered beneath the black soil. She was naked. She could feel the gooseflesh rise on her back and up her arms. She could feel gooseflesh on her buttocks. She was cold and hot at the same time. She could feel the heat of the field as she walked closer to Baptiste. She could smell him over the rich smoke. And he smelled like oil on still river water and she liked the smell more than she wanted to. There was a film on his skin that shined in the sweet night. She could see he was looking at her in the odd, smudge-lit darkness. She stepped up close enough to him so she could see his eyes, so he could see clearly that she was naked. She watched him watching her. He looked at her nakedness. He looked at her breasts for a long time. She watched his gaze as he tagged the swell of her hips, the thumb press of her belly button. He looked at the dark hair between her legs and for a moment she thought he would reach for her but he did not. He looked at her and then looked out over the reddened fields.

She had heard old stories of women pulling men inside of them and crushing them. She paced slowly toward him. She knew it was Baptiste that could pull her inside of himself. She was small next to him. Naked, she felt like a young girl beside him, a girl he wouldn't want. She wished she had her nightgown to cover her. She stepped even closer to him and felt her nipples stiffen. He did not touch her. He licked his teeth in the darkness. He was not like Mr. Bradlock, a fifty-year-old man who had not known a woman. She saw him shift his heavy penis in his trousers. He was not playing her game. She rubbed up against his natty shirt breathing his scent. His hands twitched at his thighs but he did not move to hold her. His breath was even and warm. "I'll marry you," she told him, feeling the cold weight of her heart. When he stepped back from her he laughed. Louise looked at the stiff rooster tail of his hair as he turned from her. She watched him walk up over the hill. He walked quickly across the long field. He did not trip or stumble in the darkness. His walking was sure and steady and she thought for a moment she might follow him. She saw him leap the fence near the highway. Wind lifted a tight haze of smoke up and over him until she could no longer see him. She was thinking that he would come back to her but Baptiste was gone. She did not feel his winking presence in the cattails, or his shadowed watching from the rocky hillside. She closed her arms around her nakedness, knowing he had wanted her when she could not be had.

She thought of Jules Bart in the Dixon Bar, how he turned away from her. Baptiste was turning from her too and she felt snagged by him as if he had hooked her desire to survive and had cut the line. He didn't want what she had. She heard the high rushing wind over the tops of the cottonwoods. She looked down at herself. Her skin was smudged with ashes. She thought of warriors heading into battle with snake paint on their ankles. She felt an ache of laughter in her shoulders, the low curve of her stomach. She was naked and standing out under the stars without a man or the prospect of a man. She had bared her ass to a man she sometimes hated and found he had less use for her than she had for him. She walked to the porch and sat down, weak with wanting to laugh. She was a bigger fool than Baptiste Yellow Knife.

The sky overhead sheltered white whiffs of smoke. Smoke glazed the stars. Louise saw the light puff of burr-reed and thistle gleaming at the edge of the hillside. She slipped into the house and grabbed the dress Mrs. Finger had given her. It fit her tight at the waist. It was beautiful, mint-green and shining even in the dark. She would go to the Dixon Bar and have a beer, maybe two. She thought about the burn of hard, clean whiskey. She thought about dancing and drinking and drinking until the dim bar glowed. She pulled the dress over her head and straightened it. She rubbed the ashes from her knees and ankles and decided against shoes. She was so happy she would dance barefoot to Dixon. Suddenly the world was good. She stepped off the porch like a whisper.

Charlie Kicking Woman

◆

After the Fire

I got *the call* no more than ten minutes into my shift. Some Indian disturbing the peace in the Dixon Bar. I was sick and tired of those calls, sick of the sign above every small bar and tavern across the state of Montana and beyond, anywhere there was an Indian, no dogs or indians allowed. Tired of being the authority charged to uphold a law that forbid me to enter a bar when I wasn't in uniform. Who the hell was I to haul off a brother looking for small comfort? I drove past the bar first wanting to let the poor bastard get a good buzz on before I hauled him off to the clinker. It was the least I could do I figured. I told myself I was driving over to check on the fields we had burned off that day but I was only fooling myself. I was hoping for a glimpse of Louise. I could smell the smoldering willow grass, even this far from the Magpie place. I was driving fast. The wind bleated at my windows.

I had a rising feeling in my chest, the feeling I get when I look down from the edge of Revais Hill. Rumors were flying around town about Louise because folks hadn't known where she was. Even Aida got wind of the gossip. On the way home from the field burn she told me Louise had hitchhiked to Wallace, had been working at the U & I rooms, the whorehouse in Idaho, before she had come back home. Aida seemed excited at the idea as if she had just read a romance chapter and the story was coming true.

"Everyone was talking about it at the store," she said.

"Talk like that's good for nothing," I told her.

"It's a good story," Aida had said, and her voice defied me. "It's a good story nonetheless." I felt heavy with marriage. I recognized that Aida was letting me know Louise was no good.

I felt guilty. I passed Grandma Magpie's house looking to be where I shouldn't be. The house was smudged in smoke, quiet against the sooted fields. I parked the car for a moment and scanned the hillside where there was nothing but the slow wane of smoke from ashes scattered by the breeze. I turned the car around, back to my duties and the Dixon Bar. Bradlock had called me early that morning to tell me Louise was getting married to Yellow Knife. I had burned the fields like bridges.

Behind the shaggy screen door I could see Louise sitting on a tall stool with her back to the bar. I wasn't expecting to see her; my heart leaped. Her hair was lit to shining by the bare bulb glaring from the ceiling. She had a drifting look about her, like she was thinking of someone. She was wearing a fancy dress I hadn't seen before. If she had been wearing shoes she would have looked like she was going somewhere special. I didn't think I'd been called in to pick up Louise. I surveyed the bar for a moment. I had a grim sense. A swirl of white gnats stirred above my head. I had that crawling feeling. The lights in the bar were bright, too bright, the faces too harsh, no softness. I recognized the mood from all my years as an officer. It was an atmosphere that called up meanness. One innocent quip becomes shrill. I stooped low, and squinted into the barroom to see who was there, ready for trouble. Eddie wasn't bartending. Sheila Owens was standing behind the bar with a smear of lipstick on her face. Her bun was knotted at the back of her neck. She was laughing with someone and smoking, and I remembered Railer had said Sheila liked bartending a little too much. I could see that now. She slurred even in her laughter, a tall glass perched in front of her filled, five or six whiskey shots, I guessed. I crooked my head so I might get a look at who she was talking to. I didn't want to take any chances.

I saw the polished boot of a man who wasn't a cowboy, the cuff of an ironed sleeve. It was Harvey Stoner, Harvey Stoner alone, no wife in sight. Everyone was having such a good time they didn't even notice me. I pressed my face to the screen to see Stoner leering at Louise. I never liked Stoner, a sour big shot with an ass-crack smile, who made his money off poor Indians selling their allotments. He'd cashed in on the land around the lake, owned half the waterfront property, and now he was turning his greedy eyes inland. Stoner owned so many allotments on the Flathead some Indians called it the Stoner Reservation. It wasn't funny to me.

Stoner had his eye on Louise. I could see that much. Sheila Owens was trying to keep his attention. The woman could talk to herself all night but now she thought she had company. The only trouble I could see was that Louise was stealing Sheila's thunder. It was clear that Stoner was more interested in Louise than in anything Sheila had to say. I decided to take a wait-and-see approach but the sight of Louise made me heartsick.

Louise was drunk. Her head sagged to her chest and the glass she held tipped over, spilling a foam of beer. She tried to pull herself up by placing her elbows on the back of the bar but she was slipping. I wanted to help her. I wasn't going to let her drop to the floor and offer Stoner the chance to come to her rescue. I'd seen enough.

Baptiste Yellow Knife came out of the bathroom just as I was about to enter. He was so dark Louise looked pale beside him. I stepped into the darkness and watched them. I wanted to see what she saw in him, what the attraction was. He sat down next to Louise and grabbed the back of her dress to steady her. I didn't like how he claimed her. She smiled at him for a moment and then closed her eyes. Baptiste lit a cigarette and lifted two fingers to Sheila. "I've served you," Sheila said, "now it's time for you to be going. I don't want no trouble."

"And I ain't giving you any," Baptiste said. "Just one more round," he said, "and we'll be out of here."

"I want you to know I've called the cops," Sheila said. "They'll be here anytime. You'd be doing yourself a favor to leave."

"One more round," Baptiste said a little louder.

I knew I'd gotten my cue to step in, but I wanted to see what would happen. Everything was still under control. I decided to wait. Sheila Owens took a swig of her own drink. "Can you read?" she asked Baptiste. When he lifted his head to her he was weak-eyed with booze. "The sign," she spoke again, "you read it?"

"Lady," he said, and then as if to get another start at it, "lady, I not only read the sign, I memorized it." She seemed almost pleased with the answer. "OK," she said, "but I want you to know, I'm not responsible."

"Sounds familiar," Yellow Knife said.

Louise drooped toward Yellow Knife. She couldn't drink another thing. She was ready to go under. Sheila slapped down two shots in front of him then went back to her talk with Stoner.

"I'm lining it up," Baptiste said to Louise. Louise said something that made no sense.

I watched Yellow Knife tip those small glasses to the ceiling. I watched the single rise and fall of his Adam's apple as he plied them down. Louise was close to falling and Baptiste was making a poor attempt to hold her up. I stepped forward slamming the screen door behind me, and saw Baptiste Yellow Knife set his last drink on the bar.

"About time you got here, Kicking Woman," Sheila said.

Yellow Knife braced Louise and helped her to stand. Then he scooped her up in his arms and I found myself stupidly thinking about Aida's romance novels, the dizzy covers of men rescuing women. I was stunned by the sight of her pale throat as her head tipped back and her red hair caught the light. Even her dusty bare feet looked pretty. I felt powerless again. Warm blood pulsed in my knees. "Out of my way," Yellow Knife said. The tattoo on his dark hand spelled out her name. I felt the tickling sweep of Louise's dress, the brief softness of her hair on my hands as he carried her out the door.

Sheila Owens leaned down hard on the bar top staring at me. Harvey Stoner held a glass halfway to his lips and swirled the ice in his drink looking at me too. "Hell of a lot of good you are," Sheila said, her red mouth frowning. I couldn't deny that I was of no use. The only good thing I could do now was leave too. As I was walking out the door I heard Sheila Owens say, "Damn Indians." Harvey Stoner only snorted and I wished the bastard would snort his drink down the wrong gullet.

I got in the cruiser and drove heading toward Flathead Lake. The clouds lit the high moon. It was starting to turn toward winter. Cold lined the seats of the car and I could see my breath. Summer seemed distant. I started thinking about my wife, about Louise and Yellow Knife, the way the world seems to spin us dizzy. I wondered why I had ended up with a lonesome wife and an unhealthy hankering for a woman I could never have. Aida likes to say we get what we deserve. And I didn't want to think about Aida and what she had gotten from me. I thought about fishing Dog Lake in lazy circles and the sky above me pink with dusk knowing I deserved only the dream of fish and sometimes that was enough. Now I wondered what would satisfy me. What would be enough to settle me. It seemed to me I was changing like a familiar place inching toward strangeness, because I was seeing myself differently. And I had the creeping feeling I should jump beneath a table or look out the window to see what was coming.

I was restless. Even after my shift had ended I wasn't ready to go home and entertain my old thoughts of Louise. I wanted to be finished with her then. I went to the office and stared at my pile of paperwork. I didn't get home until midafternoon, feeling guilty for the thousandth time that I had left my wife so long alone.

Aida met me at the door with news of her own. Louise had been to the house. I wanted to know what had happened, felt the desire to know rise in me. I sat down at the kitchen table and tried to act disinterested. I fingered the stitching of the tablecloth.

"I'm beat," I said. My years on the force had taught me a few things. I had learned that when people think you are too anxious to hear their stories they shut right up like they hadn't realized they were offering you something of value. It was a good lesson too. It worked.

"She was just outside," Aida said, almost breathless, "outside with that man."

I slipped off my jacket and let it rest on the back of the chair. I drummed my fingers on the table and looked at the salt and pepper shakers. After a long enough while I asked, "Did she come to see me?"

Aida shrugged her shoulders. "I think she was just looking for a place to run. They were fighting," she said.

"Was she hurt?" I asked, trying to keep my voice even.

"Her nose was bleeding if that's what you mean. But she wasn't hurt. She was fighting him." I looked at Aida. She had just washed her hair. Little dribbles of water stained the shoulders of her blouse. "She hauled off and kicked him in the balls," she said. "Last I saw of him he was hurting." I didn't care about Yellow Knife. I was pleased to hear he'd gotten a good swift kick to his best memories.

"Where'd she go?" I asked but I couldn't hide my concern. My voice had shifted an octave higher.

"How would I know," Aida said. "Is she all you care about?"

"I don't know what you mean," I said, lying, knowing exactly what she meant. But Aida was onto my game. She cooked me eggs with so much Tabasco I coughed red-faced for an hour. She hummed a high tune at the kitchen sink as she scalded every dish and stacked them in the sink rack steaming. I had to stay around the house. Aida would be wondering where I was off to. It was my weekend. I split green wood for two days, only stopping to eat and sleep. Aida stood by the window watching me work, her small face haggard and hollow in the yellow kitchen light. In the dimming cold I was chopping my troubles away. Sweat lifted from my back in a shimmering cloud. I was forgetting, I told myself, I was forgetting Louise. But I was fooling myself, I was trying to forget the man I was. At the end of that long weekend I returned to work to hear the news that Louise and Yellow Knife had married. I brought the news home to Aida like a peace pipe offered.

Baptiste and Louise

◆

The Power of Marriage

He made a wedding bed for her in his mother's house on sheets that were slick with the smell of him and oily to the touch. She scanned his room trying not to look as if she were passing judgment. She rubbed her arms and fanned her face with her hands. Baptiste did not look at her. The small room seemed to surround her. Baptiste leaned forward and tucked the bed cloth under. He did not say a word to her as he made their bed. It was cool as a root cellar in the room but a small stain of sweat puckered the back of Baptiste's white shirt. He worked without talking, straightening the sheet edge, punching the single pillow. He worked like a soldier. He did not ask for Louise's assistance. When he had finished making the bed he left the room closing the door behind him.

There was no clutter in the room, no boxes, no bottles, no paper or matchbooks, not even a shirt hung from the hooks that lined the wall. Louise was left alone. No clothing, no closets. There was one cigarette butt snubbed out on the dirt floor but it was curled with age. She wondered if a woman had smoked that cigarette but she felt no need to check for lipstick. The only thing that claimed Baptiste to this room were the four rattlers' tails that hung from his bedpost. The bed-springs trembled when she placed her small purse down.

She stood for a moment at the door listening to Baptiste and Dirty Swallow. She could make out a few words of Salish and she knew he would be a while. She was not surprised that her husband had left her in their wedding room to be with his mother. She imagined the cool breath of his mother's voice, the stories she would tell him about new brides, the ways of women. She thought of climbing out his bedroom window and going into Perma for a beer or just settling for a pop at Malick's. She wanted to sit outside as the evening cooled, find a ride with someone she didn't know, go to a place far from Baptiste, because she already knew that even though she was drawn by Baptiste he could not hold her. She knew her feelings for him were already passing. What had drawn Louise to Baptiste was the hard chase. He wanted her. His wanting her had become all that mattered. Now that he was her husband she waited.

She was in Dirty Swallow's house. The snakes would be lazy here, without power. She didn't think they would strike her in her mother-in-law's house because here it would be like striking themselves. She had married snake's blood. She checked the window. The wood was rain-split, the hinges were tight with rust. She rubbed her finger on the dust-clouded pane, still she could only see a smudge of the hillside beyond. Louise imagined snakes under Baptiste's bed, uncoiled, sleek, and long as branches, sleeping on the cool dirt floor of his room.

The voices of Baptiste and Dirty Swallow made Louise lean close to the door. She peeked through the keyhole to see a small step stool, some of the wallpaper peeling and yellow, but she could not see them. She thought she could hear her name but the more she strained to understand the more their talk began sounding like coyotes in the early morning. She heard the word "night" twice. She heard her grandmother's name. The more closely she listened the more their voices resembled wind or water or an animal wheezing.

There was a sad, smoky light in Baptiste's room. Here and there light seeped through the cracks along the edge of the floor. Small burrowed holes trapped the sun. She thought of prairie dogs and gophers, all the small animals who had been stupid enough to dig under this house, stupid enough to find themselves looking down the tight throat of a diamondback, their instincts failed.

She looked again at the rattlers' tails hanging on the bedpost. She stepped up close to count each section of growth, the length of the snakes' lives. She lifted the tails up from the bed and held them close to her face, so close she could see small patterns of color, and her heartbeat rose in her throat. The rattlers were light in her hand and smooth to the touch. She looked into the pockets of their hollowness, holding each tail to her eye, turning them in her palm, each section shifting in balance, each section shifting small weight like heaviness. Each tail whispered like it was whispering to her and she listened but could not understand the power that had guarded her husband when he was still strapped to a cradle board. What she heard was her own hard breath, the pale click of her teeth in the small, shadow-heavy room.

Louise had heard that the husband waits for the bride. The husband is left alone while the bride pinches her cheeks in the bathroom, while the bride perfumes her thighs and powders her breasts, while the bride washes herself again, cleans herself with hot water, hoping she will smell sweet as roses for her new husband. But Louise was the one who waited, knowing she smelled like tobacco smoke, a hundred swigs of beer. The perfume at her wrists had sharpened. She shook the tails again and again, finally taking the rattlers down from the bedpost, holding the tails up to her chest like small furious bells hoping the sound might startle her husband to rescue her. But the door remained closed. She could only make a sound with the tails like an old man's dry hands rubbing together. She remembered the rasp of brittle paper blown against grass before the rattler had struck her sister. She sat down on the bed. She lit a cigarette and remembered that her grandmother had not raised her voice when Baptiste had told her they were going to be married. "You'll both be unhappy," Grandma said. He had stood before her grandmother in his white shirt so stiff with starch that every time he shifted, the shirt had chafed his neck with a sound like Sister Sebastian whispering in church. In the dusky light Baptiste's hands were so dark she could not see his veins. He had frowned, and she had wondered then if he knew her grandmother had spoken the truth.

She knew she was now part of the oldest kind of marriage, a marriage of blood power. She wondered if what she really felt for Baptiste was only urgency to reclaim what Baptiste had taken from her. She did not feel romance for Baptiste Yellow Knife. She sensed Baptiste could change her. Near Baptiste she noticed the dim scent of roots, the heaviness of her own breasts, the weighted curve of her womb. She could smell the woman's blood in her and it made her long to be touched by him and long to be far from him at the same time. The desire for him was overripe in her. He made her feel unclean. She knew that Baptiste wanted to lie between the heat of her legs, but many men wanted to sleep with her, to wrench themselves inside of her, to claim her somehow. With Baptiste it was more than sex, more than just simple desire. The evening before she had left home her grandmother had told her Baptiste had sold the best part of himself to own Louise. "His spell will turn on him," she had said. "Someday, he will be bitten back."

Louise remembered stories of love medicine. Love medicine so strong it gripped, love medicine so strong men would leave their wives and families to chase a woman, an ugly woman without teeth, a woman with warts on her breasts. She used to laugh at the idea. She used to hold her sides and cross her legs when her grandmother sat stern-faced, telling her the old stories of love and desire.

She liked the story of the woman who fell in love with her sister's husband. The woman fell so hard in love with her brother-in-law, her grandmother had said, she put the love medicine on him, a bad medicine that shot up the slick cord of his spine, a medicine so strong it peeled the skin of his heart. The medicine clicked her name in his bones. He left his wife sleeping, on a black winter night. He stood up in his thin shorts with a hard-on so big it pulled him toward her. The March weeds shivered around him but he kept running toward her, toward her small house. When he found his sister-in-law with another man he chased him out of the house, chased him up into the hills and told him to never come back. The woman was so happy she took her brother-in-law to bed. Her medicine had worked better than she had hoped. He was the best lover she had ever had. He could make love all night. And when she turned from him he would still be poking her. She had found heaven. But soon she began waking up, waking up at three and four in the morning and he would be on top of her, his penis hard as a bull horn, even harder than he had been the night before. He would not eat, and when she would sit down to have a meal he would rub up behind her chair until she would slap at him. Even her dog was better company.

His wife began to stand outside her house, the wind tangling her long hair, stand outside for hours with her small children wailing, calling him back, her own sister calling. But he wouldn't look outside. He wouldn't even lift the curtain for a moment. She would tell her brother-in-law it was time to leave. She would tell him that his wife was waiting for him. He would just follow her around from room to room until his ragged shorts wore thin and fell off of him. Still she told herself she liked the looks of him. But then when she would go to visit her relatives he would put on a pair of her pants or one of her dresses. He would stand outside waiting for her, pacing her cousin's house, cupping his hands to the windows, with a hard-on, always with a hard-on, always with whining eyes, his worm lips trembling with tears. And her relatives didn't like her much either. They recognized love medicine when they saw it. She had stolen her sister's husband. And if she could steal her own sister's husband she could take theirs too, or worse.

The sister-in-law got tired of her sister's handsome husband. She went back to her sister and begged her to take him back. But her sister had finally set up with another good man. So the sister-in-law tricked the man outside and locked all of her doors and pressed cardboard to her windows. Three days later he was still standing outside her house. He began pressing his face to the locks at her doors. If there were any gaps in the cardboard at her windows he would find them. She would see his watery dark eye blinking at her. He would call her name again and again until his voice grew hoarse and whispery. Then every third day or so he would fall asleep. She knew this because he would stop knocking on her door, or pounding on the sides of her house. She would sneak away then but he would always find her. And he would chase away her friends when he walked toward her, his hard-on straining one of her old dresses. She would tell him to go away. She would shoo him like a cat but still he followed her. She threw back at him the knots of his hair that she had once carefully gathered from his favorite chair. She gave him back the small bits of clothing she had snipped from his clothesline. She gave him back all the things that held him to her but those things had gained their own power. She could not release him.

He haunted her for years. She had to leave her home and all the people she loved but even then he followed her.

For a short time Louise had thought about using love medicine on the rodeo roper to pay him back for ignoring her. When she had asked her grandmother about herbs and blood her grandmother had laughed. "You don't need love medicine, Louise. If you used love medicine on any man you'd kill him." Louise did not expect her grandmother to laugh. She thought her grandmother would scold her, warn her of danger. Her grandmother had once told her that love medicine could wear itself out, break like a tight knot pulled. Love medicine runs its course. Louise didn't really believe Baptiste Yellow Knife had put the medicine on her. But her grandmother had warned her Dirty Swallow was using her medicine, all of her medicine to hold Louise to Baptiste. "Baptiste is not the man for you, Louise, maybe no man is the man for you. That's OK, too," her grandmother had said. "Fight this. Anyone under the spell of love medicine never believes they are."

Louise calmed herself with the idea that she was staying with Baptiste because she wanted to stay. She was here in Baptiste's room of her own desire. If there was a spell on her she was smart enough to recognize it. She chose to believe she was with him because there was a strength in him she would never have. He was not ashamed to be Indian. The nuns couldn't wash the smell of spirit smoke from his hair with all their kerosene. They couldn't soap away his Indian tongue.

Sister Sebastian once told Louise that the best thing Louise could do for herself and for all of her race was to marry a white man and move off the reservation. She thought of all the young Indian women who had chosen to marry white men. They would come back to the reservation with their half-breed sons, with their daughters, faces watchful and afraid. Indian women who held their pale children back from the dance while their husbands visited other squaw men and talked about the stupidity of the tribe, the drunken Indians, all the ways in which Indians could never make things work, lazy Indians, stupid Indians, grinding talk applied to everything Indian, while their own half-breed children squatted in the warm sawdust at the edge of the arena, or stood frowning at the fry bread stand, always away from the teepee circle. Louise knew what it was to be a half-breed. She had lived on the reservation her whole life. Even though she belonged here, even though she was Indian, she couldn't claim her place here like Baptiste. Baptiste had something she desired, a power beyond medicine that she would never have.

She remembered the silver November day Sister Sebastian had looked up from her attendance sheet, her peach-colored face hardened. "John," she said, "John the Baptiste." Everyone kept still in their chairs, tracing their pencil holders, hiding their hands in their desks, keeping their eyes down, hoping not to be called upon, hoping not to be the object of the sister's ridicule. Baptiste Yellow Knife with his wild hair, Baptiste in his animal skins and high-topped moccasins had become John the Baptist eating bugs, John the Baptist thick with lice. Dirty. Dirty Indian. Louise had felt the damp heat beneath her arms, the sudden thump of her heart. Baptiste had been held back three years because his mother had refused to allow him to attend the Ursulines' until he was eight years old.

Louise recalled how Baptiste sat like a man that day at his small desk. He had sat for a very long time in his dusty clothes waiting for the school day to end. He seemed distant and sleepy, rattling his pen in the empty inkwell and turning every few minutes to glance at Louise. Ernie Matt tossed a pencil shaving on Baptiste's desk. "Eat this," he whispered. But Baptiste only put his chin to his chest and squeaked his fingers on the desk top. He sat for too long not getting the joke, not understanding he was the one being called John the Baptist. The other students began to understand too. They turned to see Baptiste, their faces tight with relief as if by watching him, by staring him down, they could chase the name of John the Baptist from themselves. They seemed to have forgotten his mother held a great power. Louise could feel something coming. Something moving along the hallway. She lifted her feet up from the wooden floor and stretched out her legs. Louise had heard Sister Sebastian as she leaned over his desk to hiss, "Baptiste," to whisper, "John the Baptiste." Louise had felt the numb center of her ears, a rushing sound move past her. She imagined for a moment she was seeing the sister's coarse hair, the pulsing red crown of her skull beneath her black veil. She had heard the clicking of the sister's rosary beads against Baptiste's desk. The sister's lips were tight, white-rimmed, close to Baptiste's ear.

The light shifted in the classroom, the strange ripening light of late afternoon, the lulling light that closes day. The light focused for a blinding moment on Sister Sebastian's half-moon glasses. And Baptiste stood up gracefully, with purpose, with an arrogant dignity that suggested he knew more than the giggling students, knew more than Sister Sebastian. He stood for what seemed a long time, looking directly at Sister Sebastian. At first she told him quietly to sit down and when he still stood standing she lifted two long erasers and slapped them together in front of his face. She had tried, Louise thought, to clap his nose. Chalk dust lifted in the air like a small cloud rising and then sifted down again on Baptiste, down on his hair and his face, down on his shoulders. He had the face of a beautiful warrior whitened for battle, his lips were pale, even his eyelashes were powdered. He opened his mouth and his mouth was dark. Sister Sebastian backed away from Baptiste, slowly at first, so slowly he seemed to be moving from her. She moved far enough back to let him pass. His shoulders were squared. He walked out of class. He did not even turn to glance back at Louise. She felt the pull of his passing so strong she had stood at the window to watch him. A few other students gathered at the window with her.

His stride was low in the dry winter grass. Dark wrens lifted from his path, their flight sudden and circling. The dead jimsonweeds rocked toward him again and again and touched his fingertips. Baptiste Yellow Knife left, shoulders strong to the gusts of wind, and he did not look back. He hadn't seen that Louise had stood up at the window to watch him leave even after Sister Sebastian had told her to sit down.

All that afternoon the wind churned the fields and chased a gray chalk dust against the school windows. Tumbleweeds and sticks struck the windows. The sky turned silver but it did not snow. Louise tucked her feet beneath her when the heavy doors knocked in their hinges. And all that day the students listened, not to Sister Sebastian and the rap of her geography stick, but for Baptiste Yellow Knife to return with his mother, to return with the power they had all lost. When the final clock buzzed low he did not return to the boys' dormitory. He never came back to sit in the stiff runner desks. When he finally came back to school he came back for Louise.

Baptiste returned to walk down the long, polished halls of the Ursulines', his snake rattles tied to the tops of his boots. The old ways clicked in his tongue. His eyes were careful but he no longer avoided trouble. He became a man with sweat-rimmed, tight-armed shirts. He didn't dress to please anyone but himself. He did not talk just because he was spoken to. He became an Indian who was not afraid of being Indian, the worst kind, the kind nobody liked, neither the Indians nor the whites, the kind of Indian who didn't care if he was liked. He had become a man who would not bathe to make a good impression. And even though he seemed coarse to Louise and she wanted to avoid him she could not stop the desire she had to stand close enough to him to feel the heat of his chest.

She found there was something in her that knit with his flinching jaw, his yellow-nailed fingers, his frowning grin, the hard hollow curve of his stomach, the straight line of his lips. She found herself thinking of the back of his head, the brush scruff of his black hair against the collars of his shirts. She found her own longing in his desire, the way he would kiss the strands of hair on her forehead and then suddenly back away from her to gulp air, to look at the hills or the ground as if he had to catch his breath.

He was her husband now, the man she had married. She sat down on the bed and removed her stockings. If there was a medicine spell on her she thought she could wear it out because it was the biggest part of her. The idea of old marriage spun in her head. Her grandmother had warned her of the many ways that Baptiste could have captured her: the razor-toothed badger close to her ankles, the claws of bears, whisper-dreams of birds swooping strands of her hair, her thoughts read by magpies, fish puffing her desires to blinking water, eagles circling her, her dreams owned by snakes. She knew his medicine could read her loneliness somehow and she thought maybe the trick was to close in on Baptiste, chase him away, suffocate his desire with the having before the venom in his blood could shrink her fast heart quicker than fire.

She had convinced herself that the only way to get past Baptiste was to stand up to him, to marry him because the more she ran from him the more he had chased her. She knew he could kiss her breasts and sleep with his nose on her pillow. He could slip his hand between her legs, but he could not own her. She held his longing now.

When Baptiste entered the room again he left the door open wide to the rest of the house, to his mother. He undid the top button of his shirt and pulled it off over his head. She could hear his starched shirt brushing his skin. Static charged his hair sending small strikes of blue lights into the room and then there was nothing but his dark shoulders. Louise watched the door as he unsnapped his pants, then closed her eyes when she heard the slow rasp of his zipper. His back was to her when she opened her eyes. She could see the tight knot of muscle in his calves, his smooth buttocks. His shoulders were broad and it seemed to Louise he undressed so slowly his muscles ached beneath his brown skin. When he turned toward Louise she could just see the dusky hair between his legs. She could trace the thick blue vein up from his groin to the thin skin of his belly. His belly looked thin-swollen, tender as a child's. He came toward her. Louise turned toward the hazy light of the window. The light was yellow now, the light of a late October night passing. Her husband was leaning over her so close she could see down the length of the frayed white scar that split his chest.

The last time Charlie Kicking Woman had seen her with Baptiste he pulled her aside. Drinking and medicine conjure a mean spirit, Charlie had told her, and Baptiste had let booze mix with his blood. She had heard the story about Baptiste many times but Charlie told her the story again with a heavy voice, a voice meant to dissuade her and she had listened. He told her that Lester Bad Road had ripped Baptiste open with a ragged butcher knife outside a bar in Plains. Baptiste's chest was bleeding badly. He shouldn't have lived through the knifing but he got back up again. He got back up again with his legs wobbling. But it's what Baptiste had done when he got back up again that made Louise listen hard. What Baptiste did to Lester became the story Louise had heard many times, the story even white people told each other when they had had one too many beers or too many belts of bourbon, a story jawed in bars or whispered after the kids had been put to sleep, a strange and funny story.

Simply, Baptiste had spit on Lester. He spit, Charlie said, on Lester with such force that Lester's whole face looked like it had been painted red. And when Lester went back into the bar to wash up, he couldn't get the blood off of his face. He couldn't scrub it off. Oil wouldn't take it off. Bleach didn't work either. Borax, Fels Naphtha, mint oil, Vaseline, kerosene, gasoline. No luck. Everyone around began saying it was snake's blood and medicine power. Charlie Kicking Woman told Louise it was nothing but superstition. "Still," he said, "Baptiste Yellow Knife is no one to mess with."

Now Louise looked at the scar on Baptiste's chest and she was moved to touch him. He had caught her up. She felt a weakness in the channel of her back. She cupped her hands to her waist to brace herself. No one could hurt her now. She had married the son of Dirty Swallow.

A rush of wind caught the door and it slammed shut like a rifle shot through the quiet house. For a short time she could hear Dirty Swallow singing and then there was silence. Louise imagined Dirty Swallow on the other side of the wall, gripping the knuckles of one hand, a snake coiled beside her.

Baptiste stood before her naked. There would be no shivaree for this marriage, no short sheets and rice, no music and dancing, no pranks and no laughter. He did not smile. Louise removed her dress and draped it over the snake tails. The room was dusk-scented, summer roots, dry leaves and overripe berries. She could smell him, smell her husband. She lay down for him. She closed her eyes. His belly was cool and slick against hers. She could feel herself sinking beneath him, the bedsprings giving way to the pressure. She could feel the steam of his breath on her throat. Her spine ached. He did not whisper that he loved her. She held him close to her and closer until she could feel him and then she let him go.

Louise

♦

Roads

Louise had only been married to Baptiste for four days when she escaped. She had begun imagining a lifetime cooped up in the soily nest of Dirty Swallow. She would wake at night from dreams of snakes to find she was struggling to free herself from her husband's arms. Baptiste and Dirty Swallow would spend early mornings visiting each other. They recounted old stories like good friends, laughing and joking, but when she would arise to join them Baptiste would leave the room to check on his horses. Dirty Swallow would busy herself in the kitchen. And Louise would stand in the living room, alone, wondering how she would fill her days, useless, not even a guest in her husband's home.

She awoke one night suddenly but lay still beside Baptiste. She could see the trailing red arc of his cigarette in the darkness, and it made her feel lonesome. She wondered how long he had been awake. She heard the soft puff of his breath sighed. Louise pretended to sleep but she watched him. Baptiste got up from bed and stood for a while on the cold dirt-floor. He looked out the window. She could see the moonlight on his skin. He rubbed the back of his neck and turned as if to look at her. In the darkness she could not see his expression.

He slipped on his pants and grabbed his shirt. He left the room and closed the door behind him with a quiet click. For a moment there was a pale shaft of light beneath the door, then the light was gone. Louise sat up in bed. She heard Baptiste's light footsteps on the porch. She wanted to move to the window, see where Baptiste was headed, but when she shifted her legs to stand she felt a cool draft moving close to the floor. She listened for the long curve of snakes beneath Baptiste's sinking bed. Baptiste had left her.

She lay still for a long while and waited for the sun to rise. She listened. She could hear Dirty Swallow moving in her room. Louise raised herself up on one elbow. She had learned Dirty Swallow's routine. Dirty Swallow would walk down to the outhouse and when she had finished her business she would head down to the river to wash her face. Louise was reluctant to swing her feet to the floor but she had to act quickly. She could see Baptiste's worn belt hanging from the wall hook. She stood on the bed and strained to grab it. Her muscles were so tight and stiff it took her four tries to reach the silver buckle. She wriggled the belt beneath the bed. She expected a furious rattle and looked to see if anything sidled the floor. There was nothing under Baptiste's bed, not even a lone sock or a pair of underwear.

She placed one foot down on the hard dirt floor and then the other. She glanced around the room making sure to check under the old magazine she had dropped on the floor. The pale, green walls made the room seem damp and mossy. She pulled her dress over her head and grabbed her shoes. She listened for the sound of her husband's voice, for Dirty Swallow's return. The house was still.

She watched the floor, aware of how thin her ankles were, the calves of her legs. She knew she was not alone in the house. Her grandmother had told her the rattlers in Dirty Swallow's house even nested in the newspaper insulation and climbed the walls waist-high. Louise had opened the kitchen drawer carefully at Dirty Swallow's, tapped the inside of the cupboards with the water ladle before reaching inside.

She slapped the floor with Baptiste's belt. She paced her steps, keen to any unexpected shadow, any hidden snake. As she walked past the kitchen, she saw again the nest of tiny rattlers curled together behind the woodstove. She remembered how Dirty Swallow had seemed unaware of their presence as if the snakes were harmless sticks. Louise pressed her back to the wall as she passed them. When she finally stepped outside she took a deep breath. She realized she had left her coat inside but she had no desire to retrieve it.

She wanted to believe that Baptiste was just outside, close by, feeding his horses, tending the field. But the sleepy horses stood in the corral and the sun was shifting toward her. She believed Baptiste would come for her, that he would leave his mother and make a home for them. She held this thought. He would come for her and yet she wondered where Baptiste had gone. She guessed he could be at Hemaucus Three Dresses' house, not because he cared for Hemaucus over her, but because Baptiste liked to catch Louise up in her insecurities to bolster himself. Louise had just begun to understand this about Baptiste. It was his nature to roam, but she had chosen to believe he had always roamed in search of her. She had wanted to leave him, not be left behind.

The day held an edge of coolness. The wind blew so hard she had to hold her dress down when a car passed. It was a long walk home to her grandmother's but she welcomed it. She shifted her gaze to the blond fields, the shadows of clouds moving over the distant hills. Now and then she would turn to see if Baptiste was following her even though she knew he wasn't.

"*You were smart to leave him,*" her grandmother said to her when Louise entered the house. She could smell sweet wood smoke, the juice of chokecherries. Louise did not wait to hear what her grand-mother had to say about Baptiste. She tried to make sense of her feel-ings for Baptiste as she walked to Malick's store. She knew her grandmother would say that Baptiste was not out of her system yet, but Louise wouldn't let herself accept his significance. She didn't want to admit to her grandmother that Baptiste had gotten to her.

Louise imagined Baptiste finding her coat. She allowed herself to think he was feeling bad he had left her alone. She imagined Baptiste looking out the small window of his room, looking for any other sign she may have left behind. She imagined he was running the dry fields toward her grandmother's house. He was running through waist-high weeds. He was running on hard stones. He was coming for her. She would teach Baptiste Yellow Knife that she was not one to be left alone.

She saw Harvey Stoner at the counter of Malick's and as she approached him he glanced back at her and leaned over the counter.

"Bull Durham," he said. She wanted to turn around to see him pur-chase the tobacco but she didn't even glance his way. She had seen him before. She could feel his attention on the backs of her legs, the curve of her buttocks, and she liked his attentions. He was watching her, stiff-eyes forward, the see-all watch that suggested indifference but Louise knew better. She lifted a can of peas from the high shelf and flexed the calves of her legs. She paused in her reach. When he turned her way pretending not to be looking she licked her finger and slowly wiped the dust off the silver top of the can.

She had known about Harvey Stoner for years but he was only beginning to notice her. He tapped his store-bought cigarettes on his silver case when she passed him, or he'd put his hands on his hips and look off beyond her like he didn't know she existed. Small things overdone. Maybe a glance her way as he lifted his car hood, his eyes on her in the rearview mirror as he pulled out of the churchyard. She could feel him like heat. Harvey Stoner. He was forty-eight years old. A Caucasian and a rich man in Dixon. Everyone said he had made something of himself. He drove fifty-seven miles to Missoula every day on government business. He lived on the reservation because he wanted to, because of the wide-open land. He drove big cars through all the small towns that Louise had spent hours walking to. The miles were easy for Harvey Stoner. There was no distance he couldn't cross, no place he wasn't welcome. She thought of Baptiste, how he could make himself welcome too, with his fist and his hard words rinsed by alcohol.

Harvey Stoner was leaning on his car trying to roll a cigarette when Louise came out of the store with her oil-stained package of cold lard. A thin line of tobacco rattled on paper, scattered to a sudden wind. He didn't look up. Though Louise had seen him many times she had never known him to smoke a cheap cigarette. He was a cigar man. She stopped in front of him. He had oiled his hair so much she saw the teeth marks of the comb. He smelled as sweet as a woman. She leaned in close to him.

"You do this, mister," she said, knowing his name but wanting the secret.

She cupped her palm and took the cotton pouch from his hand. She curled the paper with her long fingers and poured a puff of tobacco in the tunnel, pressed the paper with her thumb, rolled it forward to hide the tobacco. She licked the cigarette length then rolled it shut, licked it again, twisted the ends, then handed the cigarette to Harvey Stoner.

"There you are," she said. He looked down at the cigarette, elegant and thin in his pinkish palms.

"Looks like a girl's," he said.

Louise noticed his fat, gold ring, the square red stone that blinked back at her. His nails were clean. She thought of Baptiste's hands, his black fingernails kneading her belly, her breasts. For one small second she imagined Harvey Stoner pressing his oiled head between her breasts. She looked at Harvey as he lit the tip of his new cigarette. She heard the swift curl of fire to paper, watched the first fragrant whiffs of white smoke fade. She turned away from him.

Louise headed toward the highway. She could feel the wind at the crease of her elbows and it was cold, like rain coming. She felt that Baptiste was still gone from her. He had left her. In her heart she knew he was waiting on some other woman. She thought he was probably looking at Hemaucus now. He was probably standing outside her window while her brother sat in the kitchen. Baptiste was waiting to see Hemaucus's dark skin, waiting to see her panties fall to the floor, waiting to enter. Louise believed Baptiste no longer wanted her. He had had everything he wanted from her. He had seen the mystery of her.

Louise heard coughing behind her and she turned to find Harvey Stoner, one hand on the hood of his car, bracing himself. He was bent over, hacking smoke, the cigarette small in his hand. He looked up to see her looking back at him and he got into his car. She heard the floored engine, the little rut of tires in dirt gravel. He drove on past Louise, one hand draped on the steering wheel, cigarette in his mouth, eyes watering, while rain sizzled on the dry road and smoked back up toward sky.

She looked down the road as far as she could, drawing breath to see him coming back for her. His pale, yellow car was sleek in the rain. But when he passed her going fast the other way and all she could see was his two coyote-quick eyes looking back for the briefest moment in the rearview mirror, she stopped still on the road, surprised, and laughed toward the dust-heaving juniper, smelling the rain-heavy longing of dirt in the lightning-cracked sky. She imagined the reflection of pond grass in his chrome running boards, the quiet brown grass shining like water against the clear sun line, how she would sit in the passenger's seat of his big lazy car and roll down the windows to thunder.

Harvey Stoner had swooped by once more and when he returned his tires split the rain-slick road as he stopped, and water sprayed her. He leaned across the smooth seat of his car and opened the passenger door. She slid into the seat as the hot sun cut through the clouds. Her dress was steaming wet. She didn't have to talk to Harvey Stoner on the way to her grandmother's house because they couldn't stop laughing. Harvey Stoner had reached between the seat and pulled a beer from a tin box and had given it to her like a gift. She felt a lightness in her that she had not felt for years, if she had ever felt this way. Harvey Stoner could take her far from here.

He drove on past her grandmother's house before she had a chance to stop him. He drove so fast she felt the small muscles in her back tighten as the car pulled the curves. She felt wings lifting her belly. The rain could not hold to the windshield. Rain fanned from the windows. She had never ridden in a car that could charge the road with such speed. Harvey lifted the beer to his lips and flipped the ashtray open. He punched the lighter like he was performing some small magic. His ruby wedding ring flashed. But when the lighter popped back up he did not reach for it, instead he leaned forward and shifted in his seat.

"Take out my wallet there," he said. "In my back pocket."

Louise grabbed the wallet quickly. His wallet wasn't slim. It didn't shape to his buttocks like the wallet she had found in Baptiste's pocket.

"Open it," he said. She smiled to herself. His request was a familiarity she had never known and it made her feel both important and shy. She opened his wallet without looking at his money and placed it, straddled open, on his lap.

"Go on," he said, "count. I want to see what we have." He said it like the money had always been theirs. Louise had never seen so much money in a billfold. He kept his money like a neat cash drawer, ones, then fives, three twenties, and four fifties, all facing the same direction, heads up.

"How much?" he asked.

"I don't know," Louise said. She was surprised when she found herself thinking he was going to just give her the money and more surprised when she found herself hoping he would. She was embarrassed to be looking into his wallet. He could see her want.

"Well?" he said.

"I'd say around three hundred," Louise said, and gave him back his wallet. Before she could stop him he grabbed her hand and was kissing her fingers with the brief wet press of his tongue. She felt the heaviness of his car. The smooth rolling wheels beneath her seat.

"Let's say you and I go to Wallace tonight," he said to her.

"I'm married," she said, thinking more of his marriage than Baptiste.

He turned on the radio and the music sounded clear. He sang to a song she did not recognize but his voice was deep, almost caramel, lush in his throat. He sang to her and she felt the shade of her blood. He pulled off his ring and pretended to swallow it.

"Gone," he said.

"Don't break your teeth on it," she said, but she liked the way he teased her.

He leaned toward her a little. "Give me your hand here."

She pulled her hands tight to her lap but he clasped her left hand.

She waited for him to take his wedding ring out of his mouth, to tease her again. But he lifted her hand to his mouth. She felt his tongue between her fingers, the gentle nudge of his teeth as he slipped the heavy ring on her middle finger. She wanted to close her eyes but did not.

"Hand me a cigarette from there, will you, honey?" He tapped the glove box. She liked his slow voice, his smartness, the way his shoes were so polished they looked tight on his feet.

"Don't want me to roll one?" she said, and then she hid her eyes from him for a moment. Louise watched brilliant strikes split the sky. Sky curled back purple, gray. Rare lightning in October. She'd only been to Wallace once before. She had liked the steep mountainsides, the whistling miners. She looked down into her lap at the ring on her finger, and let Harvey Stoner have his way.

He bought her a tea-length dress, a maroon-and-white lily print that dropped to a swirl. He took her to a beauty parlor where they gathered her hair up in a twist like Lana Turner's and dabbed her lips with deep-red lipstick. And then when she had dressed for him, in the new heels he had bought for her, with sheer diamondback stockings, a rhinestone bracelet on her ankle, he took her to the Stein Club, a basement club where the men wore warm brown suit jackets and drank smoky shots of bourbon straight.

They were seated in a high-backed booth where he leaned over her once and kissed her so deeply she tasted the heat of his liquor. He ordered for the both of them, T-bone steaks speared with stacks of sizzling onion rings, baked potatoes swollen with butter and cool sour cream, red-veined beet greens with mayonnaise. She had never seen so much food, so many people eating and smiling and talking.

She loved the dark silky wood of the club. The bar shined with glasses and beautiful bottles of booze. The soft lights were crystal.

There were no beer sausages or pickled eggs, no pigs' feet, no peanut shells, no stench of ammonia and urine. There were no dirty-nailed miners here. The ladies' room did not have a rutted bar of soap or a gritty dispenser. At the Stein the women used small seashell-shaped soaps.

Men watched Louise casually, almost disinterestedly, but flashed their silver lighters whenever she reached for a cigarette. A young man smiled at her, nodded a compliment. He reminded her of Jules Bart but he wore a white shirt and argyle socks. He drank his gin with olives, slowly.

A man played the piano. And another man shook a small amount of sawdust in the corner. Women would tip their beautiful shoes in the dust not missing one beat of the music. Men paid more attention to timing, the perfect count to turn, catching the women's hands gracefully, behind their backs, stepping beside them.

When Harvey Stoner asked Louise to dance, he stood by the table and requested the honor. She stubbed out her cigarette, every ember. She stood up carefully, keeping her shoulders straight. She felt tall in her new high heels. She knew the men watched her and she tended to her step, walking sure and swaying slightly. She was surprised to find that the women were not mean here. They smiled at her as Harvey rocked her in a slow dance, nodded to her as if they appreciated the way she dressed, the way she moved. She noticed Harvey seemed pleased also, pleased that she could dance so well, that she could twirl and hold his eye, balanced-book poised. They stayed on the dance floor through three songs. When the pianist played "In the Mood" the young man who reminded her of Jules Bart tapped on Harvey's shoulder and asked for the dance. Harvey Stoner nodded.

The man spun her around and then out. He held her close. His whispers tickled her ears. She did not care what Harvey Stoner thought, she wanted to dance. She danced until she felt flushed. When she looked at Harvey Stoner he was smoking a cigar. He lifted his glass of bourbon to her and for a crazy moment she thought she should duck. But he toasted her. She lifted her arms up over her head and unpinned her hair. The young man had loosened his tie now and she was at the end of his arm. Louise had danced with many men in the Dixon Bar. She had practiced all the new steps a hundred times, but most of the men at the dances in Perma and Plains were stiff and clumsy. This man could dance.

Some of the couples on the dance floor had stepped back and were watching the two of them dance, and smiling. Women sipped pale, green drinks that smelled like spearmint and leaned against men who were too attentive to be their husbands. There were only beautiful men and beautiful women here, a music sweet as sleep. Louise let herself believe she was wanted, even though she knew she could not be obtained. Baptiste Yellow Knife would be waiting for her when she returned home.

Harvey Stoner and Louise drove home to the sound of the radio. He dropped her off just outside Dixon. She gave him back his wedding ring. He threw her a gold mesh bag of chocolate dollars and kissed her neck. The first sweet chip of chocolate had just melted in her mouth when she saw Charlie Kicking Woman. She waved to him and smiled.

Charlie Kicking Woman

♦

Powwow

Tongues were setting fires. Talk of Stoner and Louise. Talk of Baptiste and Hemaucus. Talk that made the veins in my neck tick. The kind of talk that made people furious. Talk that made people wish something bad would happen, a bad medicine in itself. I wanted no part of it.

I was headed home, and as I turned off Highway 200 I saw Stoner parked just off the road. Louise was in the car with him, not even two weeks married. I saw him lean toward her as she opened the door. She turned her cheek from him but not before I saw the kiss. She was pushing the passenger door, straining from Stoner. In my estimation she seemed bored with him but when the door swung open I saw her bare, bronze legs and then he pulled her back against him. Her throat arched, his mouth clenched over hers. I looked so intently at their kiss I felt my own lips pucker. They kissed for so long he pocketed her hair in his hands, so long I felt the mean loss of her in my groin. I watched his big, yellow Buick pull back onto the highway polished so smooth dust floated behind him. Louise looked down the road after him. I watched him leaving, with a feeling in me like jealousy. Now it seemed Harvey Stoner had everything.

I always suspected I'd catch this guy in the act but I thought it would be a jailing offense, not just another infidelity. It's strange how money will make any man attractive, because Stoner wasn't a pretty man. But Stoner had a reputation for being clean and fastidious. I had heard men in the barber shop discussing the hair oil he used, a spice-sweet oil, as if a man's grooming was a topic of conversation. I heard Stoner himself telling Mr. Malick that the secret of his boot shine was a woman, and they laughed like they shared something. I never trusted Stoner. For a white man he smiled too much, like he had a great time all by himself. I only felt good enough around him in my uniform, because he would pay attention to me then. He'd look at me with his squint-eyed grin, his handshake milking, and I'd know he wanted something from me but I couldn't be sure what. He only paid attention to Indians who could give him something.

He paid attention to Louise. Last month I saw Harvey Stoner crane his neck as Louise passed him. Aida and I were seated a few rows behind him in church. Every Sunday I had been distracted by Harvey Stoner's inattention to mass, recognizing in him my own discomfort. I had even tried to avoid him by sitting in opposing pews but it always seemed I would look over to see Stoner staring up at the ceiling murals, Stoner blowing his nose too many times and folding his linen handkerchief into a little square he slipped in and out of his pocket. I had watched Harvey Stoner as he watched slow sunlight flood the stained-glass windows. Sometimes he pinched the bridge of his nose, almost wincing, as if he wished mass would end for good. We were both caught. But I hadn't been fooled by Stoner. Stoner wasn't like the other men in church who came for their wives or their own salvation. Harvey Stoner had come to show himself off as part of the community. He wanted to fool people into thinking he was interested in more than just their money.

That Sunday, Stoner sat up front with his tight-faced wife, in the third pew. He was slumped against her and she kept shrugging against his weight trying to make him sit up. I saw the glint of his big ring when he rubbed the back of his head. He wore a buttery suede jacket. He appraised his square, buffed nails. He clenched his fist against his knee as if he were knocking softly on a door. That day nothing interested Harvey Stoner. Then Louise walked by him, slim-hipped and green-eyed, and Stoner sat up to watch her pass. Harvey Stoner was the big cat at the gopher hole. He stared at Louise without shame, like the church itself blessed his action. Mrs. Stoner's face pulled tight, then tighter. Her cheeks looked sharp. It was clear. Stoner had hooked onto Louise.

On the rare Sundays Louise had accompanied her grandmother and sister to church I had never gotten sleepy. Louise was the girl we had all stood taller for, the girl we had ignored our wives for, a chain of men straining to see her. Watching Harvey Stoner eye Louise had made me feel important. I'm not sure why. I had felt my chest tighten, my heart pumped hard as if Louise was a flag and all that she was was somehow part of me too.

Stoner could have married Louise and taken her away. But Louise would always be Indian. Louise was our own. White women may have been good-looking to me, some better-looking than Louise, but Louise had something they didn't have. She seemed fixed on something else, something better than the likes of all of us or so I thought. But out of all the men she had gone and married Baptiste Yellow Knife and now she was seeing Stoner on the sly.

I had heard a lot of Indian women say, as if it was going to hurt me, that they were going to marry a white man and move off the reservation. I said if that's what it took to make a better life, beat it. I carried the grudge that maybe it was true. Maybe marriage to a white man would have solved their problems. Maybe these women wouldn't have ended up stuck in a tumbledown house with too many kids and a man who threw the few dollars he had at the Stockman Bar. But what good had come of all of this, of all this talk, of all this fighting? While we argued Harvey Stoner had slipped into our bedrooms with a grin on his face.

The idea of Louise and Stoner burned a hole in my gut. The only consolation I gave myself with this man was that Louise was smarter than he was and I knew it. I had more to think about than one love triangle. I had gotten the news the day before that I had to police a special-host powwow. I knew the way a man followed sign that the powwow would bring problems, a powwow too late in the season for my comfort. I never minded winter gatherings, only the powwows just before the cold. After August, a powwow made us all old Indians again, hungry bears, stingy as squirrels in autumn looking for that one person to hold us through the winter freeze. I knew Baptiste and Louise would try to make each other jealous. And jealousy sparked jealousy. I had seen all the powwow love triangles I wanted to see. The triangles circled in the fall, the dead romances recharged, the old girl-friends, the first flings, the bragging men, the strutting boys. Fighting words from men so old their teeth clicked. All of them, the men and the women, circled for the first jab until rage sprayed like a beer cap blown. A brawl I had to stop.

But there had been other times, rare times when I didn't have a single drunk to chase away. Only dancing. Only laughter. I'd just been the chaperone who'd come to eat fry bread and watch. I hoped for the best but knew better.

I suspected Stoner would come for Louise. And he did. He didn't just drive past the powwow grounds. He got out of his car to have himself a look. He stood over the stick-game squatters with his new hard luck. Since he'd started seeing Louise he hadn't been looking too good. His face was haggard and drawn.

Stoner sat too close to Eneas Victor and got a mouthful of dust when Eneas started digging down in the dirt, started throwing up thick handfuls of dust, raking dust through his hair with his fingers, and rubbing dust on his big, naked belly like he was washing himself. Eneas put his head down to snort and chase the other players a little. He'd always growl and shake his head to make all the other betters forget the bones he held. I saw him growl at Stoner and I saw Stoner just standing there, fists deep in his smooth leather pockets, shoulders tight to his ears looking around slyly at all of us. And I knew deep down he was wondering about Louise, about her bronze skin and cedar-red hair, how her beauty somehow came from all that he was not and all that he could never be. And he was afraid, I think.

I saw him standing over by the pop stand, smoking, squinting hard. He looked out back past the dance circle, past the bead and candy stands, past the cooking tents to the dozens upon dozens of teepees, the canvas stretched taut over the ribs of lodge poles, the mystery of canvas or buckskin doors draped for just a small heat opening. And I wondered what we looked like to him, all these Indians, some of us in deer hides and feathers, the stick-game lines, Pendleton blankets, our old women in bright kerchiefs, the young girls with long hair and the young women with their short, black hair and red lipstick who stood back from the games aloof as deer, the toothless, the drunks, the beautiful, and everywhere the small sound of bells.

I wondered what Harvey Stoner thought of the dancers, the sawdust arena, and the high clear voices clipping the drumbeat, the drums, the singing voices that weaved the dancers. I wondered what Harvey thought about Baptiste as he entered the arena because Harvey stood for a long while watching him. I wondered because I, myself, had always stood back from Baptiste when he was sober and dressed for dancing, far back, baffled by the muscle-sleek call of his dress, the dark, chalky silks close to his neck, the white elk bones laddering the bones of his own chest, the brittle sound of his ankle bells dulled by the beat of kicked dancing dust, his quill scalp spined upward toward all of us like the needles that stitched our blood, a thousand cut-glass beads glaring on the wings of his shoulders. We all focused on Baptiste by keeping our distance. A circle formed around him by the absence of other dancers.

Baptiste would begin dancing like a great, hawking bird. He would lift his arms and we would all, all of us cower forward to watch the quick spin, the dip-swoop, his head cocked smooth and sudden, so close to the arena floor, we imagined his ear could hear the whisper of quiet dust. A bird, we would say, naming crow, magpie, eagle, hawk. Then he would straighten in his dance, the music his own, and we would see the magic of deer, the elk, or the buffalo, all the animals he had become.

The children would cry sometimes or bury their faces into the chests of their laughing parents. But I remember feeling the tingle along my spine when my cousin Baptiste would turn to face me from the dance floor, Baptiste in the heat of dance would lift his open palms like a prayer, his face painted a black mask, the whites of his eyes, then blackness again. And all the dancers stopped dancing, I think, because they recognized power, not medicine power nor the power we all have now and again to strike someone with the snake of our image. The dancers stopped to recognize the clear light that surrounded Baptiste when he chose to honor the old ways. We looked at him in the dust of that dancing day, everyone it seemed in love with all that Baptiste was in lightning seconds.

I thought of Stoner, of all the things he'd probably seen, but I didn't think he'd ever seen dancers like that, or was ever likely to see anything like it again in his life. I'm sure he didn't have a clue what it meant. And the saddest realization I've had was that I wasn't sure what it meant either.

The strangest thing happened when Harvey was watching the dancers. Baptiste had entered the arena and he was moving very slowly, not to the direct beat of the music, I guess, but somehow still in time. Baptiste held a staff of hawk feathers that I recognized but had never known him to dance with. I remember a sudden furious wind of dust in the center of the dance floor, a winding column that turned a single time with wiry force and I had an urge to draw my gun. Some of the elders had stopped dancing but I noticed Baptiste kept dancing as if nothing had happened. Some of the young kids kept dancing too. There was a kind of small drama unfolding that no one was talking about and I began to wonder if the event was all in my head. Still, something curious seemed to be happening. And then it happened.

From the open end of the arena a large mule deer entered. It was strange how nobody saw it at first. I watched the deer run headlong into the dance ring. The great deer lowered its head and kicked up at the other dancers and they were laughing and trying to keep dancing. It bucked and we could all see its antlers, and there was a small roar and clapping from the audience. The buck seemed confused and was bleeding at the nostrils. I tugged at my holster and entered the dancing arena. The dancers were beginning to clear the dance floor, all the dancers but Baptiste.

I unsnapped the top of my holster. I felt the eyes of the audience and the dance-stopped dancers. There was a low drumming and the people were singing a sad prayer. My ears felt hot and I wondered how the hell I had found myself in this situation. My gun felt heavy on my leg, the gun I had no intention of using. I was the dangerous one here. Out of my element. Snagged like a squawfish. Useless. The deer began to circle Baptiste and Baptiste lowered his head. And in the second that it took for me to notice Baptiste, the deer had bounded to the end of the arena area and I caught just a glimpse, the strange silver shine of its tail and then it was gone.

I turned to see Stoner again. I was more aware of him than any-body because I could feel him smiling at me. He had a long grin. And he clapped his hands without noise, letting me know he thought the deer was staged, a show we had worked out as Indians. I began to really look at him. I cocked my head at him and for a moment I felt like laughing. He had bigger problems than me. I looked at his face, dry as dirt at the end of summer. And I'd say he wasn't long for this life, at least not if Louise left him. But a man can live a long time on desire, an old man's lifetime. He left the powwow, his big car clipping chuckholes. If he had looked back all he would have seen was me, my hands on my holster, the powwow grounds behind me, the teepees lighting one by one a deep yellow fire he couldn't get near.

I hadn't seen Louise. Hemaucus had been dancing earlier and then I saw her go back to the campground. It was still afternoon, but a heavy afternoon over the powwow grounds. Heat pressed the sky down upon us. Over the powwow grounds a sling cloud hung low and purple. If you looked south, in the distance you could see blinding sun raining. I kept waiting for the wind to rush the camp tents and teepees. The wind to chase the candy wrappers and paper cups. But no wind came.

If the river could tick it was ticking. There was a smell I recognized in the air, a smell like wet paper and fire, and a deeper smell that was not good, deeper than the dry leaves falling, deeper than the barrow pits. I sat in my car and listened for incoming calls. But there was nothing but static, a hundred miles of it.

Louise

Blind Spot

She had agreed to meet Harvey Stoner secretly. She sat in the tall weeds, waiting for the sound of his car. It reminded her of the times she had hidden from Charlie, only this time she would get to punch the radio keys in Harvey's car, drink an ice-cold beer.

Harvey Stoner smiled at her as he opened the car door and leaned far over to her. "You're a sight," he said.

She had seen the men at the Dixon Bar glance away from their stares when she looked at them. Some of the men in Thompson Falls had looked in her eyes for a moment too long when they counted back change to her. Baptiste only smirked at her. But no man had looked at her like Harvey Stoner. He eyed her like a waterfall. Harvey drove her up behind Dixon, far up a road she had only walked with her grandmother and sister when they searched for huckleberries. She could smell the sweet light of autumn.

They sat in the car and listened to the radio. She drank her beer fast to feel the quick sleepiness settle in her chest, the drift of a good time. They rolled down the windows and watched the sky. It was dark as an Easter shroud but it did not rain. They sat for a while not talking. Louise liked the afternoon, the slow lazy sun hovering. She liked the purple belly of the clouds over their heads. Harvey Stoner drove her home, telling her next time he would surprise her. Next time. She was surprised by him this time, surprised he had not tried to kiss her or touch her. He seemed to enjoy her company. He lit her cigarettes and uncapped her beers. She was happy he wanted to see her again. Happy to have a man drive her home and pull right up next to her grandmother's house like she was a lady.

Louise couldn't have imagined the sun slanting so suddenly through the windshield of Harvey Stoner's car. She couldn't have imagined her husband would be hiding in the blind spot of her watering eyes. Harvey had just stepped out of the car to open her door. It had been Harvey Stoner she had expected to see open the car door and hold out his hand to her. But she had looked up shielding her face from the sun and it was Baptiste who hauled her from Harvey Stoner's car, Baptiste pinching her elbow so hard she felt the sting of her funny bone. She was almost smiling, almost glad that Baptiste had come for her. When she entered her grandmother's house her eyes pulsed blind in Baptiste's shadow.

She remembered Baptiste had closed the kitchen door and had fisted the hook to latch it. She heard the low rumble of Harvey Stoner's car leaving. Even Harvey Stoner could not save her. She said nothing to Baptiste. She knew there was nothing for her to say. In her grandmother's house she could hear the ragged pull of Baptiste's breath. She stood still, hoping her stillness was a remedy for the tremors that heaved Baptiste. She felt the blunt darkness of the room, the coffeepot dulled by fire, the round lip of the sink, the small thick scissors her sister used to cut catalog paper dolls.

Baptiste cracked his hand to the crown of her skull with a heat that resembled comfort. She saw a crackle of light falling to her knees. She saw the ink-pen cross and then her name on Baptiste's brown hands. She was able to bite him hard enough to taste the liquor of his blood.

When Baptiste kicked her wrist she realized she was still holding the beer Harvey Stoner had given her. She saw the splat of gold as beer bubbled out of the bottle, arching over Baptiste, striking him, spilling on the floor around him like sour light. Baptiste was drunk, drunk to falling, his eyes smoke-hazed, hard-squinting, fixed on her as if she were a distant object. She saw Baptiste holding the broken bottle by the neck, lifting and jabbing, weaving. Mean.

A crazy stillness settled in her thinking. She remembered a barn boxing match she had once witnessed in Dixon. It was so dark in the barn they had surrounded the boxers with their trucks to light the event. The stark headlamps had made the boxers seem like movie stars to her, the skin of the men so white in the white lights their whole bodies haloed a soft glow. The boxers had held each other's keen stares with a tenderness like love. Even when they were pulled apart they did not break their gaze. There was a silence she had not known before, a humid silence so heavy the only sound she had heard was the sound of the boxers' heavy fists hissing at all of them. And when one boxer fell to the floor she had witnessed the brutal ache of his sweat shimmering above his head.

She had reached up to the sink. She had pulled herself up and had turned toward Baptiste to back out of the room when he lunged at her. She felt a dull ache in her chest. The beer-splattered floor shined like the eyes of ten thousand snakes. A red sleep whispered to Louise, soles of hard shoes on slick floors, her dead mother's hair in the jar by the juniper, Arliss's white socks on wire in the wind.

She wasn't sure how long she lay on the floor listening to Baptiste's lung-hissing sobs. She told her grandmother to shut Baptiste up. "Stop, Baptiste," she said. And her sister, Florence, grabbed her hand, told her Baptiste was gone, had been gone for hours. Baptiste had run away like a coward.

"You can stop crying now," her sister said. "Baptiste won't hurt you." Louise remembered the floor grit on her cheek, the new crack in her head where the wind howled now. She began to feel the weak flesh of her tender head. It was sore and wet. She could feel the slit. She tried to get up but her left leg was asleep. She could see the boot mark, the swollen blood-blue egg on her shin. Her left side felt heavy and oddly weak. She had the sensation that her breast was being pinched hard.

She looked down to see the scowl of wet blood tightening to her chest. She tugged at her sticky blouse to keep the blood from drying to her skin. She could see the open moon, curved up around one side of her nipple, banking off the side of her head, and Baptiste's hands again, Baptiste's hands hitting, Baptiste's hands shining with snatches of her hair, Baptiste's hands slapping her face. He had hit her hard, hard enough to wake her up and set her to sleep again. Her teeth rattled and Louise thought Baptiste was at the window.

Her sister draped a small pink sweater over her shoulders and Louise imagined Florence was praying, whispering for help. Florence placed a cool washcloth at the back of Louise's neck and Louise felt dizzy.

The light in the room was yellow and so bright she could only keep her eyes open for pinched seconds. She was aware that the days of summer were mostly gone. The purple sky had delivered only the smell of rain. A bright wind scorched the cottonwoods, so dry the dust and the boards of her grandmother's house made a whispery sound like the voices of old women. To Louise it seemed to be winter. When she closed her eyes she saw snow falling, snow sifting through the guardrails, lighting on the thick tongues of cattle, slow ice growing at the windows.

The winter before Louise had married Baptiste Yellow Knife her grandmother had told Louise a story of her first marriage. At the age of thirteen her grandmother had married a son of the chief, but not the first son. The man she married was not destined to be the chief. The man her grandmother had married was an old man. His breath smelled like tobacco and old corn and he stunk up their teepee with his bad wind. Still, her grandmother had told Louise, he wanted to leave a long legacy.

This old man had chosen to sleep with another Indian woman and had gone to her teepee. Louise's grandmother had followed him, knowing he was up to no good, knowing he was going to rut like a buffalo with another woman. Her grandmother had heard him with this woman. She knew his voice, because most of his teeth were cracked and he sounded like he was whistling when he talked. Louise's grandmother lifted the flap of the teepee and had smelled them. She saw the droopy sack of her husband's balls as he mounted the smooth, flat ass of the other woman. She stood back from the teepee opening and waited. She had taken her dressing knife to this woman's lodge. She was going to kill her husband. Her grandmother had told Louise she had dreams of being free again, of being without this old man and his old ways. But she had looked at Louise as she told the story. She had looked hard at Louise and she had said, "Even when you don't love them, that is when they get you, because you think they should love you. They have you then."

As her grandmother stood next to the other woman's teepee she had felt the flush of her heart. She could hear him inside with this woman and he wasn't doing so good. The woman was laughing at him and telling him his man thing was dead and ugly like a lizard. Louise's grandmother stood in the fine silt dust of that day as the evening fanned the trees to coolness and she felt ashamed for her husband and for herself. She was so caught up in her husband's shame she didn't hear him as he sneaked from the teepee. When he saw Grandma he tried wrestling the sharp knife from her hands. He had a big smile on his face. They kicked around in the dust awhile, Grandma and the old man, until finally the old man looked up at Grandma and said, "If you want to kill me because you're so jealous then here I am."

Grandma had taken a long look at her husband, the black pigment in his knees, the sag of his pierced earlobes, his face swollen with sixty years of buffalo fat, and she never let him know she could have laughed at him. I hated him, her grandmother had told Louise. Louise let this story drift in her. She thought she understood and then she closed her eyes. She heard her grandmother and Charlie Kicking Woman. She could hear the stiff soles of Charlie's boots and she pulled her sister's sweater over her face.

There was a sudden light inside her that made her cup her hands over her face so she wouldn't see the bruises on her arms, so she wouldn't see just how dark she really was in a well-lit room with a blue-eyed white man. She noticed the man's nails shined and he smelled like clean alcohol, the kind of alcohol that didn't come from a breathless voice, the kind of alcohol that didn't wheeze in his lungs but shined on his hands when he sewed up the cut on the back of her arm. He sat her down in front of his pressed trousers, so close she could see the first three notches of his zipper. She leaned back on the damp heels of her hands and looked at the floor.

The nurse entered carrying a large, white porcelain bowl of alcohol and gauze. Louise looked up at the doctor but he only smiled at her. The nurse set the bowl down on a small table near her knee. The doctor leaned close to her. She could smell his licorice breath as he pulled her head eye-level with his waist. She tried to jerk back.

"Easy," he said.

He cradled her head with moist hands and pulled her forward so that her nose was resting in the pocket of his groin. She closed her eyes. Her breath crowded her nose. She could smell cloves, a sweet and bitter smell she could taste near the back of her throat. She jumped. She felt a small squeeze at the crown of her skull then a sharp coldness, a small fire that took hold and began to make her limbs loose as fever. She could feel a thickness at the top of her head where her skin was swelling. Her tongue seemed loose and heavy—large as a bull's, she thought, swallowing—a slick tongue slipping back from the hammer.

Louise tried to bolt from the firm grip of the doctor but he held her tight. She could hear small snips. She could see long strands of her hair fall to the floor. She could see blood on the doctor's hands and blood on the scissors he dropped in the sink. She could hear someone moaning behind the nurse.

"Louise," the doctor said, "you're fine now."

She heard her own voice coming closer to her and realized she was making a deep sound she could not quiet.

The doctor held Louise's face tight in his cool hands and asked her to remove her clothing. Louise closed her arms over her breasts and set her teeth. She had seen the ragged wound. She didn't want the doctor to see the deep smile cut on her left breast. The doctor stood for a moment looking at Louise. His face was clean-shaven and slack. He had a fine tremor that ticked beneath his right eye.

"Take this," he said, handing Louise some white gauze, a small brown bottle. "Fix yourself up there." He pointed to her chest. "I can't be responsible."

The doctor took a jar of sweet-smelling ointment and rubbed the tender spot on her leg. He held her calf and pressed firmly with both thumbs.

"I'll set this," he said. "I suspect a hairline fracture." Louise could see his scalp turning red through his sparse hair. "I shouldn't but I'm going to," he said. "Do you understand?"

Louise looked away from him.

"I'm just going to set this for you. Wrap it up in hard white plaster," he said. He took a breath. "You just take it easy. Come back in a week or so and I'll cut it off. See, when we get hurt like this it's best to protect ourselves. Insurance," he said.

The nurse brought in a pack of ice and pouched it on her leg. The doctor left the room. Louise felt the cold first at the back of her neck. She lay still for a long time until her leg was as cold as block ice. She had fallen asleep and when she awoke it was late afternoon. She heard the doctor enter. She saw the white strips of powdered gauze the nurse carried behind him in a silver tray. She closed her eyes and felt the heavy plaster on her leg. "Anyone asks," the doctor said, "they can answer to me." She could hear the beef in his voice. She could see Baptiste and the doctor entering the boxing ring.

She looked out the window to the white-grass hill beyond St. Ignatius, the small road that led out to the highway. She could see Charlie's patrol car in the weedy parking lot. Louise looked down at the cast on her leg and lay back down on the table. She would find a way to ditch Charlie. Even broken up and dizzy she could outwit Charlie. She had to leave the Flathead if just for a few days. She removed the ice pack from her leg and got up to rinse her hands, to dab cool water to her lips. She felt for a moment that she would pass out. A hand hotter than her memories of late July cupped the back of her head. She felt blood, light in her belly, and then she felt the clean, cool sting of Dirty Swallow's poison. Baptiste was in her.

Charlie Kicking Woman

♦

Chasing the Dream

*L*ouise *got away from me* and I was sick with worry to find her. I radioed dispatch, lied through my teeth, told them I was in hot pursuit of Baptiste Yellow Knife and I was crossing the reservation boundary line and heading to Missoula. I was chasing the dream of Louise, sure she had headed to town. It was a dumb-luck wager that I knew could mean both my job and my marriage, but I made the decision with my temples throbbing with fever. I was going to find Louise. I was going to save her.

I saw the loiterers of small-town businesses leaning against storefronts looking for loose change. I watched the glassy stare of the Blackfoot River worn smooth by the press of autumn. I saw women in "going to town" dresses eating ice-cream cones, wearing gloves and lipstick, men driving clean cars, men visiting men in hardware stores, and they turned to glance at me in my reservation uniform, unsure of what authority I had. I saw myself in storefront windows and turned away. With each window I passed I expected to see my shoulders twitching.

I sat at the end of the long bar at Cattleman's and was surprised when they even served me a pop. It was the warm end of a long fall, the rattling tail of summer, the drinkers were saying, the hottest part. Indian summer, they said into their sluggish beers. In the haze of slow smoke I nursed my second pop, under the scrutiny of drunk men etching quarters into the bar to leave their marks. I wondered if Louise was lost now in the nest of a tavern dark with men as mean or meaner than Baptiste. The thought worried me.

I walked down the alleys watching for Yellow Knife but looking for Louise. I checked under the Higgins Bridge thinking some of the Indians there would have seen her. They hadn't. I left a few dollars lighter. I walked past all the beer joints and listened. I knew I would find her. I could sense it. The day was slipping to afternoon and I walked the long streets, a loiterer myself now, a man determined. When I did see her I felt the weight of my own heart. If it were not for the cast on her leg, I think she would have run from me. Louise wiped her chin on her sleeve, but she was only trying to hide a smile because I must have looked ridiculous to her. I was out of place here and she knew it. She looked a little funny too; I noticed her crutches were too high for her.

"You looking for me, Charlie?" she said. She had caught me off guard.

"I was looking for you," was all I could say.

She didn't say a word to me then. I turned to her clear, sad eyes and I felt suddenly ashamed to be chasing her, no different from Stoner or Yellow Knife, my desire visible as sunrise. Louise gave no indication she noticed. She looked out over the street. I felt I had made a mistake but I was not ready to back out.

"Hungry," I said.

She ordered ham and eggs. The waitress brought us two dishes smoking with hash browns and white toast limp with butter. She ate.

She drank great steaming gulps of coffee without flinching and lit a cigarette, but did not stop eating. I watched her. I ate my toast, looked out the window too. While I was talking to the waitress, I saw Louise grab the sugar bottle and make syrup out of coffee. She looked up from her cup and smiled and I wondered where this was heading. I looked at her slender fingers, the chipped red polish on her nails. She did not wear Baptiste's wedding ring.

"You eating this?" she said to me and I pushed my plate toward her.

When she had finished, she lit another cigarette and blew a slow breath away from me. I had wanted to be with Louise off the reservation for so long that when the moment presented itself to me I was ready to take it. I felt the slow trickle of sweat beneath my armpits. In late fall the day had turned hot. I would take my chance with her and hope I could settle my desire once and for all. Maybe it was Baptiste's beating her that prompted me to this action, fear there would be no more chances.

I took her to a hotel room. On a day that sweltered like fever the steam pipes were sizzling. The room felt damp. I sat down on the bed and wiped my forehead. She limped behind me. I removed my jacket slowly, watching her face. She did not look away from me. She did not seem afraid of me. The window shade strained the late October sun yolk-yellow. I held my breath. I hated the sound of my voice then, the demands I was making on her. I had told Louise to do a hundred things as an officer of the law, now I was telling her as a man to stand in front of that shade, to undress for me slowly, one piece at a time, her summer-faded dress, her single shoe.

"Leave the stocking on," I told her so low I didn't think she would hear me, but she did. She lifted the dress up over her head. Awkward. The dim room glowed like goldenrod. She had on cotton bloomers, washboard-gray and riddled with holes. I decided I liked the holes, a hundred small scents of skin, a hundred openings to her. One crutch fell to the floor and she hopped to get it. She tried to cover her breasts with the spread of one hand. I could see the doctor had bandaged and taped her left breast. I felt the old anger for Baptiste pressing my chest. "What did that bastard do to you?" I said and wished I hadn't. She turned her back to me. "Left my brassiere at home," she said.

She covered her face. Her shoulders bowed forward. I could see the hollow of her back, how it pooled in small darkness at the base of her spine. White light sprayed though thin tears in the curtain shade to touch her skin, each rib, I thought, her ribs. I watched her, knowing something about myself I had not known before.

I stepped out of my slacks and unbuttoned my shirt quickly. I pulled my undershirt off over the bristle of my hair and felt a sudden blush of weakness for my wife who had ironed my uniform the night before. I stood naked before Louise. Desire lit my belly, so strong in that moment, I could forgive myself for what I was about to do. I was surprised when she stepped toward me. I hoped she would not notice my jaw was trembling in my effort to keep my teeth from chattering. I was so close to her I pulled her to me. Her cast was cold, rough, and heavy, as it brushed my leg. I helped her lift it onto the bed, thinking of her thin leg in plaster, the bone-break ragged beneath yellow bruises. She crossed her arms over her breasts, her head heavy on the pillow. The hair close to her neck was wet and curled tight to her throat. I tried to pull it back. My fingers were swollen fat in the heat. I poked her accidentally in the throat. She coughed, and I sat up, laughing at my damn clumsy hands. Unsmiling, she turned her face from me toward the brownish skull-like water stain that bloomed above the bed stand. I lay down beside her.

I saw the high ceiling, watched long threads of dust chase our breath. Sunlight haloed the edge of the shade, illuminated the dress she had left on the chair. The thin fabric fluttered slightly from a breeze beneath the door crack or through the mercury sliding window. And for some reason I thought of my grandmother, the day she died. She had worn her hair in tight braids all her life. But my grandfather loosened her long hair after she had stopped breathing and opened up all the doors and windows in the house. It was April. And the wind was cool and smelled of lilacs and water. All night the wind blew through her hair lifting it up to the bedposts like the pale, gray ghost of her. My grandfather sat with her body for two long days, not leaving her side, not eating, watching her still chest just to make sure she had stopped breathing.

I heard the dense breath of Louise's sleep, saw the pulse in her neck slow to dreams. Her hand slipped to the bed pulling half the gauze from her left breast. I leaned closer to kiss what she had hidden and pulled back from the sweet-rot smell. From her open breast blood oozed yellow. She had cut herself, I thought. I eased back the tape and lifted her arm over her head. She was sleeping. I looked closer. And I knew then but the thought jolted me. Yellow Knife had cut her. It was a bottle cut. I had seen the wound in bar fights. Unmistakable. I knew the jagged flesh, the puncture in places so deep, no blood. Bloated white edges like skin too long in water. Infection.

I got up from the bed and rocked back a little holding my gut. I had a snort of whiskey in my jacket that I kept for roadside accidents. I pulled the flat bottle from my pocket, sniffed it once and steamed a washcloth with tap water. I hoped she was sleeping. I pulled the tape off slowly, breathing through my mouth. I touched the hot cloth to her raggedy breast. Her eyes were closed but she was still and tight. I dabbed at the wound, touched the cloth to it, drawing blood-water. I dabbed. I dabbed. A hummingbird tongue to a delicate rose. I covered her breast with the cloth and went to the bathroom to wash my hands. I pressed my wrists to the sides of the cool porcelain basin. I could smell her blood beneath my fingernails. I dug my fingers into the soap bar, rinsed clean.

Louise was unmoving on the bed, her eyes half-closed. I opened the whiskey bottle. I decided not to tell her how I was going to use it when she opened her eyes. I felt the sting for her in the tips of my fingers. Her tears were clearer than water, smooth, steady, quiet, clean. I wanted to say, Jesus Christ. I wanted to say, Dammit. Dammit to hell. Damn.

"You should see Baptiste," she said. I didn't know what she meant at first. I didn't see the humor in it. I said nothing. Light changed from yellow to blue. I lay down beside her forgetting why I'd come here. Forgetting anything but the sound of her breath in sleep.

I knew the white moon was growing at the window shade, the Blackfoot was turning black-silver. I knew Louise slept beside me. I was in Missoula in the Northern Pacific Hotel. My name was Charlie, I said, Charlie Kicking Woman. I felt heat in the room, a strange sweat heat like there were many people standing close together under a brutal sun. Waiting. There was someone else in the room with us. Who are you? I whispered, afraid of the answer.

The shade lifted from the window and the breeze was cool. Moonlight moved on the linoleum like water, the color of cow-pasture creeks: Dead Horse, Crazy Woman, Magpie, Lightning, Revais, I whispered the names. I knew something was waiting to happen. I stood near a wide river, pressed my foot in water. I felt nothing but the pulling. The pulling down. I remembered what Railer said when we were investigating a complaint near Nairada and had found a dead man in Clear Creek. His words sizzled on my saliva-thick tongue. We are all just ghosts waiting to happen. I held on. I reached out and put my hand on Louise's thigh. She was fever-wet and smelled like the raw split center of a spud. The sun was red at the back of my neck. A hot wind dried my scalp. I was not dreaming.

I sat up to catch her and saw pinpoints of light circle my glances. The light was so bright my pupils failed. I struggled from sleep to find Louise standing at the foot of the bed balanced on crutches.

"You were dreaming," she said.

She had brushed her hair. It hung smooth and straight over her shoulders. She was ready to be going.

"Lie down," I said. I was groggy with early morning, not sure what I was seeing. I propped myself up.

She stopped at the door and then opened it fast. I jumped up to stop her. Punched the door shut with my fist. She backed away from me.

"I'm sorry to find you're like all the rest," she said.

"No," I said. "Please, Louise, sit down." She hesitated, watching me. Then she sat down carefully on the bed balancing her cast leg. I pulled the pillowcase off my side and began to rip it.

"Take off your dress, now."

I went into the bathroom and grabbed the clean washcloth. I folded it and wrapped it in the sheet strips. She had slipped her dress off her shoulders. Her skin held the copper light of October. I could see the delicate trace of her ribs, the bones of her spine. Her hands were very still on her knees. She sat straight, poised in her near nakedness as if I were going to sketch her. She trusted me and I was grateful.

She had turned the old rough bandage inside out and had put it back on. It had dried a little but it still smelled awful. I eased the tape off and gave it a toss toward the cobwebbed ceiling. She smiled away from my glance.

I felt like an asshole. I had become a man worse than the husband who had beaten her. I had wanted more from her than Yellow Knife. I had seized the opportunity of her suffering to be near her. I was the worst kind of fool.

I pinched together the sad, open breast. It was bruise-hardened and puncture-soft. She sucked a breath through closed teeth but did not cry. I had never seen a woman so beautiful. Her red-brown hair touched her shoulders like light. I pressed the cloth to the wound and made her hold it. I ripped a long strip from the top sheet.

"Hold up your arms," I told her. I wrapped her up good, tight and clean, and stepped back to help her with her dress.

"Go," I told her. She knocked a crutch to the door as she opened it, and without saying good-bye Louise was gone.

I wouldn't go after Louise this time. I was going to stay in the hotel room until I figured some things out. I hung my uniform in the bathroom and took a long, hot shower. By the time I had dressed I felt the panic of regret. I would pay for a long night that had already punished me. I looked around the sad yellow room and felt foolish for how I had acted. I felt heavy and sick. I opened the window and sat down on the bed. The night came back to me, a bad dream. Shame. I wanted to be able to go back and change what I'd done. I closed my eyes and prayed like the nuns had taught me. I said an Act of Contrition. I checked the time with a sudden second-chance realization. It was early. Early enough to make it back home, see Aida, and still make my dayshift. Blessings. I felt the surge of my blind stupidity. All I had longed for I already had. It was such a simple idea I left the hotel running, the jangle of my heart hinged on hope. I was praying I wouldn't see Louise on the roadside because I would have to pick her up. I wanted to go home without recrimination. I wanted to keep my cheating secret, give myself a chance. I rolled down the windows and noticed fall had come. The wind was cold and welcome. The leaves had died and the bright orange colors made me dizzy. A change of season had happened overnight.

Louise

Heading Home

She got a ride home in a dull blue Buick with a plump white woman from Paradise and her six kids. The woman's name was Myrna Michaels and she named off her children like a roll call Louise might remember: Virgil, Vern, Velma, Vernice, Vida, Violet. The name Michaels sounded familiar to Louise but she was too tired to place it. She wished she had a cold beer. She could see the stool where she liked to sit at the Dixon Bar, the brown lip of the beer bottle, the cap hissing white. The day was hot, so hot Louise could feel tears of sweat stream her rib cage, the breath heat rising from her makeshift bandages. She could feel the sheet strips loosening from her ribs, cool and damp. Her leg was swollen in the heat. She could barely squeeze the tip of her smallest finger into the moist opening of her cast.

"Bothering you?" Myrna asked.

Louise nodded and swallowed.

"You know," said Myrna, "I once had one of those myself. On my arm though. Saved myself the doctor bill. Utility scissors," she said.

Louise looked at her and saw that she was smiling. The road had only a hand's-width shoulder but Myrna banked off.

"I think Ed left his pruning shears in the trunk," she said, getting out. "Cut through bone, those things." The woman pulled out a large pair of clippers with a hawk-nosed blade. "This will just take a second."

Louise sat still on the bench seat of the Buick, not sure what to do. She had the feeling she should run. She felt her back on the plastic seat covers swelling with heat. Before she could wrestle her crutches to stand, Myrna had shoved the beak of her shears down the inside of her cast. Louise felt the sharp scrape on the inside, more on her leg than on the plaster. She felt a sudden sharp poke. "I'm getting her," Myrna said. But when Louise looked down she saw the opening curve of her cast blotting blood. She could feel wetness slipping to her ankle, and then a small blood bubble broke twice at the top of her cast.

"This don't seem to be working," Myrna said. "Awful sorry."

Myrna's kids had left the backseat and were running down the slope toward the river.

"Don't be running off too far," Myrna yelled. The children did not look back at her so she turned to Louise. "Might help to go over to the river and get cooled off."

"I think so," Louise said. She pulled her crutches up under her arms and stood in the sun for a minute. The sun ached at the back of her head. She could feel the stitches draw tight to her scalp. She headed down to the water. Myrna stood up on the road and waved her arms to the kids.

"Back now," the woman called. The kids ran past Louise and all she heard was the Buick's thumping motor, the small spin of gravel as they pulled back onto the highway.

Louise stood at the riverbank feeling weak in the sun. She could walk back home from here but not with crutches and a heavy cast.

She sat on the bank and let the water rush over her cast. The river was cold and her leg sunk like clay to the bottom but the cast held its shape, stiff and chafing. Louise felt heavy with sleep. She rested her forehead in her hands and noticed the water had begun to whiten around her feet. Chalky water swirled downriver and she felt the shell of the cast come loose.

She stood up and rubbed the back of her leg. Louise had heard in a bar on Front Street that Baptiste had left the Flathead and had gone to Yakima to catch the apple-picking season. She felt the burden of him and his leaving and hoped he was gone from her. She squatted near the river and washed her face in cold water. She could go home now.

She thought of Charlie Kicking Woman, how he had taken care of her in Missoula, how his eyes were heavy and when he woke up in the morning he looked like he had been crying. He held her hand. He patted her legs. When he smiled at her, she had pretended she was not looking at him. She felt the dull throb of her heartbeat, sick to know Charlie had been like the other men, and she had been too weak-willed to fight his advances. Heartsick. Sick to remember his naked-ness, his thick body, his wanting. She made up her mind to pretend last night had never happened and hoped he would too. She would behave as if nothing had happened between them because nothing had happened. Nothing really. She hoped last night would slip from her days, hide from her memory, and his. She wanted to go home without the memory of Charlie Kicking Woman's hands cleansing her wounded breast. She felt sadness in the smallest bones of her feet and hands, the same feeling she had at the end of winter as if she had been through a long, difficult time she would not see again.

It was a long walk home. She had to rest by the roadside a few times. She hoped there would be another ride, but she saw no other cars on the highway. She only wanted to see her grandmother but when she approached the hillside overlooking her grandmother's home she saw the truck that was parked in front. She hesitated. She recognized her father's old vehicle and wondered why he had come to visit. Her father had married Loretta Old Horn after her mother's death, and he rarely stopped by anymore. She felt a heaviness in her chest. She didn't want to face her father or his second wife either. Louise hated Loretta. Loretta talked incessantly and laughed whenever anyone finished a sentence, whether it was funny or not. She was exhausting to be around. Her eyeteeth were missing and the rest of her teeth were close to rotting out. Louise couldn't see what was so beautiful about Loretta that could have made her father leave her mother. And when her father first left them, Louise had to stop herself from thinking about Loretta's teeth, the hissing lisp of her drunkenness, how in the winter her hair was dirty and smelled like tanning brains. "She uses rancid bear grease on her hair. That's what makes it stringy," she had once told her sister though she had never seen Loretta's hair unbraided. She had laughed with Florence when they'd happen to chance on Loretta in the store or at Indian doings.

Loretta would smile timidly at them, adjusting her dress and touching her hair, and that would make them laugh all the harder. But sometimes Loretta would look beyond their shoulders as if she was expecting someone else. Louise would hate Loretta then. Loretta could look off into the distance where Louise's father would always be waiting. It seemed that Loretta would always have Louise's father and he would always be good to her even if her hair stunk like beaver balls and all of her teeth fell out.

Louise wondered for a moment if something was wrong. But she didn't want to think about that. She heard the hiss of wind through the cottonwoods. A few yellow leaves filtered down through the trees. Even if Loretta had come to visit, Louise was ready to go home. She crossed her arms over her chest and chose to believe everything was fine. Louise shaded her face and looked for her sister, hoped Grandma had sent her outside. Louise looked toward the pond where Florence often gathered cattails, to the white-soil hill where Florence liked to sit and chew the salty clay, but she wasn't outside.

Louise pressed her ear to the warm slat boards to hear the dim voices at the kitchen table. She was relieved she did not hear Loretta's voice. She could feel a low humming along the door frame, the sound of quiet conversation. She heard the slow-throated murmurs of her father. She heard the chair leg scorch the floor and someone skirted back to stand. A stiff wind settled the dry grass. Louise wondered if he was leaving. She peeked through the window, leaned carefully into the darkness to see, but her eyes were stained with light. She cupped her hands to the window and saw her dad standing in the doorway of the kitchen gripping his sweat-stained hat. She stood still, her heart twitching in the heat. Her father coughed and she ducked back down where she wouldn't be seen. She waited a while through a long silence. She wondered what was going on. Then a low sound rose from the kitchen, almost nothing at first, then clear and loud, pitched high like a cow caught in mud. Her father was crying. She felt blood hum in her ears. Her leg ached. Her knees jiggled. She saw her dirt-brown shoes, the hard black bruise on her leg.

Her father left the house alone and drove away slowly, without saying hello or good-bye or even looking at Louise. She lifted her hand to wave but his eyes were dazed and swollen, and fixed on the road. Louise entered the house slowly, saw only her grandmother seated at the kitchen table, her hands folded. It was quiet. So quiet. She did not hear the birds. She did not hear the sound of wind. Her grandmother looked up at Louise and her eyes were calm. "Your sister," she said, "has drowned in the river." Louise glanced away from Grandma, looked toward the stairs, out the window to where the clouds dazed the sun. She couldn't have heard right. "We have lost Florence," her grandmother said. Her voice was deep and certain.

"No," Louise said, "she's just outside." Louise was convinced her sister was close, outside for a moment, maybe hiding, but alive somewhere and waiting to be found. Grandma got up from the table and held Louise's hand. Louise noticed her hands were damp and she focused on her grandmother's hands. "She went down to the river this morning," Grandma said. "When she didn't come back right away, I looked for her. I had your dad come help me."

"Well, Grandma," Louise said, "maybe you missed her."

"She's still in the Flathead," her grandmother said, and her voice seemed strong and determined. Her grandmother was trying to convince herself Florence was gone. "We're going to try to get her out now."

"But how do you know? How do you know she's in the river?" Louise asked. She didn't want to believe Florence was dead but she found herself trying to remember the last time she had seen her sister. She tried to smile but her lower lip quivered, she was already crying.

"Louise." Her grandmother gripped her hands. "We know. Now we have to get her."

Louise did not understand what her grandmother was saying to her. The world seemed suddenly more than she could comprehend, her problems with Baptiste small, understandable. She pulled away from her grandmother and stepped out on the porch as if she could wake herself up in the bright afternoon light. She could see the green edge of the Flathead River in the near distance. The water looked thin. She could see the chalky slump of hills that crowned the banks, the tall pine trees that shadowed the water. All this time, she thought, she had been talking to her grandmother, and her sister was in the river.

"Your dad's gone for Charlie Kicking Woman," Louise heard her grandmother say. "They're going to drag the river." Several years ago a rancher had drowned in the river. She remembered the dragline, the large snag hook entering the water, the man cleaved by the brutal hook. Her grandmother stood behind her. She glimpsed the heaviness in the old woman's shoulders, remembered how clumsy her grandmother's hands were after her mother's death, the painstaking weave of her grandmother's fingers as she braided Florence's hair. She saw the burden of her grandmother's grief. She saw the scarlet willows that dipped down to the distant water and began to feel the quivering weight of her sister's death. There was no way to avoid grief.

Louise wondered if she could pull Florence from the river. She knew any foolish action would only cause her grandmother more pain, but she couldn't let Charlie drag the river. She looked toward the road. She didn't tell her grandmother what she was planning. She wasn't sure it would work or if Jules Bart would agree to help them. But if anyone could pull her sister from the river without a hook, it was him. She left her grandmother standing beside the house and fought the urge to look back. Instead Louise looked far away to the watery light at the end of the long highway, the wavering pure light she could not reach, and wished this story was like that tricking light, something that appeared to be real but was only a dream.

Charlie Kicking Woman

◆

The Still River Place

I burned the roads getting home, early enough to change my uniform and meet the day looking decent, but I arrived too late to save my marriage. Aida had left me. I guess I knew even as I sat in that hotel room she was already gone from me. A man knows these things. I drove up to our small blue house knowing it was empty. A quietness lined the rocky path to the garden. The lilac bush was turning brown. I imagined her leaving as I was driving the climb of Ravalli Hill. Sun was bleeding through the sparse winter grass as I held my breath to see the buffalo herd against all that sky, the same moment I imagined Aida closing the door on the house we shared.

Instead of going after her like I should have, I began to inventory her belongings as I entered the front screened porch, the chore of an officer first on the scene, the piecing together of the clues that would not tell me a story different from the one I already knew. Still I persisted in my task, feeling I owed myself that much, the confirmation of all my failures. Maybe I felt I owed her enough to assess the life she had left behind. It occurred to me that the belongings a person leaves behind aren't meant to suggest their return. People leave behind physical evidence of the reasons they have chosen to leave. She had left behind plenty, a note scrawled on the back of a grocery bill that simply said it wasn't going to work, the delicate china cups gathering dust in the display case I had made, four pairs of mended silk stockings, the bone-white shoes I thought she was proud of, the straight skirt I had hoped would make her look sophisticated, her white church gloves folded in the top drawer with a sprig of sage and dried wild roses, the dangly crystal earrings she mistook for diamonds. And all these things, these possessions added up to nothing, the sum total of what it seemed I had become. An old guilt spread around me like the ragged quilt she had sewn for our bed. When the clock chimed in the kitchen I had wanted to stop it to mark that moment in my life.

I resisted the urge to let her belongings stall my life. I boxed up her things and piled them in the shed. I had the uneasy feeling she would come home while I was at work, come home in love with me, and finding no trace of herself leave again brokenhearted. The thought anguished me because even though I missed her, I told myself I did not want her back. I had grown tired of it all. I was that guilty. I had fallen in love with another woman. I had fallen in love with Louise, and even though I denied any interest in her, I must have said her name two or three times a day to my wife, bringing Louise up casually so as not to imply interest. Louise was only another aspect of my job, something I could talk about when I came home from work. I told myself I was only relating my day, but more and more my day was stories of sightings or nonsightings of Louise. I was stupid enough to think I could get away with it. I realized I was arrogant enough to think Aida would come home to me at all. I had treated her without regard. I had detached myself from the small details of her life and had revealed to her only the passion I held for the comings and goings of a woman who was a stranger to her and in many ways a stranger to me as well.

I swiped my arms into a fresh uniform, ran a comb through my hair and brushed my teeth until my gums bled. I wanted just to take care of the things I could change. I wanted to return to work. I felt grateful for the job I held. I radioed dispatch, relieved when Adeline Top Crow answered me without passion. I heard the steady business of her voice as if nothing had changed. "Write up a standing floater on Yellow Knife," I told her. "I'll be in later to have the chief approve." I heard a bleat of static and then Adeline gave me the sinking information. Drowning outside of Perma between Milepost 108 and 109. I had to stop by the station and retrieve the dragline and hook. The body had been located, she said, so I wouldn't need the search boat. I didn't ask who we were talking about. I didn't want to know the details. I'd know soon enough. I had to put off the order to chase Baptiste off the reservation for now. I didn't want to think about that either.

I figured I was heading for the stretch of water known as the still river place. There'd been trouble there before, near drownings, kid dares. I should have known a drowning was coming. All the signs were there. Summer refused to leave the Flathead like it was waiting to take someone with it. There hadn't been a drowning on the reservation in years. Summer was promising to stay. The cool river was calling. I fixed it in my mind that I was headed to the drowning of a child, a difficult day growing worse. I felt strangely relieved. I wouldn't have to think about Aida and I would have a rest from thoughts of Louise.

The sky had turned yellow with heat. I saw Bradlock standing by the highway and he lifted his hands up over his head, surrendered. I parked my car off the shoulder pulling a fog of dust. Bradlock looked out of place in the tall grass, his baggy gray suit stained charcoal with sweat, his cocky brimmed hat. I had to look away from him. When I got out of the patrol car I felt an odd swoosh of coldness just over my head that chilled me.

I thought about the many hours I'd spent walking the river line. I'd walked this river in winter, fall, and summer, knowing where the marsh grass pooled to sucking mud. I knew each big rock like the highway markers, knew where the fat trout slept in lazy currents, knew where arm-length pike leaped for flies with sure snapping teeth. I didn't look at the folks gathered by the river at first. It's what I loved and hated about small-town living, everyone had license to be a rubberneck. I stood beside Bradlock, staring at the smooth dead eye of a crosscurrent and feeling the quivering bend in my knees. I went to the back of the cruiser to retrieve the dragline. Bradlock followed me around. "I think they've got other plans," he said, but I ignored him. I had work to do and I wasn't about to let Bradlock interfere. I slung the equipment over my shoulder.

They were all just looking toward the river. As I walked closer I felt the slick sweat on my back turning to salt under the drying sun. The water was so glassy my eyes teared. Everyone was quiet, quiet as a photograph. I didn't recognize her at first. I was caught off guard. My ankles wobbled suddenly under the new weight. Louise was standing by the river with her grandmother's arm encircling her. She was shivering. Her hair dribbled tails of water. Her dark nipples bled through her river-stained dress and for a moment I thought of the makeshift bandage I had taped to her ribs that morning. Logic betrayed me. I couldn't reckon the image of Louise standing here by the river with the last image I held of her. She was still in Missoula. All at once I saw myself in the nightmare my life had become. I tried to piece together what I was seeing, make sense of it. But this was like no dream I'd ever had. The day was blinding and beautiful. I felt sick. I looked past Louise and her grandmother, past the small crowd gathered to gawk, looked past the cowboy spinning his lariat at the water's edge, not making the connection.

I thought it was nothing but river grass or seaweed burnt by sun.

Something, maybe nothing. Thin strands of river willow boiling in a thick coiling current just under a smooth water surface. Up from deep smelling water, I watched the snaking black hair. I remembered long hair. Louise's sister. All of a sudden it hit me as I stood with the hook wicked enough to barb a full-grown man, still dangling from my shoulder. A coolness smiled beneath the squeak of my leather holster. My spine was a needle dipped to forty below. I thought of Florence spinning down to the silted river bottom, her wide eyes blinking back up at the mica-filtered light. Gone.

I turned away from the river, placed my hand on my hip. I thought of entering that dark water, pulling Florence dead and heavy from the depths, feeling her stiff, waterlogged fingers tap me as I reach to grab her, her cold hair around me like fish.

Bradlock came up from behind me and touched his hand to the base of my spine. I backed off so fast I nearly pitched into the water.

"I have a talk with you over here?" he said, nodding his head toward higher ground.

"What is it?" I asked, unable to mask the edge in my voice.

Bradlock was quiet for a bit. He lifted his hat off his head, airing his windworn scalp. Then he looked at me straight.

"They're convinced she's alive down there." He kept looking at me and I began to think he was believing it too. He pointed to a group of men I had known for years, both Indian and white men standing on the old Perma Bridge. I saw Sam White Elk then, standing up near the road with his back to the river, turning the straw hat he held in his hands. "Have a look yourself," Bradlock said. I put my hand over my mouth, listening. "She's out there, standing. Her eyes are open. They think," he began, looking back at Grandma Magpie and Louise, "it's just the current holding her, I know, but her arms are moving back and forth like…" and he looked away from me when he said this and stopped talking.

"What?" I said. It seemed too long a while before he answered me back.

"...like she's gesturing for someone to save her." He leaned closer and whispered to me then, "And the Indians aren't the only ones believing this." I was confused. I wanted to go to Louise but recognized it was not my place to be beside her. Sam White Elk had made his way to the middle of the bridge. He had bent over and cupped his hands to his knees staring into the water. He looked as if someone had just knocked the wind out of him. Some of the men had straddled the railing on the bridge. Others were just peering over the side. Some of the old ranchers had taken off their cowboy hats and I understood this was their small way of showing respect. Ordinarily the death of an Indian, even an Indian child, would have gone unnoticed by the whites, but this death had caught everyone up. I knew this would be a story even the old ranchers would be telling for years, not a ghost story or an eerie story, but an inexplicable story turned sideways, almost funny, so it could be dismissed. I joined the men on the bridge with a burdened heart.

I looked down into the clear green water. I could see the large round rocks, the smooth colors of water stones, and then I saw her standing upright beneath the bridge. She was dancing in the river water, a traditional dance, slow and sustained, dancing to a song we could not hear. I pushed back from the railing, felt the clank of the drag hook at my back. I didn't want to see what I was seeing. I was afraid these people would look to me for answers I didn't have. Logically I knew she was just caught in a deep crosscurrent, a current that was pulling her, a trick. But in my heart I felt the Indian in me trying to understand what this all meant. I scanned the length of the river as if I could find answers. The river ran milk white over rocks a good long way then seemed to stop and still to this channel that held Louise's sister. Here the water ran deep and surface calm, thick as oil.

Rocks shined. Branches bowed deep to dark, green currents. I tried not to look at the spot in the river where Florence's hair tangled in the twisting flow.

I thought of this story rising from here, Florence standing in water with her eyes open and her arms reaching. They will say that Florence was dancing in the water, and not just dancing, dancing dead. I knew this story would soon lead to mistrust and anxiety. I have my stories too.

I have seen a sudden wind swirl up so fast it has a voice, even in a room with all the doors and windows shut, and it talks and talks until morning. I have seen my grandmother rise up above the flames of a campfire as she danced to become well. I have seen the medicine man turn his back to a crowd of people and turn once again to show his eyes colorless as silver dimes, and for the rest of that year money had come to me.

When I became a police officer these stories took a backseat to small houses filled with hungry children. These stories disappeared when headlights met on a moonless road or I found a young man sleeping under a white man's car on a night so rainy half his face was dark with mud.

I wanted to shake these people who held to these stories when their children were waking up with the smoke of cold hissing through their wood-split homes. I saw so many Indian families with such pitiful houses—Louise and her grandma and this poor girl for one. I saw the damn chinking was crumbling. Their house was stuffed with rags. I'd stopped by early in the morning and I had seen the snow on their floors. Poverty is a story that doesn't seem to get told.

I looked up to see the rodeo man from Revais Creek and began to put the pieces together. A coil of rope was slung over his arm, another on his shoulder, on the curve of his hip hung a thick cable rope black-green with oil and heavy-looking. And it struck me, he was going to try to lasso Florence out of the water. I saw the long throw of his lean arm, heard the rope pelt water, sinking fast. I admired him. At least he was doing something and didn't seem caught up in all the nonsense. I sucked in a full breath and let it out slowly. Something was tugging the end of the line, then the rope shot back empty, skipping water. He reeled the rope in fast, looping it tight, a dripping coil. He cupped his hand and tested the water. Then he removed the heavy cable from his hip and looped it. I watched him lift the lasso above his head. He had to rock back on his heels to spin it, to get some lift. And then he was leaning forward and the wiry line was flying, caught on a curve of wind riding just above water. I heard the wind whine as the cable cut the air. He jerked the line and dropped it clean into the water. I watched the river swallow the looping noose. The cowboy tightened the lead. He had cinched something. You could see the strain on his shoulders. He began pulling, hand over hand. Water was dripping down the front of his pants, dripping down the length of his arms. I squinted to see what he was pulling. When I saw Florence's head lift from the water I rushed to lend him a hand.

Louise

♦

The Long Length of Day

She couldn't shake the image of her sister, Florence, still and beautiful in the shallow, lapping water. She saw again and again Jules Bart kneeling down in the water. Her sister's head tilting back, her long hair trailing the ground as Jules lifted her in his arms and carried her from the river that had claimed her. Charlie had made a difficult situation only more difficult.

Jules Bart had done what the other men could not do. He had passed the body of her sister, Florence, into the shaking arms of her father. Her grandmother had covered Florence's face with the shade of her hand as if to protect her from the onlookers. Louise even thought of Loretta, how Loretta had stood bird-small beside Louise's father, the heels of Loretta's moccasins dark in the thin-crusted mud. When Loretta had glanced at Louise she had smiled and cried at the same time and Louise had felt a lonesomeness for her own mother then. And they had all stood together by the sharp edge of the river, a family, her grandmother's voice a prayer over them.

Louise couldn't bear up under the weight of all that would follow the death of her sister. She knew the family was preparing to gather for the wake, the long procession of aunties and uncles, cousins and distant relations. Charlie Kicking Woman had suggested they take Florence to Ferron's Funeral Home in Mission to prepare her body for the wake. Grandma had resisted the idea. Grandma said she didn't want to be apart from Florence, didn't want Florence to be alone in the cold funeral home far from her. Charlie had listened to her grandmother with his hat in his hands, nodding carefully, the patter of river water dripping from his trousers. Finally Grandma released the body to Charlie's care. And Louise wondered if her grandmother had only said yes to spare Charlie's pride. But Louise recognized her grandmother was grief-weary. She had prepared too many of her loved ones for burial. She had grown old with death.

Louise watched as Charlie Kicking Woman placed the body of her sister in the back of his car and covered her with a blanket. She saw her sister's brown hands, unmoving, and tried to imagine Florence stopped. Forever stopped. As Charlie closed the door on the image of her quiet sister she knew he was closing the door on one of the last memories she would hold of Florence, and without her forever, a rush of memories tapped at Louise, brief as summer rain. Florence smiling. Florence reaching toward the winter-blue sky. Florence in the August fields. Florence dressed in beaded buckskin, turning slowly. Ready to dance.

Charlie pulled onto the highway and Louise saw the sun for one brilliant moment glinting on his windshield, forever summer for her sister now. Florence had passed away. Passed away like a car going in the direction Louise was not going, geese across the dark night sky traveling to a safer place, wheels turning wind, and then the wake of silence.

Jules Bart stood tall beside her, handsome. She had not noticed before how his eyes were the mint-green color of summer. When she took his arm she smelled the sweet sweat of horse near his throat.

Louise pressed her face to the cool window of Jules Bart's truck and gulped air. She remembered she had gone to the still river place with Baptiste, the day after they were married. She had stripped down to nothing while Baptiste peed in the bushes behind her. Louise had her feet in the cold water and was ready to dive in when Baptiste had grabbed her. She had thought he wanted her then and she had struggled to free herself. She had wanted to bow her head in the cool current, to scissor her bare legs in the cold green river. But Baptiste made her sit on the rock to watch the smooth surface of water changing, to see the small movement of waves beyond the calm of a circle the size of her grandmother's house. She remembered that when the shadows of clouds passed over the river she could see the texture of silver currents writhing water within the deadly hoop.

"There," Baptiste had showed her, pointing, "the water is hungry."

He had told her a story that day and she hadn't paid attention to him. Now the story came back to her bitter as bile, a warning story, and she felt panic wrench her chest to recall Baptiste's words of drowning. The story came back to her without her wanting it to, as if Baptiste was beside her as Jules Bart fiddled with the dial on his radio.

Charlie Kicking Woman

◆

Duties

The drive to Mission was the longest ride of my life. I'd promised Grandma Magpie I would stay with the body of Florence
White Elk, but I had to go home. I felt I had done my duty. There was
something about Florence's death that brought back all my failures.
I had saved her from the rattlesnake bite for another death more terrible. Florence's death served to remind me of other Indian kids I had
let down.

I remembered this Indian kid from Browning. One night this kid
goes downstairs to the basement of the Ursulines' and bleeds himself.
He cut the tendons in the backs of his legs, then cut his wrists. He
had wanted to die. Even now when I dress a deer out, I see his slick
blood flowing toward the drain. I always thought he was trying to say
something by doing that, but I had saved him. It was the same night I
ran into Harvey Stoner up Pistol Creek, parked in his fancy car surveying land sites, and somehow I put the two things together like it
was Stoner's fault this damn kid takes a deer knife to himself, a deer
knife sharp as obsidian, and slices into the heat of his own blood.
Stoner's fault this kid lies on cement for maybe an hour without tears
or prayers but with a clean, dry face and the belief that maybe he's

going to a better place. Stoner's fault his skin's so white this kid would have stood almost black beside him. But they never would have stood beside each other, this dark kid from some small reservation in Montana, this white man from Spokane. And I have tried to think of this kid by himself without Stoner, but I can't.

With so much gone I wondered what more Stoner wanted to take, because he seemed to have taken everything. Mr. Malick polished the hood of Harvey's car when he dropped a quarter for gasoline. Eddie the bartender set up Harvey's drinks before he walked through the door. Free drinks too. I'd seen women, even older women, flutter around him. His money bulged from his back pocket like a good-time promise. But I didn't imagine Stoner would ever accrue enough land to parlay his money to future generations because he thought only of himself. He had the look of singular greed that made me angry. The loss of an Indian child always made me furious. An old anger rose in me that stretched back years, back beyond my ability to make sense of anything. I realized I was looking for answers. I spent the night alone thinking too much.

I could feel the bad times coming. I forced myself not to think about my wife far away and through with me or about what had happened to Louise. I'd had a burning in my gut to throw myself into my work. Cold was coming. I saw the warm days slipping to the hiss of my white breath. And I knew what that meant. I'd seen Indians in the dead of winter sleeping on door stoops. And I had thought they were drunk. I'd gone up to them thinking I was going to enforce the law and all I found was someone too poor to have a house to sleep in. Someone who had lice in his hair and cloth moccasins, twenty below, a coat so ragged the wind whistled through it.

I didn't blame the white man for everything because I had seen Indians around here with less than a spit of Indian blood in their veins, the bastards of bastards left over from the French fur trappers, who rode herd on the rest of us. The Indians who had their fingers in every pie because the rest of us were too busy fighting each other. While we knocked ourselves out to heat the cracks in our paper-insulated homes they ran cattle with the white man. Those Indians were the first to tell us how to save money while their icehouses were stacked with beefsteaks and commodity butter. The kind of Indians that Indians themselves didn't recognize, the kind of Indians who claimed to be white when it suited them.

Sometimes I thought Louise married Yellow Knife because he was a black Indian. Baptiste couldn't walk into any place and pass for white. No place. It was Baptiste and no dogs allowed. He scared all the white people. He could have been walking down the street, dull sober, and those white people would have charged to the other side of the street without even the pretense that they weren't afraid. Yellow Knife entered a bar and got served just because the bartender was afraid to kick him out. It didn't matter if Yellow Knife cleaned every other customer out of that bar, that bartender still served him until someone finally called us to haul him out.

I'd been glad to get the news that Yellow Knife was in Yakima. Even though he was five hundred miles away I had to stay watchful for his return. I remembered several years ago when I had found Baptiste sleeping in the woods just past the Ashcroft place. He was curled under a small outcrop of soft pine that smelled sweet as gin. I had known not to wake Yellow Knife from sleep, especially when I was alone. I had turned to get a stick to poke him just in case he was dead and when I looked back again he was gone. I'd never really been sure I saw him that day but the details of him were still clear. He wore a red-and-white scarf knotted tight to his neck. He slept like a fawn, without moving, without scent. I felt sick at the sight of him, a dizzy sickness that hummed in my skull. I remembered seeing his shoes scuffed with dust and the thread worn off at the soles. As I left the woods the pale sun touched only the tops of the trees, and it was difficult to get my bearings. I thought Baptiste was playing a trick on me, that he was around me, hiding behind bushes or shimmied up a ghost tree. I just couldn't see him anymore. He was a fish in shadowed water, a fleck of mica in a dust wind. He was gone.

I knew to keep an eye out on Louise to make sure she was safe. I wasn't about to let Yellow Knife fool me again. I kept on the lookout for Yellow Knife, and minded Harvey Stoner.

Louise

◆

Dead Sight

After Florence died the weather changed. The sun turned cold, and dark owl days perched over Louise's life. The approaching winter light blinked through the windows of her grandmother's house to find her still slumped in bed. Louise would wake to a sun so bright she would cover her face with her hands. She would sit on the porch until late afternoon waiting until she could return to bed.

Two weeks after the burial, her grandmother placed a sack of fry bread in her hands. "It's time," her grandmother told her, "to thank those who've helped us. You take this on over to the cowboy." Louise didn't want to leave the house. She didn't want to comb her hair or get dressed. She looked out to the wide road toward the cottonwoods that stood black against the far hills.

When she left the house the clouds that had been in the distance were moving in fast. Trees were creaking with wind. She felt the sting of cold and wished she had grabbed a jacket. Rain pelted her like hail. She began running to stay warm. She crossed the highway and followed the old Dixon trail. It cut a mile or so off the highway. When she reached Miner's Hill she walked under the pine trees to get out of the storm but wind drove thin needles of rain down through the branches, so she ran again. She ran to forget her sister, to forget Baptiste, to forget the hollowness that lined her chest. Grouse drummed the bushes with the pounding of her heart. She had forgotten the way the cold wind could feel in the heat of running, clean and cleansing. And sooner than she would have liked she came upon the land where Jules Bart lived. She followed the hill slope that dipped down to a wide corral. She saw his white barn. A few horses were running the far fence line. She thought of Baptiste and the horses he carefully tended. Baptiste would talk to Champagne and the horse would rub his muzzle on Baptiste's chest. She wondered if his mother was caring for her son's horses now. She thought of Champagne, winded from running, turning wild without Baptiste. The storm was purple over the hills and moving fast. Wind pushed at her back. Wind pressed the grass flat and the horses ran hard. Rain dripped from her face, from her hands.

She had not seen Jules Bart since the day her sister died, since the night she had gone home with him. She had followed him down a dark hall. She had seen the glint of his spurs hanging neatly on the wall. Cowboy hats and silk scarves hung from dusty antlers above his bed. A spiderweb laced the top of his window but his house was neat and orderly. She noticed small details of lace on the nightstand and dresser, the signs of a woman who had lived there long ago. She looked at the bubbled glass—covered photographs of a thin man with a handlebar mustache, an unsmiling young woman in a severe black dress. Yellowed newspaper clippings curled back from the walls, pictures of Jules smiling too wide under World Champion headline titles, and she had wondered what the point of it all was. Jules Bart champion rodeo roper. Her sister sleeping in the dark room of Ferron's Funeral Home. His house had been so dark that night she had been aware of little else but him. She had leaned into Jules Bart, closed her eyes to his room, because he smelled sweet as juniper.

His house was quiet and still. The door was open and she pressed her face to the dusty screen. All the windows were open too and a shrill wind battered the window shades. "Hello," she called. "Is anybody home?" There was no answer. She opened the screen door and stepped inside. She noticed one clean plate, a single fork in the drain rack. On the kitchen table she saw an ashtray filled with cigarette butts. Ashes spilled over on a fan of bills. A cup sat on the table, half-filled with black coffee. A sack of empty bourbon bottles leaned against a chair. She stepped closer, saw the fan of bills, the red stamps on each one. past due. unpaid. final notice. On the corner of the table were more bills, a stack of them left unopened. She took a hard swallow. "Jules," she called, her voice soft. She was going to leave the fry bread on his counter but she looked past the kitchen toward the hallway. She believed he was in the far field mending fence, or herding cattle up to his winter fields. His house seemed empty to Louise as if he had been gone a long time.

She knew she should leave. She felt she was violating something beyond just his privacy, she was learning something about herself. She wanted to see the room he slept in again, the room she had slept in with him. She had a desire to see all the things he possessed, the life he led alone. She walked down the dim hall aware of the faint sour smell of mice. She stopped for a moment to listen and heard the sound of someone sleeping, the slow, even breath of Jules. It was early afternoon, too late to be sleeping, much too late for a rancher to be in bed. Her heart quickened and she had an urge to leave again, but she was drawn to him because he was unaware of her presence. She was hidden from him, a snake in the grass coming closer. She peered into the bedroom.

She saw Jules on the bed, sprawled on his back. He was in a deep sleep, his eyes half open, dreaming. Naked and uncovered. Even though she had slept beside him she had not seen his naked body until now. He had pulled the shade down in a room already dark before he had undressed, and she had felt disappointment. She had seen him shirtless across the pasture at twilight but she had never really seen him unclothed up close. The night her sister died he had crushed her with the weight of his body, his insistence, but he had not let her touch him. He had pressed his palms to her shoulders to keep her at a distance, even as she felt the heat of his legs against hers. The sharp edge of his lower rib cage had been hard against her own, unyielding, almost painful. She had had to push him away to catch her breath and she realized he had been inside of her and she had not even felt his heart beating. When he was finished he had gripped the covers to his armpits before he lit a cigarette. He had fallen asleep that night so soundly he seemed to be sleeping alone.

Now she looked at him, shaken by what she saw. His legs were long and beautiful but his torso was badly scarred. She had seen the faces of many rodeo cowboys, the small, white lines that split the bridges of their noses or creased their lips, the knots of flesh at the base of their hands that had once been their thumbs. Cowboys' scars were supposed to be sexy, the mark of toughness, but seeing Jules's old injuries, knowing he had hidden them from her, made Louise aware he had not healed from them, might never heal. She had heard a broken rib cage, if left untended, could carve through a man's middle and eventually tighten around his torso like a bucking horse cinch. She saw that Jules Bart carried that scar and more. She could see the broken line of his bottom rib, the suck-hole scar as big as her fist where a bull horn must have pierced his stomach. He had been wounded. She knew now that Jules had kept himself alone and hidden for many reasons, a man who drank to forget and be forgotten. A man who was not connected to the world that had used him up. Jules Bart had never sought her out. He had only wished to be left alone.

He closed his hand and jerked in his sleep. He startled her and she felt suddenly ashamed. He was not the man she had imagined him to be, neither sure of himself nor at ease in the world. Jules Bart, a man without family, looked to be losing his ranch. She turned back toward the hall. She didn't want him to catch her. She walked quickly away from the sight of him and then she was running. The door slammed shut behind her.

The storm was closing in, growing darker. She wanted to run from herself. She took off for the hills. She bounded over weeds and tall grass. She dropped the sack of fry bread but didn't stop to retrieve it. She looked behind her, hoping Jules was not watching her from his window. She decided to head for the trees where she could not be easily spotted. For now she was only interested in putting distance between herself and Jules Bart. She kept her eyes on the far hills.

She was running so fast she caught her foot under a rock, maybe a fallen branch, and she was flying. She was falling. She saw wet grass come up at her face, heard the grinding thud of her bones. For a moment she lay still in the cold grass listening to her hard breath. Her knees were hot. She could feel the little stinging rocks buried in her palms, the deep throbbing pulse of her heart, and she felt foolish. She had gotten what she deserved, seen something she was not supposed to see. She had also shirked her obligations. She felt her sides heaving. She looked at her aching hands. She had taken a hard fall.

There was a weakening sweetness in the air that made her want to inhale deeply. She saw a large rock and made her way to it. She needed to calm down. The wind shifted and the smell turned suddenly ripe. She sniffed the air but the breeze had already turned from her. Her back was stiff. She sat down on the rough rock and looked at her bleeding knees. The storm was whipping the bramble. It was still raining. She brushed the wet hair back from her face. The fall had made her feel like laughing or crying, and she thought if she started either she would never stop. She tried to gulp air, catch her breath. Her toes were rain-soaked too. She busied herself with untying her shoes, but as she bent over she spotted something in the grass. Her heart shot to her throat. She looked again.

Something lay still in the grass. She hoped it was a dead deer, hoped it was anything other than what it was. She saw a woman. She saw Hemaucus Three Dresses in the grass, her eyes clouded and wide-open, unblinking in the falling rain. Her arms stretched back above her head, her black hair caught in the weeds. Louise stood up. She could see the dirt under Hemaucus's nails. She was dead. Louise felt the muscles in her back curl up to her neck. She knew someone had put her there. Her legs were tired from running, but she ran.

When she got to the highway she kept running. She heard a car coming up from behind her and she wanted to hide in the ditch. Blood itched in her tight fingers.

The car pulled off on the shoulder behind Louise. She turned to see Harvey Stoner looking at her from the open window of his big car. She couldn't remember when she had been so happy to see anyone.

"You're a sight for sore eyes," he told her, licking his lips. As she approached him his expression changed. "Hey," he said, "are you OK? You look like you've seen a ghost." She wanted to tell him she was not OK, there was a dead woman on the hill and she had recently lost her sister but she felt too weary. She got into his car without an invitation.

"There's a dead woman up on the hill," she said, "right up there."

Harvey looked at her as if he could not comprehend what she was telling him. He looked at her strangely. As he was getting out of the car she was locking the doors. When he came back down the hill, his face was gray. He ran his fingers through his thinning hair.

"I'm sorry you had to see that," he said. He paused and spoke softly, "I heard about your sister. I'm sorry."

Louise reached for the pack of cigarettes on his dash.

"I've been thinking about you," he said. He traced her breastbone with light fingers.

"Shouldn't we call someone?" she said. He pulled away from her and slammed the keys in the ignition. Her hair was running water. He grabbed his leather coat from the backseat and tossed it to her. "Try not to get that wet," he said. She pulled the coat up to her throat, shivering. Hemaucus Three Dresses was openmouthed under the cold silver sky.

Before she could stop him Harvey turned into the lane going up to Jules Bart's house. "Guy here has a phone," Harvey said, but he noticed she leaned her elbow up on the door to shield her eyes. "What's wrong?" he said, reaching for her. "What's going on here?"

"I don't think we should be up here," she said, but Harvey cocked his head to her. He knew when she was trying to hide something. "What were you doing up here?" he asked. She had nothing to tell him. She pulled Harvey's coat tighter around her.

"Something's up," Harvey said.

They pulled up in front of Jules Bart's house and Harvey honked his horn. They waited a moment. Harvey was just about to open his door when Jules Bart stepped outside. He was tucking his shirt in his jeans but when he saw Louise he stopped still and adjusted his cowboy hat. Louise had to turn her face from him, unsure if Jules was aware of her recent visit. Harvey rolled down his window. "Can we use your phone?"

"Is there a problem?" Jules asked.

"I suppose you could say that," Harvey said. Jules Bart rubbed his eyes and glanced at Louise but did not acknowledge her.

"A girl's been found up on the hill," Harvey said. "We need to call someone."

Jules nodded his head and Harvey Stoner walked into the house alone.

Jules walked up to her side of the car. He kicked at the mud. "Rain's stopped," he said. She looked at his face but he did not give her any sign to indicate he knew what she had done. Louise looked at his boots wanting to say something, but Stoner leaned out the door then and called to her.

She assumed Harvey would call the state police. She was surprised to hear Charlie's voice on the line. "What's going on?" Charlie said, and the sound of his familiar voice brought back the tight feeling in her chest. She swallowed, not wanting to cry. "What are you doing with that guy?" He began to scold her about Harvey Stoner but she did not listen. She waited until he was finished and then she told him the bad news.

"Hemaucus is dead," she said, and she told him where he would find the body.

"Louise," he said, "you didn't find her, did you?" Before Charlie could apologize she hung up on him. She couldn't bear his kindness now. It had begun to rain again. A hard rain. She saw rain pouring from the bill of Jules's cowboy hat. She got back into Stoner's car and watched Jules in the side mirror as they left him.

She was relieved when they reached the highway again. Harvey stopped his car and turned to her. "What're your plans?" Harvey asked. He shifted in his seat and rubbed the length of his legs. "We could go to my house," he said. He slipped his hand beneath her armpit and tried to pull her to him, his thumb ticked at her nipple. She could see a blue crack of sky over the faded hills. He leaned across the seat and kissed her ear. "I've been missing you," he whispered. She felt the warm lick of his tongue and she brushed her cheek to her shoulder trying to wipe him off. Harvey leaned even closer to her. His voice was sharp. "I need to see more of you," he said.

"I'm sorry," she said, "it's been a hard time."

He gripped her thigh and she crossed her arms over her chest. She had wanted just to go home but she knew Harvey would not accept that excuse. "I need to go to Baptiste's place," she said and closed her eyes.

"You're not getting back with that guy, are you?" he asked. She knew then he had not heard the news of her husband, had not heard Baptiste had to leave the reservation. She figured Harvey Stoner probably didn't listen to all the gossip of Perma. Harvey was thinking Baptiste was still around.

"I'm going to go for a ride," she said.

"I'll bet." Harvey winked at her.

"A horseback ride," she said and pulled back from the steam of his breath.

He drove fast toward Dirty Swallow's house, dipping potholes, tapping the steering wheel with his ruby ring. He was reckless. She felt the shifting weight of his car as he wheeled the corners. He was angry with her. She felt the sudden need to make amends. She didn't want to lose Harvey Stoner's attention. He was the only person who could get her off the reservation. She folded his coat in her lap and stroked the sleeves. "I love his horse," she said. "It's the reason I've stayed with him."

"His horse," he snorted. Harvey Stoner was ugly when he was jealous.

Louise didn't reply. She did want to see Baptiste's horse, hoped in some way she would feel close to Baptiste too. It occurred to Louise that Baptiste was the only man who seemed honest to her. He didn't have any secrets. He didn't hide anything from her. Harvey stopped the car short and she lurched forward.

"You'll be sorry," he said.

She gripped the door handle. "What did you say?"

"I said, you'll be sorry," Harvey Stoner said again, swatting the keys in the ignition. She felt the threat of his words even when he finished the line, "...you didn't come with me."

The engine ticked. Stoner pressed his open palms into the seat. The heater struggled and wheezed. She tapped her fingers on his flat hand to get his attention. His face was tight-lined, his lips white-edged and dry. Harvey Stoner was a man used to getting his own way. He was not looking in her direction, too much set on gaining her full attention. He had seen Hemaucus Three Dresses dead in the field and he was still only concerned with getting his own way.

"Honey, if it's a horse you want, I can get you a damned horse," he said, and then he looked at her hard, as if he was willing her to choose him. And she knew Harvey Stoner could buy her a hundred horses. He believed he could replace anything, and that everything was replaceable.

She got out of Stoner's car and he turned away from her, but he had stayed, stayed long enough to see Champagne running the fields toward her. She was happy to be free of everything for a while. She didn't care if Dirty Swallow found her there. She lifted her arms to Champagne and nuzzled his neck. Champagne rubbed his throat on her back and she buried her face in his soft coat. When she looked up again she saw that Harvey Stoner was still watching her. It frightened her a little. He was a man who demanded too much. She was suddenly aware that he was capable of taking away the things that she loved in order to secure what he wanted. Her instincts told her she was revealing too much of herself to Harvey Stoner. She stepped back from Champagne and sat down in the tall grass. When Harvey Stoner finally left, she talked to Champagne and realized she wished she were talking to Baptiste. She tried to shake the image of Hemaucus Three Dresses dead in the tall grass. She remembered the day she had seen Hemaucus walking with Baptiste, Hemaucus alive and smiling. She thought of Jules Bart, plagued with debt, desperate, and hiding. She was beginning to understand many things she had not known before.

Charlie Kicking Woman

◆

Reservation Death

I had failed to gather all the information I needed from Louise in order to do my job. I didn't respond to the call like an officer, because I'd been too busy giving Louise advice about Harvey Stoner. I couldn't get the grinding voice of Stoner out of my head, the image of Stoner beside Louise in her time of trouble. They were together again. I imagined Stoner comforting Louise, stroking her hair, cooing to her. I wanted to find the two of them more than I had wanted to find the body of Hemaucus Three Dresses.

Dispatch wasn't able to get ahold of Railer right away. He'd been called to an accident scene outside of Polson. By the time Railer arrived in Perma dusk was settling. I had searched the bottom land first. I wanted to narrow the area, make Railer believe I was on top of things. Railer found me at the base of the hill, searching, wandering. "What are we looking at?" he asked. I explained to him that I'd gotten a call, possible murder. I pointed out the area I had already covered, a pitiful patch of ground. Darkness traced the edge of the fields. The clouds had lifted but sunlight was only a thin line at the top of the hills, fading.

"Where did Mr. Stoner say the body was exactly?" Railer looked at me intently.

"Here," I said, sweeping my arm. "Here someplace."

"Right," Railer said. "Great." He headed up the hill. I grabbed my flashlight from the car and followed him. I was worried the coyotes would find the body of Hemaucus before we got to her, and it would be my fault. I scanned the fields, walking quickly. I could see Railer on the far side of the field. I could see him kicking at tufts of grass. Now and then he would stop, place his hands on his hips, and shake his head. I tried to stay focused. I looked the ground over carefully for any sign, a dip in the grass, a telltale trail. I was finding only rocks. I was aware my eyes had adjusted to the encroaching dark but now the night was swallowing the fields. I could see the narrow path of Railer's flashlight, and sometimes not even that. I jogged from one end of the field to the other, plotting my own grid. It seemed hopeless. Railer had come up behind me and when he gripped my shoulder he startled me. "Easy," he said. He took his hat off and slapped his leg. "We're not doing a lick of good out here," he said. "We won't be finding that girl tonight." He flashed his light on a small patch of grass. "We'll try again at daybreak," he said. "We might even have to call in Harvey Stoner." I tried not to grimace. I followed Railer back to the road, still searching the ground, circling my flashlight toward rocks and small bushes. I was unwilling to admit Railer was right: we wouldn't be finding Hemaucus tonight. I rubbed my eyes, already weary. My stomach was churning. By morning the crows would gather. I had failed.

I returned to the scene before the sun cleared the Missions. The morning was still gray. It was November and it should have been cold. It wasn't. A bitter frost was steaming off the fields. I knew people would shed their winter coats and step outdoors with renewed vigor, unaware they were welcoming sickness. There would be more death from this trick change of season. It was a mock spring that had claimed Annie White Elk, Louise's mother. She had hiked up Magpie Creek to search for her husband. She'd been gone for two days with only a shotgun and a sack of jerky. The warm days had deceived her. She came home fever-chilled, dreaming, Grandma Magpie said, of a white root-cellar filled with yellow apples. She died within the week.

I brought a bright roll of surveying tape with me. I wanted to mark the ground I covered. I'd been at work for over two hours when Railer finally showed up. He sipped a cup of coffee and nodded his head toward the bows of pink tape I had tied so carefully to weeds and trees. He was amused with my efforts. "An old Indian trick?" he asked. I ignored him. He ambled past me, stopping now and then to take a gulp of coffee. As luck would have it, he wasn't out in the field for more than ten minutes when he yelled over to me. "Scout," he said, "she's over here." I was convinced he was pulling my leg, but he lifted his hand to me and motioned for me to come. When I realized he wasn't kidding I ran to him. I was suddenly winded, not up to the task. I was breathing too hard and Railer looked at me. "Nothing to get excited about here," he said. "She's been dead a while, I'd say."

I looked down at the face of Hemaucus Three Dresses, reality setting in. Her mouth was open. Her lips had split like the tender skin of ripe fruit. Railer pressed his foot to her side to rock the body over and I reached to stop him.

"What's the matter with you?" he said.

I swallowed hard as Railer pushed his shiny black boot to her thigh. I looked down at Hemaucus's face as he turned her over. Her long, loose hair, shiny and thick as horsetail strands, threading weeds. I saw the hole in her back that pierced straight through her shattered breastbone. A single bloodstain, round and dry as a quarter, lay beneath her. She had been shot somewhere else and brought to this place. Her shirt fell open, exposing one breast. I saw she was already returning to the mud cradle that held her. The weave of grass stamped on her soft skin held a warm, sweet smell that made me uncomfortable. Death. Railer called the ambulance to transport the body. We covered Hemaucus with a blanket, then waited by the roadside.

Mist smoked above the river. The sun had risen to meet our eyes. The light was so bright I was almost blind. The top ground was thawing and we packed the grass like straw as we lifted her out. Her body was heavy. I felt the weight of the task. If Yellow Knife had been in a hundred-mile radius I would have tracked him down, but the word was out that he was still in Yakima. That was one thing in his favor.

I ran suspects through my head. All the people who might have had some connection to Hemaucus. But I kept coming back to Yellow Knife and his slick grin, the way he liked to shine his cheeks with oil when he was looking to fight. I was looking for an easy answer. I felt my scalp tighten. If Yellow Knife was back on the Flathead I wouldn't have too much to investigate. The thought didn't make me feel any better. The only thought that consoled me was that old Stoner would be in a world of shit if my suspicions proved true. No amount of money could save him from Yellow Knife. I knew I had to include myself in Yellow Knife's list of "get-evens." I didn't want to put myself in Stoner's category, but as much as I hated to admit it, where Louise was concerned, I was no different than Stoner.

I knew Yellow Knife had been with Hemaucus the night he'd beaten up Louise. Everybody knew that. And though I had word that he had lost himself in Yakima, I could not keep myself from seeing Yellow Knife lifting a rifle to his shoulder. Taking aim. It was the story that Hemaucus could no longer tell me. I had a gut feeling Yellow Knife had returned to the Flathead. I had learned to trust my instincts but they troubled me just the same. I wanted to gain my knowledge through hard work and sweat. I didn't want vague certainty, animal wisdom. I wanted evidence. I found it.

Baptiste Yellow Knife sat outside Malick's store in a black LaSalle that didn't look half bad. The car door was open and he was sitting on the passenger side with one leg swung out, the kind of stance that told me he possessed more than the car. He'd been picking more than apples. He tossed a cigarette toward me and looked away. I was sick to remember I hadn't taken care of the floater order on Yellow Knife when I should have. If I couldn't prove he'd murdered Hemaucus at least I could get him off the reservation. I'd been too lax. Now the weight of Yellow Knife's return punched me.

"Hello Baptiste," I said, feeling a little smug in my knowing.

He didn't answer me. He looked across the street with a stiff smile on his face that told me I shouldn't come closer. I was reading his signs too well. I hated myself for taking his cue. He was leaner than I remembered. His arms were vein-lined and hard-muscled.

I drew in my breath. "What are you doing back here?" I asked.

He stretched his arms out in front of him and wrapped them around his chest. He tapped his fingers on his ribs.

"Look," he said, "let me be."

I put my hands on my hips, easy, and practiced control. I didn't know whether I was mad at him or just scared. I thought about calling for backup.

A woman came out of the grocery store. Her hair was black and she was wearing too much Indian jewelry, but she wasn't Indian. She was carrying a bag of groceries. She wore a nice coat and a smile.

I looked down. "You want to tell me where you been the last couple days, Mr. Yellow Knife." A statement.

"Ask me straight," he said.

"He's been with me," the woman said, standing taller. "We just got here this morning."

Baptiste Yellow Knife rubbed his cheek.

"You seen your mother yet?" I asked, wanting to ask him about Louise but knowing better. He looked up at me and got up to grab the groceries.

"Hemaucus Three Dresses is dead," I said without emotion.

He looked off, far off.

I tipped my hat to the woman, but I could see the brutal recognition in her trembling mouth. She had just stepped into a mess of trouble. I opened the back door of my patrol car and motioned for Yellow Knife. It was a signal, a polite gesture to show him I still held respect for him. I didn't want to nail Yellow Knife with a choke hold, I told myself, but I knew my act was cowardly.

"I'm not going anywhere," Yellow Knife said and hawked spit at my feet. I stood there with my useless gun, wishing I had called for backup even if it meant Railer.

"We're heading to Ma's place," he said. "Just let me have that."

Yellow Knife swung his leg back in the car and slammed the door. They drove off together. I followed like a mutt after its owner, knowing I should have taken action at Malick's.

Yellow Knife and the woman were together. More trouble. I thought about the brewing mix of personalities. Yellow Knife, Louise, the strange woman, Stoner, and me. I was a stir stick in a pot of fuel, a wick to their anger. I hoped I was wrong. I hoped they would keep their distance. But even I had a sense about these things. And I was getting smarter all the time.

The drive was long and uneventful until I saw Louise on the roadside. I tightened in my seat wondering if Yellow Knife would have his girlfriend stop the car so he could speak to his wife. Louise stood on the roadside for a moment, shaded her eyes to watch us all pass. I wondered what occurred to her as she saw her husband traveling with another woman, not bothering to lift his hand or even look her way. Louise did not return my wave. I glanced back briefly at her, saw her face, then turned again to my business. I wasn't going to let Yellow Knife pull anything.

I followed the LaSalle down Dirty Swallow's road. The house was small, a rough shingle house among rocks and black-trunked junipers. The rattler's haven.

I got out of the car and opened the door of the LaSalle for Yellow Knife and stood at close attendance. I wanted him to know I was in control.

"You're an asshole," he said, but I didn't respond.

Dirty Swallow was coming out to meet her son. She didn't seem surprised to see me. She gripped Yellow Knife's hand. I went back to the cruiser and let them have their time together. I radioed the dispatcher to let them know where I was. I watched the black-haired white woman nodding to Dirty Swallow. And then Dirty Swallow turned to me. She walked slowly, stiff-kneed, toward my car. I rolled down the window.

"Stem," she said to me, a Salish greeting. Her face was round and tight. Her eyes were so dark I could not read their expression.

"Come in," she said. "Come in. Have coffee." I wanted to sit in my patrol car where I held some authority but even as an officer of the law I couldn't refuse custom.

I followed her into the house. She had a pleasant way of humming to herself, almost like she was answering someone I could not see, but as we entered the house I felt the coolness of a drafty dirt floor, a constant restless breeze at my ankles. I knew to remove my hat and sit down.

She poured me a thick cup of coffee and waited for me to take a sip.

Yellow Knife leaned against the kitchen sideboard and looked at the floor. I noticed the ink stain of Louise's name blue-black on his hand. And then I saw Louise's name again on his forearm, encased in a broken heart, a twisted thorny rose wound around the bottom of the heart, a blue-and-red genuine parlor tattoo. I had entered the wrong place.

The black-haired white woman sat across the table from me with a polite nonsmile on her face. She held her car keys as if she were counting them over and over. Baptiste spoke to his mother. I understood a few words, less than I thought I would. They used many old words that were only hints of something I could understand. Dirty Swallow shook her head and dabbed her eyes when he said "Hemaucus."

There was a long silence. A silence that made my muscles squirm, the silence of sleeping snakes and flat rocks, a silence only Dirty Swallow could settle or conjure. I drank hot coffee, let it line the long length of my throat. I held my hands still on the table, afraid to look at my watch and see no time had passed at all or see that hours had gone by. The silence sifted down on me, heavy, quiet. In that silence I saw Hemaucus smile and turn her face away from me.

Yellow Knife was quiet in the backseat of my patrol car. He looked down at his hands. I could smell the cigarette smoke in his thick hair, the sour clothing of a man who had been drinking too long, enjoying too much pussy. I pictured Louise rubbing his forehead, lighting another cigarette for him.

The drive to Polson was long. I couldn't let go of the stories I had heard about him, the stories I knew to be true. He moved like a snake, quick and quirky, suddenly at you and suddenly away from you. His skin gleamed with every turn of the road, every shift of light. I had to stop myself from thinking about his breath coming through the diamond slats at my back.

I used to think Yellow Knife would give up the booze and his anger. But I understood he would always be edgy, unreadable. I believed I had the most dangerous man on the Flathead seated behind me, looking at the back of my head and knowing how much pressure it took to rattle my brains with a puff of his breath, his spell turned toward me. I tried to shake the notion, tried to believe it was only superstition. I had to believe I was the one with the power.

I heard him scratch his head. "Lousy," he said. "I must have picked up something." He scratched his head again hard enough to bug me. I was glad to surrender Yellow Knife to Lake County for holding. Railer was one of the officers who led Yellow Knife down the jailhouse steps. Railer seemed leery around Yellow Knife even after he had handcuffed him. Railer did not look back once to smile at my lack of authority. Murder was out of my jurisdiction but I could still do some checking.

On my way to Dixon, Railer radioed me with a smile in his voice. "Nothing to hold Yellow Knife," he said. "He's a mean Indian on the loose." I clicked him off.

By the time I got home all the Indians had their ideas about who had killed Hemaucus. If there was any magic or power in Indian country it was the moccasin telegraph. As far as I knew only one car had passed Railer and me as we lifted Hemaucus's body into the ambulance. My job had suddenly become more difficult. I imagined by tomorrow I would be receiving tips from Browning, theories on the murder of Hemaucus Three Dresses from a thousand Indian grandmas. My auntie stopped by to fill me in on the details as she knew them. She told me how Hemaucus had been cooking and had left the table set. I was tired but nodded politely. I'd be getting plenty more advice. The dough for the fry bread was on the counter, she said, a pot of eggs boiling on the stove. I looked past Auntie to the cookbooks Aida had left behind. The small daily particulars of Hemaucus's life were story now.

Auntie reminded me that when Hemaucus was a young girl she had kept house for a man over at Dirty Corners. I remembered. It was a BIA job. Many of the Indian girls were sent away in summer to be housemaids for nickels. Hemaucus was lucky to stay around home but Sam Plowman had a "thing" for Hemaucus. He used to wait around the school yard to see what boys she talked to and where she went. Hemaucus was never pretty. She had a plain, almost handsome way about her that seemed to come from her quietness. Whatever she had, Sam Plowman desired it in the worst way, and I remember when we were kids we thought it was funny. It had something to do with shame, with wanting so bad it didn't matter that he was forty-three years old with a facial tic, with bad breath and body odor. In fact that seemed to be a big part of it all, an undesirability that was beyond appearance. He'd been born with unmistakable grief. It was something you couldn't love out of him, something no white or Indian medicine could cut from him. He was flawed. Loneliness quivered in him and we could see it.

I had a hard time in school myself. I listened to my auntie, not wanting to recollect the hard times I'd had. The kids would make fun of me. Call me "pansy" and "pussy." But when old Sam Plowman came along skunking around the school yard in his skulky clothes, I could laugh at him too. When I was eleven, Sam Plowman became the joke. For a short time I could feel like I belonged. I was part of the group.

Then the feeling changed for me. The more I called him names, the more rocks I threw at him, the more I felt connected to him. He could bear the brunt for both of us. So I threw even more rocks at him. I stood beside all the other boys. I pitched rocks fast and hard, pelting his sloped shoulders, grazing his ears. We'd sting him bad. I'd run away laughing with the sound of his whimpering roaring in my ears. I turned once to see him rubbing his knees, sitting on the Mission steps and no Hemaucus in sight.

It wasn't until I got older that I began to see he was neither funny nor one to be made fun of. Like the time he beat Hemaucus up outside of school when we were fourteen. We stood in a circle, maybe fifteen of us boys, our hands in our pockets, all of us vaguely embarrassed because we did nothing but watch. His fists were grinding. When he finished with her, her eyes were small, red-rimmed as a sow's, and bleeding. Nothing was ever done that I know of. We didn't know who to tell. Hemaucus walked home alone snuffling through a fist-sized nose. And that was the last time Hemaucus came to school. I understood people had reasons to suspect Sam Plowman. I was sticking to my suspicions about Yellow Knife.

I went early to the office with my big plans. I had to show my head supervisor I was being methodical, careful, and objective. Lately, I'd seen Hemaucus around Mission with a Hidatsa cowboy from Wolf Point. He'd gone to Rodeo Days over in Ritzville, and so he would've been far away when the incident occurred. In fact, I told the supervisor, he'd been gone quite a while. I had to tread lightly, convince the men in charge I'd considered all the angles so I could make a solid case against Yellow Knife. I knew it was Yellow Knife. I could feel it. My head boss was a BIA bureaucrat, as white as Stoner. I couldn't talk to him about intuition. He listened to my story, jotted down a few notes, then turned to me. "I can understand why the murder of this woman concerns you," he said. "You knew Miss Three Dresses, didn't you?" He eyed me with measured understanding. It was his business to deal with zealousness, misplaced vengeance, cops like me. I nodded my head. "I'm sure you have plenty of good ideas," he said, "but this murder is not in your jurisdiction. The case has rightly been turned over to the state."

"Of course," I said, "just wanted to help." I knew then I had to investigate Yellow Knife on my own. I backed out of his office and quietly shut the door. I figured Yellow Knife must have shot her first and then moved her body to the field a few hours later. Maybe his new girlfriend helped him. I was thinking I'd go out to his mother's house again, have a good look around.

I saw the two men in their clean-whistle suits head for the office I had just left. I nodded to them but they ignored me. Men that high up don't talk to road officers. I wasn't in their league. I was just about to leave when the supervisor stuck his head out the door. "Officer Kicking Woman," he said, "I'm glad I caught you. You may be interested in this." I walked back into his office and stood by the door holding my hat. I'd been offered a privilege and I had no misconceptions that the offer had made me welcome. I did not sit down even when the two men began to speak. It was a dead end, they said. They weren't going to be able to do much. I had heard that line before. They estimated she'd been shot in the field about ten o'clock three nights back. They'd been asking questions and all the leads were cold. They'd keep working on it, they said. The matter was in their hands now. I looked at my supervisor, knowing this was shit. When they left he grabbed my shoulder hard and said it was best to drop it.

They picked up Sam Plowman two days later, apprehended him at the Dixon Bar. They held him less than thirty-six hours. His mother had found a sterling alibi for him. That's my theory anyway. I don't know, maybe a person like Plowman has only one obsession in a lifetime. But I hate to speculate on bullshit. It was Yellow Knife I was after. I saw my work cut out for me, a thick cloud I couldn't blow away.

I stopped in at the 44 Bar but Yellow Knife hadn't been there. The bartender didn't even know Yellow Knife. I considered the possibility that Yellow Knife had bullied the man but that didn't seem likely. Baptiste had other watering holes. It was always dark in the Stockman and the booze was cheap. Only hard drinkers patronized the place. A few regulars came for breakfast beers and stayed until closing. There were no mirrors behind the bar. Nobody wasted their nickels on the jukebox. The Stockman seemed the most likely place for Yellow Knife. These men couldn't care less if an Indian drank beside them. They were looking for anonymity themselves.

I poked my head into the Stockman, but the afternoon sun was so bright I had to let my eyes adjust. My vision pulsed for a moment. I could make out the men at the bar. The bartender looked to be playing solitaire. He glanced up at me as I entered the bar. I was going to ask him a few questions but then I spotted Stoner and the rodeo cowboy sitting at the back table. The two of them together in the piss-reeking bar made me stop for a moment. The cowboy blew smoke through his nostrils and his boot heel ticked the floor, a nervous bounce, tight, anxious. Bart was leaning just far enough back from Stoner that he looked put off, but he was nodding his head. Stoner was doing all the talking. He looked to be laying some ground rules when he placed his hand flat on the table. And then they both nodded in unison.

As I left the bar I had to shield my eyes from the sun. I noticed Stoner had parked his car around back, almost hidden from view. I wondered what the two of them were up to but I had work to do. I couldn't give much thought to two white men jawing in a bar. Yellow Knife was on the loose. I would have to keep a closer watch on Louise if I was going to keep her safe.

I understood I had to be straight with myself too. I couldn't lie to myself about Louise anymore. I desired to possess her, and in many ways I wasn't much different from Plowman, not much different from Stoner. I wanted Louise in all the small ways a man can want a woman, probably in some ways as bad as Sam Plowman had wanted Hemaucus. I didn't have the high ground here. I knew I had a lot to be ashamed of. This morning I had let a white man press a mud-boot to Hemaucus and talk about bullet trajectories and possible motives when I should have leaned over her with respect and closed her eyes.

I still chased Louise, looked for her, told myself she needed to be looked after. I should have backed off a long time ago, when my wife still loved me. There's a point in love where we all can choose to be in love or not to be in love. Maybe something deep in our lives beyond instinct and hope makes us weary and too damn wanting, the slow time when we look out our morning window and we don't see the new sun or the grass shining. We only see that something is missing in our lives, something we're not quite sure of, like the feeling of losing a good, deep breath to restlessness. I jumped on the hope of solution and it turned out to be love again, which in my opinion was just more wanting, the worst kind of wanting after you had already stood at the altar with a shit grin on your face that didn't look like a happy glow after five years.

I'd been thinking maybe I'd try to move off the Flathead for a while. I'd been wondering what it might be like in California free from all my troubles. But deep down I knew I'd just be staying here. I was stuck with wanting something I knew I'd never have. And Louise was the woman I felt myself pulling in my breath for, my soft gut. A woman who saw only that my boots were polished and holeless, the leather on my holster had a nice sound, that I always had a good meat sandwich in my jockey box. I guess maybe that's all the Indians saw in me. It's what I saw in myself, a whole lot of nothing everybody else didn't have.

Finally I caught Louise drinking in the bar. I've hauled her out of the bar a hundred times and a hundred times more I've let her stay.

That night I just wanted to be in the same room with her, Yellow Knife or not, legal or not. She turned to me with her wind-sweet smile and leaned so close to me I could smell the sweat in her hair. She put her head on my shoulder and said so low I almost couldn't hear her, "Where would you like to be?" And I didn't expect her to say that. The question caught me by surprise. I suppose the question could have meant a lot of things but what it meant to me that night was more than I wanted anyone to see. It was a question that drew me to her. And standing there in my uniform with the threat of getting tossed out on my butt, with the threat of losing my job and my standing in the community, I slipped a tight arm around her waist. We were quiet together for a long while. I left the bar alone. About the time I got close to home my belly was shaking and I was grinding my teeth thinking there was a stupidity born in me I could never escape.

I knew I had to clamp down and focus on the business at hand. I couldn't let myself be caught again in a compromising situation that wouldn't do Louise or me any good. I wanted a little rest, a break from work. I had planned to stay home on my day off. Sleep in.

The phone woke me too early. I yanked the covers up over my head. The phone didn't stop ringing. I pulled myself up. I picked up the receiver not bothering to say hello. "Charlie?" the voice said. "Is that you, Charlie?" The woman had only spoken a few words but the voice was unmistakable. Dirty Swallow. I rubbed the bristle of my hair, blinked into the dark morning looming through the windows. "Can you tell me what this is about?" I said. I could hear the low buzzing wire humming between us. "Just you come," she said.

It was five in the morning. I'd been in bed for three hours. Sleep was calling me, so I washed my face and pulled on my trousers. Dirty Swallow wasn't a person to ignore. She had no problem getting even, and I didn't want to add her to my long list of troubles. I wondered if this concerned Yellow Knife. "Son of a bitch," I said, as I buttoned my shirt. "Son of a bitch."

The day was so dry with cold my heater rattled. The mountains were edged with morning light. The stars were thinning. I thought about my warm bed, heavy blankets over my back, sleep. A thin skiff of snow powdered the highway. The cold swelled my knuckles. I could see Dirty Swallow's house in the distance and knew I had to wake up.

I turned my car in the drive and spotted the pelt of an animal hung on the corral, heavy as an Indian blanket. Skinned. A bad dream. The thought occurred to me that Yellow Knife had gutted his best horse and had hung it up to dry. Maybe he needed money and had concocted this idea, but I was straining for answers. I pulled my car up and stopped. I busied myself for a moment. I opened the jockey box and looked for a stick of gum but knew I wouldn't find anything. I was stalling the inevitable and probably making things worse. I grabbed my notebook and made my way to the corral.

Dirty Swallow stepped up behind me. She had a way of sneaking up on people and it had always made me nervous. "What happened here?" I asked.

Wisps of her hair had threaded loose from her braid. I saw the pale puff of her breath and realized she was having difficulty speaking.

"This was here when I got up this morning," she said.

I reached in my pocket for my gloves. It was a horse hide, folded; as I pulled back the skin a bitter smoke rose above us.

"Baptiste do this?" I asked, but she shook her head. "Someone took his horse," she said.

"Stole it?" I said.

"He thinks so. He's out looking for that horse now," she said.

"I don't follow," I said. She seemed frustrated by my stupidity.

She crossed her arms and raised her voice. "This isn't the horse," she said.

I wasn't getting anywhere. I thought for a while. Dirty Swallow seemed to be telling me someone had stolen Yellow Knife's horse and had left a skinned one in its place.

"Whoever done this, wanted my son to think this was his horse."

It was a cruel deed to do to any man, even Yellow Knife. The man had plenty of enemies. I knew that for sure. The kill was fresh. Blood tapped the snow.

My toes were beginning to feel the sting of cold. I looked toward the field, saw a few Indian ponies. I didn't see Yellow Knife's prized horse.

I checked the hide for a brand but found none. I scribbled in my notebook. The hide appeared to have the markings of Yellow Knife's horse. I tried to remember the animal's name, but knew it wasn't important. I only remembered that Louise loved the horse.

"You got any ideas who might be trying to get back at him?" I asked with a tight jaw. I didn't wait for her answer. "I'll write up a report," I told her. "Do some checking."

Yellow Knife had more problems than I could solve. I planned to head back home and hit the sack. I tried to put the incident to rest but it stayed with me. I drove home wondering who would go to such lengths to get at Yellow Knife. The deed was meant to shock him. I figured someone had Yellow Knife's horse in their pasture but that story didn't hold together. The person had purposely left a horse for Yellow Knife to find and it had to be somebody from here.

Louise

♦

The Long Hunger

*T*he winter that Baptiste had told her to prepare for finally arrived. Cold crawled up the windows of her grandmother's house and stayed. Snow fell for three blind days, a dry snow that chirped under her shoes and drifted so high she had to fight to open the door of the outhouse. The Flathead River, the highway and the hills became the same white plain. Snow piled up against the root cellar and caught up under the eaves of the house. Dry snow snaked through the walls, sifted through the weather-cracked floors. Louise would wake to find the siltlike snow covering her face and her chin-high blankets. Even the red-bellied stove couldn't chase an early-winter cold that dipped to fifteen below.

When Louise would go to Malick's store, her grandmother would wrap Louise's feet in so many newspapers she would have to struggle to get her father's old boots on. She would wrap each finger in catalog paper and shove her hands deep into wool socks. Mr. Malick always scolded her when she arrived with her face burning with cold, her eyes small and watering. He told her she could freeze to death in ten minutes with a good wind. Linder Schultz had frozen to death on a walk from his house to his barn, Mr. Malick told her. Lay right down and died. She pulled her scarf up to her mouth.

A few weeks earlier a wind had caught her. It had come on her suddenly when she was almost home. She heard a breeze at the top of Perma Hill, like an old man wheezing. It didn't seem like anything at first but as she reached the crest of the hill she saw the snow-swirling fog. Louise couldn't see the road anymore. It was like stepping into deep, white water. She drew a stuttering breath. A low wind hissed over her head and stung the backs of her legs. She took her hands out of her pockets and pulled her coat tighter around her waist. She tried to remember a story that Baptiste had told her about the cold and the Indians who had danced for good days to come, but her thoughts were confused. She had seen Baptiste in Dixon with the bossy white woman. He had attempted to approach Louise but the woman had tugged at his shirttail and he had given in to her. Baptiste's eyes had been strange, the pale-rimmed eyes of a man who had lost sleep. He had become thin. He had become another man around this woman, and Louise's grandmother had told her to forget him. It was best to let him go. But she could not forget the brutal slap of his hands, the numb scar at the crown of her skull. He had beaten her, and she could not forget him. She could not forgive him either and the thought of Baptiste nagged her. She looked down at her feet and tried to feel the rut of the road, but she could only feel her dry fingers curling up in the catalog paper. A slow burn.

She tried not to cry. She kept her eyes down. She tried to watch her feet and keep walking. Her wool coat scratched her back. There was a dryness in her nostrils that was beginning to sting. She could feel the sharp snow scrape her neck. She took her scarf off and her hair lifted away from her head and snapped silver lights. She couldn't tie her scarf back on with her stiff fingers so she tucked the ends down into her coat. Louise wasn't sure she was on the road. She couldn't see anything familiar. The wind sprayed a fine sheet of snow over her. Her coat snapped at her knees. Then as suddenly as the storm had descended it lifted and Louise saw her grandmother's house.

She would make it through the winter even without Baptiste, even when most days she had little more to eat than fry bread and beans. She belted her skirts now to keep them from falling down. A few days earlier the health nurse had placed two fingers at Louise's chest and had tapped until Louise could hear the dull hard thump of her bones. She knew the nurse thought she had TB. Louise knew her sickness was only hunger. All winter long she would wake up nightly, shivering in her frostbitten dreams of eating venison. She woke remembering how Charlie had chased her up the narrow canyon, how she had hid in a rock split that would swallow her now. She knew this hunger would grip her into spring. A hunger that would stay with her long after the Indian celery had blossomed. A hunger that had made her stingy and jealous.

She hadn't seen Harvey Stoner in a while and then one night he pulled up just outside her grandmother's house and parked. She had grabbed her coat and left with him. Harvey Stoner had taken Louise to Kalispell, a dark bar no different from the bar in Dixon. She kept her coat on even though the snow melted from her shoes. She was afraid Stoner might see how thin she had become, how hungry she was. She had hoped he would take her out for a meal so she could save her food for her grandmother, but Harvey did not talk about food. It was early December. Dusty red lights glowed in nests of angel hair above the bar. A string of red and green lights was tacked in the narrow window that overlooked Main Street.

Stoner talked to the bartender and gave her four bits to play the jukebox. She pocketed one quarter and slipped the other quarter into the machine. She heard Harvey shake for the jukebox. She could hear the bartender whispering, feel the lazy approval of Harvey's gaze on her backside.

"Get some peanuts, Harvey, will you?" she said, hoping he would not hear the hunger in her voice.

"She wants my nuts," the bartender said, and both men laughed.

She felt the floor cool with a thin sheath of snow as the door opened. She read the jukebox list and punched until she felt the hand on her shoulder. It startled her but she had learned not to show fear, not to jump at sudden advances. She looked up and saw her husband. She felt her heart strike her chest. She glanced past his shoulder expecting to see his girlfriend, but he was alone.

Baptiste Yellow Knife stood before her, the husband she no longer recognized. He was so thin, thinner than she had remembered. His pants revealed his leanness. He had lost his soft summer belly. "I need some help from you here," Baptiste said, just to her. Louise stepped back from Baptiste and was surprised to find she held no anger toward him. He weaved slightly but not from drink. He seemed feverish. The bartender had come up behind her.

"You know this character?" the bartender asked her, his eyes on Baptiste. Louise remained mute. "You read the sign?" he said, this time to Baptiste alone.

Louise stepped back and hoped the man would not see how she twisted her hands behind her back. Louise could see Baptiste as she thought these men saw him. She recognized the pink ringworm curl, his scalp worn in places. She knew he was hungry. And that he had had trouble with the woman from Yakima, trouble he had brought on himself like a hail of bricks. He had struck the woman maybe or had looked too long at another woman. Every day there could be a hundred reasons to leave Baptiste Yellow Knife. Louise imagined Baptiste pissing by the side of the road, the woman's black car roaring off in a stinging wind.

"Hey, fella," the bartender said to Baptiste, "time to go."

Baptiste stood by the jukebox. He placed his hands on his hips and tried to hitch his pants. Christmas lights glowed through his sparse hair. She had not caused his problems, she told herself, but in that moment she could not deny him. The bartender had grabbed onto Baptiste's arm. Harvey opened the door. It was so cold Louise felt an aching heaviness in her knees.

"Read the sign," the man kept saying to Baptiste. "Read the sign."

"Come on, Louise," Baptiste said. He lifted his hand to her. Louise heard the jukebox sift the record stack and pull her song.

"Make her read the sign?" Baptiste asked.

The bartender turned toward Louise and looked her over. She wondered how she appeared to him, if he could see the Indian in her.

"You know this joker?" the bartender said to her. He seemed ready to toss her out with Baptiste. She saw the long road back home winding all the way through the sleeping woods, the ice-edged lake. Her shoes were so thin she curled her toes to warm them and looked down at her feet.

"No," she said. The bartender shoved Baptiste out the door and then latched it. Harvey patted the bar stool next to him for Louise to sit down. She took a hard swallow of whiskey, watched the narrow window to see her husband pass by. She thought for sure he would rattle the window with his fist. Accuse her. But she waited a long time and did not see Baptiste. She knew she did not love Baptiste, had never loved him, but the idea that he might love her crushed her. She had held no warmth for him in this dark place. She had found no kindness, no acceptance in herself or the company she kept. She was over a hundred miles from home, a hundred miles but Baptiste had found her. It would be six months until summer again. Six months before the rattlers would find the sun. She could have walked home alone and felt less lonely. Her heart was the tablet of seltzer Stoner threw in his water glass.

Louise tilted her head back in the seat of Harvey's car. It was a cold, clear night, but snow dropped from the trees and froze on Harvey's windshield. Louise tried to see beyond the car's headlights. She peered into the darkness, looking for Baptiste Yellow Knife. Looking for the self she had denied. She had never been ashamed to be Indian, except in that moment when for a meal and a warm ride home she had denied her husband.

Her grandmother would tell her the love medicine was gone for certain. But sometimes Louise would sit at the kitchen table with her grandmother and dream that her sister was alive again, that Baptiste Yellow Knife was almost to their home, a deer straddling his shoulders. She told no one how she watched and waited for him to come to her. She listened to the hiss of wind. Snow rattled at the windows like sand but still he did not come. She would curl up at night beside her grandmother under a few thin blankets and old clothes and smell the palms of her hands until she fell asleep.

A pressing ache in her hollow chest made her long to sleep near the soft bellies of old men for warmth, the yawning smell of bacon fat in their wet breath, their cupboards lined with food, jars of yeast, barrels of flour she could knead to sweet bread, the golden batter of honey, smooth and clear on crisp toast, hot coffee with thick cream, full to the top rung of her ribs as they pushed into her. But the hungrier she became, it seemed, the more the men stayed away.

It was a long drive home and Louise began to think about Harvey Stoner. He acted like he had other places to go, better places, places where she knew she would never get to. Sometimes he talked to her about how the Rio Grande in Texas was no bigger than Pistol Creek or how the mountains in Italy looked like the Mission Mountains. She liked his distance. She didn't want him to be close to her. She wanted him to go away at the end of the evening. To leave her alone.

Maybe it was the long crawl into winter. Maybe it was seeing her once-powerful husband without power that made her want to understand her own intentions. She tried to figure out why she was interested in Harvey. He fed her. He was always good for a two-dollar meal in Plains and a warm night at the Syme's Hotel in Hot Springs. He'd buy her little things too. He bought her a rhinestone ankle bracelet and a pair of Mary Jane shoes with straps. A dress. Not much of anything she couldn't live without. The gifts he gave her didn't matter to her. But he had power. She knew, because any time she was with him, Charlie Kicking Woman would leave her alone.

She could stand up at the bar and swig bourbon from the bottle and Charlie would look right at her and not do a damn thing. She felt safe with Harvey Stoner. He could go anywhere and be welcome. He could pay for a room with solid doors and chain locks. If his car broke down he could get it fixed anywhere. If he couldn't get it fixed he could buy a new one. He could write a check and have enough sudden cash to pay for a month of good groceries. He would never go hungry.

But Louise had begun learning that power ran two ways. She had started turning down Harvey Stoner. As long as the Indian summer had held she liked saying no to his car ride offers. She liked lifting her thigh up between his legs and saying no when he rubbed against her. He had everything. And she had heard he wanted more. More land, more women. It didn't make sense to her. He had lost himself to his desire. He had become an object himself.

All she could remember of him when he drove away was the rough smell of his smooth leather seats, the pink-lit panel of his car in the darkness. She remembered wood-sweet oil and lavender shampoo, not him. She remembered the black silk stockings, not that he had put them on her. She remembered the purr of his big car driving dirt roads so fast her stomach dropped. She never thought of Harvey behind the wheel. She thought that being with Harvey Stoner was like trying to love every small thing that could be bought. He was tiring.

Once she had slept with another man just to get the scent of Harvey Stoner off her skin. Harvey Stoner could touch her now and it didn't matter anymore. She felt only small tugs on her skin, a heat in her belly, and then he was gone. And the less he mattered to her the more he wanted her. And the more he wanted her the less he mattered, until he had become small to her. She wasn't sure what she wanted from him, if she had ever wanted anything from him.

She had left her rhinestone ankle bracelet to gather dust on the windowsill. There was a run in one of her silk stockings and she had thrown them both away. Seeing Baptiste again had made her turn from Harvey. Everything he could give her seemed suddenly unimportant.

"Louise, you love me," he had said, half-asking.

She looked at the deep shine of the dashboard. She blinked at the reflection of her face, black and silver in the plum-painted metal.

"You don't have to, you know?"

"I don't," she said.

"You don't what?" He leaned closer to her and was tapping his chin on her shoulder.

She knew what he wanted to hear. She could smell a faint lick of sage through the open window. There was a look some men got when they had lost themselves. A look that wasn't in their eyes but in the way they carried themselves. It seemed their place in the world had changed, as if they had lost the ability to stand alone. She noticed first the knee crossed inward, toward her. Then more and more they leaned in her direction. And all of their questions began to be directed toward her. What did she want from them? What did she feel about them? What did she think about them? Harvey was pressing toward her. Wanting to know. Wanting to know himself through her. He made her feel sick and closed in, like she needed to press out with her hands, a victim who needed breath.

"Let me out here," she said to him.

"I want to know if you love me," he said.

Louise watched the road. He banked his car on the edge of a drift and Louise felt the veer of his tires, the suction of snow. Harvey reached for her hand. She pulled her hand away from him and he grabbed her wrists so tightly she felt the burn of his grasp.

"I got to take a leak," he said. Louise nodded. She let Harvey Stoner calm down. He kept the car running but he turned off the lights. She could see the outline of him in the puff of cold, the amber haze of his parking lights. A shoulder of wind hit the car and she felt a thousand slivers of ice. She knew the narrow snaking dips of the road, the place where the barrow pits plunged and the places where they bridged to the hillside. In this snow, if she had to make a run for it she could ditch Harvey Stoner.

"I want you to love me," he said when he had gotten back into the car. Louise could smell the bitter tar of cigar smoke in his hair. He began to rub her thigh. She kept her leg still. He leaned toward her and whispered to her, "I want you to love me."

Louise watched the road. From far away she could see the head-lamps of another car coming. She waited and watched. She let Harvey roll his thumb along her panty line. When he unbuttoned his slacks she pulled her arm tight to her side and kicked the door open. He was outside the car with her. She could feel the weight of him, the chase of him behind her. Her shoes slipped on the ice-rutted road. Snow ringed the headlamps of the advancing car, created a shimmering glow that lifted around them. Harvey held her wrists behind her and nod-ded grimly as the car passed them. "You're showing me plenty," he said to her.

He slammed her against his car door. The cold had not numbed her. She felt the sting of blood along her spine. She put one hand over her closed eyes as Harvey reached up under her dress to cup her ass. She felt his hard knuckles between her legs as he stroked himself. The wind blew so hard it split her hair to the scalp. She felt the deep ache of her bones. A pulse of heat hit her thigh. For a moment Harvey dropped his head on her shoulder. She grabbed his testicles then, and squeezed until her nails bit through skin. He slugged her the way a man slugs a man, the arm back and rounding with drive, a knuckle-burning blow to her chest. She felt stunning blackness, circling silver bees. She let go of him. Her lungs were dull and heavy in her chest. She saw Harvey slumped over the hood of his car. She shot for the hills.

Harvey waited for her on the bleak roadside like a cat waits for a wounded bird. She scooped beneath a willow bush, down beneath the layers of snow where summer grass had swirled a small tight nest. She pressed her feet into the cold pocket and crouched among the branches. Her grandmother had taught her how to stay warm, how to survive. She thought of her grandmother and rubbed her hands. She would have to keep moving and soon. Harvey Stoner leaned back on his car door and reached through the open window. He began to spotlight the fields along the highway. He directed his brooding light over the soft landscape. Each hill curve became Louise. He could not see her.

The cold had entered Louise. Her skin was becoming gray. Harvey stayed so long he began begging her. He had dropped to his knees with a proposal of marriage. And even in the sleepy cold Louise almost revealed herself. She could have laughed at the idea, Harvey Stoner believing she wanted marriage from him. He got up from his knees not bothering to brush the curds of snow from his slacks. "You're nothing," he finally said. "They don't call you Perma Red for nothing." She knew people called her Perma Red, but until that moment no one had dared to call her Perma Red to her face. She knew Harvey had only spoken the name to call her out, a dare for her to show herself. Perma Red, Harvey said in a smudge of breath lifting to the hills and the river, his wet breath making the name sparkle then fade. This was the darkest name they called her, the ranchers and the schoolboys, Mr. Malick and Eddie Taylor, the whispering Indian boys at the end of the school yard, the wet-lipped women sipping coffee at their kitchen tables. It meant all the bad names polite company could hiss. Red-light district. Slut. Louise understood the meaning of the name, a label that said she was Indian and nothing more. She came from Perma and she could never change her life standing. She wouldn't let that name claim her.

Louise stood to watch Harvey leaving. She could see him for a long way down the slow curving road heading back into Dixon. He was almost gone when she saw the red flash of brake lights, the swooping turn back toward her direction. She saw the driver's floodlight strobe the hillside and the fields, traveling up one side of the road and then the other. A shattering picture, a jarring light stuttering over the land in search of her.

She imagined Harvey Stoner looking through the dense trees, staring at the flat fields, blinking at the stunned mullien sparkling on the roadside. She realized then that he had wanted her to stay hidden in the cold. He wanted to ice her then thaw her, nothing better than a doll mute to his desires.

She was miles from home. Charlie Kicking Woman's stretch of land glittered under a hard field light. She felt the cold crack in her ankles. She nearly jumped the fence surrounding Aida's garden. She worried about getting trapped. She could hear the pop of the apple trees in the orchard. She thought of hoisting herself up in the branches of an apple tree but knew that the branch might snap. She edged her way around back to see the lights of Harvey's car light Charlie's driveway. She ran to the side of the house breaking snow. She could not breathe. The moon burned like crystal. She flattened her back to the house's shadow as Charlie's porch light snapped on. Harvey pulled his car short. Fence posts wore hats of snow. She saw Harvey open the car door and look toward her as if he were considering approaching the house. Charlie's voice was hoarse with sleep as he called out to Harvey. She thought for a moment he was speaking to her but she watched as Charlie stepped from his house, shivering, to have a talk with Harvey Stoner. Charlie had left his back door unlatched and she ducked into the safety of his home. She did not hear Charlie as he reentered the house. She was watching Harvey pull himself back into his car, his headlamps so bright she was sure he could see her standing at the window. He backed out of Charlie's road slowly, and the sparkling snow churned behind him, wolfing his misery.

Charlie Kicking Woman

◆

Trouble

I *knew I'd have* a run-in with Stoner but I never imagined he'd show up at my doorstep at two in the morning. I'd slept most of the day. A Northern cold front swept into the valley and in a matter of hours the temperature slammed to zero. I could feel the edge of cold seeping through the walls of my house. Ice laced the windows. I sat by the stove a long while, listening to the hiss of pitch. I thought of the small rising breath of all the animals sleeping. The Jocko River purling white. Dry snow was snaking the highway. I was glad to be home. At least I didn't have to be out in this.

I was restless. I'd paid the bills, read the paper. I had too much time on my hands. I remembered the name of Yellow Knife's horse. "Champagne," I said to myself, thinking of Louise. I suspected Yellow Knife would be looking for that horse in all the wrong places. I imagined him in a swirl of snow, his thin shirt flapping in the wind. Baptiste creeping up on honest men's pastures looking for revenge. I told myself it was only the cold settling, the frost etching the windows, but I couldn't shake the feeling I was being watched.

I saw a sudden light strike the wall behind me, and I knew someone was driving up my road, traveling too fast. Light bounced on the walls. Trouble. No one brings good news to a country house past midnight.

I pulled my rubber boots on over my socks and stepped out on the porch. I held my arm up to shade my sight. Slivers of snow rode the silvery light. A man got out of the car and stood beside it. Harvey Stoner. He cupped his hands and I saw the red tip of his cigarette.

"Stoner?" I called. "What the hell's going on?" I saw the smoke of his breath. He rubbed his chin and squinted at me through the roiling light. I walked a few steps closer, but not too close. I imagined he'd been drinking.

"I'm looking for Louise," he said. His voice needled me. He looked at me without looking away. I realized I was the last-ditch effort of his search. I felt a small wince of pleasure at his predicament, but I remained guarded.

"She's a grown woman," I said. I'd had enough of this conversation. I wasn't interested in this man's woes. He threw his cigarette to the ground and blew breath into the pocket of his hands. His eyes were watering and I realized that even a rich man broken could be pitiful.

"I think she's in trouble," he said, trying to bait me. I wasn't up for it. I turned back to the house.

"I guess you don't care what happens to her." He had raised his voice to catch me. "She's looking for Yellow Knife," he said. "He's going to beat the tar out of her again." His voice was accusing.

"So what makes you think you'd find her here?" I said, stopping to face him again.

He folded his arms over his chest and glanced away but not before I saw the smirk on his face. "You're not fooling me," he said. I felt the rise of sudden heat in my chest, the muscles in my back pulling tight. If I had been closer to him I would have thrown a wild punch at him, a haymaker slam that would have rattled his gold teeth. I didn't have time to put up with this asshole, not in my driveway, not on my night off. I went inside, leaving him.

I closed my door tight to Stoner and sighed. I heard his car start up. His headlamps flooded the room, a wash of light that illuminated the walls, the cracked linoleum floors, and Louise standing still beside the window. She was breathing hard, her hand pressed to her belly as if she'd just stopped running. Stoner was gone. The room settled gray. The stove glowed red. "You want to tell me what's going on?" I said.

She sat on the sofa and wrapped her arms around her waist. I snapped on the table lamp and stood beside her. I could see the white tattle of pale frostbite on her bronze face hadn't quite taken hold. If she had been out in the cold much longer she would have been in trouble. I wanted to hold my warm hands to her face, heal her.

"I'm having a hard time," she said. I saw the sudden gloss of her eyes, but she did not cry. She leaned forward and grabbed the toes of her shoes to warm herself.

"You'll stay here for a while," I said, "at least until this blows over."

I wanted her to be grateful but she seemed resigned. "OK," she said, and then, "yes." The room seemed suddenly warm. I lifted the window to catch a breath of air.

"Take the bedroom," I said. She looked at me and suddenly away from me.

"I'll sleep out here," I said. She eyed the short sofa. "It's fine," I said. It didn't look like I'd be getting much sleep anyway. Now I had Stoner and Yellow Knife to contend with. I stuffed Aida's small hand-knit pillow beneath my head. Louise was in my house and I would have slept on the porch steps to keep her here.

There was no door to seal my bedroom; the room opened wide to the living room. I could see Louise clearly in the soft light of the moon, and I slowed my breath and pretended to be asleep, but I was watching her. Louise undressed in that light. Her hands were slender and smooth and beautiful at her throat as she unsnapped the fastener, as each button opened to skin. I watched her hands as she undid the buttons on her blouse, as she unzipped her skirt. Her thin slip fluttered to the floor. I held my breath. Louise stood naked in my house. Light was moving like dust over her shoulders, turning Louise's hair the color of smoke. Her bronze skin looked pale and gray as rain. I saw the perched line of her nipples, the round curve of her hips.

I pulled the covers up over my head as she tiptoed past me to the bathroom. I heard the rush of water in the basin. And then she returned to the room. She turned on the table lamp and I pulled the covers back from my face. I rubbed my eyes and squinted hard to adjust my sight. She didn't seem to mind that I could see her or maybe she thought I was sleeping. I didn't care. I propped myself up to see Louise standing naked beside the bed I had shared with my wife. A pan of water steamed on the bedside table. I could see everything in the lamplight. I saw the purple swell of blood above her left breast. I saw the black grip marks at the tops of her thighs, and I thought of Yellow Knife's hands, the bruises to Louise's hips where the imprint of his fist was so deep you could count the knuckles. The smooth cups of her breasts were lavender-edged. I could see Yellow Knife's work there too, the scar that puckered her left nipple. I wanted to kiss that nipple but I sat back to watch her. I watched as she put her foot on the chair and washed the inside of her leg, from the hollow of her foot up a long length of calf. She didn't use a washcloth, only her hands shining like oil. I stared. My cock was so hard it lifted the covers. I could smell her skin. I wondered how many people had seen her in her nakedness. I felt my stomach tighten to think of Harvey Stoner touching her.

She sat down on the bed and I had been so busy gawking at her body I hadn't noticed she was struggling to keep her emotions in check. Her hands were trembling. She turned off the light and lay down slowly. She was quiet, so quiet. I couldn't hear her crying but I knew she was. I was ashamed of myself, my hard cock and my desires. I couldn't go to her. I sat up on the couch. "Louise?" I said, my eyes adjusting again to moonlight.

"I'm OK, Charlie," she said. I could see the outline of her face in shadows, sad and dark like mountains. I lay back down and closed my eyes to it all, to Louise's sad face, to the long night. I felt a cold breeze lift the curtain up and knew she had fallen asleep.

I slept on and off, waking to Louise's shifting movements. I got up reluctantly and washed my face. I had a night shift. I was grateful that Louise slept on through the day. She didn't wake until late afternoon when I was already dressed and ready to go.

The cold night would be full of urgent calls but I was determined more than ever to find Yellow Knife. I was going to make sure he was off the streets for good.

When I left Louise, she was sitting in the big chair with one of Aida's romance novels open on her lap, but she wasn't reading. She looked out the big, black window to something I couldn't see. All I could see was me, my hard badge glinting in the window's reflection, a beautiful woman turned away from my glances.

It was a tough night for driving. Snow sank over the ruts in the road like soft ground sifts over a grave. I seemed to be the only one driving the road that night; the back roads were quiet with snow. My wheels made no sound. Snow was so light it sprayed from my car, a silence that made me edgy. Yellow Knife was out there someplace, ready to jump me. I was looking for him, looking hard, but all I found were annoyances, a lot of little annoyances.

There were traveling nights where I felt the need to keep searching. And then there were tangled nights. Long night calls, drives to disturbances where even the fighters have given up and gone to bed. Even when the shades were drawn and the houses were quiet I had to investigate the complaint. And I pounded on doors only to be met by the half-woken complainer peering from behind a half-open door, a woman clutching her nightgown to her throat, the man behind her blinking at me in his sagging underwear, drink turning to the dull dream of regret and headache. Heartache. That was one of those nights. I crossed off the sour complaints and chased the next call. I turned toward Hot Springs from Perma, passed the turnoff where Florence had drowned. A new-moon night. The river held light the way soft stones do.

I should have determined a plan of action to find Yellow Knife. I was chasing hunches. I could have been driving toward Baptiste or way the hell away from him. I spotted some car tracks headed up Bluebird Road and followed them. The road circled back over the river through the badland peaks. Land where the farmers grazed their cattle but no occupied homes existed anymore.

I imagined I wouldn't find anything out of the ordinary, probably a cheating couple looking for privacy on a dark road. I'd flashed my searchlight on too many breath-frosted cars, saw the startled faces of lovers, the sudden gleam of skin as they scrambled to cover themselves. I expected I'd have to warn another couple about the dangers of asphyxiation, a job that required diplomacy, not quick wit.

My headlamps cuffed the potholes but I continued to drive. I came up on the Chefler place, an abandoned homestead built on Indian land. A cheater's stake. The house and the outbuildings had that wind-whistled look, gray and rusted-wood entryways open to sky, the only legacy of the family's forgotten dreams. Story had it the Cheflers broke every plow blade they buried in the earth. I realized, almost gratefully, that our land would not always surrender to the plow. The bare asses of rocks jeweled their fields. They'd had to give up their blades, dig in the earth with their bare hands only to expose more rocks. A field of them, rocks, big and deep-centered. Their harvest had become rock. Piles and piles of rocks.

The snow was deep here. If there was a sunbelt on the Flathead, this was the snowbelt. Snow could bury this house and be nothing more than a sprinkling just a meadow over. Now the outbuildings housed bats and swallows, another haunted place where old wishes remained, a place the farm kids laughed at and then ran from.

I saw the tracks of one car cut around back one of the outbuildings. The other tire tracks seemed to lead to a rock outcropping. I parked my car just off the road. I didn't want to risk getting stuck. I took my flashlight with me even though there was something about the way the hills surrounded this place that made it seem to throb with light. I had to take a leak. I was standing by the sagging outhouse when I heard an animal sound. The sound a deer makes when its backside's been grazed, a lung-wheezing sound. I stepped around the old barn keeping my back covered when I saw the LaSalle with Washington plates. I took a slow, deep breath. I wasn't sure what I would find but images of Louise and Yellow Knife charged me. I pulled my gun and checked the safety. I was ready. I heard the low pummel of fists. If you hear the dull thud of a man's fist on another man's body you will never forget the sound. It's a sound with consequence beyond the action. The bystander can feel the fist slam deep in his own gut, a heart squeeze, a rush of hot adrenaline like a booze shot that can either sicken you or addict you. I wasn't going to step into trouble with only one gun against Baptiste Yellow Knife. I went back to my car.

I backed the vehicle up just far enough to get some forward momentum. I had to bank my car up in the snow to spotlight them. I figured if I could spotlight them I could scare them. I should have radioed but I didn't. I acted.

I hoped I'd get some power beneath my wheels in the powdered snow. I didn't need torque on this snowy road. I needed to move fast. I started the drive forward with my headlights off, slipping only inches forward, and then my car fishtailed, and I had enough speed to sail. I cleared the first hump of snow and then I shoved up over the hill flipping my light switch, whooping my siren, stopping in time to catch two men running. I got out of my car and yelled for them to stop. Then I fired into the air. I felt the crawling unease of someone looking at me over my shoulder.

I used my spotlight and chased the hills until I caught Harvey Stoner. He had placed his hands squarely on top of his head. He flinched into the light. "Who's with you?" I asked. I refused to call him by his name, refused to recognize him or admit he had any power here. "We meet again, Officer," Stoner said, but I looked away from him. Someone was slumped on the ground. He was heavy-drunk, a gunnysack of meat. I shined my flashlight on a man. He turned to me and mustered the strength to stand. He was only recognizable by his stance, his unshakable stance. He'd taken a mean hit to his eye. Baptiste Yellow Knife.

"Charlie," he said, "you come here to save me?" Even at my distance, I could smell the juniper berries on his breath, the stench of cheap gin. I looked at Baptiste. Stoner may have gotten one good punch in but that would be the end of it. Yellow Knife was too drunk to harm. He was like the drunk in the automobile accident, the limber-loose scarecrow.

"Who else is here with you?" I asked. I could see there was someone else.

"Here."

I turned my flashlight on Jules Bart. He lifted his hand to his face to block the light. "Just making things fair," he said. "Evening out the score."

"Don't leave me here with these candy asses," Yellow Knife said. "I'll be here all night." Yellow Knife reminded me of the Blackfeet warrior who had been captured by the Flatheads. The Flatheads plucked his eyes out, they cut off his fingers, branded him. And after every torture he would laugh at the Flathead men and call them women.

"You come around here, Charlie, sniffing for my wife? Join the line."

I pulled myself up. I had been trained to let things be. Be slow to anger. Be patient. Be courteous. I remembered seeing Louise on the floor of her grandmother's house, beaten. I remembered seeing her earlier. Yellow Knife had beaten her again in the worst way, in the hidden way a man can beat a woman, so there are no bruises, no true signs, only the light in her begins to die. I remembered Hemaucus Three Dresses.

I stepped back from these men. I trudged to the car letting myself believe in simple justice. I put it in reverse and tapped the horn for help. When Stoner responded I rocked my car, forward and back, spun my tires to make him strain to help me. I would leave Baptiste Yellow Knife the way Baptiste Yellow Knife had left Louise. Beaten. I figured Yellow Knife would take a few more hard punches and then they would all go home.

But as I pulled back onto the highway I felt the urge to turn around. I wanted to spin my car back down that odd haunted road and pull Baptiste Yellow Knife from the hands of those white men. I turned this thought over and over in my mind but I did not turn around. I heard the wheeze of my compression wipers as snow clotted my windshield. I kept thinking Yellow Knife deserved this treatment. He deserved at least one good beating. But I wasn't sure I was the one to make that call. The truth was I was more concerned about my own health when Yellow Knife got loose from Stoner.

I was relieved when I found Louise still at my house that morning. She had pulled her hair up on top of her head, and I noticed how thin her face had become. It looked like she had washed her dress in the sink. It was bunched in places but she looked rested. She had made me breakfast. "Stay for a few days," I told her. She wouldn't commit. "Stay," I said again. "I'm just offering for a few days," I lied. My heart had lifted to come home to Louise, to see her sad face smiling and know she was safe. She slept in my bedroom and I slept on the couch, content. There would be time now. I could finally see my chance with her. I went to work with a light heart, a grin I couldn't hide.

Two days later the black-haired woman came into the office looking to file a report. Her face was almost pretty, but her eyes were hard. She looked like a woman who had been left too many times. She said Baptiste Yellow Knife had disappeared. I wanted to tell her Yellow Knife running wasn't my problem. He'd been looking for Louise and I knew it. I felt the sharp squeeze in my chest, the sinking. I figured Yellow Knife would have made it back to her by now. He was looking for Louise and I wondered if he would find her at my place.

I looked at the woman, listening to her, not talking. I was going to call somebody else in to write up a complaint we could toss in the waste bucket when she left. She licked her lips so many times I found myself licking my own lips. I found myself looking at the crack in the doorjamb when she wiped her eyes. I wanted to tell her how sorry she looked loving a man like Yellow Knife when someone like Louise was first in line. Someone beautiful and wild and tough as Louise. I wanted to tell her to give it up. Go back where she came from. Yellow Knife was gone for good. A woman like her could never hold him. But I felt like I was hearing a part of an old story that was my own, the story of liking Louise too much, of wishing for attention that was never going to come my way, of that old desire, the want to hold somebody down because you want what you know they can't give you or never want to give you. You can't make somebody love you, my mother used to say. I learned that lesson the hard way, over and over again. And even knowing Louise was hidden safe at my house didn't make it any easier.

I tapped my pencil on my leg and then I began to hear what she was saying. Here I'd been listening to my own problems and she was telling something to me as an officer of the law. I sat up, not sure I was hearing right.

"Come see for yourself," she said, "if you don't believe me. Just have a look yourself. I went up to Lake County, and once I said 'Baptiste Yellow Knife,' they wouldn't even talk to me." I could believe this. She stood up and gestured for me to come outside. I followed her.

"Just look," she said. "Now, I'm not making this up."

The wind was blowing hard outside. It snapped her coat up. I wanted to go back in and pick up my coat but felt guilty somehow for not listening earlier to what the woman had been trying to tell me. There was something in her voice, a dryness, like resignation. She wasn't fooling herself.

"The night before last, Baptiste took the car or I thought he took the car. I've been drunk," she said, "I don't remember. The next morning the car's back without Baptiste." She looked at me then, hoping, I guess, that I could tell her why, that somehow I was the man to solve her problems with Baptiste Yellow Knife. I thought she was lucky to get her car back at all. I was lucky I didn't have to be looking for a vehicle.

"That's Yellow Knife for you," I said, thinking I knew more than this woman about the ways of Baptiste. I thought about telling her she was better off without the son of a bitch. And then I was going to go back inside because I was freezing my balls off. I didn't consider anything was wrong. It seemed just like Yellow Knife to get a long ride with a woman, chase all over the countryside for Louise, and then dump the woman when he found her. That was Baptiste Yellow Knife. The woman went to the car door and kind of pushed it open with her fingertips to make her point.

Blood was splattered on the dashboard. It looked like someone had taken a beating in the car. I looked to see if the blood had splattered in a certain direction, if there was any kind of clue to what had taken place in there. I figured they'd jumped Yellow Knife in the car before taking him out to the field. But as I squatted beside the car and checked under the seat, the thought of Stoner and Bart hit me, clubbed me. I could feel the heaviness of Baptiste Yellow Knife. I wanted to think that this woman was trying to pull something on me, that she was up to something with Yellow Knife. This was my payback for having left him to the white men. It was my own guilt speaking to me.

I leaned farther into the car, still believing in the possibility of a hoax. My open hand pressed the seat. Thick blood welled up between my fingers sticky and rust-smelling. I wondered why Stoner and the cowboy had returned the car to the woman, but I had my ideas. And my idea was we'd never find Baptiste Yellow Knife again. They'd moved the body and ditched the car. I fought the idea because I didn't want to face the fact that I was responsible for his death. But I knew I was. I had known Yellow Knife was dying even as I drove away from the Chefler place. Something had happened between the time I left Stoner and Yellow Knife and the time the woman found her car. And from the feel of it and the smell of it Yellow Knife had gone down hard.

I went back inside not wanting to call Lake County and the feds, beating my brains for a different plan. I had a sudden idea that I realized might be either a life jacket or a lead vest that I was too eager to strap on. I wouldn't file a report on Yellow Knife. I straightened my tie, tightened it around my throat. Yellow Knife's girlfriend followed me. I sat her down across the desk from me. I had to believe Yellow Knife had it coming to him. If it hadn't been Yellow Knife dead it would have been Louise. I had saved Louise, I told myself.

I pulled my handkerchief from my pants pocket and wiped my hands. I told the white woman to forget about Yellow Knife, to go back to Yakima. I looked into her face and then I had to look away, because I could see she believed I would somehow save Baptiste Yellow Knife and, worse, that I would save her too. I understood the pinched corners of her eyes, the intent stare. All my instincts, all my suspicions seemed thin now. I questioned my reasoning and my ideas about Yellow Knife. I could have hated him because he had what I would never have. He had Louise.

I followed the woman back out to her car. She did not answer me. Her lips drew together tight and straight. She opened the trunk of her car and removed an old Pendleton blanket like she had been expecting my reaction. She flapped the blanket on the car seat. I thought she might stick around, haunt me like a white woman on a mission. But she left without questions, without answers, and I realized she had little more power than an Indian, a small voice she was quick to silence herself, maybe because she had never been heard, and she would never be recognized. She could come back a week later with a posse of officers. She could come back with a lawyer, a detective, a team of investigators. She could change her mind a year from now and return to Lake County with her blood-rusty seats and her long list of suspicions, but I knew she would never return. I was safe from her. I was safe from little else but I was safe from her. I turned to see the woman looking at the blood on my hands, dry-eyed, accepting this end for

Baptiste Yellow Knife, expecting this end, I thought. Now the only grief was work.

Before I went home to Louise I paid the killing site a visit. I parked my own car a mile from the Chefler place and stumbled toward the spot I'd last seen Yellow Knife. The thing I will remember most is the blood. There was so much blood at the site where Yellow Knife had been beaten, my knees trembled. I tried to find Yellow Knife's body but when I couldn't find him, I walked the long mile back to my car. I grabbed the fire shovel from the trunk of my car. I walked fast, so fast my head throbbed. My lungs gripped breath. It was cold but a steam of fog was hiding me. I ducked at every sound and I prayed. I prayed like the nuns had taught me because I figured the devil had something to do with all of this. I needed to be rid of him.

I dug down to tough rocky soil. I ignored the shrill scrape of metal on rock and frozen ground. I churned up dirt with the same urgency I used to save a man because I was saving a man, I was saving myself and all I had worked for, for the good I believed in. I was working to save Louise.

I worked so hard the calluses that claimed my hands chipped off and stung with blood again. If it had been summer I would have scrubbed my hands with lye soap and salt until they bled clean to hide my own guilt from the rattlers. I realized this was a crazy thought because I couldn't escape. The story was set now. I had to stop myself from saying this is what comes of deceit and treachery, because I was already bloating, filling up with poison. Choking bile. When I had covered up Baptiste's blood with dirt I shoveled fresh snow over it. I shoveled enough earth and enough snow to create a new hill. But it was the hard work of a fool. Blood seeped through the snow again.

The death of Yellow Knife came with the death of what I had long wanted. I had looked to the day when I would be able to tell Louise she was free of Yellow Knife and his fists, that Yellow Knife had met his end in a barroom brawl, or a tight curve on a hard drinking night. I hadn't planned for this. I ran stories through my head, plausible stories of Yellow Knife's death that didn't include me in the scenario. But in the end I was faced with the simple hard task of telling Louise her husband was dead. That was the beginning and end of my story.

I could see the lights of my house and I counted the miles with sighs. Louise met me at the door, and she seemed so glad to see me I considered not telling her. I went to the kitchen sink for a glass of water. I could see Louise at the corner of my eye, waiting. I drank another glass of water, a full one this time. I drank slowly and listened to the hard gulps catch in my throat. I looked out the kitchen window in my avoidance. Late afternoon was clear now over the valley. I could see in the distance small trails of fog lifting to sky, clouds. I felt the leaving. An ache in my ribs. There was a part of me that just wanted to sit in my kitchen and remember better times.

Louise approached me. I had been surprised by her light step. She walked softly on my creaking wood floors, walked like a dancer, a sure hunter. She never made a sound. "Is something wrong?" she asked. I placed my hand over my heart and braced my chest. I thought of saying a prayer but knew I had already said one just by thinking I should. I had stalled long enough. I felt the importance of what I was about to say welling in me. I didn't have answers for Louise. I would tell her what I knew, what I had found, and it wasn't a body but the evidence of death. I didn't think we'd ever find the body. I kept seeing Stoner and Bart after I had left Yellow Knife. They had beaten him to death. I imagined they cut him up like a fryer and tossed him down the outhouse. From the looks of it they had pulverized him with field rocks. Come spring a good hot sun would lift the stink of him up over the fields, a smell that would bring mice, a few tight-footed coyotes sniffing a circle of stones, and his smell would find me. I knew it would. Come spring Yellow Knife wouldn't be anything but old stink.

I reached for Louise's hand and held it to my throat. In my years of service I had learned not to begin news with the statement "I've got some bad news." Saying those words never prepared anyone for what was to follow. Anticipation of bad news never softens the blow. I couldn't look her in the eye when I told her the hard story. I had to look away. I did not tell her who had killed Yellow Knife. I told her the story as if I had just discovered it. I recounted only the details I had found, not what I had done.

Louise did not cry when I told her. She did not collapse in my arms. She sat down, dry-eyed and staring, her hands heavy in her lap. In the mournful silence I could not speak to Louise about all she had been through. She accepted Yellow Knife's death. I made a pot of coffee and sat down to meet the night.

"I should have gone with him," she said.

I stood close to her and pressed my hand to the cold window.

"You dying wouldn't do any good," I said. "What good would that do?"

"No," she said. "I never should have left him in the first place. I knew something would happen to him."

"Something bad was bound to happen," I said, "the way he lived his life."

"He's not what you think he is," she said. I had no answer to that. Yellow Knife was an angry Indian, a mean drunk, but I could not speak ill of him now and not to Louise, his wife, so I said nothing. I considered for one moment that I hadn't known him. I had only passed judgment on him. I thought of my own father and the stories I had heard of him after his passing. So many of those stories were strange to me. It was like they were speaking about someone else, not the man I knew. I felt a sudden rising sadness in my chest, the certain feeling I had missed something that would haunt me. There would have had to be more to the man Yellow Knife than all of my shallow pronouncements. He was dead and gone and I could consider him. Not long. I closed my eyes and remembered Louise limping, her sad and sorrowful breast. I thought of the Indians I had picked up off the floor after Yellow Knife had lit into them.

Images of Yellow Knife returned to me. Yellow Knife at the post office in Perma. Yellow Knife slamming a dime down on the counter. Yellow Knife turning to me, the damp smell of him pungent as highway dust before rain. Yellow Knife always looking at me for a second too long, the prickle of sweat at the slap of my back. Yellow Knife exiting rooms by hitting doors with the butt of his hand.

Yellow Knife returned to me like that one mean Indian who had hid in the shadows of my matinee memories, a knife pressed between tight lips, the nickel-movie Indian who frightened real Indians. In death that image seemed ridiculous to me and yet I knew the image I had conjured of Yellow Knife would be the only memory that remained. Unreal and permanent. Yellow Knife larger than life. The ghost of Yellow Knife already spooked me. I swallowed hard. Even with all the trouble I was facing as the result of my hand in his death, I felt relief.

Louise lit a cigarette. I heard the slow exhale of her breath, the stuttered inhale. She was putting on her coat and lacing her bootlaces.

"You're not going out in this weather," I told her, but she turned to me, her eyes etched hard. "Get away from me," she said. I moved to stop her but she yanked her arm from me so quickly I lost my balance. "You could have helped Baptiste," she said. "Of all people, you could have helped him."

I wondered what she knew. She left the door open to the cold and I did not follow her. I had done enough damage. I had let Yellow Knife die, and whether I had let him die in Cheflers' field or in a bar fight I was still responsible.

I didn't have to work again until early morning. I considered my options. I had none. I went to the kitchen for another glass of water and then I went out to my car. I pulled the whiskey from the glove compartment and I stood out on the icy roadway with no one to see me, no one to watch me take the fall. I slugged a belt from the bottle.

Louise

♦

Old Ghosts

Louise felt the blistering welts of anger at her back. The cold wind felt good at first and she walked quickly toward the highway. If anything had happened to Baptiste, she blamed Charlie. Charlie who had spent more time looking for her than minding his job. She placed her hand to her heart, tried to measure the absence of Baptiste. But she didn't feel the dull panicked ache of death. She was certain that if Baptiste had passed she would have felt his leaving. She was sure she would have felt his spirit leaving. If she marched to Dirty Swallow's house she would find him with his girlfriend. He would laugh at her jealousy. He would catch her up in his arms, spinning, and Charlie would be wrong. She lifted her thumb to the approaching car, heard the crack of blue ice beneath heavy tires behind her, watched the wake of swirling snow in the taillights' glare.

Night was pressing hard over the hills, a charcoal face, Louise thought, the chest and front legs of a giant horse running, clouds turning. She stood on the road and looked over at the dull river. She could see the black water where the animals had chipped a hole in the ice. Day was sinking. Through the naked trees she heard the river's voice. A sound like a woman moaning across the water bank. Louise told herself it was only the ice, the fingernail-thin ice pulling on the shore. Louise squinted at the water skin rattling on the river, the place where the current ran hard. The still river place where her sister had died last summer.

She stood for a long time watching the spot of her sister's death hoping she could call her sister back. For a moment there was no sound. Winter had laced the trees along the riverline. Snow snaked the road. She watched with her eyes clear and seeing. She watched without moving, her heart slowing. She could feel the day around her slipping. The closer you are to life, the closer you are to death, her grandmother had told her. She wondered if now was one of those times.

A mule deer leaped from the dense brush and clipped across the changing river. Louise heard its hollow clocking steps and then its hooves shattered the river skin. Ice creaked like an old door closing. She saw the deer's dark eyes roll up white, a clear splash of water gurgling. And then the river was silent. There was only the jagged black hole. Smoking water. The deer was gone.

The wind chattered in the red bramble.

She was sleepy. She decided to sit down by the roadside, to rest for a minute. The hills were black against the pale sky. She thought of summer, the hushed noises of birds, the smell of sweet nettle on a hot day. The huckleberries, sarvis berries, Indian celery were hidden beneath the knee-deep snow. Louise blew breath into the cup of her white palms, then stuffed her hands back into her pockets. She curled her fingers tight and felt the burning pulse of blood.

She blinked her eyes to the cold. Florence stood among the tall grass, half-hidden in the orange thicket. She wasn't looking at

Louise, and Louise felt no fear in seeing her. Florence was looking toward the river. Louise tilted her head and looked, looked closely. Louise knew she was seeing the dead. Her sister had died. Louise didn't want to think the old stories of life and death were not just story but procedure, stories that revealed something sure and unquestionable. Signs to follow. If you drop a rock in water it will sink. If you touch your hand to the red-bellied stove you will burn. When you near your own death, you will begin to see the dead. She felt she was in the first stages of a great wind; it was hissing now at her ankles.

She thought to chase Florence, to run back toward the river in the deep snow that cupped the base of tall trees and buried the stickery bushes. She thought to chase her sister and she thought she might catch her, hold the tail end of her and pull her back. But as Louise strained to see Florence, Florence turned into the torn shirt of a rancher. An old fence marker. Louise rubbed her forehead.

She sat for a long time by the road, for an hour maybe, before Baptiste showed up and sat beside her. She wasn't startled by him. She knew he would find her, but she did not know where Baptiste had come from. He was beside her. She was sure she could feel the warmth of him. She held her head in her hands resigned to the past they shared. The Yakima woman was nowhere in sight.

"Looks like we didn't do it right," she said into her coat hoping Baptiste wouldn't detect the heaviness in her voice. Baptiste only nodded. For the first time Baptiste did not twist her words back on her. He remained quiet, sitting beside her on the cold roadside. He sat close enough to touch her but he did not. She began to wonder if he was sitting beside her at all, if she was only wishing him back. She glanced at him sideways not wanting to look at him and see the new bad times he had to offer. He held his hands together, a lazy man's prayerful hands. She saw her name again etched in his skin forever.

No one would ever love her again like Baptiste Yellow Knife. No one would care to chase her with rattlesnakes, look up the outhouse knotholes to find her, wait for her everywhere, care who she liked, chase her across the countryside, carry her home. No one would ever love her like Baptiste again, with his love so hateful it made her wish for peace. She rocked the heel of her rubber boot into the gravel. She pulled her coat up over her head and was grateful her chest was warm.

She waited a moment for a response from Baptiste. The road was quiet. She thought she could hear the ice puddles cracking. She felt as alone as she had ever felt, alone from the roots and bushes, disconnected from the road's path, separated from the trees. The mountains were the clouds. She pulled her head up from her coat.

Baptiste was no longer beside her. She looked around. She looked on the high road toward his mother's house but he was nowhere. He was gone. She remembered the times when the thought of Baptiste Yellow Knife had risen in her throat like purpose. She felt herself fading from him, the knots of her hair loosening, her ripped clothing turning to powder. When she closed her eyes again she could see the pale sun.

It was Jules. Jules in his blister-blue truck, his headlights smoking. He had lifted her from the roadside and carried her to his truck. He had made her mad. She had slapped him for waking her when the good dreams had just started to come. The windshield was frosted with his breath. The moonlight was white. Jules had thrown two horse blankets over her. She could smell the sweat of horses from the scratch of heavy wool at her face. She couldn't open her eyes even when she knew Jules was pounding the dashboard to wake her. The heater hummed. And she turned toward sleep. He slapped at her face until the roots of her hair were fire. "Christ," he whispered. "Christ." There was white moonlight. The curve of the river flashing. The sleepy shift of the truck rounding curves. And Jules whispering. Whispering to the sound of the slick hum of wheels.

He had taken off her clothes, jerked her arms out of her sleeves. She opened her eyes to see him as he was pulling back the blankets on his bed. She felt the heavy tug of sleep again, the blankets, the thick heat of Jules's hands cupping her buttocks, the way her teeth chattered even in sleep.

"Jesus," he said. "You could have died out there."

She heard him in the morning as he was leaving but he did not say good-bye.

Charlie Kicking Woman

◆

Seeing

I wasn't a drinking man. Whiskey made me sputter. I didn't need a drink that night. I drank like a sick man drinks medicine, a tonic to help me sleep. But I couldn't sleep. I couldn't shake Louise's words, that I could have helped Yellow Knife. I was responsible for Yellow Knife's death. Maybe I should have thought that was a good thing. I was ridding the world of a nuisance, a killing man who would have eventually killed. I told myself I had saved Louise, but I had told myself that so many times I no longer believed it.

I looked around the room and saw only Aida's belongings, the things I hadn't thought to store away. Her hairbrush rested in the medicine cabinet beside my shaving cup. I looked at that brush, stroked the stray hairs that remained. Aida's hair. Her favorite coffee cup hung from a hook in the kitchen, plain and unadorned. Simple. Easy, like the life we had had together. I had been wrong. I didn't know why I hadn't seen it before, why I had been so determined to chase after Louise and forget my own wife. I sat down on the chair beside the woodstove. The heat made me sad and sleepy. I could feel heat pooling in my chest, a heaviness I couldn't carry. I got in my truck and drove.

It was a night of too much lonesome that gave me the harebrained idea to call Aida. I would call her and beg her to come back to me. It was the call of a man too desperate, a man with nothing to offer but regret. I stopped at Malick's and stood out in the crusted snow, my breath a fog in the receiver, wet as tears I wouldn't cry. I got her sister Arnette on the phone. "It's Charlie," she said to the family I imagined had gathered around the kitchen table. I heard the scuffle of footsteps. I heard the whisper of my wife. "Tell him I'm not here," she said. The urge to speak to her was so overpowering I considered taking my patrol car to see her, driving all the way to Toppenish with my lights flashing. I wanted to forget about Louise. She had suddenly become a hard knot in me, the worst of my wrong choices, something beautiful turned ugly. Louise had made me face the fear that clenched my gut, made me see the side of me I had tried to hide from myself. I should have done better. I could have done better. I could have saved Yellow Knife, but I chose not to. Louise's condemnation called back the voices of all the nuns I had ever known. I was immoral. I was forever soiled. Yellow Knife was the cousin I had forsaken, the brother whose wife I had coveted, the brother I had allowed two white men to bludgeon. I was the worst kind of Indian, an Indian without loyalty or love for self, and I wanted Aida to love me again, the way I imagined she loved me for who I really was with all my faults. "Please," I said to Arnette, "please, I just want to tell her I'm sorry."

Aida answered me. "Charlie," she said, and her voice was steady and certain. "Charlie," she said again, and I answered her, ready, at attention. "You're heading toward trouble," she said. "I can't save you."

I stood in the cold of a Montana night coming down hard. I could feel my bones ache with a loss that would sink me when I was old. "Just come home," I said. My chest quivered but my voice remained steady. "Come back to me," I said, but the line buzzed. I was talking to myself.

I drove home, my mind racing with ideas on how to win back Aida. If I had to dance at the powwow, dress up in Indian feathers, and paint my face, I would. I would get Aida back. I took a belt of whiskey and went to bed. I wanted to get some sleep before work. In the sleepy darkness I began to see the murky moonlight as hope. But in the middle of the night I woke and she was pressing against me. I felt the soft roundness of her thighs, the heat of her. I buried my face in the sweet hollow of her throat and heard her sigh and lift her hips toward me. The bed swayed under the pulse of my hips. I felt the slow rise, the hot blush in the pocket of my groin, my eyes strung tight in my skull. I felt the slick sweat of her belly and I was rising, rising. Aida had come back to me. I had heard the taps of Aida's footsteps on the walkway. I was with Aida. I felt a crushing love for her, for my wife. I awoke startled and shaken and alone. I turned on the light and rubbed my eyes. I had only been dreaming. I stepped outside and called my wife's name but heard only the sound of my own voice ringing. My piss steamed in the powdered snow. She was far away. The moon failed and the high clouds passed over me, and I knew I was caught by the choices I had made. I looked down the valley and saw the thick mat of fog, ghostly and hovering. I felt the wet chill of it, the slick roads shining. It was so cold my toenails ached. My bare feet stung so bad I hopped back to bed. The covers were still warm with my own heat. I could taste the smudge of liquor in my lungs. I'd been breathing hard. The room was so quiet I imagined I could hear the breath of fog hissing toward me. I felt suddenly afraid. It was the night, the fear of being forever alone but I had the childish feeling someone was watching me. My eyes gathered the dark room slowly and then I shut my eyes. I moled down in the covers and breathed a full breath.

I heard someone call my name. Yellow Knife was speaking to me. The old ghost stories slammed my chest. Instead of meeting my fears I burrowed deeper in the covers, my knees shaking.

I heard someone fumble with the light on my bed stand where my gun rested in its holster. I threw back the covers and saw a man I could recognize only as Baptiste Yellow Knife. I wanted to bolt. I wanted to grab my gun and shoot the apparition but he stood before me grinning. "Scare you?" he said. "Think you could get rid of me that easy?"

I sat up. My heart squirmed with pain. I grabbed my chest and Baptiste left the room. "Don't be a pussy," he was saying to me. I couldn't be seeing right. I sat for a moment stunned and then I grabbed my gun and hugged the wall. I inched my way slowly toward the living room wishing I had a door to hide behind.

"Take it easy, pal," Yellow Knife said, like we were old buddies. I switched on the living-room light and sighted down my gun. Yellow Knife had been beaten so badly his face puffed twice its size. His left eye ran pus and rolled back red, as if the muscles of that eye couldn't hold. If I hadn't been so scared I would have thought he looked piti-ful, and he did. He didn't seem afraid of me. He shuffled to the kitchen table like an old man. I saw a festering black wound at the back of his head. His right arm was wobbling in a scarf sling. His legs trembled when he sat down.

He tried to focus his attention on me but his head seemed too heavy for him.

"You look worse than me," he said. "If you're going to use that gun, you better do it quick and put me out of my misery."

I held the gun in both hands, my legs braced and straddled like I was on the firing range. I couldn't believe what I was seeing. I lowered my gun and walked cautiously to the table.

"Have a seat," he said. "I didn't come to settle any scores."

I sat down and rubbed the back of my neck wondering if I might be dreaming still, but Yellow Knife was real and sitting at my kitchen table.

"Jesus, Charlie, you look like a man who needs a drink."

I did need a drink. I picked up the whiskey bottle and chugged a good swallow.

"As you can see," he said, "I'm in no condition to hunt for my wife. I think you can tell me where she is. Save me some time."

I didn't answer Yellow Knife. I figured if he was alive again and talking to me he was up to something.

"She's in for trouble. I know what's been going on," he said.

I couldn't shake the feeling I was talking to a man I'd killed. Yellow Knife was like Coyote. He kept coming back from the dead. "I can't help you," I said, remembering Louise's words. My voice cracked. "I don't know anymore. I don't know anything."

"I know about Stoner," he said. "It's not you I'm blaming for my troubles."

I sat with my chin in my hands, an ache in my chest. Grief. I wanted Yellow Knife to leave, hobble back down the road and leave me be. The alcohol was roaring in my belly and I wondered how people could stand to drink the stuff.

Yellow Knife was quiet for a long while, what seemed like hours. He bent over holding his side, and he rocked back and forth. He didn't look like the Yellow Knife I knew. I knew he'd taken a beating that would have killed another man, would have killed me. I thought he still might die, and I was still the mean bastard whose only thought for the moment was that I didn't want him dying in my house.

I was strapping on my workboots when Yellow Knife began talking as if he was talking to someone else. But Baptiste Yellow Knife was talking to me and for the first time I didn't have my badge pinned to my chest. I wondered if he was delirious and I think he was. Baptiste Yellow Knife was telling me a story, and I heard in his voice a memory of the man he could have been. I didn't want to listen to this Indian talking. I had to get my wife back. I rolled my head in my hands and saw the long night of work stretching before me, and then I found myself leaning forward just a little, straining to hear what Yellow Knife was saying. His voice was a light inside me pulling me up the rock cliffs behind my house, and I could see, see beyond the valley, see beyond myself.

Louise

♦

Going Home

*S*he didn't want to stay in Jules Bart's house. He had probably
saved her life last night, but she could not forget the day she had
entered his house uninvited. She felt she had betrayed him and he had
been good to her more than once without any reason. As Louise
reached the edge of the highway she sniffed the cold air and felt the
good pull in her lungs. She was going home again. She walked, glad
for the walk. There was fog on the low hills, a mist on the road that
felt good on her face. She saw the car in the distance, the round
repeating rings of light, the dense lit darkness. She knew the sound of
Harvey Stoner's car, and Harvey Stoner was heading up over the hill
toward her.

She looked off the road into the snowbound fields, into the swirled
trick of hills where she could sink to her thighs in a drift. She decided
she wouldn't run from Harvey Stoner. She was smarter than him. She
would not run from anybody. It was dark on the road, though in some
places she walked through the spare breath of clouds as if she were
hidden in a strange light. Harvey Stoner might not see her. She could
be a ghost in the murky light. But as his car entered the road mist she
lit up, glowed like an apparition. She could see the light her hands

gave off. She echoed with light, and Stoner slowed his car and turned out on the shoulder. She would not give herself away. He would never know he frightened her.

"You owe me," she said. She tried to smile at him. The corner of her mouth twitched. She held her hands cupped over her ribs to steady her quaking stomach and bent down just enough to see him. She did not walk over to him. She stayed to her side of the road. In the sifting haze of his car lights she saw the rainbow skim of ice on the highway. No one else was on the road. She knew Baptiste was dead or he would save her from Harvey Stoner. She was on her own.

She squinted into the light. Harvey looked down as if he was ashamed to be seen. She saw the thin fringe of his eyebrows frowning. "You shouldn't be out here," he said. "I'll take you home."

The passenger door opened and she saw Jules Bart grinning. He couldn't have jumped out at her and made her heart pound any faster. Jules Bart and Harvey Stoner together was a wrong sight from the start. She felt it before she could reason it, knew that they had plans for her. She didn't believe Jules Bart would harm her on his own, or he would have acted by now. But Jules Bart and Harvey Stoner together bred a different man. Stoner had the money to manipulate a man in Jules Bart's situation.

Harvey Stoner had his own reasons for desiring her silence. She used to think Harvey wanted to make sure at any cost that Emma Stoner never found out about their affair, but Louise had begun to see that everything Harvey Stoner needed had suddenly become invested in her. His desire endangered her. There was something these two men wanted from her. She would run. She imagined long-legged Jules Bart running over the top of her like a horse over a bunny. Her only defense was ignorance. Ignorance would save her.

"Two handsome men," she said. "I must have died."

Jules got out of the car and stood by the door. She braced her legs and walked over to him. He pressed his arm on her shoulder urging her into the seat between them. "Where's your truck?" she asked. Jules didn't answer her.

"It gave out," Harvey said. "This is the second time the clunker's failed. I picked him up down the road."

Harvey seemed to be explaining too much. He'd talk himself into telling her what she didn't need to know. Louise backed out of the question with more talk. "Turn up the heat," she said, and she saw the men smile at each other. She rubbed her hands together and smiled at both of them, first one and then the other. She noticed the look that passed between the two men.

"A drink," she said. "A drink is what I need." She would be safe in a bar, able to ditch them.

They drove past the Perma Bar in the seething fog. They drove in drowsy silence all the way to Paradise. Louise sat stiffly in her seat, careful not to lean on either one of them as the car made the curves. She could feel the tires slipping at times, the quick slide to berms and back again to the road's center.

The Angler Bar in Paradise was set up for a night of dancing. A live music sign was taped to the door. A group of four or five women was sitting at the bar in lively print dresses that were more suited to summer. They did not smile at Louise when she smiled at them. Harvey Stoner came back to the table with three clinking glasses, a special bottle of Four Roses for the lady. He poured them each a tall drink. Louise lifted the glass to her mouth and gulped the whiskey until she coughed.

"Drink up," Harvey said. He pulled a pack of cigarettes from his coat pocket and lit one.

Louise drank more, hoping for a plan, an idea to get out of the bar without Harvey and Jules. The only other men present were with women themselves, women who seemed anxious to hold onto their men. The group of single women at the bar eyed Louise with flat humor. Tight-lipped women who had chased more than one man to the altar, women too eager to be with a man again, and Louise looked to have two. They plumped their lips and dabbed at the corners of their mouths. Louise was the girl at the Ursulines' eating the last sandwich. She lifted her glass again. Jules went to play the jukebox. He played the cattle-call song and Louise felt the dull liquor in her chest.

Harvey Stoner leaned on the table and winked at Louise. "What do you know?" he said. He seemed to be teasing her, but when Louise looked over at Jules he was waiting on her answer as if she had something important to say. They were both waiting on her answer. Jules poured her another belt and she shot it down. He poured a tall drink for himself and gulped it down fast. Then he had another. His drinking seemed desperate to her. She could see the lazy loll of his eyes. Her eyelids felt puffy, swollen in the barroom heat. She saw the smoke haze of the women's cigarettes. They were crossing their legs now. They were smiling too much.

"Nothing," she said. "I don't know."

She slipped out of her coat to wake herself. The door opened and two men came in carrying guitars. They turned off the jukebox and headed for a small, lit area. Louise looked at the door and then she saw the back of a man's head. He was a tall Indian man, lean and strong. His hair was thick and black and stiff. He was wearing only a thin white shirt, a pair of moccasins. His pants looked stiff and dirty. She felt the heat of the drinks in her chest. The room was moving a little faster than her head. She looked at this man but he stood at the bar and bent his head down over his drink. She knew he wasn't Baptiste and yet she had a strange, shaking feeling in her shoulders that if she took her eyes off of him he would disappear. Harvey Stoner saw him too. "What do you hear from your husband?" he said. He had never asked her about Baptiste before. He drew hard on his cigarette and smiled at her but his eyes remained fixed. Jules Bart lifted his head, listening. "I don't hear much," she said. Jules shifted back in his chair and tipped back another drink. "And you're not going to hear nothing," he said. She saw the quick shift of Harvey's eyes to Jules. She could see Harvey pressing his knee into Jules Bart's thigh. Jules pulled away from him with a start. Harvey had been caught. Louise tried to read their gesture but Harvey Stoner stood up. "Time to go," he said.

The night air was so cold she felt the sober press of it on her hands and face. They shouldered her into the car. Louise closed her eyes and rested her head on the back of Harvey's seat. She could feel their eyes on her. She knew they thought she was so drunk she couldn't make out their talk. She heard their grim whispers to each other like lovers. She couldn't help but laugh, and her laughter sounded loud and harsh in the car as if her lungs had exploded. "Are you two together?" she said. She had only meant to tease them, to break the ice. Jules turned to her. His face was heat on her. She knew. Right then she knew. She turned to Harvey and he tried to smile with her like he was laughing too, but now she knew the both of them had done something terrible together. They had conspired together. She could feel something pass between the two men. Harvey Stoner's cigarette lighter popped up and when he lifted it to his face she saw his teeth turn red.

She felt the buzzing spin of booze circle her thoughts. "I know you killed my husband," she said. Before she had said the words aloud they were just crazy thoughts but as she listened the words fell around her like sharp stones. Both men were turning on her, stricken, their eyes suddenly hollow. "Louise," Harvey said, "you've had a few." She had shaken them. Fog surrounded the car. Fog so thick there was only the three of them and the words Louise had spoken. They had killed her husband.

Harvey pulled the car to a stop on the roadside. Louise tightened the muscles in her legs.

"What are you doing, Stoner?" Jules asked.

"What do you think I'm doing?" Harvey Stoner slammed the gear into park. Before Jules could speak Stoner was out of the car.

"You're helping me on this one too," he told Jules. Louise pressed her hands to the seat ready to run when the chance opened. Jules sat beside her, his eyes wide. He would look at the dash and then he would glance sideways at Louise.

"Out you two," Stoner said.

Jules opened the door and Louise slid over the seat to standing. She walked toward the front of Stoner's car. She could hear the ticking engine cooling. She tried to think of a plan.

"You did me a favor," she told the men.

"What are you talking about?" Jules was flexing his hands like he was working his strength up.

"Killing Baptiste," she said. "You did us all a favor." She pulled her hair to one side of her neck and leaned over to tug her stocking up to her thigh. She hoped they were watching her and that they couldn't see that her hands were shaking. She thought of Baptiste dead, how she was standing on an open road, no other car in sight for miles, with the men who had killed him. She dropped her skirt quickly and tried to smile at Harvey. Harvey was looking at Jules. "You know what we have to do," he said. They spoke a code Louise understood. She looked up to see the grimace on Jules's face, knowing he was turning toward the idea of her death.

Jules looked at Louise.

"What's up?" She tried to make her voice sound light. "I'm not talking. I won't be telling anybody about this." Her knees were trembling. Jules leaned on the car and swiped his hands through his hair.

"Let's just get this over with," Stoner said.

"I can't," Jules said. "I won't."

Louise knew their plan was closing around her. Stoner glanced toward the river. She looked for the clearest path in the darkness and then she made a run for it. She could think of nothing else to save her. She pushed hard. She prayed and her prayers smoked behind her in the cold wind of her passing. She decided to head for the river. She would take her chances on the ice. She could hear them running behind her. She heard one of them slip and fall and she turned to see Jules catching himself and then lifting up again in his run. She jumped the barrow pit and sank for a moment in a swell of snow.

When she reached the river edge she held her breath and took to the ice. The moon lifted through the clouds she had hoped would hide her. She heard the crack and then the low moan, saw the black cobweb beneath her feet as the frozen river gave way, the sudden pool of water to her ankle. She leaped to catch the opaque ice and then she was clear of the river. Jules trailed her. She turned to see Jules's leg plunging into a black swirl of water, the ice shattering around him. He yelled to Harvey but Harvey pressed past him in his run. They were far behind her.

Harvey clipped the ice and was reaching the bank as she grabbed the thick horsetail weeds and pulled herself up the embankment. Harvey was puffing hard. He was slowing his pace. He'd had too many easy days to run fast enough to catch her. She was feeling strong, even cocky. She reached the hill and took the down trail. The snow was deep, too deep, it cupped her chest. She had stepped off into the powder of a high snowdrift. She struggled to free herself but she was trapped. The snow was fine as silt. As soon as she brushed a path it sifted over her chest again.

She felt the blow of his fist so hard on the top of her head that light stuttered, and she was being lifted from the snow, heaved over his shoulder. She could feel the wheeze of his lungs. Her ribs ached. He had knocked the breath from her. She caught a glimpse of Jules sitting on the bank edge, his clothes dark-edged with water. She saw a glittering circle of stars.

"Jules, get in the car."

"What will we do?" Jules asked.

"Just get in the car," Stoner replied.

Jules followed Harvey as Harvey carried her like a sack of grain, as Harvey fumbled in the car to turn on the overhead. She let them believe Harvey had knocked her out. She had to think. She could see her blood tap the snow and she wanted to touch her face, but she remained still. Jules dropped to his knees, his clothes steaming in the cold.

"Christ, get up," Harvey turned to him.

The moon moved from the clouds clear and bright and Louise closed her eyes for a moment.

"Get up," Harvey said again. "Help me here. We'll have to take her up to the Chefler place. This was a bad idea anyway. We can't just stand here by the road."

"What about Charlie Kicking Woman?" Jules asked. Louise could hear the high pitch of his voice. She wondered if he was scared.

Jules opened the back door of Harvey's car for him, but Stoner heaved her in the front seat. "She can't get away from us up here."

"Not now anyway," Jules said.

She heard Stoner reach in the glove box and saw him grab a flashlight. "I'm going to see if I have a rope in the trunk," Stoner said. She knew Jules was looking at her so she kept her eyes closed, her head resting on the seat back. She stayed very still.

"Jesus," Jules said. "Is she dead? I don't see the point of this." Stoner was so busy in the trunk she doubted if he had heard Jules.

Jules got in the car beside Louise and she allowed herself to slump against his shoulder. She could feel his cold through her coat. His teeth chattered so hard she had to clench her jaw to keep from shaking beside him. She could feel the line of blood that ran from her nose up to her forehead pulling tight, drying. She felt a cold rag on her face and knew Jules was dabbing the blood from her nose. His hands were shaking. An anxious cold was settling in her chest. He reached across her and started the engine.

"What the hell are you doing?" Stoner yelled.

"I'm freezing my ass," Jules yelled back. Louise heard Jules mutter. There was trouble brewing between the two men.

She heard an approaching car, and opened her eyes to see the haze-ringed headlights of a truck. This was her chance. She punched Jules with a sidelong swing and reached for the door handle.

"Grab her, dammit," she heard Harvey's urgent voice. She felt the crack of Jules's fist to her jaw, and then he pressed her face into the shoulder of his coat with such force she felt the smothering blood bubbles in her throat, her nostrils. She tried to push him away, but he held her tight, then tighter. She felt the scratch of his coat against her face and then she felt the sudden, dizzy heat of sleep.

She thought she heard another man's voice, a voice she didn't recognize.

"No problem here," Harvey was saying. "Looks like they made up."

She heard the crunch of footsteps beside the car door, and Jules Bart clamped his hand to the back of her head and held her very still.

"Lovers' quarrel," Harvey said.

Louise heard the car as it was passing them. Jules released his hold. She felt the driver's door open, the seat dip as Harvey got in. Her tongue was swelling and she wanted to spit. "Hold her down this time," Harvey said. She felt Jules lean toward her. She lay still, snorting blood.

"She's out now," Jules said.

She had fooled them twice. She began to believe she had another chance.

Harvey's foot weighed the pedal. They passed into the dense lifting heat of the river. Louise could hear the lick of tires on wet ice. She braced herself knowing the steep bank of land that rose up from the left and then the right side of the car, the high whining curves, the places where the road shot off to darkness. She struggled to wake, but everything seemed to be whirling around her. She lifted her head and opened her eyes. She saw Harvey's grim face. She could feel the car fishtail the road but Harvey drove on faster. It seemed to Louise he was trying to chase the fog. She tried to concentrate.

Jules turned to Harvey. "What are we going to do?" he said, his voice quavering. "What the hell are we going to do?" He wasn't looking at Louise. He was leaning toward Harvey Stoner. He was slapping the back of his fingers in the palm of his hand but he wasn't looking her way. She leaped for the door handle and before Jules could grab her she had his side door open. "Shit," Jules said. She could hear the hollow loud wind as she shoved at Jules. He grabbed the dashboard to hold on. The car weaved on the road and she could feel the pull of the open door. The wind woke her. Harvey slammed his elbow deep into her throat and she coughed. She grabbed the steering wheel and tried to punch the brakes. She was slapping at Harvey's head. She was gouging his eyes with her nails. Jules was trying to grab her hands to hold her, but she was determined to get out of the car. The deep fog curled around the hood then lifted again to night. Harvey yelled. Jules threw his hands over his face. Ice so slick they seemed to be flying, and then the car was. They were flying. Wind sailed past blinking stars for one moment forever.

Charlie Kicking Woman

◆

Bad Roads
Mile Post Marker 104

I did what I felt a good man would do. I took Baptiste Yellow Knife home to his mother. He wouldn't let me help him into the house even though he needed my help. He yanked his arm away from me and I thought about the young boy he had been, stubborn, pigheaded, and knew that part of his nature would always be dependable. Beaten to hell and still refusing any assistance, my assistance. I tapped the horn and waited for Dirty Swallow to help her son into the house. After all I had done, I wanted to do more. An old woman's help was all I had to offer him.

I thought about what Louise had said, that I didn't know Yellow Knife. I learned that night she'd been right. I didn't know the man and I figured I never would but I found something out about myself. I had been wrong about many things. Seeing Yellow Knife as a beaten man and hanging onto life changed the way I saw the world that night.

It was closing in on Christmas. The days after Christmas were always my worst times working. The dream of Christmas was over. People found the last push of winter burying them. Hope wasn't even a word they lisped. People drank too much. People fought. Men shot their wives and called it suicide. Too many men had gone to war and returned broken in some way, or were just sick of being married, or trying to swat women away.

Two days before Christmas and out across the miles I could see a string of red Christmas lights around a small window, and every time I looked in that direction I remembered Yellow Knife was alive and kicking and I had something to hope for. Yellow Knife had made me promise to find Louise. I was looking forward to bringing her good news, looking forward to putting the past behind me. I had a light feeling straddling my chest, a hopefulness I couldn't deny. I figured I'd take a few days off starting Christmas. I'd take the bus to Yakima if I had to, but I'd get my Aida back. I'd be a better man. I'd bury my pride and chase after the dreams that would make my life easy. I still had a chance.

I drove first to Grandma Magpie's house with my squad lights racing. Even the fog didn't deter me. Around the last turn I doused the lights. I didn't want to scare Louise's grandma. I was unnerved when my headlights flickered through the cottonwoods to find Grandma Magpie standing on the road to her house. I switched the fan on and a breeze blew at my face, cold, iced. I didn't want to see Louise's grandmother standing outside in deep snow in moccasins, only a thin scarf covering her head. I rolled my window down and she met my car. "Have you come with news of Louise?" Her breath was puffing damp clouds.

I had to take her back into the house. She looked out the dark curtainless windows and told me she had heard Louise call her name. She couldn't sleep, she said. She'd gotten out of bed to make a pot of coffee and wait for Louise. She had heard Louise's voice plain as day, she told me. "Something has happened to my granddaughter," she said. I couldn't shake her of the idea though I tried. I suggested she'd been dreaming still. That could have happened. She didn't buy my faithless notions. I did what I could for her. I chopped some wood and built up the fire, but even the fire didn't help much. She shivered so hard I could hear her bones knocking. I wrapped her with a blanket and told her to sit by the fire. I'd bring Louise home. But as I left the house I couldn't keep my belly from shaking. My nerves popped in my legs and I had to steady my breath. I gripped the wheel. Maybe it was the night drifting in fog, the uneasy blindness of low clouds. Maybe it was the story that Yellow Knife had told me, the old stories that ached in my stiff hands, but I had an ominous feeling settling on me, and I didn't want to let go of the hope I had found.

I turned on my brights, a poor idea. Bright lights churned the fog, an eerie swirl that reminded me of blood clogging the drain. Road ice was gray, the color of scaled fish, and so slick the bite of chains did not prevent sudden slips. I found myself praying for road markers, praying my way through fishtails, praying for prudence. The night would bring accidents, I knew that much. Finding Louise was a bright spot on my long-night agenda. As soon as I found Louise, I assured myself, the night would go easy no matter what else happened.

My mind raced with stories I thought I had left behind. As I drove into Dixon I remembered the ghost story of the young girl who froze in fear when the Dixon ghost followed her. The story goes that a girl was traveling in the back of her grandparents' wagon, and as they passed over the Jocko Bridge the old white man ghost came up from the river and followed the travelers. I was like a kid, frightened to turn a glance at my side windows, afraid the white man ghost was seeking my attention, a ghost tapping my frosted windows calling me. I remembered the story of the Mission ghost who was said to haunt the church, a woman who appeared to people praying in the early-morning hours, the ghost dressed in black who liked to light the church stove for the prayerful, a fire that never gave warmth. It just popped and hissed and scared everyone. I remembered the crying grave that I had been called to many times, hearing for myself the high whining cry of a child. And I had to tell these people they were hearing a distant voice carried to the graveyard on wind when I didn't believe my own explanation. The thought prickled my neck. I was scaring myself and I knew I had to settle down.

I was relieved when I heard the crackle of static on the radio, a connection with firm reality, even a grim reality. Railer's voice was high-etched, a choirboy pitch. There had been an accident, a bad accident involving Harvey Stoner outside Perma, and I'd have to turn back around. It occurred to me that what goes around does come back around but I found no good feelings in Stoner's misfortune. I was only annoyed I was called to his rescue when I should have been looking for Louise. I didn't want to go but I had informed Railer of my location. He had me. Railer was just outside of Polson and in this weather he wouldn't be on the scene any time soon. I was the man. I bit the inside of my cheek. I didn't want to see Stoner under any condition but this was the worst of circumstances.

I turned on my squad lights. I couldn't help but think about Stoner's beautiful car rolled in the ditch or top-up on the road. Stoner's yellow Buick towed to the junkyard in Ravalli where it'd be set up on blocks like a monument. Fog steamed the road. I searched the dim roadside for his car. My high beams couldn't shatter the white darkness. My eyes watered. I switched my beams on low and crawled. I could have walked faster. I prayed Aida was safe and sleeping in my mother-in-law's house. I saw only the snowdrifts of fog, then blackness. I wasn't much concerned with Stoner's plight. He was getting what he deserved. Even in my anxiety, there was a laziness about my search, an eerie calmness that came with driving so slowly, driving so deliberately almost as if nothing had happened.

The initial call for help had been made from the Perma Bar. Sanders County would be called too. Railer was called because he was a close backup but I wished he'd been left out. Everybody would be on their toes because Stoner's power knew no boundary lines here. But Stoner would soon be getting his comeuppance. Yellow Knife was alive and healing.

My headlamps roiled in the haze. I could make out the lights of Grandma Magpie's house and I didn't feel good about abandoning my search for Louise to help the likes of Stoner. Just past the White Elk allotment the fog became so thick I rolled the window down and felt the wet chill on my face. I was afraid I would run into the wreck or worse. I stuck my head out the window desperate to find a marker and then I saw the tracks, the distinct box trail where the car had passed and then fallen to the tracks below. I saw a man making his way up to the roadside. His face was busted up so badly I thought he was Stoner but he was not. I pulled my car over.

"Sir," I said. "I'm Officer Kicking Woman. I was called to this accident."

"I know," he said. "I was the one who made the call."

"Sir. Stay where you are. I'm coming," I said. The man kept walking toward me. He tried to wipe his face on his coat. I saw his nose had been so badly cut it needed compression. He staggered a bit toward me and I recognized Jules Bart. I found myself thinking he wouldn't be so good-looking now.

"I'm no good," he said. "I'm sorry." He nodded down to the tracks below. I grabbed a first-aid kit from under the seat and blankets from the trunk. I tossed a blanket to Bart and I headed down the steep embankment. And then I was falling. I felt the sharp bite split the leg of my pants, a rock bruise. I cussed and then pulled myself up. The car was on its top on the railroad tracks and I was worrying about a scratch on my leg.

I looked at my watch. I would have to cancel the train from Pend d'Oreille. One headlight of the car cast its long light down the length of the tracks. I could see the light from the car's dashboard, pink and green, almost pretty. I heard music, the soft sound of the radio playing a tune I had not heard before. I wanted to stop, listen hard enough to identify the melody. Stoner lay next to the Buick. He held his ears from the cold. I wrapped the blanket around his shoulders. His cheeks were flaming red and circled white. Frostbite was near him. "Pull that up over your head," I told him. I could see the car was unsteady beside him, pitched on its side on the track edge.

"She's over there," he said with such a grimace he looked to be grinning.

"I've got to make a call," I told him. "The train's still coming. I've got to stop it." Stoner tried to lift himself up from the tracks like I meant "this very moment." He looked down the rails both ways.

"I'm glad it's you," he said. I didn't talk. I knew his statement was the voice of implication, not flattery. I scrambled up to the car and radioed to stop the train. It was almost one in the morning. Then I headed back down to Stoner to survey the damage. "She's over there," he said. He grabbed my arm. "Let her die," he said. "She knows too much." I shined my flashlight on a form. They had covered her with a blanket, a blue Pendleton blanket with a red border. I shined my flashlight on the woman, steadily, carefully, because the new dead hold fragile information.

I saw what I did not expect to see. I saw the sweep of an arm beneath the blanket. I saw the flutter of her fingers. Then I saw breath. The halo of labored breath rising from the blanket. Beads of frozen breath collected on top of the blue blanket, small silver drops. I thought. Or maybe I didn't think. They had left her to die in the brutal snow. The woman lay parallel to the railroad tracks. I looked at Stoner. He had turned his back to me. I could not see his face but in the darkness I heard the crack of his smile.

"This is a peach, isn't it?" he said.

I couldn't see anything at first. I saw the round red pulse of my blood on the night sky. I had to look back into the darkness several times before I saw the light. I had to get her up out of the snow fast, but I wondered if there was any hope for the woman. It was so cold the stars were brittle. Snow was so tight it squeaked beneath my boots. I was sure I saw the mist of her breath. I pulled the blanket from the woman's face as she struggled. I felt the push of her hand. Her head tipped back and for a moment her eyes opened on my face, but there was so much blood running from her scalp I could not see her. I could not tell what color her hair was from the blood. And then my teeth were throbbing with chattering. I couldn't quell my panic.

"Charlie," Stoner said to me like a command but I couldn't hear the words that followed.

I lifted her head up with one shaking hand. My palm warmed by her blood. The breath of her blood rose around us.

"She knows it all," he said.

"What are you talking about?" I yelled. My heart exploded. I felt the thunder of my wild pulse. They had left Louise to die because of a mistaken idea. "You crazy sons of bitches," I said. "She knows nothing."

Sickness kicked me. My hands shook violently. My worst fear had struck. Years of the nuns' cruel words buzzed in me like hornets in the ribs of deer. I would learn one thing, they had told me, I was good for nothing. I felt the lump of my heart sinking. The last thing Louise would see, I thought, was my failure. My life's work boiled down to this moment. In the snow my skin pulled up so tight my bones knit. I knelt down beside Louise, removed my jacket and clutched it to her thin shoulders. There was no wind, no sound at all except for her breathing etched, her lungs squeaking. The tight cold moving tighter around her. Her eyes were colorless in the darkness, the pupils opening, pulsing, then opening again. But I remembered the color of her eyes in sunlight, how she would turn to me and her brown eyes could change to green. Her breath labored to clouds. I caught for a moment the gleam of the river, the black, pulling current beside our grim vigil. Seconds ticked in me.

She was dying.

I wasn't going to let this happen, not to Louise. Louise was not going to die by the roadside. I clasped her wrist in my fingertips and checked her pulse. I felt the strong beating will of her heart. "Hold on, Louise," I whispered to her and she squeezed my hand.

I heard the screech of the car slipping and Stoner yelled to me, "Get me the hell out of here." I detected the hysteria in his voice and felt a sense of satisfaction, a sense of power. I didn't have time to rescue the bastard. I had to save myself. I had to save Louise. I pulled Louise to my chest, and her body was frail and light in my arms. I remembered carrying her mother from her deathbed, and closed my eyes. "Give me a chance," I said, hoping it would suffice as prayer. I prayed as I carried her up the steep embankment, prayed I wouldn't fall, prayed for strength for the both of us. I could hear gasoline hissing from the punctured tank of Stoner's car, gasoline gurgling along the outline of the car's fractured frame. I had to move fast.

I heard the cowboy sniffle and knew the man was crying. I laid Louise close beside him. "Help me here," I said to him. I had to trust him then. The cowboy opened his arms to shelter Louise in the folds of his blanket. "I'm sorry," he was saying and I realized he was speaking to Louise. "I'm sorry for everything," he said.

"I've got to go back and help the other guy," I said, refusing to say Stoner's name. "Help is coming," I said, but realized I was not trying to be reassuring. I knew it was my own wake-up call. If I was going to act, I had to act now. I skirted down the hill, feeling the blunt swell of my own injury. The smell of gasoline made me swoon. I could detect the sweet shine of it spilling toward Stoner, lining the sleeves of his butter-soft jacket.

"It's about goddamned time," Stoner said. I stepped closer to him and gasoline wheezed in my chest. Stoner grabbed my leg then and I was startled by the strength of his clutch. I recognized the grasp of a desperate man. "Everything's going to be OK," I said. "Just take it easy. I can't help you if you don't let go of me here."

"That's the spirit," Stoner said. "That's the spirit," he said again, coaxing me, urging me. "Now get me the hell out of here," he yelled.

I lost my resolve. I saw myself trudging back up the embankment with Stoner in my arms, waiting impatiently by the roadside for Railer to smirk at me. My heart was sinking. I didn't have the guts. I squatted before him then, steadying myself for the pull. I was helping the enemy. I had my cheek to his and I was beginning to lift him, ready to hoist him on my shoulder and pull him to safety when I felt the bite of his words close to my ear. "The bitch dead yet?" he said. I knew I had heard him right and I didn't want to hear those words again but I stopped dead-still. I was embracing him. "What?" I said.

"You heard me," he said. "Is the bitch dead yet?"

I dropped his weight then and stepped back where he couldn't reach me even though he scrambled to swipe at me again.

"You think you can manage to walk on your own?" I said, not really certain if he was a man too injured to move.

I removed my flashlight from my belt-loop sleeve and though my hands were calm the light stuttered over Stoner's body. The cuff of his pant leg was spilling blood, the left leg so badly broken the bone had slammed through his pants.

"Does it look like I can walk?" he said, his tone softer.

"No," was all I said. A calmness plunged through me. My heart was still. "I can save the whole Flathead Nation," I said only to myself but Stoner answered me.

"You just have to save me," he said, and there was relief in his voice.

I shone the light into Stoner's face and looked at him for the first time without flinching. I held the light to his blue eyes and knew he was the enemy. I saw the chickened-yellow jowls of his sagging jaw-line, and in that moment I suddenly saw the bleak face of Sister Simon even when I blinked. Stupid Indian, she was saying, stupid, stupid Indian. And the answer was easy. There were no more choices. There was only this one duty before me, this one responsibility.

"Hold on there," I said to Stoner. I patted my chest for the matches I knew I didn't have. I moved toward Stoner and squatted down before him once again. I began patting his coat pockets and he grabbed at my wrists. Stoner was wild-eyed and glaring. "What the hell?" he said to me. "I don't need comfort here." His voice was shrill. I lifted Stoner's cold silver lighter in my palm and held it above his head. He knew now. There was no doubt. He grabbed at me but I managed to step back from him, out of his reach forever.

The first spark erupted in my heart. A blue blinding flame of light was the first and last light I would ever see. A flush of heat rocking me, exploding, and then no sound. Silence. A rushing, fierce wind I could not hear. Stoner's voice flaming, then gone. The river flashed red as purgatory, suddenly summer. I knew without knowing that the heat had seared my uniform buckle to melting. My sleeves were flaming, the front of my shirt was flickering with light and falling from me. I could smell the dense smoke of my singed hair. My eyes pulsed with light. It was over. Stoner was gone. The fire consuming, roaring, a blaze beginning to quiet. The Buick ticked in the dying heat. I felt a singe of cold, my skin pocketing.

"Holy shit," I heard the cowboy say above me. "Holy shit."

"It just blew up," I found myself saying, dazed and unblinking.

"That's what I would say," the cowboy said.

"Louise," I said. "Is Louise OK?"

"She's tough," the cowboy said. "She's still with us."

I could hear the sirens. The bank above me lit up red with new traffic. The lights were frantic. I could make out the familiar slam of emergency doors, men about their business. I thought I heard Railer calling me and I turned to see. The men were coming down the hill with lamps and flashlights. Their headlamps shined above my head. My eyes were dry. When I touched my fingertips to my eyelids I felt the watering blisters.

"We've got an officer injured down here," someone yelled.

"Over here," a man said. He was standing by Stoner's body. "We'll need the tarp."

Someone flashed a light in my face, then the light flickered on my arms, my torso. I could see I had a belly blister big as a pregnancy. "I'll be damned," Railer said to the others. "It looks like we got ourselves a hero here."

I recognized another voice in the darkness, the voice of the Lake County sheriff. "You did what you could, Officer," he was saying. "We'll get you some help now." He had never spoken to me with respect before.

They eased me onto the stretcher and carried me carefully up to the ambulance. I heard the cowboy giving his statement to Railer. "All I know," he said, "is Officer Kicking Woman risked his life to try and save Mr. Stoner."

They slid my stretcher in next to Louise. I watched her. I couldn't take my eyes off her still face. And I watched until I saw her chest expand gathering air. The fog had finally lifted. The night sky was so clear smoke rose from the wreckage like sparkling dust, so high, so high, then gone. I heard the small silver bells of chains nicking the road as we headed toward the hospital. I closed my eyes. Safe.

Baptiste Yellow Knife

♦

Gifts

Even the smallest bones in his hands and feet were lit with pain. He had to brace himself against his mother to make it to the bed. Stars rushed his head, burning stars glittered his backbone. The ground seemed to drop from him and rise up again suddenly. He couldn't get his bearings. He wobbled in his walk.

His mother had smoked his room with sweet grass and lined his blankets with sage. She wanted to sit beside him, to tend to him, but even her watchful eyes were heavy on him, painful. He wanted to be alone. He told her to leave him. She left a jar of bitter juniper-berry and black-moss tea steaming by his bedside. Fever thrummed his temples and he woke to find his hair damp. He could taste the salt crust on his dry lips. His spine swelled in the sagging bed and he had to rock himself to turn over. Sleep would not come, only wakeful glimpses of dreams. He took gulps of the tea his mother had left him and found it thick and cold. His belly trembled. A dark fog pressed on his chest and he struggled to breathe. The backs of his ears were hot and he felt something breathing behind him. He braced his arms to the bed and pushed up with all his strength to stand.

The room seemed to be closing in on him. He needed to open the window. He pressed his fingertips beneath the wood-frame window casing. No budge. He pushed hard and heard the crack of old paint. And then he felt the thin mercury window shattering, his palms tender with slivered glass. Cold startled him awake. His mother called to him and he told her he had only broken a glass, he was OK. He stepped around the shards to pull a cigarette from his shirt. The room held an odd glowing light. He pulled smoke deep into his broken chest and saw his blood in the sawbands of glass that glittered the floor. In his blood he saw a crimson salamander. He pressed his good eye with his thumb and looked again. His blood had hit the floor in the shape of a salamander. He could see Louise's great-grandmother, the lick of the salamander brief in the August grass, the sudden red tail humming.

Death was close. Death came to warn him with glimpses of events he couldn't understand. He wanted to shut out the things he was seeing. He dragged the blankets from his bed to the living room. He wanted to sleep on the dirt floor, wanted to smell the sleeping dust, hear the dull sound of his heartbeat against the earth, not see what death had come to show him.

He is standing in the snow-frosted fields again. Wind ticks through weeds. He sees the men as they slam their fists to his chest, to his belly. He hears his arm shatter. Sharp silver tips of boots crack his ribs. His lungs fill with brilliant water. In the brittle cold he is glass.

Death rattled the windows of his mother's house, tapped, then pounded at the door for Baptiste's notice, for Baptiste knew death. Death rose up over the powwow grounds in the hottest part of summer. Death waited at the edge of the highway fluttering silver water. Death could enter the dance arena sleek as a silver deer. Death bones rattled in the hands of stick-game players when they began thinking of spending their last silver dime. Death was the glittering light the hunters followed, the light Annie White Elk had followed. Death was the weak-hearted smell waiting in the sweet huckleberry bushes. Death was the silver smile along the river line that had called Louise's sister. Death was clear light, the film of night fading. That night Baptiste knew death was the blue light sinking over the valley, the holy light of winter. He closed his eyes to see the Flathead River smoking. Fog whispered over the valley floor. He could see the white puddles of ice on the highway, the whitest frost on the thin branches of silver trees. The highways, the trails of animals lit by low clouds. The gleam of winter was calling him. He felt the ache of sleep pulse behind his eyes. He covered his head and whispered a prayer.

It is summer. The sun so hot and dry he hears the green whisper of leaves. Baptiste runs to Louise. He lifts her tight in his arms, so tight the back of her skirt hikes up to her panties. He spins her around. They are laughing.

"I didn't think you would find me," she says. As they kiss Baptiste strokes Louise's hair and holds it back from her face. The wind blows hard.

He sees the pale yellow car pull over. The car is stopping for Louise. Louise lifts her hand to Baptiste but he doesn't wave back to her. "Don't go, Louise," he calls. "Please," he yells. He is pleading. "Don't leave, Louise." He sees her duck her head to enter the car. He knows if she leaves him she will not return. "Please, no," he says. He hears the dry rustle of wind through grass and turns to see that Louise is still standing beside him.

Louise is entering the dance arena. Her hair is wrapped in otter skins and she begins to dance. She is turning in the dance. She is turning toward Baptiste. The drumbeat is the sound of her fast heart, but she dances slowly, slowly toward him. And she is so beautiful the sun blushes behind her, touches the crown of her sleek braided hair. Blue beads glitter on her shoulders. Dance, he whispers to her, don't stop dancing.

Light was a presence. Light filtered through horsehair blankets covering his face. Light touched his eyelids and he didn't open his eyes at first. He felt heat in his lungs, a hard run heat. His heart was slow. For a moment Baptiste thought he might be dying. He opened his eyes to witness the room lighting up slowly, becoming sky, changing in the way a tarp darkens slowly when touched by water, light penetrating the room like a cool shadow. Baptiste could only find comparisons in darkness, things turning dark, things surrendering light to understand the white light that was entering the room.

He tried to think but no thoughts came, only more light, more light and more light, until one long moment stretched in his lungs like a new breath and told Baptiste he could lift from the room. He opened his eyes and felt peace and for the first time recognized what it was. He heard wind rattle the door and the door suddenly opened. The night was a beautiful, prayerful sight to him, almost painful to behold. He blinked his eyes. A sheath of snow smoked over the floor and Louise was outlined in light. She lifted her hand to Baptiste and he tried to get up from the floor, but he couldn't move and he knew that he was only dreaming. He held the thought that Louise had come back to him. He saw a brilliant flash of light, a fire that calmed him. The thought was a light so warm Baptiste slept. Death glimmered for one moment over the smooth rocks. Death glinted on the hills above Perma.

Baptiste slept.

He was aware that his blankets were rising up and dropping down heavy on his face. He could not shake the feeling that someone was lifting the blankets from him and letting them fall back down. He tried to turn. He rocked his sore hip on the dirt floor and the blankets began to rise again. He thought his mother was teasing him but that didn't make sense. "Stop it," he yelled. He heard his mother's clipped laughter. After a breath or two, he felt the familiar rise of his blankets again, something tugging at his covers. Baptiste inched himself up and there in the clear morning light stood a horse, a big horse, a horse snorting and hoofing the dirt floor. His mother was standing in the doorway. "He's been trying to wake you," she said. "He's been at you a good long while."

Baptiste sat up. The sky was pink with dawn. He rubbed his sore eyes and blinked at the horse he did not recognize. He could see the split hooves of the horse. The animal was nothing but an old sack of bones. The horse looked worse than he felt. He clucked his tongue to soothe the snorting horse. "How'd you get in here?" he asked. Baptiste saw the door was wide-open to the cold day.

"I'd close that door," Dirty Swallow said, "but I'm hemmed in here."

Baptiste struggled to stand. He felt weak and sore but better than he'd felt since the beating. The horse switched its tail. "Easy," Baptiste said. He closed the blanket around his shoulders and reached his hand to the muzzle of the horse. He brushed the horse's back with his palm. The horse was so burr-ridden he couldn't distinguish what color it was. Ribs shined through its pitiful coat. He'd been bitten by barbed wire. A chunk of flesh dangled from his withers. His mane was so matted and flea-bitten it had fallen out in places. Baptiste looked closely. The horse's left eye was swollen with pus, but his right eye looked shyly back at Baptiste, unwavering. He wasn't sure he was seeing right but he recognized this horse. "Champagne," he said, and the horse flinched and tossed his head. Dirty Swallow touched the horse's nose and he did not shy from her.

Baptiste stood stunned by the sight of his horse. He had given up on ever finding him. He remembered seeing the pelt of the dead horse strung on his corral fence. At first he had thought it was Champagne, but he knew his horse too well. He knew the delicate shading of his coat, the small scar split above its tail. He had kissed this horse and rubbed down every inch of him with his hands. He thought the cowboy had put the horse down. But now Champagne had risen from the dead.

"It seems you and I have a lot in common," Baptiste whispered.

Last night seemed far away, a fog he could not remember. He told his mother he was going to mend his horse in her living room and she had nodded her agreement. "He must have wanted to come back to you," she said. Dirty Swallow lit the cookstove fire and put a kettle of water on. Baptiste had some oats in the barn. He put on his coat. He stepped off the porch into snow a foot deep and let himself fall back into it. He saw veils of snow that had drifted over the corral. Snow cradled his back and the cold was soothing to him. He blinked into the bright sun and suddenly remembered. He dusted off his backside and walked back to the front of the house. Louise had come to him in the night. He was sure of it and the thought startled him. He saw the horse's tracks. They began out of nowhere, a few feet from the porch. He brushed his hand over the crusted snow looking for a drift that hid the horse's hoofprints but there were no indentations in the snow beyond the perimeter of the porch. He knew then something was wrong but he wasn't sure what it all meant. There was no sign of Louise's footsteps.

When he entered the house he saw his mother dabbing a steaming cloth to Champagne's wounds but the horse did not flinch. He told her he had to go into town, but she was too busy with her task to hear him.

He went out to the field where the old farm truck had stood neglected since September. He wondered if it would start. He turned his attention to the small details of living, the feel of the cold wheel burning in his hands, the strain of seeing in the bright sunlight. He heard the low grind of gears, the high whirring spin of the engine turning, and then turning over. He did not brush the snow from his windshield. He was driving to Perma. The sun lit the white fields so bright he squinted through the ice-sparkled windshield. He drove as fast as the truck could drive, dipping over scoured ice roads, crunching over potholes. He had to scrape a peek hole with his fingernail but he did not slow down. He was determined to see Louise again but the day chipped at his resolve. He had been desperate to see her and now the day had found him weak and pitiful, ashamed. The silver-blue sky told him Louise was alive and well. He wanted to see her and he would, he told himself. He would find her in Dixon if he waited in the bar. He knew this was a story a drinking man would tell himself to defend his drinking, but he wanted a drink. He needed one, he told himself. If he just had one drink he could face Louise. He would find her well and probably still angry with him. He could have another chance if he didn't rush it. He drove to Dixon blinded with the idea that he could find some strength in one drink. He was driving so fast over the whirring ice, he had to pump his breaks to stop.

He entered the dim bar and found he had to take in the room slowly, allow his eyes to adjust. He smelled Purex and piss. He could see that Eddie Taylor had placed his hands on his hips and was eyeing him. Everything seemed the same. He believed the familiar could hold him in place, secure him. He longed for everything to remain the same, but knew the world was always changing. He wished he could tell himself the stories he could tell others, that he could find peace in his heart the way he had the night before. Baptiste braced his knees beneath the bar and refused to look back at Eddie. If he was stubborn he knew a drink would come but he was still surprised when Eddie Taylor placed a double ditch in front of him without being asked.

"On the house," Eddie said.

Baptiste took a gulp of the drink but the burning draw did not make him feel better.

"You must have heard about the accident," Eddie was saying as he wiped the back counter. Baptiste ignored him. Eddie Taylor always talked too much. "Hell of an explosion," Eddie said. "Of course you'd know," he said, and then fell silent. He glanced at Baptiste but Baptiste did not look at him.

Baptiste could see himself in the mirror above the liquor bottles and pigs'-feet jars. He had not looked at himself after the beating. He had never been good-looking but now his face was slashed with a puckering scar that looked to be healing his left eye to closing. His lower lip was still split. He put his tongue to the cut and tasted blood. His right eye sized him with a hard mean stare. He could not face the man he knew others saw.

He looked out the window to see a small group of people gathering in a line, a straggly gathering of people he recognized and most he knew. He watched as people stepped from the livery shop, the grocery store, and post office. People were lining up on the highway's shoulder as if a parade was going to pass by. The feed store clerk was waiting, arching his neck and gawking down the road. Eddie Taylor was removing his bar apron and heading for the door.

"Baptiste," Eddie said, "this might be something you'll want to see." And before Baptiste could answer him he was out the door. Baptiste downed his drink and slapped money on the bar. He didn't want Eddie Taylor's charity. He wanted to see what the commotion was. He wanted the distraction. He squinted into the sunlight. He saw a cowboy across the street pull off his hat and shift his gaze down the road. And Baptiste looked too. He looked down the long road and realized suddenly what he was waiting to see and the sight of it made his heart leap. The slow moving procession appeared on the road curve. The Lake County sheriff preceded the hearse and as they moved through Dixon the sheriff's red beam swirled in silence. A Sanders County sheriff flanked the rear of the hearse.

The small group fell to silence. The livery man removed his cap and clutched it to his chest. A white woman Baptiste knew as Mrs.

Wing placed her hand over her heart. Even in the bright sunlight a swoop of solemnity had settled. The road gleamed with melting ice. Baptiste's eyes watered. He saw Eddie Taylor cup his hands above his brow but he did not stop looking at the hearse. Baptiste had seen hearses before but this hearse was dazzling. Mirror chrome glinted and flashed. The black hearse was so shiny he could see the town and its people passing in its reflection.

Baptiste heard a woman he did not know whispering beside him but he did not turn to glimpse her. "A big shot," she was saying.

"Harvey Stoner," another woman answered. She dabbed a handkerchief to her eyes.

Baptiste felt woozy. He felt as if he had been in a battle for years and had managed to win a skirmish but instead of victory he felt the heaviness of it all, the long struggle of the fight. Weakness shined his ribs. He was as thin as his long-lost horse, so thin that if anyone looked at him they could have seen his heart spilling the tears of relief he couldn't allow himself to cry. He was rattled by the emotion he felt. Harvey Stoner's death meant a lot of things, but to Baptiste Yellow Knife Harvey Stoner's death meant that Louise would be free of this man's influence, that Baptiste might finally get the chance to right the wrongs he had done, another chance to save the marriage he had been convinced he had lost. It seemed suddenly easy, too easy. He lowered his face, and his eyes met the passing hearse, the heavy velvet curtains pulled shut.

"Poor sucker," Eddie whispered to him and Baptiste grabbed Eddie's arm. "You telling me that's Harvey Stoner?" he asked. He was oddly stunned.

"His wife's sending the body back east for burial. Even dead, the guy's so important he gets a police escort all the way to the county line." Eddie whistled low. "First class to the bitter end."

Baptiste could taste the whiskey on his tongue. His lungs were sour. The onlookers could smell him. He stood by his truck for a while and knew he should go find Louise. He had his chance now, but he was weak. He heard the engine ticking but he could not climb inside. He went back into the bar. He lay a twenty down on the bar, the only money he had. "Give me a bottle," he said. "Anything."

Eddie only leaned back on the back bar and crossed his arms. Baptiste wondered if Eddie was going to get him the booze he had asked for. Baptiste pushed himself back from the bar and drew up his shoulders ready to fight if he had to.

"You got it," Eddie said, moving quickly, lifting a fifth from the top shelf, but when he placed the bottle down before Baptiste he did not remove his hand. He looked at Baptiste straight on, something few men ever did, let alone a white man. "I've got to say this," Eddie said, and Baptiste gripped the bottle Eddie held and waited for the chastisement. "Why the hell are you here, Baptiste, when Louise is busted up in the hospital?" Eddie asked him.

The news of Louise pitched Baptiste back a step. He felt the drink reeling in his empty stomach. "Just give me the bottle," he said. He wouldn't let Eddie know he had not heard about Louise. Eddie was ringing the money in the till as Baptiste was leaving the Dixon Bar.

He knew that Louise needed him, that he should be there for her, but he couldn't face this trouble, not now. He needed to think awhile, he told himself. He planned instead to drink the day away. He planned to forget his troubles, find a place where he could drink in peace. He walked toward the river, heard the slow water struggling in the channel. He thought of the fish, cold and sweet beneath green water. He saw a magpie, white-and-black against the blue sky, and remembered Louise's great-grandfather in his cap of magpie feathers. He stomped a path in the deep snow and cleared a place to sit. He would forget, he told himself. He would forget everything. But he did not forget.

Baptiste felt the sting of snow. He felt old anger rising in his throat, anger with himself. Anger sizzled in his belly. He sat for a long time, alone, and the snow was so cold his hands shook. He looked at the whiskey bottle and thought of the Indians who didn't drink. He drank because the white man had told him he couldn't drink. He had convinced himself he was winning the battle, but even with Harvey Stoner dead and gone he was losing his own life to drink. He had already lost the part of himself that gave him the will to fight. He lifted up the bottle and sloshed the amber fire. The drink called to him, but this time he wouldn't answer. He threw the bottle with all the strength in his arm, threw it so far from himself he didn't hear it hit the ground. And then Baptiste Yellow Knife stood up. He knew what he had to do and yet he felt powerless and small. His face was wet with streaming tears.

The whole sky lit. He turned his face to the sun and closed his eyes. He listened and he waited. He could see the red pulse of his blood. He could hear his slow and easy breath. He waited for what would come to him.

When there was death, the holy man would come, the man with his long hair wrapped in white silk. Baptiste could see him riding. Baptiste could feel the clean heat singing in the man. And he knew who the man had come for. He had come for Louise. Wind was blowing so hard it lifted Baptiste's hair from his scalp. He could smell the sweet ring of cottonwoods, spearmint lifting from the low hills. Baptiste remembered how his mother had taught him to pray with his hands open and his arms outstretched, with his hands empty to the sky for he had nothing in this world. He braced himself and opened his palms to the spirit and he prayed. "Give my life back to me," he prayed, knowing he was asking for the life of Louise.

A great wind rose up from behind him and whistled through his thin coat, and the smooth river dimpled then turned white. And this was what he knew, what had always been before him, a healing within his grasp. And he saw the great light, a simple gift, that was all the light he had ever seen, from the smallest lick of the moon on a black river to the shine of long grass on a windy day.

Louise Yellow Knife

♦

Returning

She was groggy. A weakness had settled in her muscles, and her lips were swollen dry. Her grandmother had opened the window in her room and the breeze was cool and Louise longed to sit out on the porch. She pulled herself from the heavy blankets and sat up. It occurred to her that she had been sleeping on a bed, a real bed, and not a nest of cattails. She pushed her hands into the mattress to feel the spring of it. She sat for a while and it felt good to be sitting upright, good not to feel the cradle of the pillow pressed against her skull. She felt dazed with light. She squinted and touched her eyes. She traced the outline of her nose and her lips. She found that a scar pinched her hairline, but it was numb and tight-ridged, not sore to the touch. She combed her fingers through her hair and snagged on the matted knot at the back of her neck.

Louise felt she had slept through a lifetime, a life that had changed around her. She was vaguely aware of a recent past: needle pricks, her hands cold and stinging, a bag of fluid dripping through a tube, her heart heavy then fluttering. Moments sparked: someone lifting her, someone carrying her up steps, someone resting a warm hand on her forehead. There was a ring of kerosene light sputtering in darkness so black she whimpered, wind battering the house, a window opening then shutting, a breath of snow passing over her. Through long nights she could hear the voice of a man she knew to be her great-grandfather, long dead. Night after night, while the wind swirled snow in great sheets over the house, she had heard him praying. His voice shivered in the corners of the room, then passed like light to morning when she would hear him outside, circling the house with prayer. She had heard her sister whispering in her ear, the sound of laughter. Once her mother had held her hand. Once Baptiste had placed his hand over her weak heart and bowed his head. And she knew she must have been dreaming because she knew her sister had drowned; Baptiste was dead. The room had filled with a thousand people then emptied, and she did not know if the people who had visited her were living or dead.

She had traveled over a field so blue with snow her soul shined silver. She had found a broken horse in that field and had returned him to Baptiste. She had danced in the dance arena with Baptiste and the sun had capped her head. But most nights were heavy iron pressing down upon her, colorless, nights when she was only aware of drawing breath, breath, exhausting breath. There were birds tapping the windows, black ice creeping over the edge of the pond, owls flying swiftly over her snatching her breath, her breath.

Her thoughts rattled then stopped, clung about her like an ill-fitting dress that puckered at her breasts and pinched her arms. Memories that were not memories: soup dribbling down her neck. Cold fingers gripping her wrists, thick fingers thumping her numb chest. A thin stinging prickle in her hip that swirled her head like the chamber pot spilling, flushing over her thighs, the backs of her legs.

She looked out the window and the sun was high and cool above the house. She thought it was winter. It was winter yesterday, she remembered, but could remember nothing more. She heard her grandmother in the kitchen and she wanted to be near her. She strained to stand. Her feet were tender on the bare floor, raw, but the stretch renewed her. She pulled a blanket from the bed and slowly walked toward the kitchen. She winced to see Florence's shawl hanging on the kitchen wall beside the stove. She remembered suddenly and too clearly how her grandmother had carefully beaded each red rose, had knotted every fringe, and, when her sister had died, had hung the shawl where it would always be seen and where it would always remain, unfinished and beautiful.

Her grandmother stood at the sideboard kneading fry bread. The old woman turned suddenly as if startled and smiled broadly at Louise.

"Granddaughter," she said, "I've missed you." And Louise realized she had been gone a long, long time. Her grandmother wiped her hands on her long skirt and grabbed Louise to steady her. "Sit down here," she said, and Louise felt her legs so weak she thumped into the chair the old woman placed before her. Louise looked at her grandmother's face, saw the swollen tender skin beneath her eyelids. She reached for her grandmother's hands and saw her turn away to touch her fingertips to the corners of her eyes.

She wanted to ask her a lot of questions but knew her grandmother did not want to talk about what had happened. Louise looked out the open window. She saw the swirl of thick smoke, smelled the smoldering tamarack. Her grandmother was tanning. Grandma had set about her chores as always. The old woman had known difficult times. She had known long hunger, disease. Grandma had fed and clothed two daughters and had lost them. Louise's mother to pneumonia, Rosalie to TB. Both had died in their twenties. Her grandmother kept a photograph of them hidden upstairs. The bubbled-glass frame had failed to protect their images. Every year they faded a little more as if they were being encompassed by white light. Grandma had never hung the photograph. It was too special for that, her grandmother said. And Louise understood that her grandmother's grief was a private thing. She knew there were things her grandmother would never tell her.

She wanted most to ask her grandmother about Baptiste, for she was certain she had heard him while she was sleeping. When she had fluttered her eyes she had spotted glimpses of him, scar-worn and sober, different toward her, attentive and kind. She wanted to ask her grandmother if maybe Baptiste had visited her but she knew it would be like asking if Florence had stood by her side, if her mother had returned from the dead. He had appeared to her alive but perhaps only the way the dead can appear in dreams.

She thought of Baptiste, how he could be shy, how soft his voice had been, how he had once been there for her. She felt sorrowful and weak, uncertain about what life held for her now. She saw the beautiful day as endless, unforgiving, but she was awake and alive. She wanted to sit outside for a while and find some peace in the day. "I'd like to sit out on the porch," she said, "if you think that's OK?"

Her grandmother nodded and wiped her hands on her skirt again. She placed her hand beneath Louise's arm and Louise was taken with her grandmother's firm strength. They moved together slowly. Louise clutched the blanket to her chest and bit her lip. She had to concentrate hard to make her legs move, but when they reached the porch she gulped the cool sweet air and felt new energy. Her grandmother held onto her arm as Louise strained to sit down. "I'm fine now, Grandma," she said. "It's OK."

"I'm just inside," her grandmother called. "You holler if you need me."

The highway stretched out before Louise but she was no longer restless. She didn't have any desire to walk the road looking for a good time or trouble. She folded her hands in her lap and willed her past to return to her. She remembered Mrs. Finger but could not recall the daughter's name. That was good, she found herself thinking, she didn't want to know. She thought of riding with Baptiste, the whip of her hair, the pale sky lining the high Mission Mountains and fusing with heaven. But the memory of Baptiste was as elusive as he had been. The nuns had tried to lock Baptiste in the storage room because he had refused to speak English, Louise remembered. She shifted her gaze to the field dazzled green in early spring, tufts of black-eyed Susans, Indian paintbrush flamed the low hills. When the nuns had come to release him, he was gone. The nuns had tapped on the walls and the floors believing he had found a hiding place. But Louise knew Baptiste had possessed something they had prayed for. He could not be bound by walls or locks. The nuns could not release Baptiste because he'd always been free.

She tried to recount the days she had lost but it was like trying to clasp water in the pocket of a closing hand. She wanted to revive the story she had heard, but only Baptiste could have told her the story. It had been Baptiste's voice, clear and low that had spoken to her, but when had he told her this story? She pressed the heat of her palms to her eyelids and spoke his name believing he had loved her once, and she had loved him. She recalled the hollow of Baptiste's neck, the shape of his hands fluttering around her when he had told her stories. She heard the ripple of pond water, the wind graze the cattails. Her grandmother had taught her to remember the dead with respect, to forgive.

She took a deep breath. Home was quiet. She felt suddenly chilled and she pulled the blanket more tightly around her. She was going to stand, she told herself. She was going to make her way back into the house without her grandmother's assistance.

She flattened her hands to her sides and pushed herself to standing.

"That wasn't so difficult," she said aloud, but it had winded her. "Each day will get easier," she reassured herself. These were the thoughts she held as she reached forward to steady herself, the promise she made as she heard the small tinkling of bells in the distance, the sound growing louder, the distinct clop of a horse's hooves on pavement. The sound panicked her. She didn't want to be seen by anyone just then, weak and sun-stricken, blinking painfully into the light, her hair matted and unwashed. She was vain, she knew, to be thinking such thoughts, but she wanted a fresh start, a new beginning, not this. She tried to move quickly but her muscles wouldn't cooperate.

She pulled the blanket over her head and peered out from beneath it. She rubbed her eyes. She was dreaming, more addled than she had at first believed. She blinked hard, but the vision remained the same. She wasn't dreaming.

Up over the hill she saw him coming toward her. Baptiste Yellow Knife was alive. He rode straight-backed and proud. He was wearing his finest silks. Silver bells trembled around the chest of his horse. Champagne's beaded harness was glittering in sunlight. Louise let the blanket drop from her shoulders. She stepped from the porch and had to catch herself. She didn't care if her hair was matted and dirty; her husband was beautiful. She wanted to run to him. She stepped forward.